"He's Lining Us Up," Dobbs Warned.

Cy Allen had no choice but to use his power and speed advantage . . . He unloaded the F-4, and in afterburner accelerated to Mach 2 in a dive from twenty thousand to ten thousand feet.

The MiG-17 fell behind but continued to pursue. At ten thousand feet, Cy pulled back on the stick, and zoomed up to thirty-five thousand feet. At the top of his climb he saw the MiG, about six thousand feet below, run out of power and fall off on one wing. Instantly Cy pulled the throttles out of burner, kicked rudder to fall off to his left, and turned into line behind the steeply banked, almost stationary enemy plane.

"You're in range," Dobbs said at the instant Cy Allen fired.

"Skip it." He didn't need Dobbs' radar-guided Sparrows. A heat-seeker would do the trick . . . The Sidewinder streaked up the MiG's tailpipe and detonated inside the airframe.

The MiG broke in half.

HENRY ZEYBEL is a retired Lieutenant Colonel in the U.S. Air Force. He served in both the Korean and Vietnam wars, and was awarded the Silver Star, eight Distinguished Flying Crosses and nineteen Air Medals.

THE FIRST ACE

Henry Zeybel

PUBLISHED BY POCKET BOOKS NEW YORK

To Jan and Karen and Jeni

This novel is a work of fiction. Names, characters, places and incidents are either the product of the author's imagination or are used fictitiously. Any resemblance to actual events or locales or persons, living or dead, is entirely coincidental.

An *Original* publication of POCKET BOOKS

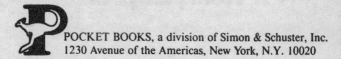

POCKET BOOKS, a division of Simon & Schuster, Inc.
1230 Avenue of the Americas, New York, N.Y. 10020

Copyright © 1986 by Henry Zeybel
Cover artwork copyright © 1986 by Franco Accornero, Inc.

ISBN: 0-671-62868-2

First Pocket Books printing August, 1986

10 9 8 7 6 5 4 3 2 1

POCKET and colophon are registered trademarks
of Simon & Schuster, Inc.

Printed in the U.S.A.

Acknowledgments

Mega-thanks to MiG-killer Phil Combies and Aviator Valor Award–winner Jerry Dobberfuhl without whose help the sex would lack violence.

Also my regards to Jon Mallard, Bob Schneidenbach, Jerry Haynes, Sam Ross, Ted Baader, Carl Ross, and Harry Kocian for sharing pieces of their lives.

Prologue

Betty Vaughn's body had ripened exactly as Cy Allen had anticipated. She always carried a sweaterful, but the rest of her used to be thin, angular. Her long legs often had reminded him of a newborn filly's. During the two years at Penn State when she had been his steady, Allen's friends had called her Bones. In defense Allen had told them, "The closer the bone, the sweeter the meat." He wished they could see her now. She was softly rounded in all the right places, and those super long legs curved way up into a tightly packed ass. Absolutely fabulous, he thought, and felt his heart slip in an extra beat.

Betty's black hair was shorter, fuller, and shinier than he remembered. And her green eyes were more brilliant than he recalled. He was pleased. After all, he hadn't seen her in five years. He never had owned a picture of her, said he never needed one, claimed her portrait was engraved forever in his mind and in his heart. Surprisingly, her face hadn't changed: the same exotic, almond-shaped, eyes, the high cheekbones, the wide jaw, and that unforgettable mouth with its ruby lips and perfect, dazzling white teeth.

1

A wave of desire made him tremble like a jet fighter waiting to launch. Looking up at him through long, black eyelashes, Betty smiled and Allen wondered if she knew his thoughts, felt his excitement.

Her Craig Street apartment was only living room, bedroom, kitchen, and bath, but the rooms were enormous (the ceilings were high enough for clouds to form, high enough for dogfighting, Allen thought). He recognized furniture from her parents' home. She wasn't hurting, he decided.

Betty poured him a bourbon and water and they talked of trivial things. He failed to move the conversation in his direction and regretted that he hadn't worn his uniform with his silver wings and rows of ribbons; they would have given him an opening for stories about his exploits in Korea. In civilian clothes he felt dull, like another taxpayer, a real limp dick. To make matters worse, he couldn't come up with one genuinely funny line. It used to be so easy to keep her laughing with streams of far-out nonsense, he thought. Now, his attempts at humor sounded either juvenile or sarcastic. In frustration he poured himself more bourbon while Betty rambled on about her life.

She had been married for a short time. "He married me because he thought I had money," she said. "I was confused after my parents died. It was—sudden. First, Mother; then, Dad. Both had heart attacks, within five months of each other. So suddenly . . ."

Cy got the impression that she had the story down pat. "I'm sorry," he told her. He had disliked her parents because he believed they had come between them by transferring her to Carnegie Tech at the end of her sophomore year.

"He showed up at Dad's funeral—the mourner, professional mourner—there was nothing he wouldn't do to help. He always was there when I needed something. He was so understanding. He fooled me. I trusted him, ended up marrying him. Then I saw: He wanted my money." Her voice lowered to a confidential level: "There wasn't that much. At least not as much as he expected. I had the marriage annulled as soon as I saw what was going on." She finished with a self-righteous ring: "And I took back my maiden name."

How many times had those two consummated their short marriage, Allen wondered. During the two years he had gone steady with her, they'd never fucked. They'd survived on oral sex because she had been paranoid about becoming pregnant. No contraceptive was safe enough to satisfy her. Furthermore, she had argued that they should save something for after they were married. She had pussy-whipped him right from the start, Allen thought.

"My health is borderline," Betty said. "Practically every other day I see a doctor for vitamin shots. My medical bills nearly equal my rent." She went on to explain at great length the function and intricacies of her ailing liver. Jesus, did she ever, Allen thought. She knew her body, got into it with both feet, sounded like a transcript from *Gray's Anatomy*.

He wasn't buying any of her sorrow. He saw her as a healthy, young woman. She looked capable of mining coal. What she needed, he thought, was one of Lieutenant Cy Allen's pure protein insertions. His thoughts and the drinks heated him; he took off his coat and rolled up his shirt-sleeves.

Betty moved on to the minutiae of her career as a department store sales promoter.

After more drinks he moved next to her on the couch and wrapped an arm about her. She didn't resist. He rested his head on top of hers. She was warm and soft and her flowery fragrance made him dizzy. "I still love you," he said.

After about a ten count, she said, "Cy, you don't know me anymore."

He protested: "You're the same person. Only more beautiful. Remember when we were—"

"We were children back then."

That wasn't true, he thought. Stupidly, he said, "Let's get married."

She gave him a frozen smile. Was her expression an answer or a question?

"Why not? You have a boyfriend?"

"No. Yes." She waved aside his question. "That's not the reason."

"Marry me and I'll get out of the Air Force and we'll go to Europe and . . ." Plans stopped flowing from his mind.

"Why go to Europe?" she asked.

He didn't know. He wanted to go to Europe. He thought everybody wanted to go to Europe. He said, "To live. Have fun. Be together. Make love. I can get . . ." He calculated rapidly. ". . . twelve, maybe fifteen thousand dollars together, maybe eighteen. That should last a year, at least."

"And after that?"

He sat with his mouth half-open. He didn't have an answer. His vision didn't go beyond one glorious year with her.

"You're drunk, Cy."

He kissed her silky lips. She returned the kiss. He got an erection and slid her hand onto it. "Let's go in the other room," he said. They never had spent an entire night together, he thought. The incompleteness of their love depressed him.

She moved away from him and matter-of-factly said, "Cy, you're drunk. I think you should leave."

Without even token resistance, he felt defeated. Her tone of voice made him feel immature. Damnit, he'd show her. "Let me see you tomorrow," he said. He'd wear his uniform and stay sober and show her that he was the returning, conquering hero. And he was ready to settle down.

She stood, moved to the center of the living room. "Call me tomorrow."

"Would you like to go out for dinner?" He mentally damned himself for begging.

"Maybe. Call me."

He took the hand she held out to him. "When?" he asked.

"Tomorrow. After I get home from work."

"What time will that be?"

She looked at him as if he were mentally deficient. "Seven," she said and led him to the door.

Betty Vaughn had been Allen's first real love. She had done him like he never knew he could be done. And nobody ever matched her. Nobody came close. He considered her to be his "natural soul mate." She possessed the uncanny ability to sense his exact degree of sexual excitement, as if she were mainlined into his central nervous system. With hands and mouth she transported him to the edge of sexual release and held him there for minute after minute after minute. Each minute seemed a lifetime . . .

He was locked in a state of incredible and inconceivable delight, agony, excitement, and confusion: he had to come but didn't want to; he wanted to come but she wouldn't permit him; he didn't want to come and feared she was going to make him come. She balanced him on the brink with flicks and licks of her soft tongue and tiny movements of her silky lips. All the while, her smooth, long fingers explored elsewhere . . .

When he believed he couldn't hold back for another moment and had either to go off or to go crazy, she elevated him to a higher plane. Magically, she gave him the ability to receive more pleasure. It was like getting a second wind when running. It was a dimension that only she had ever shown him and he worshipped her for taking him there. At the new plateau, she lured him to the edge once again and fixed him on the spot, filled with boiling energy and an overpowering expectation of relief, filled with a pleasurable tenseness and tightness that she controlled. He felt charged with a nameless force . . . weightless . . . airborne . . . awash in sex, he transcended his body . . . Betty and he became one . . . soul mates.

Then, always unexpectedly, with long, firm strokes she released him and made him explode again and again and again while she milked him and nursed from him and reduced him to a blubbering, drooling idiot capable only of whispering, "Thank you, thank you, thank you. I love you, I love you, I love you. Oh, thank you, thank you, my love. Oh, Sweet Jesus, I do love you, love you, only you . . ."

By comparison her orgasms were calm. Her lack of response made him wonder if he satisfied her. She claimed he did. Inhibitions kept her from being demonstrative, she said. Their lovemaking took place in borrowed cars, in secluded spots around campus, and in back rooms of fraternity houses. She never denied him gratification. But often she rejected reciprocation for fear of being discovered. He felt selfish when he took her love and she went without. At those times he silently vowed that, after they were married, he would repay her with endless pleasure.

At exactly seven o'clock the following evening Allen telephoned Betty from downtown. His rings went unanswered. He tried every ten minutes until eight o'clock when he tired of window-shopping and ducked into the Cork and Bottle Lounge for a fast drink. He'd not been in the place before. From what he'd heard, he'd always believed it was a little too ritzy for his taste.

Before Cy had a chance to look around, a red-faced middle-aged bartender said, "Hey, you're the guy . . ." He rapidly snapped his fingers, then pointed a forefinger like a gun. ". . . the guy in the paper. The aviator." He searched behind the bar and came up with a day-old copy of *The Pittsburgh Lighthouse*. Cy's picture and an account of his combat exploits were featured on the first page of the second section. "Lieutenant Cy Young Allen," the bartender read aloud, "the MiG killer."

Allen gave his best smile, offered his hand.

"Shit oh dear, how about that? Ten friggin' MiGs." The bartender pushed the paper in front of Cy. "Autograph this thing. Drinks are on the house, my pleasure, kid. I'm Irish Jim Conley. Crewed a P-51, World War Duece. Long-distance brothers-in-arms. Damn, if I'd stayed in, I'd be over halfway to retired by now."

Allen laughed. Every old-timer who had once been in the service figured that out after it was too late, he thought. They always sounded as if, in some way, they had been cheated.

By ten o'clock Allen lost count of his drinks and the

frequency of his phone calls. For a long time he left the lounge's pay phone off the hook with Betty's telephone ringing at the other end of the line.

Irish Jim's patter helped pass the time. He kept his voice low; his eyes looked everywhere but at Cy while words poured from a corner of his mouth: "Good-looking broad came in the other night. I says, 'Hi, honey, I'd sure like a little pussy.' She said, 'So would I, buster, mine's as big as your hat.' I offered to buy her a beer. She told me to make it a champagne cocktail. I says, 'Champagne? You think I'm a sucker?' She said, 'Don't get personal.' She leaned close and said, 'When I drink champagne cocktails, the man I'm with becomes the world's greatest lover. But when I drink beer, I fart.' She was my kind, kid. I gave her a beer and told her, 'I'll do things you never had done. I'll kiss your breasts.' She said, 'I had my breasts kissed.' I told her, 'I'll kiss your navel.' She said, 'I had my navel kissed.' I says, 'From the inside?'"

Around eleven o'clock Betty answered the phone. Cy was smashed. "Hi," he shouted, "can I come see you?"

"It's too late."

"Betty . . ."

"What?"

"Marry me."

"I need more stability than that."

How could she refuse him, he wondered. Didn't she read the paper? Didn't she know who he was? Even the bartender knew who he was. What was wrong with her? "Betty . . ."

"What?"

"Let's go to Europe."

"Cy, you don't understand. I'm not healthy. My metabolism isn't right. My doctor . . . my job . . .

Even if I wanted to, I couldn't leave Pittsburgh. I have too many commitments here."

"Betty, I'm gonna come see you." She needed his meat loaf, he thought. "I'll catch a cab—"

"No."

"Why the fuck not?" he shouted. She didn't reply. "Aw, horseshit," he muttered. "Can I see you tomorrow?"

"I don't think so."

"Betty, I love you."

"Cy, can't you forget that? We were children back then. That—"

He wasn't hearing her. "Betty—someday, someday, someday I'm going to have you, marry you, make you mine. I don't care if I have to wait. Someday. I don't care if we're—forty years old."

Betty exhaled loudly.

Cy was in tears. "Someday," he bawled. "I don't care how old we are. Forty. Even fifty, maybe."

"I'm spoken for," Betty said.

Cy heard that. He felt as if somebody had punted his heart clear out of sight. "Who?" he whispered.

"A man I've been seeing for about six months. A widower. A furrier. He and I—"

Cy surprised himself with drunken insight, softly said, "You're going to marry a rich, old Jew."

"Who is a gentleman and has made something of his life. He has stability. He and I—"

"A rich, old Jew," Cy shouted in amazement. The guy wouldn't simply take Betty to Europe, he would buy Europe for her, Cy thought before Betty hung up on him.

He tried her number several times and got busy signals. He returned to the bar where Irish Jim took off on an editorial: "Pro comes in. I know her specialty, around-the-world. Lots of guys told me, gives the best face in town. I pour her a drink. She complains, 'This glass is dirty.' Who knows where her mouth has been, right? I should break the glass she drinks out of. Can you beat that?" He topped off Allen's bourbon on the rocks. "Comes in here once, twice a week. High-tone. Calls herself Beverly. Once when she was in the can, I sneaked a peek at her driver's license. Real name's Betty, just plain Betty."

Without thinking, Allen automatically said, "Betty Vaughn."

"That's her. Address out on Craig. She's a looker, I'll give her that."

Cy felt as if a burst of .50-cal had riddled his heart. Was this some kind of practical joke? He stared at Irish Jim who shrugged, winked, said, "Takes all kinds to make a world, right, kid?"

Allen smiled crookedly: "You shitting me?"

"About what?"

Cy croaked out the name: "Betty. Vaughn."

Irish Jim pursed his lips. For several seconds he didn't move. Then he tried to top off Allen's already full glass. His hand shook. "You know her?" he asked softly.

Allen nodded.

"I mean, she's not some kind of friend, or something, is she?" Christ, he'd accidentally let his motor mouth run up a tab that his ass was going to pay, Irish Jim thought. Beads of perspiration popped out along his forehead and upper lip.

The man was actually sweating, Allen thought. It was no fucking joke, goddamnit. He felt his riddled heart disintegrate into a million pieces.

He was reminded of a time in Korea when a new jock reported in from Germany. His first night at the O-Club, the new guy hogged the spotlight by describing the great stuff he'd banged while in Europe, but especially one cute, little, oversexed, blond nurse in Wiesbaden. "I think I know her," Baldy Ryan had said, "a lieutenant named Sally from Philly?" The new guy clapped his hands, stomped his feet, laughed and nodded. Baldy finished his drink, leaned toward the new guy, and snapped, "You asshole motherfucker, she's my wife." And it was true. The new guy actually farted in distress (an act he never lived down because he was henceforth called Flate, short for flatus).

At the time Allen had felt sorry for Baldy Ryan, the victim of a one-in-a-million coincidence. Now he was in the same fix. Trying to sound casual, he asked Irish Jim, "You ever had her—Betty Vaughn?"

Irish Jim's eyes got big and he shook his head emphatically. "Me? You kidding? I can't afford that kind of stuff. I mean—" Irish Jim was at a loss for words.

"You're wrong about her," Cy Allen said. "She doesn't give the best face in town. She gives the best in the world."

Instantly Irish Jim lightened up, chuckled: "You had me going for a minute." He poured himself a drink. "You fighter pilots're all alike. I'd settle for what you guys pass up." He nodded. "More ass than a toilet seat." Smiling, back in control, he took off on another string of jokes.

None of them registered with Cy, who pictured himself as a cuckold. He could and he couldn't believe what he'd heard. Betty . . . Beverly . . . part-time pro . . . Queen of Heads. In a perverse way the idea made him want her more. He considered calling her, offering to buy it. No, that wasn't the answer. He wanted more from her than that. He felt he owed her, had something to prove to her. But she didn't want him.

The bitch was going to marry a rich, old fart. What a waste. Here he was—six-two, a hundred ninety pounds of raw dynamite, and with a long fuse—ready and able. Two weeks ago he had been over Korea looking for another kill. Two weeks ago he had been the toast of his fighter wing. Now he was a casualty, shot down in flames, shot down by the whore he loved.

Irish Jim finished his patter without Allen cracking a smile. "Come on, kid, wake up." Young guys today couldn't hold their booze, Irish Jim told himself. "On second thought, don't bother. I'm going to have to cut you off." He shook Cy's hand. "Good night. And good luck, lieutenant. Keep 'em flyin'."

Cy Allen hired a taxicab to drive him to Betty's apartment house. The operator asked, "I ever haul you before? You look familiar." Cy shook his drooping head.

For visitors the building's front door lock was electrically controlled from each apartment. Allen pressed Betty's buzzer. After a short wait, her voice came over the intercom: "Who is it, please?"

"Me. Cy Allen."

She didn't reply. He waited and then rang and called her name to no avail. He rang another apartment and, when there was no answer, rang one apartment after another. Suddenly five or six persons were talking to him. "I forgot my key," Allen shouted, "let me in." One by one they turned him off until a single voice remained to challenge him.

"What's your name?" the voice asked.

Allen read from one of the mailboxes: "Simon Dermott."

"You're not Simon," the voice said. "I know Simon. Who are you?"

"Rumple-fucking-stiltskin. Let me in."

"You better go away before I call the police."

"Do that. Yeah, do that. And I'll find out who you are and come back and shoot down your fucking apartment."

"Fuck you," the voice said. "I'm calling the cops."

"Watch your language, asshole."

"Fuck you twice," the voice said and the intercom went dead.

Cy Allen circled the apartment building. To get to the rear he climbed a high wooden fence; in the process, he ripped a pants leg from ankle to knee. Two basement doors were firmly locked; the rear fire exit also was secured. Goddamned distrustful bastards, he thought, what if he really was locked out? He'd have the manager's ass. The hell with it. He'd prove he was smarter; he'd get in regardless. . . .

Ornamental brickwork extended up the wall around the fire exit and passed what obviously were hall windows. Protruding bricks formed a pattern that, to his eyes, resembled a gigantic ladder. Stairway to the stars, he thought.

"Don't look down," he whispered and, using finger- and toeholds, he slowly scaled the brickwork. Each brick was a little shelf, he thought. He was surprised by how much space he had. But he was scuffing the shit out of his cordovans. Sacrifices were necessary when principle was at stake, he told himself. The moment he had both feet off the ground, Cy Allen transformed himself into the Human Fly. He buzzed quietly, crooned a fly lullaby while he crept upward, cautiously moved one hand and one foot at a time. The bricks were cool against his cheek. Stick like glue, his mind said.

He found the second floor window locked, decided to climb to the roof if he had to. Nothing stopped the

Human Fly. Slowly he buzzed his way to the third floor and discovered the window latch undone. Ha! Noiselessly he raised the window and loudly fell into the hallway. He had a fleeting notion to phone the manager and to chew him out for leaving the window unlocked: piss poor security.

He was going to surprise the shit out of Betty. He went down a flight of stairs and, locating her apartment door, hammered it with his fist. There was no response. He pounded harder and called her name until, from inside the apartment, a man's voice said, "Stop that at once and go away. Betty doesn't care to see you."

Fuck that noise, Allen thought. He was tired of people telling him to go away. Betty would get a chance to speak for herself. He rammed his body against the door which bowed inward before he rebounded and fell to the floor. Leaping to his feet, he hit the door again; locks and hinges strained but held. He backed off, built up a head of steam, and roared forward. A fraction of a second before he reached the door, it was jerked open. He practically flew into the apartment. By the time he caught his balance, he was towering over a short, gray-haired man who looked old enough to be his father.

Betty stepped from behind the door. "Cy—"

Allen didn't believe his eyes: "This guy?" He could have shaken the old fart apart with one hand. "This is the guy?" He noticed that the man was wearing a perfectly tailored suit that appeared to be cashmere, probably cost more than Allen earned in a month. "This is him? Is this the guy?"

"Yes," Betty shouted. "Cy, you better—"

"Fuck!" Allen hit the nearest wall with an overhand right and drove a fist-size hole at head level through plaster and lath.

"That does it," Betty shouted. "That's enough." She burst into tears. "Get out, get out—"

From the hallway, a man in pajamas and robe leaned into the room and outshouted her: "Hey, hey, hey, we are trying to sleep down the hall. Do you mind? Knock it off or I'm calling the cops."

Allen saw that the intruder was about his size, an equal match. The voice sounded familiar. "Hey, hey, hey, yourself," Allen shouted. "You the asshole who knows what's-his-face Simon . . ." With fists ready, he stepped toward the man. "Simon—Dermott?"

The intruder stared in surprise: "Hold it a minute, don't I know you? Didn't I see your picture—"

"Excuse us," Betty said to the man in the hall and shoved the door closed. She gave Allen a strange, panicked look. "You are going to have to get out of here," she said, "forever."

"That's a long fucking time," said Allen. He breathed heavily through his nose and looked back and forth from Betty to the gray-haired man. "I wish you were my age," he said.

"So do I," the man said with a hint of a smile.

Allen walked in a small circle, then stopped and banged his head against the edge of the hole he had punched in the wall. Without looking at Betty, he said, "Okay, this is it. Make up your mind once and for all. Betty, will you marry me—"

"No," she said.

He jerked his head toward her: "Goddamnit, let me finish." He glared at her: "Marry me and we'll go to Europe."

"No," she said without hesitation.

Allen looked her up and down. Even with puffy eyes she was beautiful. "You sure?"

"Yes."

"Positive?"

"Yes. Yes, yes, yes. Now just leave."

Allen closed his eyes, pressed his knuckles against his temples, and inhaled loudly through clenched teeth. His head throbbed. His mouth tasted like ox snot. Opening his eyes, he noticed his torn pants. The toes of his cordovans looked like suede. Never spit-shine those beauties again, he thought. He brushed plaster dust from the front of his coat. At the last minute he had decided not to wear his uniform; he would look twice as bad if he had. Jesus, he was a walking wreck. He really was shot down. He didn't belong here. He wanted to be back in Korea, in control, raising hell, flying, shooting down MiGs. He looked up and saw the other man watching him. "Who the fuck are you?" Allen asked.

The man smiled: "I'm Simon Dermott."

"No shit?"

"No shit."

Allen laughed, said, "You going to marry Betty?" and laughed again when he thought: No fool like an old fool.

"In three weeks." He took one of Betty's hands and patted it. With a thumb he gently wiped a tear from her cheek.

You better wipe her mouth too, Cy thought, and said, "You a Jew?"

"Yes."

"You got a number tattooed on your arm?"

Dermott shook his head: "I was born in Squirrel Hill."

"Jesus Christ, Betty, he's not even a real, one hundred percent, honest to god, genuine Jew. Have you checked him out? Is he circumcised?"

Betty's nostrils flared: "Cy, you—"

"Save it," Allen told her, "I'm leaving." Shaking his head, he walked to the door.

"You rotten bastard," Betty whispered after him.

He turned and studied Simon, then said, "In case you don't know it yet, Beverly here . . ." He pointed at Betty. ". . . is the world's greatest cocksucker. Ask anybody at the Cork and Bottle." Exit smiling.

In the morning he regretted having said it. The statement was unbecoming an officer and a gentleman. But he wouldn't have taken it back for less than five more MiGs. He decided that as a present he'd pay for the hole in the wall, if the wedding was still go.

That afternoon Simon Dermott phoned. Allen wasn't difficult to find: he was staying at his father's home in West View. He still was in bed when the phone rang. Dermott said: "I know Betty's past. I met her in the place you mentioned. I understand that phase of her life. I understand her motivation. And I love her. I suppose I also understand how you feel. But this ends it. The hole in the wall is on me." He paused, then said, "By the way, I explained to Betty who you are. Good luck in your career." And he disconnected.

Allen smiled at the old man's cool, at the reference to his career. How could he have more luck? As a fighter pilot he was at the pinnacle of his life. Then he suddenly realized that unless the United States fought another war, from here on his career was all downhill.

1

Trotting along at pretty good speed, the four Phantom jets in Rambler flight were hunting for something to kill. Echeloned left at four thousand foot intervals from eight up to twenty thousand feet, they headed southeast paralleling Thud Ridge. The Ridge was a twenty-five mile long mountain range that pointed directly at Hanoi, twenty miles away.

Riding atop the stack of F-4C Phantoms, Lieutenant Colonel Cy Young Allen felt he had his ass hung out. At any moment he expected a surface-to-air missile to pop through the undercast, a solid cloud deck between six and seven thou, and home on him. By the time he saw the missile it would be up to speed, humming along near Mach 2. He would have about a tick and a half to dive and turn into the missile and hopefully outbend it, hopefully watch it attempt to fly up its own exhaust hole and thereby miss his likewise orifice. Another fun-filled day of technoviolence, Cy Allen thought. But if the day came off as planned—if the ruse worked—he expected to be a MiG-killer by nightfall.

Over the headset he heard the "scree" of a ground-based search radar as its scan swept across his fighter. The Phantom's radar homing and warning (RHAW) gear converted radar energy to sound for detection by the crew. Cy wondered if the radar was Ground Control Intercept which vectored MiGs to attack, or if it was Fan Song which launched and guided surface-to-air missiles—the hated SA2 Guidelines. Korea had been far less complicated, he thought, and asked Lieutenant Jerry Dobbs who was in the F-4's rear seat, "You watching that RHAW gear back there?"

Dobbs also heard the radar sweeps. In addition he had scopes that reported hostile radar activity with light signals. Since entering North Vietnam his eyes had been locked on his warning equipment. He answered, "Yeah."

"Yeah?" Cy repeated mockingly.

"Yeah, *sir!*"

"I don't want any last-minute surprises from one of those big white bastards. We don't have a lot of room to play with." The Dinks would shoot white today, Cy decided, tougher to see against the clouds. SAMs came in assorted colors: white, black, and the ever-popular camouflage brown and green. The last was identical to the Phantom's paint job. "You see the tuxedo jacket Hawk had made out of that camouflage material Raja got in?"

"Negative."

"If you do, don't get ideas . . ."

"Yes, sir."

". . . because all that stuff turns to junk back in the real world."

"Yes, sir."

"Knock off the gab and keep your eyes open. Stay alert," Cy said half-jokingly. One pair of eyes wasn't enough when over enemy territory and up against an array of technological threats—MiGs, SAMs, radar-

controlled antiaircraft artillery. It was reassuring to
have the kid in the back seat, reassuring to have the
extra set of eyes focused on the gee-whiz electronics
inside the cockpit while his eyes took in the world
outside. About then the four Phantoms of Rambler
flight swung right and headed back to the northwest.

Rambler was the third flight launched that day—2
January 1967—as spearhead for Operation Uppercut,
a plan to lure North Vietnamese MiG-21s into battle.
Operating from five principal sanctuaries—Phuc Yen,
Kep, and Gia Lam airfields located near Hanoi, plus
Kien An and Cat Bi outside Haiphong—the MiGs
were free from attack when on the ground because, at
the time, the United States government prohibited
strikes against North Vietnamese airfields. With such
immunity, North Vietnamese Air Force tactics were
to scramble MiGs early and have them feint attacks,
or make a single slashing high-speed firing pass
through target-bound U.S. formations. In either case,
grossed-out F-105 Thunderchiefs who lugged most of
the bombs were forced to prematurely jettison their
racks of ordnance in order to generate speed for
self-defense. Once the strike force was thus neutralized, the MiGs fled to their airfield sanctuaries rather
than join in air-to-air combat.

Since 1964 when U.S. airstrikes began against
North Vietnam, air defense forces had responded
unpredictably. However, USAF analysts recognized a
vague cyclic air defense reaction geared to the experience levels of MiG pilots, the seasonal weather, and
the pattern of offensive strike forces. Operation Uppercut was predicated upon the latter factor—a familiar strike force pattern. The intention was to lull
North Vietnamese radar operators into thinking that
Uppercut was merely another routine day-in, day-out
Thunderchief mission.

Like most successful tricks, Uppercut was uncomplicated. Fundamentally, F-4s were substituted for F-105s, a change that put the Americans into a ready-to-fight posture with tremendous numerical superiority if the MiGs came up. In addition, F-4 combat air patrols were pre-positioned to deny the MiGs landing privileges or retreat routes to China. Most important, however, the F-4s were made to appear as lumbering, bomb-laden F-105s: the F-4s flew F-105 mission profiles (used Thunderchief refueling tracks and altitudes, target approach routes, airspeeds, radio call signs and procedures) and, for the first time, F-4s were equipped with electronic countermeasure pods to jam enemy radars, a recognized F-105 capability.

Now everything was in place—Buick flight had arrived over target at 1500 hours, Ford flight at 1505, Rambler at 1510—and the three spearhead flights were poised in motion, independently trolling as MiGCAPs ahead of the inbound eighty-four ship main force.

And now it was up to the North Vietnamese radar controllers. Would they be deceived? Would they scramble MiGs?

Fly around and wait, Cy Allen thought, same old story: hours of boredom broken by seconds of absolute terror. On the lookout, his head and eyes constantly moved: he searched the horizon, the sky above and below. Actually, he was happy to be where he was. For his entire adult life he'd been a fighter pilot—F-86s, F-100s, F-102s—building toward this day.

After Uppercut had been delayed an hour because of clouds over target, while cranking his Phantom's twin jet engines he'd discovered that the plane's left-hand generator would not stay on line. To repair it would have required down-loading Sparrow missiles, an act that would have thrown him out of takeoff sequence and probably would have resulted in an abort. Knowing there was no spare airplane, he had decided to "overlook" the malfunction. After all, it was a maximum effort day. A crew chief who had a leg in a cast had been feverishly hopping about the parking ramp, readying an F-4.

Now, nothing was happening and yet Cy Allen felt as nervous as a whore in church. Whatever was going to happen had better happen fast, he thought. Today the F-4s had short legs, carried only outboard fuel tanks, no six-hundred-gallon centerline tank. The streamlined configuration left the Phantoms ready to dogfight instantly.

Then, without prelude, over the radio he heard the two flights that had preceded them—Buick and Ford —roll into an attack. Somewhere, MiGs were up! The voices of comrades in battle put Cy Allen on the edge of his seat. But where was the action? Amid radio calls between Buick and Ford flights, Lieutenant Colonel Rocco Monge who was Rambler Lead asked, "Where are you? Where are the MiGs?" The voice of the Buick flight leader rumbled back, loud and clear: "These are mine. Find your own."

To Cy Allen it was the ultimate frustration to listen to the battle rage without being able to join in.

Then he saw them, was first to spot them—six flashing drops of quicksilver suspended in space. He called, "Two o'clock low, six bandits." The delta-wing shapes were unmistakable. In a shallow climb, six sleek MiG-21 Fishbeds had slipped out of the clouds about eight miles away, almost parallel to Cy Allen who felt a warm spot deep in his gut at the sight of them. The nerves on his hands and forearms tingled.

After all the years, he thought, just like Pavlov's dog . . .

Rambler flight made a hard right turn and Rocco Monge called, "Lead's in." He dived at the MiGs, followed immediately by Major Mike Hawk, flying Two position.

Number Three sat there like a dead-ass and Allen gave him a two count, then hit both afterburners and rolled into a dive toward the enemy. "Yow," he yelled to Dobbs. He flashed by Three who was still flying straight and level and saw him again only after the fight ended. He remembered calling, "Four's in. Three?"

After days of briefings on tactics and discussions about covering each other and working as a team, all the words and promises were ignored in a blink. The meat was on the table and suddenly it was every man for himself—catch as catch can, no holds barred.

The MiG-21s turned too late for a head-on pass at the F-4s. Nevertheless, they started shooting. The tracers from their twin-barrel 23-mm cannons looked like flaming red golf balls as they curved away from the diving Phantoms.

Cy Allen's body was atingle as he leaned forward against his shoulder straps. But his mind was calm. He had one objective: get behind the bastard he had picked for a target before he dived. Nearing his prey, he kicked the rudders; he horsed the control stick with his right hand and hot-rodded the throttles with his left, in and out and back into afterburners: boom! boom! Rudder-rolling through a high angle-off attack, he wasn't thinking about his physical movements: the plane was as one with his body, an extension of his physical being. He could have just as easily been running down a street after the bandit. The rotating horizon went unnoticed: to a fighter jock the aircraft was always right side up. Cy Young Allen had eyes only for his target.

He pulled the control stick right, back, tighter right, back more. He had been warned that an F-4 was at a disadvantage in trying to out-turn a MiG-21, but he was doing it and pulling only four to five Gs, nowhere near the G-load he had expected necessary to beat one of those guys. Barely a minute after selecting his target, with unimagined ease, he rolled out in line directly behind it.

The C-model Phantom wasn't equipped with a lead computing gunsight; therefore, he ignored the fancy illuminated reticle and steering dot projected on his center windscreen. Instead, he flew so that the MiG appeared to be perched atop the F-4's nose radome. Eyeballs were best. The two airplanes went around once in a tight circle and Cy had his prize: a big silver delta-shaped MiG-21 with a big red star on each wing. "Jer?" he said and caught himself grinning inside his oxygen mask.

Dobbs replied, "You got a radar lock. In range."

Cy pulled the trigger on the head of his control column. With interlocks out, the mechanical genius of the radar fire control computer was bypassed; the missile should have launched instantly. Instead, the radar-guided AIM7 Sparrow missile fizzled—simply fell off the airplane. Nothing? Goddamn son-of-a-bitch, he thought. In a left turn at around twelve thousand feet altitude, he squeezed the trigger again. A second Sparrow flew home—a darting journey of less than a mile. A moment before the missile impacted, the MiG pilot ejected. He'd probably seen the rocket fire from the Sparrow's tail and decided it wasn't his day, Cy thought. Then the ninety-pound warhead hit the MiG in the wing root and a large orange ball of fire momentarily hid the airframe. Pieces of the plane came loose, hung suspended in the wake of the MiG's slipstream. An instant later, the empty fighter lost momentum and entered its final gravitational arc. Corkscrewing downward, the abandoned airframe bored its way into the cloud deck below.

"Hey, you got one," somebody shouted.

The radio was filled with a flow of words, gasps, pants.

"There's one, three o'clock."

". . . afterburner. Goddamn . . ."

"See him."

"Go get . . ."

"He's mine."

"Three, break right."

"Fuckin' . . . Check six. Check my six."

"I got him." A crow of triumph from Major Mike Hawk. It was amazing how, in the heat of battle, one man recognized another's voice. Hawk's kill was made with one of three AIM7 Sparrows triggered at the target. The missile hit the fuselage, just aft of the wing root, and set the MiG-21 ablaze.

"Check my six, damnit."

"You're clean. I got him."

Off to his left Cy saw a smear of black smoke extending toward the clouds.

"I got him!"

"Good show, Hawk. Now get off the air," Rocco Monge ordered, keeping tabs on everyone and everything. Time enough to celebrate back on the ground. . . .

Moments later Monge quietly killed a MiG-21 with one of a pair of AIM7 Sparrows. The target exploded in front of him, forced him to fly through debris, thereby damaging the underside of his Phantom—the only damage inflicted on Rambler flight. Surprisingly, the pilot escaped from the shattered MiG and apparently parachuted safely to earth, as did the pilot of the MiG set afire by Hawk. Monge later shot another Sparrow at another MiG but it passed approximately two thousand feet in front of the enemy fighter.

After his first kill, Cy Allen at once began searching for more MiGs. Breaking hard to clear his six o'clock position, he heard Dobbs grunt while flexing his upper body in an effort to stave off the effects of heavy G-forces pulled in the tight turn. Cy glanced quickly at his armament panel: every switch was in the correct position. Good. The Sparrow had fucked up, not him.

A couple hundred feet below he saw another MiG cutting a circle slightly inside of him. Putting back pressure on the control stick, he slightly decreased his bank angle, then arced the jet's nose upward. The laws of physics went to work: in a wink, gravity sucked off the Phantom's excess speed and reduced the angle between the aircraft. The jet climbed for an instant before he rolled it onto its back, then pulled its nose down toward the enemy fighter's six o'clock position, thereby slicing the circle in half. The maneuver, a high-speed yo-yo, placed the Phantom directly in trail behind the MiG: it was almost as if the guy had waited for him. In the slot where the MiG pilot couldn't see him, Cy paused a heartbeat, admired the same silver delta shape, the same red star. Beautiful! "Jer . . . ?"

"Lock. In range."

Happiness is a radar lock-on at the speed of sound, Cy thought and pulled the trigger. The third Sparrow fell off the airplane—a stillborn bird, exactly like the first. "Fuck," Cy shouted and squeezed again. The fourth and last Sparrow missile failed to fire—died on the rails. Fuck this bullshit, he thought. He was flying like hell to stay behind that guy and his technological advantage was the biggest handicap he ever had. He would have traded his left nut for a .50-caliber machine gun.

Stretching forward and flipping a T-bar switch with his left hand, he changed over to the AIM9 Sidewinder missiles—heat seekers with twenty-five pound warheads. In a five-G turn, he fired two. The missiles slued wide of the target. They had been designed ten years earlier for use against slow-moving bombers, not hard-turning fighters. Sweating now, Cy Allen mentally damned antiquated technology.

The MiG pilot solved every problem: he leveled his fighter and dived for the cover of the clouds. "Wrong move," Cy told Dobbs. Glancing at his Mach meter, he read 1.8—nearly twice the speed of sound. "Fantastic," he whispered to himself and triggered his last two Sidewinders. Both came off the rails cleanly and tracked perfectly—parallel snakes of white smoke. Both hit—bing! bang!—and the MiG came unglued.

Much better, Cy thought. He felt good, like after a hard driving piece, winded but deeply satisfied. Flipping his oxygen control lever to one hundred percent, he took several deep breaths of cool pure oxygen, then peripherally saw two MiGs hightailing it in formation and turned after them. He was gaining on the enemy survivors when Dobbs asked, "What're you doing?"

"I got two MiGs visual," Cy snapped. A passenger was a pain in the ass, he thought. He had forgotten he was out of ordnance.

Dobbs quietly asked, "What're you going to do, throw rocks at them?"

At that point Cy would have tossed in his right nut too in exchange for a .50-cal. Breaking off the chase, he started looking for the rest of Rambler flight.

Dobbs didn't leave it alone: "Let's go after them. Maybe you can talk them into surrendering."

Cy Allen was ready to tell him, "Shut up and we'll damn well discuss it on the ground," when Dobbs said, "Hey, Colonel Allen, thanks for the greatest day of my life."

Slipping the throttles into maximum afterburners, Allen stroked back the control pole: upside down at the top of a perfect loop, he told Dobbs, "Thanks for the help."

On the way home they decided that if they ever lined up another MiG and had only Sparrows, they were going to climb above the target and drop the five-hundred-pound missiles on it.

Headed for Ubon Air Base in Thailand—home of the 8th Tactical Fighter Wing Wolfpack—Allen reflected that he wasn't as quick as he'd been in his mid-twenties, but he knew what to do and when to do it. Experience had made him more intense, controlled, deliberate. By his age, maneuvers were instinctive. That more than made up for being half a mo slower. Most important, however, he still had great eyeballs. He had spotted airplanes at twenty-six, twenty-seven miles and told Dobbs to wave the radar over that way, and Dobbs then locked on them. Naturally if he saw enemy planes before their drivers saw his . . .

He smiled to himself at the idea that he had probably shot down the pappies of some of the young Zips flying around out there today.

He fell into a pattern of thought that was a carry-over from his experiences in Korea. In a dogfight, it

21s. A nice day's work. If the missiles hadn't failed, or if he'd owned a gun, he might have had four. His heart took a couple extra knocks at that idea. In Korea he had been a double ace—a total of ten kills—but he had never downed four in one day. Few Americans had.

The beautiful knowledge that he was to become the first ace of the Vietnam War crept onto the edge of his mind. He let it slumber there. He wasn't ready to examine it in detail.

He appreciated that Dobbs had been perfectly in sync when he called on him:

"Jer . . . ?"

"Lock. In range."

Pull the trigger.

The kid was an extra arm, an extra pair of eyes. The last of Cy's doubts about Dobbs vanished. Best of all, the kid had enjoyed the action too.

What a day it turned out to be for the Wolfpack: seven kills. Rocco Monge's squadron, the 555th— Triple Nickel—downed four and the 433rd Tactical Fighter Squadron—the Haloed Devils—went in right behind them and bagged three. Seven in one day and it was only the Second of January. What an auspicious beginning to the year. In all of 1966, the entire United States Air Force had destroyed but seventeen MiGs; in 1965, only two.

Debriefing revealed that the F-4 pilots had fired— or had attempted to fire—twenty-nine air-to-air missiles: sixteen AIM7 Sparrows to down four MiG-21s, and thirteen AIM9 Sidewinders for the other three MiGs. Cy wasn't the only crewman who claimed he'd rather carry a gun.

Rambler flight had scored Triple Nickel's four victories. The bundle of nervous energy named Mike

Hawk crowed to the world about his kill and was drunk before he left debriefing. Squadron Commander Rocco Monge who got the other hardly said a word. Rocco had been instrumental in keeping Cy Allen at Ubon despite a change of orders, and thereafter made certain that Allen flew in his flight, especially after he heard Dobbs boast that with the naked eye his pilot could see airplanes twenty-seven miles away. At debriefing, self-effacing Rocco literally shoved Allen and Dobbs into the spotlight. And Number Three—old Dale Vestik—just sat there on the fringe, doing on the ground exactly what he did in the air. Cy decided that he had picked off Vestik's share—and if the fucking missiles had worked. . . .

The air battle hadn't been half as rough as the party that followed. From debriefing, the crews went to the Officers' Club where the atmosphere was like a World Series winning team's dressing room. The men poured as much beer and whiskey on each other as they drank. By nightfall the club was littered with soaked, hoarse, fatigued, staggering men in tattered flying suits.

To put life back into the party, Rocco organized a MiG Sweep. He assembled the biggest lieutenants at the quietest end of the barroom. They linked arms and formed a flying wedge as wide as the room, then charged in an all-out run down the length of the room. When the other drunks saw the MiG Sweep approaching, most leaped onto or over the bar or climbed the railing that separated the barroom from the dining room. Less agile persons and a few diehards who deliberately opposed the wedge formation were knocked down and trampled or ultimately crushed against the opposite wall. At that point, MiG Sweep personnel did an about-face, rejoined arms, and roared back through the barroom in an unopposed, full-speed run that terminated with a building-rattling impact against the wall from which they started. Listing twenty degrees to the right, Rocco emerged from the center of the formation and stated, "Someday we'll take out that whole wall and sweep the entire base."

Rocco's backseater, Lieutenant Greg Wiltrout, who was the only person in the room more muscular than Rocco, shouted, "Base, my ass. All the way to Hanoi."

Eventually the party moved to the Noncommissioned Officers' Club and then to the Airmen's Club. The flyers owed the respect of a visit to both. They had taken the machines that the enlisted men had painstakingly made ready and had shot the dick off the North Vietnamese Air Force—and without suffering a loss.

Compared to the Officers' Club, the atmosphere of the NCO Club was reserved. The senior ranking enlisted men had, as usual, placed the bedding-down of their airplanes as their first responsibility; as a result, the NCOs got a late start at the bar. Therefore, the relatively sober senior enlisted men pretended that the officers weren't absolutely shitfaced: everyone stood around and shared a gentlemanly drink and congratulated one another with handshakes and pats on the back. As it turned out, the flyers needed the brief respite.

The Airmen's Club was like open house at the loco weed factory. The assistant crew chiefs and other flightline knuckle-busting wrench turners were drunker than the flyers. Drink throwing started over again. There were deafening cheers and unheard speeches and unintelligible toasts and locomotor chants: "Ho —Chi—Minh—fuck him" and "Hey, hey, LBJ—how many MiGs did we kill today?"

About the time Rocco tried to organize another

MiG Sweep, somebody decided it was souvenir time. Airmen swarmed over the pilots who had scored the MiG kills and tore the flying suits off them. Then they stripped the backseaters. Laughing all the way, and finally dressed in only boxer shorts and flying boots, Rocco Monge leaned against the bar and told a similarly clad Cy Allen, "Fuckin' rock and roll stars get this shit all the time. Can you believe it? Even if the crowd was full of young pussy, it'd still get old in a hurry—I think."

Then Rocco offered to arm wrestle all comers. He knocked off opponents one after the other until a brute of an airman from the Armament and Electronics Squadron whipped him fast, fair and square. The moment Rocco's arm hit the floor, red-faced Greg Wiltrout began bellowing: "What the fuck? What the fuck?" Wiltrout, who wore his blond hair clipped to a quarter-inch length, was one of the last pilots flying in the rear seat of the F-4. He grabbed the A&E airman by the shoulders and shook him: "What the fuck? You're a maintenance man, man. You can't whip a pilot."

"I think I just did, lieutenant," the A&E airman said.

"What the fuck? Like shit," Wiltrout shouted. Thick veins swelled out on his neck. For three years he had been the Texas Aggies' starting fullback. "Before you start claiming you whipped a pilot, boy, you gotta whip me." He opened and closed thick meaty hands: muscles ridged along his forearms. "Colonel Rocco and me are a team. It doesn't count unless you whip both of us. So let's go."

The young lions stretched out on the floor and, a moment after the referee let them go, Wiltrout slammed down the airman's arm, leaped to his feet, roared, pounded his chest. Nobody called for a rematch. The power of Wiltrout's drunken rage fractured the airman's wrist. The outcome didn't slow the party. The airman wasn't the only casualty of the day. The MiG Sweep of the O-Club had scored a fractured collarbone, a broken foot, and sixteen miscellaneous stitches. Nobody cared, not even the injured.

Later, while the A&E airman's right arm was in a cast, Wiltrout frequently saw him working on an airplane using one hand. The smiling airman always had the same greeting: "Sir, I truly do believe I whipped half a pilot." Crew chiefs were ballsy guys, a lot like aircrewmen, Wiltrout decided. He remembered the old crew chief who broke a leg and never missed a day of duty, full leg cast and all.

About the time Wiltrout was avenging Rocco's loss, Cy Allen decided he was badly out of control and close to spinning and crashing. It was time to taxi home. He found Dobbs asleep against a wall. Unable to wake his backseater, Cy picked him up in a fireman's carry and away they went, from pillar to post. Dobbs was his responsibility. The young man he once had considered a liability had developed into a precious asset.

2

___

When they were assigned to fly together in training at MacDill Air Force Base, Allen had wondered if Dobbs was physically tough enough to last in jet fighters. Dobbs, who was directly out of navigator training, was gangly, a couple of inches taller than Allen who stood six-two. However, at an even two hundred, Allen outweighed him by forty, maybe fifty pounds; Dobbs never admitted to an exact weight. Allen's first impression was that the younger man looked too fragile to stand up under physical pressure.

The first day they met, talking between classes, Dobbs said he had played some basketball, Industrial League, while in college.

"Semipro, hunh?" Allen said. He had played a lot of basketball, including varsity college ball, but had never earned a dime for any of it. Kids today didn't do anything for the fun of it, he thought. "Get paid much?"

"Enough to get me through school," Dobbs said quietly.

"You in shape now?"

"Sure. I take care of myself." Dobbs knew who Cy

Young Allen was: he respected the man, his accomplishments, and his senior rank. But he wasn't going to be intimidated by him, no matter how big he was. Korea was a long time ago, nearly ancient history, Dobbs thought, and Vietnam was new. Going there, they were equals.

"How about a little one-on-one?" Allen offered. "Today, after classes."

Dobbs fidgeted. His footlocker hadn't arrived and he didn't have gym clothes, but he wasn't going to use *that* as an excuse. He nodded agreement. He showed up on the base gymnasium floor in cutoff jeans, black uniform socks, and crepe-soled Hush Puppies.

The black socks were bad enough, Allen thought, but street shoes. . . . And the frayed jeans made him look like some raggedy-ass hippie refugee. Cy considered calling the whole thing off.

Using both hands, Dobbs bounced the ball four times and said, "Ready when you are."

About then the noncom in charge of the gym came steaming out of his office: "Hold it, hold it. You can't play in here with black-soled shoes. You'll mark up the floor."

Allen was about to say, "Another day then," but Dobbs nodded, said, "Okay, sarge," pulled off his shoes, and threw them beyond the endline.

"You going to play in socks?" Allen asked.

"Sure. Why not?"

Because after I beat you I don't want you to have any excuses for why you lost, Allen thought.

"You better take it slow," the sergeant said. "I don't want to have to write up a busted ass."

Dobbs thought for a second. "Right," he said, "too slippery. Thanks." He stripped off the black socks, stuffed them in a back pocket, smiled at Allen. "Ready when you are."

Allen and the sergeant exchanged glances of mutual resignation, hedging acceptance of a value system unlike theirs.

May as well get it over with, Allen thought, and told Dobbs, "Take the ball out. One point a basket. Game's eleven."

Dobbs moved beyond the free throw line, dribbled a few feet, and, when Allen didn't come after him, put up a soft one-hander. It missed, but Dobbs out-jumped the older man for the rebound and scored. Allen took the ball out and, when Dobbs didn't come after him, swished through a two-hander from twenty feet. The game followed that pattern: from outside Allen pumped through set shots while Dobbs scored from close in. Allen won the first game, 11-10; Dobbs took the second, 11-9. Allen had been putting out at about seventy-five percent and guessed that Dobbs had been doing the same. They took a break and Allen said, "Enough of this messin' around. Let's play best of three to see who buys dinner."

Dobbs agreed.

"Winner buys."

Dobbs held up a hand: "Wait a minute. I've always played 'Loser Buys.'"

"That so? Well, *I* always play 'Winner Buys' because that really proves how much you want to win."

Dobbs thought about it, nodded: "OK. Winner buys. Take the ball out."

Allen moved beyond the free throw line, turned, and found both of Dobbs' hands in his face; with no chance to set for a two-hander, he drove to the basket and took off for a lay-up. Dobbs cleanly stole the ball out of his hands and, before Allen recovered, spun around and slipped in a reverse lay-up. At that point, the tempo of play went out of control. Suddenly Allen was giving "a hundred and ten percent" and still couldn't keep up. Dobbs blew him off the court, 11-4.

Allen resorted to pure strength and muscle the second game but it didn't change things. Dobbs won easily. He refused to be intimidated by the deliberate use of force. Only once did he complain and that was when he was tripped: "Hey, now that's *really* a foul," he shouted. But he didn't lose the ball or interrupt his dribble; quickly rising to his feet, he drove to the basket and scored.

Dobbs made it a clean sweep by winning the third game which Allen insisted on playing and called "The Consolation Round." The skinny kid sandbagged him, Allen decided. Deep inside he felt a touch of admiration that he refused to voice.

At dinner Allen offered to pay despite their bet. Dobbs asked, "Did you play as hard as you could?"

"You bet your sweet ass I did."

"Then I pay."

After that they played daily, but only on the same side, and never lost a two-on-two game. Allen's long two-hand set shots from both chest level and over-head delighted Dobbs who laughingly said, "God-damn, nobody shoots like that."

"So what? They go in. Don't forget, I learned my game in the late Thirties, early Forties."

"I was born in the Forties," Dobbs said. "Nineteen forty-two."

"Don't rub it in."

"I think my folks did me before my dad enlisted in the Army, for the Great Hate. He's a warrant officer— thirty-year man—United States Army, all the way."

On his best days, with amazing consistency Allen bombed in two-handers from as far as thirty feet. He felt free to fire at will because when he missed Dobbs went up like a goosed kangaroo for a tip-in; nobody on base, black or white, outjumped him. "We're the perfect pair: Mister Inside and Mister Outside," he told Dobbs. "I'm surprised they let me set from out there, especially when I'm hitting. They never come out after me."

"All the fucking bunnies want to do is score," Dobbs said. "To them, playing defense sucks. Same, they believe nobody can hit from out there time after time. They're too fucking dumb to believe it even when they see you do it. Of course, you're a relic. You wouldn't be worth shit today in a real five-man game. Your team would be down court and have a dozen shots by the time you got open and set for a two-hander."

"Jerry, I don't want you to be afraid to say exactly what you think. Don't ever let my rank get in the way of your frankness."

Having always gone up against the enemy alone, Allen decided that if he had to be stuck with another body in the airplane—and, of all people, it had to be a navigator—Dobbs was as good as anyone he would have selected. Dobbs was near the age that Allen had been when he flew F-86s in Korea. The similarity caused Allen to strongly identify with the young man. He respected Dobbs' basketball skills, his overpowering honesty, and the facts that he didn't smoke and drank only moderately. Above all, he admired Dobbs' professional competence. The young man was a quick study who never needed the same lesson twice: he paid attention in class, studied his F-4 Flight Manual nightly, and frequently sought information beyond what was provided.

When they finished ground school and entered the flying phase of training, Dobbs displayed an ecstasy that made Allen recall the rapture of his early days of jet flying. Filled with nostalgia, he desired to be young again, to start his career and his life over. His career was his life, he thought. The idea pleased him. If he had it to do over again, he would probably do it exactly the same. He recognized that the act of returning to combat was a new beginning. Even before they took to the air, Dobbs' reactions brought memories to Allen. He flashed back in time while watching Dobbs go through the ritual of being fitted with flying gear designed specifically for jet fighter operations, a ritual like preparing to enter another world.

The white flying helmet was a symbol of strength and purity to Allen. Maybe the helmet's two retractable visors, one clear and one tinted, gave him that impression: when he pulled down a visor he often thought of helmeted knights in shining armor. Or maybe the white color did it: putting on the helmet always made him feel like the "good guy." He never understood men who defaced their helmets with lightning bolts or tiger stripes or personalized forms of graffiti. He noticed that each time Dobbs donned the helmet he stood a little straighter and sneaked admiring glances of himself from reflecting surfaces.

Numerous fittings by personal equipment specialists were necessary before the helmet's shaped foam rubber liners perfectly matched the contours of the wearer's head. The night after the fittings, Allen entered Dobbs' room and found him wearing the helmet while studying. Although they had private BOQ rooms connected by a common bath, Dobbs obviously hadn't expected the visit and hastily explained, "Breaking it in. Getting used to it. Finding the hot spots." He hadn't needed to say a word. When given his first helmet, Allen had spent the evening shining it until it glowed in the dark.

After having his facial features measured with calipers, Dobbs' oxygen mask too was individually sized and shaped until it formed an airtight seal covering nose and mouth. After one fitting, as if sensing Allen's thoughts, Dobbs unclipped the mask and said, "The Man in the Iron Mask."

The webbed harness, designed to connect to a parachute and survival equipment in the airplane, was cinched down until the wearer was required to walk in a seated position. Trapped in the gear and with knuckles scraping the floor, Dobbs did a monkey imitation for Allen's amusement.

Dobbs also reacted to the anti-G suit that covered the wearer like kneeless cowboy chaps. The suit contained inflatable bladders that stretched over the abdomen, thighs, and calves. Inside the airplane the suit connected to a pneumatic system that, upon sensing positive G-forces, inflated the bladders which squeezed the lower body. Centrifugal force developed by high positive G-loads normally drained the blood from the upper body. However, the inflated bladders restricted the flow of blood into the lower body. The result was that supplies of blood and oxygen were held in the heart and brain and the chance of a blackout was reduced.

The G-suit was snugged up with corset-like laces down the back. "Tighter the better, sir," a personal equipment sergeant told Dobbs. "Long as your toes don't turn black, you're in good shape." The first few times that Dobbs wore the suit, he walked with an exaggerated bowlegged stride that reminded Cy of Matt Dillon in the opening frames of "Gunsmoke." To make the image perfect, Dobbs needed only a six-shooter, and a hundred pounds of body weight.

It was in the air, however, that Dobbs truly reopened Allen's eyes. On their initial flight, they had barely broken ground and were climbing toward the Gulf of Mexico when Dobbs pointed out several sea-going tankers: "Look at those big mothers. Oh, shit! How could you miss? I wish we were armed."

"And over North Vietnam," Allen added. A long time before, from the air he had stopped viewing *everything* as a potential target. As it was, it had required years to break himself of the habit. Now, instantly, Dobbs' enthusiasm recalled that definite sense of power produced by being in a small, fast, and highly maneuverable warplane. He loved it.

On that initial flight, Allen had put the Phantom through its paces. He wasn't interested in wringing out the airplane; he already knew what it could do. With an instructor pilot in the back seat, he had spent two weeks checking out the Phantom before Dobbs arrived at MacDill. Now he wanted to wring out Dobbs, to find out at once if the rookie could handle the stress and strain of combat maneuvers. If not, he wasn't wasting another flight on him. Allen went through the book of aerobatics: rudder rolls, maximum G breaks, Immelmanns, vertical rolling scissors, spirals, split-S's, whifferdills, and high- and low-speed yo-yos. To be fair and to give Dobbs a chance to appreciate the test, he explained each maneuver before he executed it: "Now, a whifferdill. Used to change direction one hundred and eighty degrees. First, the nose is raised thirty to sixty degrees. Lot of room for error. Then into a ninety degree bank, reverse direction, and pull the nose below the horizon. Nothing more than a half-assed split-S. And so. . . ." He smoothly accomplished the maneuver. When he reached the end of the list, Dobbs wasn't saying much. "You all right, Jer?"

"Sure. Fine."

"Then hang on," Allen told him and he put all the

maneuvers into a medley of aerobatics that would have turned an eagle green with envy, or with an upset stomach. The interphone system between the Phantom's front and back cockpits was an open, or "hot," microphone. Allen listened to Dobbs grunt and suck wind and belch, but never say a word. When Allen finally bottomed out after a long descending vertical rolling scissors maneuver and skimmed low across the water toward MacDill, Dobbs voluntarily spoke for the first time since they began: "Jesus Christ, that was insane. Fucking unbelievable. Jesus!" He laughed loudly. "Let's do it again. One—more—time."

Allen considered that maybe he had a winner.

The F-4 Phantom originally was designed for the Navy as a single-seat, carrier-based, all-weather interceptor. It quickly evolved into a two-man fighter-bomber, with a back seat for an observer, and became operational in 1961. In 1963 the Air Force purchased the C model, added flight controls and an inertial guidance system in the rear cockpit, and manned the F-4 with two pilots. When a pilot shortage developed, navigators were assigned to the back seat.

On subsequent training missions, Allen taught Dobbs the fundamentals of controlling the Phantom. He demonstrated flying techniques but mostly, in the few spare minutes they found, he let Dobbs handle the stick, get a feel for the airplane and how it responded. On the ground they discussed what they didn't have time for in flight. Allen made one point emphatically: when aiming a machine that moved at ten to fifteen miles a minute, every wiggle of the stick profoundly affected speed and direction. He explained how each change in bank angle or pitch moved the aircraft into a new geometric plane and, as a result, the laws of aerodynamics and physics applied new forces on the airframe. Dobbs was inquisitive. In answering a few of his probing questions regarding high performance aircraft, Allen remembered long forgotten principles behind causes and effects that, for years, he had been taking for granted. He didn't admit it aloud but, after thousands of hours in airplanes, he suddenly felt a new enlightenment toward flying. Dobbs had renewed his desire for perfection, absolute precision. He recognized another reward from his efforts: Dobbs' mental growth was reflected in his flying too. Deciding that his backseater had a flair for handling the stick, he asked, "How come you never went to pilot training?"

"My far vision's messed up. Too much reading, late at night, poor light."

"That's a shame. Don't get the big head, but I think you have a touch."

"A touch of what?"

"Insanity. Jeez. . . . You know, that's one system I never understood: a guy has to be twenty-twenty to enter pilot school, but after he gets his wings he can practically go blind and still stay on flying status—as long as he's correctable to twenty-twenty."

"I don't understand half of what the Air Force does."

"Don't start playing the cynical role. You haven't been around long enough. Really though, I once had a squadron commander who wore glasses . . ." With forefinger and thumb he indicated a thickness of at least an inch. ". . . like this."

Dobbs laughed: "And he had a dog that flew with him."

"No. Really, one day we swiped his glasses and used the lenses, you know, by focusing the sun through them, to set fire to a newspaper on his desk."

"Come on . . ."

"It's the truth. How come you don't wear glasses?"

"My eyes aren't *that* bad. My near vision is twenty-twenty. Hell, I can see everything in the cockpit, perfectly."

"You own glasses?"

"Yeah."

"Ever wear them?"

"Only driving on long trips."

"If it's vanity—"

"It's not vanity," Dobbs snapped.

After several seconds, Allen said, "You ought to rethink all that, before we get overseas. I'd hate to get zapped because you missed seeing something beyond your range."

At their next preflight briefing, Dobbs put on his gold-filled, steel-framed, Air Force-issue glasses and from then on wore them everywhere. In that regard, his only comment came after they were airborne: "I'll be damned. The Florida coastline isn't made of felt after all." On the basketball court Dobbs' outside shooting improved greatly. Allen was gentleman enough not to point that out.

The third or fourth time Dobbs had control of the Phantom, he said, "Not too many studs get their first stick time in a jet fighter and are as good as me."

Allen said, "I got it." Grabbing the stick, he snapped the F-4 inverted for a second, then rolled back to level.

Dobbs shouted, "What the fuck . . . ?" The contents of a cup of coffee that he had been sipping spattered around his cockpit. "Thanks a lot, Colonel Cy."

Cy watched it all in his rearview mirrors. "This isn't a cafeteria, bighead. Just remember, these training sessions are premiums on my insurance policy.

I'm the important guy on *this* team. Don't you forget it."

After a respectful silence, Dobbs said quietly, "Sir, I promise to be humble as long as you don't make me look at your scrapbook again."

Genuinely surprised by the comment, Allen laughed delightedly. He had yet to speak seriously to Dobbs about his victories in Korea.

Dobbs never ceased to surprise Allen. Whenever they weren't scheduled to fly, they honky-tonked and generally acted ill-bred up and down the western coast of Florida. And why not? Allen was divorced, not too long ago either. Dobbs was a bachelor. And they were headed to war. They owed it to themselves. "Who knows what evil lurks in the far Far East?" Dobbs often asked. Allen had no answer but, one night in a mean waterfront bar outside of Tarpon Springs, he encountered as much evil as he wanted while on the ground anywhere.

In Scene One, he and Dobbs met a bleached blonde who was turned on by the idea of doing both of them. She played with Dobbs' glasses and called him "Professor." When she got around to playing with other things while seated at the bar, they decided to take the show on the road.

Scene Two was set in the parking lot. A stranger taller than Dobbs and huskier than Allen called out to them, "Hold it. Where the hell you all think you're going?" He had jumped from a pickup truck and had left the engine running and the door open.

The blonde said, "Shit fire, that's my beau. Lemme—"

Dobbs took three or four steps to the side and said, "Move on, mister, unless you want trouble." Dobbs hadn't had enough to drink in order to act that way, Allen thought. As far as he was concerned, the big asshole could have his girlfriend. Good riddance . . .

"Why, you skinny four-eyed motherfucker, I'll break you in two," the stranger said. With raised hands, he advanced menacingly. He snorted and puffed up his body until he looked twice as large as Dobbs.

They were about four feet apart when Dobbs brought his left hand out of his pants pocket. The movement wasn't flashy: the hand merely appeared at his side and from it a double-edged six-inch blade flicked into sight. Allen later doubted that the stranger saw the weapon. The huge man reached for Dobbs who stepped inside his raised arms and sank the knife blade upward into the stranger's right thigh as easily as if he had slid it into a tub of butter, right to the hilt. The big man never touched Dobbs. He gasped and dropped his hands to the punctured leg. Dobbs shook the knife and the man groaned. Taking a step backward, Dobbs pulled the blade free. With a loud sigh the wounded man sank to the gravel. Face down, he silently clutched his thigh. Dobbs bent forward and Allen expected him to cut the stranger's throat. Although it seemed an appropriate thing to do, he wanted to stop him and, with a very dry mouth, softly called, "Jer . . ."

Dobbs wiped the knife on the back of the man's shirt, closed the blade, then looked up: "What?"

"Nothing. Let's go. Let's get out of here."

The blonde was bug-eyed and rocking on her toes. With one hand she pulled at her hair and with the other wadded the front of Allen's shirt. She allowed herself to be guided into their van without taking her eyes off Dobbs who casually climbed into the driver's seat and even took time to fasten his seatbelt. What a cool, cool guy, Allen thought and wondered if maybe Dobbs was more than he could handle.

They didn't make it to a motel. By the time they reached the highway, the blonde was all over Dobbs. After a mile or two Dobbs pulled the van onto a road that she pointed out and they got lost behind some dunes for most of the night.

On the way back to the base, Allen said, "She was so hot for you, I thought she was going to get on you on the get-off ramp."

Jerry Dobbs shook his head and frowned, as if puzzled: "Small-town Southern girls . . . Vio really turns them on. It's sort of disgusting."

Days later Allen asked, "How long you been carrying that, you know, sword."

"I threw it away," said Dobbs. "I started carrying it after some niggers waylaid me coming home from an IL game. I knew them. I'd just scored fifty points against them. The fuckers . . . They didn't hurt me, much. But they scared me, really scared me. And they insulted me, made me feel completely helpless. Those bastards are masters at intimidation. And at the same time they're so fucking ignorant. I decided that I was never going to be anybody's fool again, black or white."

On the morning of outprocessing from training at MacDill, Allen was handed amended orders which reassigned him from Ubon to Danang. Ubon Air Base in northeastern Thailand was a miniature resort, according to returned pilots: "Great facilities. Great club, great food—lobsters, steaks, you name it—and a nifty downtown—lots of sweet, young things." One returnee added: "Comparing my old lady to those little Thai girls is like comparing an old combat boot to a silk-lined slipper." Danang Air Base on the northeast coast of Vietnam was like Sparta: ten thousand feet of concrete and not much more. It was nicknamed "Rocket City" because nearly every night the North Vietnamese sailed a rocket or two into the base, just to remind everyone that a war was in progress. And the Vietnamese women . . . One returnee said, "Anyone who would screw some Viet is too lazy to jackoff." With the flip of a page, Park Avenue to the Bowery, Allen thought. Furthermore, Dobbs' orders were unchanged which meant that the two men would be separated.

Being a career soldier, Allen could have lived with those conditions. Reassignments were part of the game. However, this particular reassignment had greater impact: it eliminated his chances of killing MiGs. The war's ground rules were clear: fighters stationed in South Vietnam operated primarily over the South; fighters stationed in Thailand operated over North Vietnam and were banned from the South. MiGs flew only over the North. Far in the back of his mind Allen had toyed with the idea of becoming the first ace of the Vietnam War, his last hurrah. Now he had been robbed of any chance at it. "That Personnel . . . I never got such shabby treatment in my career," he told Dobbs. "Those fuckers . . ."

Around noon the two men went into Tampa; a "farewell" drink lengthened into bar crawling. They reminisced about their short time together as if they had been comrades for years. The Air Force environment promoted such feelings. The mental and physical intensity of flying together, whether in the same airplane or in the same formation or in the same squadron, rapidly created bonds similar to those found among men who played on championship athletic teams. Angry that they were being split apart for no apparent reason, both men got drunk. At sunset in a sleazy bar on the edge of Hillsborough Bay, Allen declared, "Fuck it, Jerry, I am too great to waste a whole year dropping bombs on groundpounders in the fucking South when there is air-to-air up North. I mean, fuck it!"

For the thirtieth or fortieth time Dobbs said, "I know how you must feel. But that's the Air Force. Hunh? Right? Nothin' you can do about it."

Allen rolled his head and grew wild-eyed. "The fuck there isn't," he shouted. "Wait right here." He stormed out of the bar. After several minutes he returned with a handful of paper and yelled at Dobbs, "Follow me." Banging his way out the back door of the bar, Allen broke into a run along the pier and, with an overhand sweep of his arm, threw the papers high into the orange sky. A breeze scattered them across the bay.

In disbelief, Dobbs asked, "Your new orders?"

"Fuck 'em all. We're going to Ubon," Allen said. "I have my original orders. As far as I'm concerned, I never heard about a change. Let's face it, if you can't take the word of a lieutenant colonel, who the fuck can you trust?"

Neither Lieutenant Colonel Cy Allen nor Lieutenant Jerry Dobbs would have confessed to the interdependence that had developed between them. At most, Allen would have said he patronized the young man: "He's all right to drag along. But, shit, I can still do it alone." If pressed, Dobbs might have admitted, "Sometimes I like the old fart. Other times he's nothing but an old-fashioned hardass."

Naturally, a father-son relationship existed between them: Allen was thirty-nine and Dobbs twenty-four. It was the mature type of relationship in which the father understood that he no longer had a great deal of control over his son in most situations; in turn, the son recognized that the father maintained the role of "appointed" leader. Allen would have denied all of that too. He didn't want the responsibility of another son. He already had three: Frank Luke Allen, the firstborn; and the twins, Richard Bong Allen and Thomas McGuire Allen, named after the top American fighter aces of World War II. The names made sense to him. He and his younger brother, Ty Cobb Allen, had been named after their father's favorite baseball players. Actually, the names were his father's second and third choices; he believed that his first choice, "Honus Wagner," was too heavy to hang on any baby. For the same reason, Cy Young Allen didn't name his oldest son "Eddie Rickenbacker" and, instead, settled for the name of America's second highest ace in World War I.

Separated by fifteen years in age, Allen and Dobbs were, at times, light-years apart in experience. Allen frequently made Dobbs laugh with what he considered to be worn-out jokes. During a briefing, Dobbs whispered, "I have to pee."

Allen hissed, "Request denied. Resubmit in writing in thirty days."

Dobbs barked out a laugh that befuddled the briefer.

When they were about to climb into a Phantom for their first flight together, Allen said, "All aboard that's going aboard. And if you can't get aboard, get a plank." Dobbs liked the line so much that he repeated it before every mission.

For a time Allen suspected that Dobbs laughed at the old jokes to curry favor. As a test he told Dobbs the Air Force's oldest shaggy-dog story. He fabricated an air battle over Korea in which he found himself outnumbered twenty-five to one. His ammo was gone.

He had his flaps shot away, was driven over Red China, ran out of fuel, and was gliding earthward with two MiG-15s directly on his tail. "They opened fire," he said, "and tracers were hitting all over the Sabre. Smoke was pouring into the cockpit. I pulled the ejection handle and the seat didn't go. I couldn't even get the canopy off." He paused for effect. "Then you know what happened?"

Dobbs nodded. With a bored expression he said, "You got killed."

"Right," Allen said happily. He had known that it was virtually impossible for Dobbs not to have heard that most-told tale.

By the time they reached Thailand, their jokes were original and elaborate. During mission planning Allen said, "Somebody broke into my room and ate my pillow."

"Really?" Dobbs was listening with one ear. "That's too bad."

"The Air Police have the person who did it."

"That's good. Was it a houseboy?" Dobbs worked on his chart for a moment, then looked up and said, "*Ate* your pillow?"

Allen nodded. "The APs caught who did it. They arrested a guy who had a down-in-the-mouth look."

A few days later they had an early morning takeoff and, during their climb on course, met the sun coming over the horizon. Dobbs said, "I just had a big yawn and you know what I felt?"

Cy Allen thought for half a minute before saying, "Yep."

"You don't really know, do you?"

"Yes, I do."

Dobbs had to say it: "Dawn in the mouth."

"Yep. That's right."

Dobbs won the prize, however, the morning they

shot down the two MiG-21s. The squadron killed four that day and everyone was excited. They were the first crew into Intelligence debriefing. The wing commander and his staff eagerly awaited the details; the Intelligence officers had their pencils poised. Allen had experienced it many times years before and, although the glamour never faded, he turned to Dobbs and said, "Jer, tell 'em what happened."

"Me? You want *me* to tell them?"

"Who the fuck else was with us?"

The staff officers laughed boisterously.

Dobbs looked back and forth between his pilot and his wing commander. "Well . . ." He cleared his throat. ". . . you see, to make a wonderfully long story short, the MiGs lost."

3

Allen's first low-level pop-up bombing mission to the Thai Nguyen iron and steel complex located thirty-five miles north of Hanoi was a masochist's wet dream. For years after, the word "suicidal" popped to Dobbs' mind at the mention of Thai Nguyen.

Both Allen and Dobbs were surprised when they learned that over North Vietnam not every day was pure air-to-air fun and games for the F-4 Phantom jet flyers. MiG-killing decidedly took second place to bombing.

"The objective of the air offensive over the North is to destroy the North's ability to support operations against South Vietnam," a four-star United States Air Force general told the world in 1967. "MiG-killing is not our objective. Air superiority is necessary only to protect the strike force so that ordnance can be placed precisely on assigned targets with the least possible loss of American crews," he explained. "Any MiG kill is a bonus. The loss of an American strike aircraft automatically classifies a mission as a failure regardless of the number of MiGs destroyed."

As a result, planners at Seventh Air Force Head-quarters located at Tan Son Nhut Air Base outside Saigon repeatedly employed F-4s as bombers to augment the F-105 Thunderchiefs, constructed fifty- and hundred-plane armadas reminiscent of World War II and Korea. Seventh Air Force planners issued weekly and daily Frag Orders which dictated where and when each F-4 would deliver its six seven-hundred-fifty-pounders. Primarily they were used against "strategic" targets located within a one-hundred-mile radius of Hanoi.

Unfortunately for the USAF aircrews, the North Vietnamese Army and Air Force knew that their nation's prime targets were grouped around Hanoi. As a result the NVA and NVAF packed the area wall-to-wall with antiaircraft defenses, namely: SA2 Guideline missiles capable of boosting three-hundred-pound warheads to an altitude of sixty-five thousand feet; antiaircraft artillery ranging from 23-mm to 130-mm in size, the largest of which fired seventy-five pound projectiles to thirty thousand feet; early warning and height-finding radars; and GCI radar systems that controlled MiGs. The North Vietnamese could afford to be prodigal; the Soviet Union paid the bill.

As a sort of sideshow to the USAF armadas, Phantoms often flew four-ship low-level pop-up missions against the North, a tactic designed to unbalance the defenses listed above. A flight of four aircraft was the basic operating unit.

During a staff inspection visit to Ubon, a major who flew a desk at Seventh Air Force Headquarters briefed the F-4 crews: "Your little four-ship soirees . . ." He actually said "soirees" and Dobbs was puzzled when he was the only listener who laughed in scorn, felt smug until touched by the chill of a ghost army of French soldiers who died in Vietnam. "Your little four-ship soirees," the major began anew, "are calculated to keep the pressure on, constantly."

"On the North Vietnamese or on our crews?" Mike Hawk said. "I'm ready to head to the peace talk table right now."

The *Operational Procedures Manual* recommended a pop-up maneuver to crews attacking "a high priority target in a SAM environment." According to the Manual: *The aircraft approaches the target area in low-level penetration to enhance survivability, achieve deception, and surprise the defenses.*

Low-level penetration to enhance survivability was moot. The SA2 Guideline/Fan Song was a medium-to-high-level missile/radar system which meant it was unable to track fast-moving aircraft flying below three thousand feet. The Russians possessed an advanced low-to-medium level missile/radar system, the SA3 Goa/Low Blow, which tracked aircraft down to the deck. Fortunately for the USAF crews, the Soviets opted not to provide that system to the North Vietnamese. (The mere knowledge of the existence of such a system caused a few sleepless nights to deep-thinking crewmembers. In that regard, Dobbs recalled his father saying, "Too much imagination is worse than none at all," when he learned his son was headed to war.) Therefore, by flying below three thousand feet the fighter-bombers were safe from surface-to-air missiles. However, they then were inside the small arms envelope where they were exposed to being gutshot by every Dink who owned a pea-shooter.

Deception and surprise also were relative. Every clear day, fighter-bombers climbed out from Thailand, roared in formation above Laos, then burned a low-level streak across approximately a hundred miles of North Vietnam before reaching their targets. When Dobbs first read the Manual he said, "The defenses would be more surprised if we didn't show up."

The Manual spelled out the pop-up tactic:

After passing the initial point (a well defined landmark) the aircraft is maneuvered until the target falls within a desirable angle extending from the nose of the aircraft to the target. Airspeed is increased, and at pop-up point the aircraft initiates a wing-level pullup, climbs to an apex altitude above the target suitable for strafing or dive-bombing.

A successful attack using the pop-up tactic depends on the pilot's ability to maneuver his aircraft to a precise position in space relative to the target. This position in space is determined by the type ordnance carried . . . and characteristics of the aircraft.

Withdrawal following weapons release depends on target environment and subsequent intentions.

At one tactics briefing Rocco Monge said, "That last sentence sounds like porno to me."

"The whole war's porno," Mike Hawk told him.

Allen read the pop-up procedures several times during his tour and with each reading the instructions grew more amusing: they were classics of understatement. Theory took place in a vacuum. Practice happened in steel-filled air. In reality an F-4 low-level pop-up bombing mission reminded him of "The Charge of the Light Brigade." During briefing for their first attack on the Thai Nguyen iron and steel works, he told Dobbs, "My family is in the iron and steel business—my mother irons and my father steals." Dobbs groaned but loved it. It was the last laugh of the day . . .

* * *

Allen and Dobbs were Three in a flight of three Phantoms. Each fighter-bomber lugged the standard load of six seven-hundred-fifty-pounders. A scheduled fourth aircraft aborted on the ground after its pilot declared the left generator wouldn't come on line. The spare failed to taxi for reasons Cy didn't hear.

Rocco Monge was Lead and Junior Eliot Two.

Rocco reminded Dobbs of the Incredible Hulk of comic book fame. The muscular Dago's body was as thick as Dobbs' was wide. He completely filled a Phantom's front cockpit and literally strapped the warbird to his ass in order to fly off to battle. Rocco and Wiltrout could have been stand-ins for Stonehenge, Dobbs thought. On the other hand, Rocco was intelligent, talented, and refreshing as hell.

The day's plan of attack was simple: through the hills and into the murk. The three-ship formation blasted off from Ubon, roared high above Laos where it refueled from an orbiting KC-135 Stratotanker ("Sure wish I could go with you, sir," the boom operator said and Junior Eliot answered him with a screw-loose swirling gesture around the ear), then flashed down to the deck for the dash across North Vietnam—seventeen minutes in, seventeen out at no more than twenty feet off the ground. Rocco believed that low-level meant *low*-level.

Of course, the NVA knew they were coming. An hour earlier Seventh Air Force planners had sent another flight of four Phantoms along the same route and against the same target. The tactic ensured that everybody in the area was awake and scanning the sky.

The final leg of the low-level route, from the initial point inbound to the target, was along a narrow valley where guns lined the hilltops. Every gun was manned.

Entering the valley, Rocco said, "This is it, guys." He had been there before.

> "Forward the Light Brigade!
> Charge for the guns," he said.

Until then, the trip had been fairly quiet. Dobbs had done a little map reading to check out his inertial navigation computer and to make certain they were on course. Allen mostly kept an eye on Rocco and Junior while flying low and avoiding scooping grass into the engine intakes.

Then they ripped into the valley and the whole world lit up. The sky filled with streaks of glowing tracers. Looking up, Allen saw a woven pattern of crisscrossing fire, a solid red ceiling of death. He heard Dobbs breathing twice as loud as normal, then realized he too was hyperventilating. As they raced along near the valley floor, he looked up again and, seeing hummocks around the guns, joyfully recognized that the gunners couldn't depress their weapons far enough to hit the planes. Nevertheless, the gunners kept shooting. Some blasted away along the length of the valley while others wildly sprayed fire across the valley. Small bore and large bore weapons pumped endless streams of rounds. Seeing tracers stretched from hilltop to hilltop, he said, "The bastards are shooting each other."

"So?" Dobbs replied. He whispered to himself, "If I could get my hands on my ROTC recruiter right now . . ." He was thinking ahead. In a minute, they were going up into that layer of flaming steel.

Four miles from the target the Phantoms had to climb to two hundred feet, an altitude necessary to permit the bombs to arm after they were dropped. At release, the bombs' high-drogue fins extended into wide X-shaped spoilers which rapidly braked the weapons' speed and converted their horizontal glide path into a vertical drop. The broad spoilers permitted the delivery aircraft to leave the bombs quickly behind and thereby escape their effects.

Approaching pop-up point, a railroad spur, Rocco said only, "Ready?" He expected his wingmen to be paying attention, watching him rather than worrying about groundfire. Eliot and Allen checked in: "Two." "Three."

Rocco went up first, an instant before the others, and immediately an antiaircraft artillery round exploded under his right wing. The shell blew a hole completely through the wing and Allen called, "Lead, you're hit."

Rocco calmly answered, "I know it." Fuel poured out of the gaping hole.

> Theirs not to make reply.
> Theirs not to reason why.

Allen was in his climb and, thinking he saw flames licking off the trailing edge of Rocco Monge's wing, said, "Lead, you—" Then there were two "Cracks" and a "Whump" and a "Thump." "Three's hit," Allen shouted and in that instant found that his airplane was upside down, fifty feet off the ground, traveling at five hundred fifty knots. The right panel of his windscreen was gone. Wind roared into the cockpit and he couldn't hear, could hardly see. Shards of glass were on his face, down his collar, all over the cockpit. More shards were breaking loose, blowing in at him. But the plane was flying!

Pulling down his clear helmet visor, he shouted to Dobbs, "Jerry, don't go. Don't go, Jerry. Don't go. No, no, no." Instinctively he held the throttles forward: he had to keep his speed, his only defense. Without time to glance at the instruments, with eyes on the inverted horizon and flying by the seat of his pants, he pushed forward on the stick, kicked left rudder, and rolled the Phantom upright to a straight and level attitude. Then he resumed his climb, had no choice but to steepen it a bit.

> Stormed at with shot and shell
> Boldly they rode and well

By then Rocco Monge and Junior Eliot were far ahead, nearing the bomb release line. Allen glanced at his engine instruments; everything appeared normal. What the hell, the airplane was flying. What more could he ask? He hadn't come that far for nothing. Leaning on the throttles, he tried to bend them beyond one hundred percent power in order to catch up. Then he again remembered he wasn't alone: "Jer, you still there? You all right?"

Dobbs quietly answered, "Affirmative."

Allen saw bombs drop from the other two planes. Below them were three tall smokestacks lined up north to south and several long, three-to-five-story, gray buildings. If those buildings were the steel mill, he thought, the lineup looked perfect: the bombs would be exactly on target.

Pushing harder on the throttles Allen thought he felt the airspeed increase slightly. Had he forced a hundred and one percent power from the engines? Then he was at the bomb release line and the buildings looked exactly like the photographs he had studied back at Ubon—a lifetime ago. He had time to tell Dobbs, "Just like the pictures," before he pickled his load. The six seven-hundred-fifty-pounders came off cleanly and he mentally thanked Sweet Jesus for that much. Then the world came apart again.

In falling behind, he had unwittingly distanced himself so that he arrived over target the moment when the bombs from the other planes detonated. He felt the concussions, the shock waves from their blasts. His plane buffeted, bounced, yawed. Then the control stick went dead and Allen's heart nearly stopped. Tracers were still crisscrossing around him. If the gooks didn't get him, his own guys would, he thought. What was he doing there? Another lifetime passed before he again had control of the plane and a moment later, somehow, he was through the danger.

He spotted Rocco and Junior in a right bank, turning to make the exit dash. He cut inside their circle and rejoined them. Rocco called, "Glad to see you again." His plane had holes everywhere. Bands of daylight showed through its vertical stabilizer. Amazingly, Junior Eliot's airplane was unmarked, had not a nick. How in hell had that happened, Allen wondered while the trio lined up for egress.

The easiest exit would have been to bore ahead after release and, flying low, follow the Red River Delta out to sea. That course would have avoided most of the small arms fire. But the Navy owned the territory in that direction. Air Force planners had dictated that the three Air Force pilots make a U-turn and fly outbound along the route they had followed inbound. Rocco led them back down to ten feet off the valley floor.

> Cannon to right of them,
> Cannon to left of them,
> Cannon behind them
> Volleyed and thundered.

A misty veil appeared along the horizon and Allen said, "I'd call the vis 'piss poor.'"

"Or worse," said Dobbs.

They tore through the valley while what seemed like the entire population of North Vietnam shot at them.

Finally they were out of the valley but people continued to shoot at them. Men stood in open fields and banged away with rifles.

Suddenly, out of the mist a row of hootches sprang up in front of the trio. The pilots pulled up to clear the buildings and there, on one of the roofs, stood an unarmed man. A spectator? When he saw the Phantoms bearing down on him, he spun about and broadjumped off the far side of the roof. All elbows and asshole, Allen thought and, for a moment, worried that the poor SOB broke both arms and legs. Then he worried that they were off course.

To make matters worse, without warning, ground effect increased: the Phantoms wanted to climb. To counteract the aerodynamic lift, Allen pumped the stick forward to hold the plane low. As a result the fighter bounced like an ocean-going speedboat leaping from wave to wave. Rocco and Junior fought the same problem. Nothing seemed right. "Jer, any of this country look familiar?"

"Say again," Dobbs replied. He had a fleeting thought that they were on spin dry cycle.

"Where the hell are we?" Allen demanded. The kid had inertial and computer units out the ass back there. . . .

Everything was shaking: the airplane was bouncing too hard for Dobbs to read his navigational aids. "Sir, you see that little stream off to the right?"

"Affirmative."

"Well, we're about a quarter mile to the left of it."

Goddamnit, thought Allen, just as he'd suspected: they were lost.

Ahead, clouds blended with the ground. Unexpectedly Rocco Monge shouted, "Pull, pull. Climb! Burners!"

In formation flying everybody does what the leader

does. Instant response to any movement or command is ingrained by years of training. Allen and Junior Eliot obeyed orders reflexively: they jerked back their control sticks and fired their afterburners to give their planes maximum thrust.

Following Monge, they pulled eight Gs, stood the jets on their tailpipes, and climbed straight up the face of a piece of karst that had been hidden in the haze—a piece of solid rock that jutted to seven thousand feet. In the climb Allen felt close enough to reach out and touch the blackish stone wall. If he lowered his landing gear, he thought, he could taxi to the top.

Clearing the karst, they pushed forward on their sticks and took the Phantoms back down to the deck. The remainder of the way out, they were in the weeds or in the murk. Allen thankfully wondered how Rocco had seen or known the chunk of rock was exactly there. If it was pure luck, all the better.

> When can their glory fade?
> Oh, the wild charge they made!

They exited North Vietnam and went to altitude. During the climb, Allen remembered a long ago day before an air show when, with a group of allied officers, he'd watched the practice flight of a nine-ship Indonesian Air Force aerobatics team—the show's host team. The tight, huge formation arced over the top of a low-altitude loop and, maintaining a perfect diamond pattern, flew straight into the ground about a quarter mile from the end of the runway. "Holy shit," Allen muttered. "I say, rotten luck," a Royal Air Force type next to him agreed. "That definitely leaves a gap in tomorrow's program. One of their chaps had best find the band director, have him come up with an extra tune or two."

Without Rocco's instincts, their three Phantoms would be metal plaques hammered against an unknown mountain, Cy thought. Follow the leader . . . he owed Rocco.

By the time they rendezvoused with another KC-135 Stratotanker, Monge was pissing fuel all over the sky and Junior Eliot told him, "Lead, you better see the flight surgeon when we land; you're dripping."

"Ho, ho," Wiltrout answered.

Because he was losing so much fuel overboard, Rocco was first to drink. How had he made it that far?

The refueling boom in the tail of the tanker lowered and the probe extended out and down. In the belly of the tanker, stretched on his stomach and facing aft, the boom operator watched through a window. By controlling small wings attached to the boom, he flew the probe home to the air-to-air refueling receptacle atop the fighter's fuselage, immediately aft of the rear cockpit. Flying on fumes, Monge was inches from hooking up when the boom operator abruptly retracted the probe: "Sir, I can't refuel you until you put out your cigarette."

A couple of seconds of dead air followed. Then Rocco said, "Give me fuel right now or I'll shoot you down."

For a time it seemed as if fuel ran out of the hole in Rocco's wing as fast as the tanker pumped it into his refueling receptacle. Then he had enough and gave way to Eliot and Allen.

While Rocco and Junior tapped the tanker, Allen pulled shards of glass that reminded him of porcupine quills from the upper arms of his flying suit. A few of the shards had penetrated his skin and after he popped them free he saw blood on them. What an easy way to win a Purple Heart, he thought. Then he told himself he wouldn't mention it to anyone. Then he saw that his sleeves were spotted with blood and finally decided: Fuck it, he'd take it. He earned it.

After everyone topped off, Monge hooked up again and hung on the boom with gas pumping into his refueling receptacle while the KC-135 dragged him to Ubon.

Monge landed first and set it down hard. He barely turned off the runway when the plane's main wing spar collapsed and the Phantom broke in half on the taxiway. There wasn't enough fuel in the tanks for a real fire. Monge and Wiltrout walked away from the wreck.

The Wing Director of Operations greeted Allen and Dobbs after they parked. He handed a fifth of Ten High to Allen who broke the seal, took a pull, then passed the bottle to Dobbs. Jerry took the longest drink of straight whiskey that Allen had ever seen any man swallow.

Their airplane's fuselage looked like a colander. The airframe wouldn't be ready to fly again for a week, or more, if ever.

"Rough?" the Wing DO asked.

Allen faked a puke.

Dobbs said, "As far as I'm concerned, that goddamn fucking steel mill can stay there for eternity."

4

After the trip to Thai Nguyen, Jerry Dobbs wrote to his father:

I finished the Larteguy and two Bernard Fall books you gave me. In one place Larteguy wrote, "Men are all alike; they all did the same thing at one moment or other of their lives. They chose what belonged to them: their wife, their house, their lands, their money. It's stronger than the rest: ideals, friends, memories." I read that paragraph and immediately thought of Colonel Allen. He puts ideals, friends, and memories ahead of everything. I really admire his individuality.

Then I compared him to you and began to wonder if his attitude was selfish. You have equally strong ideals, plenty of friends and lots of memories. *And* you also have Mom and our family and the house and the property in Carolina. Colonel Allen is divorced and has three sons. He never talks about his ex-wife or his sons.

Isn't the man who does it all, who balances the choices, really the better person?

This letter is not meant to knock Colonel Allen. I respect him tremendously. I guess this letter really is to thank you for making *all* the choices, especially for sticking with Mom and for keeping our family together through the hassles of a military life and two wars—three when you make it over here. What do you hear on that?

(Not until years later, when he read the letters his father had saved, did Dobbs recognize that as a subtle cosmic bonus for eluding death at Thai Nguyen he'd been granted his first incisive glimpse of a meaning for life. Had combat brought the beginning of an appreciation for adulthood? If he had died at that business, what then?)

Larteguy also wrote, "Table companions are easily found, companions in death are rare." I know what he meant but I'd still like to tell him, "I prefer companions in life." Why do writers turn war into poetry, or propaganda? I enjoyed Bernard Fall's books because they are straightforward.

Somehow all of this is leading up to the fact that we went on our first low-level bombing mission two days ago and bombed a steel mill (which I never saw) about thirty miles north of Hanoi. The flight was like being shot down a chute . . .

At that point Dobbs stopped writing. His memories of the mission defied his ability to describe them. In his mind the chute was a seamless tube coursing through other dimensions of time and space, through an anti-world to all that was familiar.

The frightening part of his passage through the chute was that he had not been afraid. He should have been. Even when the Phantom was upside down and about to be swallowed by the earth he had not been afraid. He should have been. But somehow he had known that he would survive, that today was not his turn to die. (He would feel ridiculous expressing such ideas to his father, he thought.)

Despite his certainty of survival, Thai Nguyen had infected Dobbs with helplessness, made him a mote in a very endless universe. His helpless sensation brought back the night he'd been waylaid after a basketball game: the pack of blue-lips had made him feel equally helpless, but also had frightened him, made him believe he perhaps might die. Those tormentors were flesh and blood violence facing his vulnerable flesh and blood loneliness. A very personal helplessness fed his fear back then. Why hadn't helplessness brought fear at Thai Nguyen? Had the speed of the Phantom's cockpit/cocoon provided an aura of salvation? Or had Colonel Cy's presence made the difference?

Whatever the cause, at Thai Nguyen fear had not been his psychological partner. Anger had. Helplessness bred anger. Anger bred hate. He'd felt an incandescent hatred for everything within that anti-world. His hatred focused on stupidity—the stupidity of the invisible people shooting at them, the stupidity of the mission's demands, the stupidity of Allen's daring, the stupidity of his needless participation—the stupidity of his helplessness.

Helplessness—anger—hate—stupidity—helplessness: Dobbs' circle of emotions had closed on itself. Had he possessed limitless power, he might have risen above the battleground and . . . he saw no end to the destruction he might have caused. His anger had crested in an evil passion that he had not enjoyed.

". . . like riding through a nightmare," he abruptly ended the letter to his father. "Love to you and Mom. Your son, Jerry."

Air war was a secret life, Dobbs thought. A secret life that flyers lived alone.

About the time Dobbs was puzzling through his letter to his father, Allen was over North Vietnam making good on a dare, voluntarily flying a freebie mission that counted for nothing but experience.

That afternoon he had been sitting in the club and describing the shit storm that smacked him at Thai Nguyen when Lieutenant Colonel Ted Joseph, a curly haired nickel-plated instructor pilot from the 497th TFS Night Owls, said, "You ought to try it at night."

"In a pig's ass," said Allen.

The Owls formed the only Air Force squadron "to keep the pressure on" by flying night bombing missions against targets in North Vietnam.

"In a pig's ass is a little bit brighter than at night over the North," Joseph said.

"I've never been either place," Allen said with a grin, "and don't care to go."

"Why not? Come on, if you're not busy tonight, you can ride with me." Joseph's black eyes stared long and hard, put down the challenge. "Once in a lifetime chance to learn what the war's really like," Joseph said softly.

Ted Joseph and Cy Allen blasted off three hours after sunset, second ship in a two-ship formation. Their target was the Viet Tri transshipment area on the northwest railroad out of Hanoi.

Once they crossed the Mekong River, left Thailand and were over Laos, it grew black below. Very black. Their sole companion was the neon glow of Lead's fiery pale blue exhausts. Joseph read Allen's thoughts, said, "Black as a well digger's ass."

Flying was for sunny days, Allen thought; he even

disliked clouds. Why had he been suckered by a grade school dare?

The tanker was an airborne Christmas tree of red and green lights that Allen spotted from seventy-five miles. "You got champ peepers," Joseph said.

"Born to fly," Allen told him and they shared a laugh. Cramped in the back seat, unable to look out over the nose, Allen thought: This was how Jerry saw the war. He didn't like the view.

The Phantoms dropped low and Joseph pulled into trail position, made Lead invisible to Allen who spent his time watching negatives of landscape flash by to his right and left, negatives that became clearer as his eyes adjusted to the dark, that revealed a range of subtle grays far beyond his imagination. At the same time, his depth perception played games with him: as terrain elevation changed his eyes told him the airplane was climbing or descending when actually it was straight and level.

The moonlight glitter of the Black River stretched across their path like a band of metal foil, a strip of Christo's environmental art.

Then the silver Red River reflected up from the grayness ahead along with the railroad that paralleled it. Allen sensed Viet Tri lined up on the nose.

Lead asked, "Ready, Teddy?"

Joseph answered, "Two."

Allen expected a wham-bam-thank-you-ma'am hit-and-be-gone pass. Instead the two ships began flying low-level search patterns, looking for the best target of opportunity, poking like rubes on their first trip downtown.

"You should have been along the night we zigged over to Thanh Hoa barracks, caught them with all the lights on," Joseph said. "Surprise, soldiers!"

"Laugh a minute, I'll bet," said Allen. Banking

through the grayness at low altitude made him uneasy: he preferred to hold the stick in his hand, to control his destiny. Poor Jerry, he thought. He repeatedly glanced at the altimeter to confirm he was wrong to feel that the airplane was dipping lower and lower.

"Train ho," called Lead, "ten o'clock."

"Tally," said Joseph.

Lead announced, "All aboard," and climbed, released a flare that burst overhead, hung in the night sky like a single poolhall lamp, produced living shadows that stretched and contracted as the descending flare oscillated on its parachute. To Allen the entire landscape was alive with movement: artificial or real?

The flare's deathly pale yellow-orange light produced only brighter shades of gray, added frost to the landscape.

North Vietnamese antiaircraft artillery provided the color. Orange and red tracers patterned giant fans seemingly snapped open by giant hands. Huge peacock tails of blazing steel rose around the fighter-bombers. A phantasmagoria of earthly stars burst across the somber gray night, left flak puffs of salt and pepper dotting the sky.

"They seldom shoot before we find something," Joseph said, "probably hope we'll overlook them, go elsewhere."

Allen still hadn't located the target. From his perspective it appeared as if Joseph was about to fly through a fan of fire. He held his breath, involuntarily reached for the control stick.

Joseph fooled him, slipped into afterburners, broke hard right, climbed steeply, turned left sharply, cried, "Two's in," and dived on the target.

Allen's G-suit expanded and contracted like a polka accordian. Unseen forces pushed and pulled him from all directions. He wanted the control stick, wanted to be up front, to see over the nose. Then he felt the bombs drop free and he was sucked deep into his seat, smothered by gravity's grayness. His helmet tried to squash his brain. His oxygen mask slid off his chin. His tunnel vision eyes strained to see the G-meter, to read a fading seven.

"Lead's in," he heard like a voice from a distant galaxy.

Joseph kicked out of burners, eased the G's by half. Allen searched over his shoulder, glimpsed Lead pancaking through the bottom of his high-speed trajectory, reaching for altitude, cutting white wingtip contrails.

Allen finally saw the train. An automatic weapon mounted on a flatcar was pulsing streaks of orange at the juking fighter-bomber. Allen weakly said, "Gun on train." A hollow moan of question or fact?

"Twenty-three mike-mike," Joseph said. "SOP."

"Let's book," Lead called.

"Two has you vis," Joseph reported, then plugged in afterburners and raced low to catch up.

Outbound, Allen asked, "How many of your hundred will be night?"

"Ninety. Ninety-five," Joseph said brightly. Climbing toward the tanker, he apologized: "I'm sorry, really. You didn't get to see them launch a SAM. At night, one of those things looks like an Atlas lifting off the pad, lights up half the sky. It's a sight you'd never forget. I'm really sorry you missed it."

He had enough bad dreams pressed into his mind for one night, Allen thought. If its destruction depended upon night attacks then, as far as he was concerned, Viet Tri could stay there for eternity. He smiled tiredly. He'd found a new affinity with Dobbs.

5

Allen met Pensy at a fair in Ubon Ratchathani, near a booth for renting popguns that fired corks. The booth was a shooting gallery whose targets were plastic toy infantrymen spread in attack formation across a green felt plain. Unlike American shooting galleries, the booth offered no kewpie doll or stuffed animal prize; the reward was in the game itself.

Allen and Dobbs were knocking down the miniature soldiers as fast as the giggling booth attendant could stand them up. The two Americans had attracted a crowd of cheering Thai children. To amuse them, Dobbs was clowning, lobbing handfuls of corks between shots, mimicking explosions and death cries.

Allen spotted Pensy at an adjoining booth. She was watching Dobbs with a half-puzzled, half-amused expression. She was nearly six feet tall, he guessed; surprisingly full-bodied, she contradicted the normal reed-like appearance of tall Thais. Her jet black hair reached to her waist, was parted down the middle. Later she described her hairstyle as "hee-pee way" and laughed from deep in her throat. Her laugh as much as anything else was what attracted Allen.

The moment she caught Allen watching her watch Dobbs, her dark eyes spontaneously crinkled at the corners, then the full lips of her wide mouth parted, arced upward until she squinted. Her head tilted backward. She had big, strong, dazzling white teeth and she showed all of them in a free and open expression of happiness. Then she caught his eyes again, covered her mouth with a hand, and turned away, moved off at a stroll. Embarrassed or coy?

Later Allen learned she kept her teeth white by brushing with salt and water, nothing more. In a like manner, she used no perfume or deodorant, yet exuded a fragrance that reminded Allen of tropical flowers, flowers that grew along the floor of a hot, steamy, fertile jungle. Eventually, in the oriental manner, he learned to enjoy inhaling the aroma of her face and breasts instead of kissing as foreplay.

Now he handed his popgun to one of the children and walked after Pensy. She stopped at the next booth, looked over her shoulder, watched him approach.

"Good evening," he said.

In reply, she faced him and did the whole Thai greeting ritual: lowered eyes, hands pressed palm to palm, deep bow. Then she tittered: "Sawadee." She looked into his face and said, "I see you kill many VC."

Allen frowned. Was she jerking his chain? "I never met a VC I didn't like," he said, figured the humor to be totally wasted.

She surprised him by salvaging a fragment: "How come? You friend of VC? Some kind of spy?"

He smiled at her comeback, shook his head. "My name is Cy Allen." He waited, linked her coal black eyes to his. He knew the almond eyes, long black lashes, high cheekbones, wide jaw. . . . .

"I am Pensy," she said, lowering her eyes. Her head bowed slightly, a reflexive movement.

"Would you like to have dinner with me?"

She looked toward Dobbs: "What about your friend?"

"He knows how to feed himself."

"You take him too. Then I go."

She led them to a restaurant on a sidestreet, a place where Allen and Dobbs were the only foreigners, drew surprised stares from the patrons until they noticed Pensy. "Educate us," Allen said and Pensy ordered for the three of them. Then she asked, "You Night Owl?" aimed the question more at Dobbs than at Allen.

Dobbs made a sour face and shook his head emphatically, then grinned maliciously, said, "Colonel Cy would like to be."

Pensy focused on Allen. "Colonel?" It sounded like two words: "Coal. Nell."

"Half," he said. "Lieutenant colonel."

"Three nickel, maybe?"

"Right," said Dobbs. "Triple Nickel. We fly together, same crew."

"Who the pilot?"

Dobbs pointed to Allen.

Pensy winked at Allen and, when he returned the wink, gave him her big laugh.

The food was a plate of translucent pieces of meat and a plate of fried rice. Dobbs took a quick look and said, "Raw fish?"

"Chicken," said Pensy, irritated.

"Raw?" said Dobbs.

"No." Did he think Thais were barbarians, Pensy wondered. The thought of eating raw chicken nauseated her. She served portions of the meat to Allen and Dobbs, took only rice for herself.

The skinned and boned chicken breasts had been marinated in lemon and then grilled exactly to done, not a second longer. Allen took a bite and said, "Perfect." He served a piece of the meat to Pensy but she barely touched it.

After dinner she asked, "Want to see Chinese movie? Titles in Thai. But special booth for Americans, speak English." Less confidently she added, "Or you want go club, listen music and dance?"

"I think I'll head back to base," Dobbs said.

Allen and Pensy went to the movie and then club hopping. Allen felt he was on a college date. And that was how it turned out—like a college date.

At the Jaguar Club and then the Playboy Club, Pensy enjoyed a few grins at Allen's expense—his dancing style was as outdated as his basketball style—but he didn't mind. He was smooth and she recognized that quality. At the clubs, places he wouldn't have visited on his own, Pensy exchanged few greetings, seemed as much a stranger as Allen.

After leaving the Playboy he proposed, "Want to go to the base?" He roomed alone in half of a two-bedroom trailer divided by a common bathroom.

"Go where you live?"

He nodded.

"I no think." Her tone whispered, "I'm sorry."

The idea of offering her money never entered his mind. It was late. He was tired and suddenly didn't care if they went to bed together or not.

Did she sense his shift of mood? Did she recognize she was losing him? "Meet me tomorrow," she said. "Same place restaurant. About six?"

He nodded, wondered why he agreed, wasn't certain if he would or wouldn't meet her. This all seemed so familiar. He was too old to play these games.

"You sure?" she said.

He nodded again with half-closed eyelids.

She pressed her cheek against his neck, brushed his chest with her breasts, inhaled him for a long moment, left a trace of her flowery fragrance in his nostrils. Then she walked away with purpose, knew exactly where she was headed.

Without a definite idea of where he stood, Allen hailed a pedicab, told the driver, "Air base."

That night Cy Allen dreamed of Betty Vaughn, a girlfriend from his first years of college, his first love. The dream was frustrating: Betty and he were naked but did nothing except desperately stroke each other, found no release or satisfaction. In the morning, he did not recall the dream.

Pensy understood Air Force punctuality. She arrived at the restaurant at precisely six o'clock, met Allen at the door. She gave him her biggest smile. He asked her if they had to eat immediately and when she said it didn't matter, he told her, "I'm hungry for you more than for food." If she hadn't understood the meaning of his words, his staring eyes would have told her what he wanted.

Considering the possible profit, her investment was nothing, she thought. In a way, she liked his directness. Allen rented a room at the Ubol Hotel.

Naked, she matched his expectations. Her body was unblemished, tightly fleshed, a primitive golden brown that reflected eternal summer sunlight from the deepest shadows of the shaded room. It was as if she wore a golden veil that covered her even when she stood naked.

Her body was all about pleasure, he thought. He explored the golden ridges and valleys of her body's landscape with hands and lips and tongue, made a feast of her, made love to her for his own pleasure and to give pleasure. He lost himself in an unreal paradise, a fragrant jungle Eden of satisfaction, a dreamworld of souls that he unconsciously had sought for years.

If passion begins with a sense of uniqueness, then Pensy was attracted by Allen's concentration on her, his giving as well as taking, his leisurely tempo of lovemaking. So unlike Americans, she thought. In an unfeeling world she saw promise of a man who cared.

But hadn't she seen similar promise before?

When they were leaving the hotel, on their way to a late dinner, the Thai desk clerk courteously nodded to Allen, then coldly stared at Pensy. Malediction by sight. "I no like," she told Allen. "Man on desk look at me like I some whore. Not so!"

A week later they leased a bungalow in Warin Chamrap, a town across the Mae Nam Muo River, on the side of Ubon opposite the air base.

Unknown to Allen, Pensy kept her single, rented room in Ubon, a room she had let since moving to the city. The room had evolved into her private retreat. The first American she had slept with had lived there. His name had been Ronald Poindexter, from Knoxville, Tennessee. A technical sergeant with two children, he had promised to divorce his wife, a woman who had trapped him, and marry Pensy. Or so he had said. During his last month at Ubon, all he had talked about and planned for was their life together in the United States. Pensy had believed every word, dreamed of their future.

After Ronald Poindexter's year in Thailand ended, she had never heard from him again. It had taken her a long time to realize that there was no mistake: he had abandoned her. She'd seen the story in movies and read it in books. But living it had been different, much more difficult to believe.

She had truly loved Ronald Poindexter from Knoxville, Tennessee. Often, she still thought of him and imagined how happy her life could have been with him. He had broken her heart.

When she had finally understood that he had lied, she'd renounced love and had gone to work in one of the city's massage houses. By then, she had spent the seemingly large sum of money that Poindexter had left to tide her over. Being exposed to officers and recognizing the wide economic gap between them and enlisted men had been a reeducation for Pensy and the start of a new life. Pensy had quickly learned that it was easier to play "wife" to one man than to slave in a massage parlor and be a "girlfriend" to many. Also, there was always hope that one of her "husbands" would take her to the United States.

Cy Allen was the first lieutenant colonel in Pensy's line of majors and captains. Naturally, his rank stood him above the rest, added to the promise she saw in him. He differed in one more important way: he never questioned her about the past. As a result she told him many things about her life, details she had not revealed to other men even when directly questioned. She disguised her experiences by attributing them to friends, and cousins, and nieces. When she finished a story, however, she usually felt that Allen knew she had been talking about herself. She couldn't forgive herself for her lack of discretion, just as she couldn't forgive Allen for listening, for encouraging her with his nonjudgmental silence.

6

While flights of Phantoms periodically made their "Charges" into North Vietnam, major air strikes employed F-105 bombers. A typical strike force was composed of twelve to twenty F-105 bombers. Each single-seat F-105 carried six seven-hundred-fifty-pounders or two three-thousand-pounders.

Four F-105 flak suppressors. Each plane carried six Cluster Bomb Unit (CBU) cannisters which opened in the air and evenly spread one hundred eighty-two fragmentation bomblets in an oval pattern sixty by thirty yards. About the size of baseballs, the bomblets randomly exploded for several minutes.

Eight F-105F SAM suppressors. This model of the F-105 carried a two-man crew and was armed with four air-to-ground Shrike missiles.

Four or eight F-4s for Combat Air Patrol. The number depended upon the current MiG threat. Each F-4 was armed with four AIM7 Sparrow missiles stored in the fuselage well and four AIM9 Sidewinder missiles hung from a wing pylon for use in engaging MiGs. The element was called a MiGCAP.

Additional F-4s, in flights of four. Armed with six

seven-fifties on pylons and four Sparrows in the well, they trailed the F-105 bombers and played a dual role.

One KC-135 tanker for every four airplanes in the strike force. Everyone refueled going and coming.

Two EB-66 Destroyers for electronic countermeasures. The EB-66 was a reconfigured version of the B-66: its bomb bay carried a capsule which housed four ECM specialists and their equipment. As in the B-66, a pilot and navigator rode up front. The two-engine EB-66 was unarmed when flying over the North. Isolated in the windowless capsule, the ECM operators frequently questioned exactly who the Destroyer was designed to destroy.

Last of all, when needed, the strike force could call upon a standby array of search and rescue aircraft: four to eight prop-driven A1 Skyraiders, two HH-3 Jolly Green Giant helicopters, and a C-130 Hercules.

The F-4 Phantom and F-105 Thunderchief, the latter cynically but affectionately called the "Thud," perfectly complemented each other. They were approximately the same dimensions: sixty-five feet long, thirty-five feet across the wings, twenty feet tall at the tail. Naked, they weighed fourteen tons; gassed and armed, their weight jumped to twenty-seven tons. The Phantom had two engines, each with seventeen thousand pounds of thrust; the Thud had one with twenty-seven thousand pounds of push. Both aircraft were capable of speeds near Mach 2.2 at altitude and Mach 1.1 at sea level. The Thud's "Coke bottle" shape and thin wings accounted for its straight-out speed. As originally designed the Thud was sleek: its wing area was under four hundred square feet while the Phantom's was over five hundred. The F-105 had been built for high-speed delivery of an internally stowed tactical nuclear weapon. So that the F-105 could lug multiple conventional weapons into North Vietnam, heavy metal racks were attached to its belly. The racks disrupted the F-105's smooth profile and made it react like a "Lead Sled," another of the airplane's nicknames.

Strike force aircraft launched from several bases. F-105s from Takhli and Korat joined up over central Thailand and cruised northward at an airspeed of four hundred eighty knots indicated and an altitude of fifteen thousand feet. Before entering Laos, they rendezvoused with F-4s from Ubon. Over Laos, every plane hooked onto a KC-135 and topped off its fuel load.

Entering North Vietnam, the airspeed and the pucker factor increased: the strike force accelerated to five hundred twenty knots indicated and the crewmen grew alert for MiGs and SAMs. The MiGCAP preceded the other planes by five minutes and swept the skies (the MiGCAP continued to fly cover until the last Thud departed North Vietnam). MiGs usually made their passes while the strike force was inbound, five to ten minutes from target. The MiGs' objective was, by threatening the lumbering bombers, to intimidate them into prematurely dumping their loads on the foothills and rice paddies west of the target areas. Without MiGCAPs for protection, statistics verified that when threatened by MiGs fifty-five percent of the bombers jettisoned ordnance. In instances when the bombers cleaned themselves in preparation for offensive air-to-air action, the MiGs frequently broke off the engagement and withdrew.

In the strike force formation, flak and SAM suppression aircraft were next in line behind the MiGCAP.

Once beyond the Annamese Cordillera, the wild

and rugged saw-toothed mountain range that separated Laos from North Vietnam, the strike force was over rolling green-carpeted hills. Reaching the Black River, twenty miles into the North, the pilots again pushed the power forward until the indicated airspeed read five-forty. From there, on clear days, the crewmen could see the Red River Delta in the distance. Forty miles apart, the Black and Red rivers ran from the northwest, out of China. They paralleled each other for nearly four hundred miles until, thirty miles from Hanoi, the Black hooked north and joined the Red. East of the confluence, a five-thousand-foot-high, twenty-five-mile-long ridgeline paralleled the Red River and pointed directly at Hanoi: it was nicknamed "Thud Ridge." At Hanoi, the Red River spread and formed a fifty-mile-wide delta before emptying into the Gulf of Tonkin. The lush Delta looked quiet and inviting. Most targets were in that region, surrounded by defenses.

At the beginning of 1967, one hundred fifty SAM sites provided continuous coverage from Yen Bai, seventy miles northwest of Hanoi, to Vinh, one hundred forty miles south of Hanoi. Within that same area, antiaircraft guns (23-mm and larger) numbered several thousand with more arriving daily. Guns smaller than 23-mm were too numerous to count.

Approaching its target, the strike force flew in formation with one to three miles separation between flights of four. The F-105s and F-4s frequently carried external electronic countermeasure pods which supplemented more powerful equipment in the EB-66s. For self-preservation, the slow-moving EBs worked the fringes of the target sector and conducted jamming from afar. If the fighter-bombers maintained proper flight formation, the radiations from their ECM pods overlapped and effects were intensified.

When everything worked perfectly, they flooded fire control radar screens and denied altitude, azimuth, and range readings for accurate aiming of larger antiaircraft guns; they also degraded the Fan Song radar operators' ability to isolate individual airplanes in order to guide SAMs toward them by radio command. Separation between aircraft ensured maneuvering room, however, if AAA or SAM fire became accurate.

When the fighter-bombers were within range, larger antiaircraft guns sent up barrages in an effort to disperse the formation: explosions from twenty- and thirty-pound shells filled the sky with black clouds of flak. Although the guns were visually controlled and scored few direct hits, the intensity of fire unsettled the aircrews who had to fly into the barrages. At times, the flak was so thick that, as F-105 pilots often said, "we could've lowered the gear and taxied on it."

Veteran flyers claimed that by watching the muzzle flashes of the antiaircraft artillery they could tell whether or not a battery was aimed at them. If so, they moved a thousand feet left or right to avoid the burst. Allen had a surer method: he watched the big shells on their upward trajectory and reacted accordingly. Other pilots agreed that they also saw the shells, but only when the light was right. Hearing Cy Allen talk about AAA trajectories, Junior Eliot said, "Come on, colonel, you never even saw that *huge* piece of karst that Rocco took us over." Everyone laughed but Dobbs who was convinced that *that* mission had been a Seventh Air Force plot to kill all of them.

Four flak suppression Thuds comprised the lead wave of bombers. On their own to fight separate duels, the pilots of those craft attacked what they decided were the most formidable AAA guns or batteries in sight. They pressed their bomb runs to the lowest limit in order to put CBU patterns tightly around gun emplacements. AAA was configured so that weapons or groups of weapons of varying sizes supported each other. In that way a bomber that made a pass on one site was vulnerable to fire from other sites. The arrangement also allowed gunners to maintain the maximum rate of fire on an airplane throughout its approach, attack, and withdrawal. The flak suppression pilots' excessive courage in the face of overlapping defenses caused many losses. They knew their role was ridiculously dangerous, but they zealously planted their cluster bombs. The CBU bomblets' delayed explosions discouraged AAA gunners from exposing themselves for several minutes. In those intervals, the following waves of bombers roared down the chute four abreast. The few flak suppression aircraft never silenced all the guns from the multitude of AAA batteries. Therefore, the bomber pilots saw their share of flak.

Reaching target, the F-105 and F-4 bombers climbed a thousand feet, rolled in, and dived earthward at five hundred fifty knots, a fraction under Mach 1. The planes were speed-limited by their external ordnance. At that point, the 57-mm and 37-mm antiaircraft guns commenced firing. Their projectiles were much smaller than those from the larger guns; however, their rates of fire were five to ten times greater. Layers of flak followed the bombers downward.

To avoid groundfire, the diving pilots juked their planes right and left while trying to line up on their assigned target. They were briefed to release at eight thousand feet: the whole load! Most pilots let go at between nine and six thou; a few madmen pressed lower. Each plane made one pass only. As soon as bombs were away, the pilots busted the sound barrier and performed jinking climbs at maximum power to escape the area. The bomb run was over in seconds but the adrenaline rush lingered for hours.

(Between eleven and fifteen F-105s were needed to deliver a bomb load that could have been equaled by one B-52 Stratofortress drop. However, Washington strategists hesitated to risk the invincible Strategic Air Command bombers against surface-to-air missiles. No politician wanted the onus of losing a "battleship" to a Soviet puppet. The massive bombers were reserved for safely smashing the jungles of South Vietnam and Laos and Cambodia to pulp, until December 1972. Then, in a frenzy of hate and frustration, the President sent hundreds of B-52s over the North for two weeks—centered around Christmas—and systematically destroyed every target the smaller fighter-bombers had been chasing for years. Yes, the United States lost fifteen B-52s during those two weeks. But the losses came early, before the North Vietnamese used up their stockpile of surface-to-air missiles. And the cost didn't begin to match the thousands of United States aircraft lost over the North during the previous campaigns. The B-52 raids ended the war, by the way. But that's another tale. Of course, if the B-52s had bombed earlier, Allen's story might never have happened.)

Allen and Dobbs thought that MiGCAP was the easiest job in the strike force. They argued about whether the flak suppressor or bomber role was more difficult, meaning more dangerous. They wholeheartedly agreed that the toughest job in the strike force belonged to the SAM suppressors, two-man crews who flew special models of the F-105, appropriately called "Iron Hand."

* * *

Iron Hand crews loitered above the target area and waited for SAM sites to activate. A SAM complex was a small network of roads that resembled a wheel with a Fan Song radar control van at the hub and SA2 Guideline missiles positioned at the end of the spokes. SAM complexes were spread over most of North Vietnam but all were not occupied every day. Launch controllers and missile crews continually changed locations. Therefore, Iron Hand crews never knew which sites posed a threat to the strike force. As a result, with calculated aggressiveness, the crews played a form of Russian roulette: the pilots flew directly over SAM complexes in hopes of attracting attention. Iron Hand's objective was to destroy control vans and kill their radar operators before they launched SA2s at the strike force. The SA2 missiles were radio command-guided and, in flight, had to be directed to their targets.

Fan Song radar operators often sat in their vans and played cat-and-mouse with the strike force. By not coming up on the air they remained undetected. When they thought the time was right, they activated and launched as quickly as possible. Weather permitting, Fan Song operators used optics to align the radar antennas; in that way, when they transmitted, they immediately were tracking a target. When emitting radar signals, the operators knew they were liable to be attacked.

Iron Hands were armed with ten-foot-long Shrike missiles that delivered a one hundred forty-five pound fragmentation warhead. The missiles were beam riders: they locked on a radar signal and, when launched, homed directly to the signal's transmitter at twice the speed of sound.

Listening to tape recordings of Iron Hand attacks

made Allen break out in goose bumps: the flights were dashes deep ". . . into the jaws of Death, into the mouth of Hell . . ." He decided that his reaction was caused by tremendous empathy coupled with the fact that he had no control over the outcome. The tapes produced an uneasiness similar to that which had overcome him as a Night Owl backseater. In one sense, however, the tapes were more emotional. On his Night Owl flight he knew that if disaster struck the frontseater, he had the capability of flying the airplane, of taking control of stick and throttle. The tapes provided no such course of action. His sole consolation as a listener was that he knew the crew survived, otherwise the tapes wouldn't have been available to him. His insight gave him a keener appreciation for what Dobbs endured, being along only for the ride. Allen knew that what was un-heard on the tapes was as dramatic as what was recorded . . .

A typical scenario found an Iron Hand aircraft orbiting the day's target. (On the tape, in the background, there is a "scree" at several-second intervals. The sound resembles a fingernail being dragged a short distance across a blackboard. The noise is too persistent, too grating to be ignored. It represents the three-hundred-sixty-degree search sweep of ground radar.)

IRON HAND NAVIGATOR: I have a SAM activity light. (On his Radar Homing And Warning gear a light has just come on to indicate search radar is sweeping across their F-105.) Three o'clock.

IRON HAND PILOT: I hear it. Think it's that site there? (He turns the airplane until the site in question is lined up under the nose.)

NAVIGATOR: It's twelve o'clock, now.

PILOT: Roger. Got it.

(In the background the "scree" increases in pitch, becomes a squeak that repeats every other second. The change indicates that a Fan Song radar has been switched from search to track mode: its sweep is narrowed to several degrees in order to follow a single target.)

NAVIGATOR (His RHAW gear scope shows one ring, a red circle of light. There is no humor in his voice.): I think we got his attention. He's tracking.

(In the background the squeak grows higher in pitch and is heard every second: the radar scan has been narrowed to a few degrees and paints more frequently back and forth across the Thud.)

PILOT: Sounds like. . .

NAVIGATOR (His RHAW gear shows two rings. His voice takes on a distinct edge.): I have a SAM lock.

PILOT: . . . a lock.

NAVIGATOR (tightly): Roger that.

PILOT (He pushes over the nose of the airplane, lights afterburners, and from fifteen thousand feet dives at the site. He throws switches rapidly: activates his Shrike missiles, sets up his armament panel . . . He is as busy as a one-handed piccolo player): Ready, ready, ready. (He inhales loudly.)

At this point the Fan Song operators have two choices: one, shut down their transmitter and have the Iron Hand break off the attack; two, try to launch an SA2 before the Iron Hand launches a Shrike. Fan Song operators know the game as well as the Iron Hand crew: to play on either side takes balls as big as the Ritz.

(In the background, the squeak becomes a high-pitched rattle, like a snake about to strike. The radar sweep has been narrowed to approximately one degree for aiming the SA2 missile.)

NAVIGATOR (Three red rings flash on his RHAW gear.): I have a SAM ready-to-launch light.

PILOT: Got it.

Now is the time. The Iron Hand pilot can launch his Shrike at any moment. He presses down through ten thousand feet, however, without firing. He wants to be lower, as close as he can get (if it were possible, he would like to be *inside* the van) when he launches. The closer he is the better chance he has to score a devastating hit.

NAVIGATOR: I have a ready-to-launch light.

PILOT: I hear it.

(The SAM complex grows larger in his center windscreen panel. The rattle leaps out of the background, increases in volume to voice level.)

NAVIGATOR (loudly): I have a solid lock, ready-to-launch light.

PILOT (Lined up on the SAM site with his finger on the trigger): Affirmative. (Through the center windscreen he sees every detail of the complex: the command van, missiles, launchers, supply vehicles, trucks, and transport trailers. Everything is identical to the photographs he has been shown countless times at Intelligence briefings. The rattle grows louder, nearly overpowering, as loud as it will ever get.) Any second.

NAVIGATOR (His words are like a plea.): I have a ready-to-launch light.

PILOT: Any second now.

NAVIGATOR (A red "X" fills his RHAW gear scope. He shouts): SAM launch. Break. I have a SAM launch light.

PILOT (He sees an SA2 missile emit a billowing cloud of white smoke an instant before it lifts off the rails of its launcher. In that instant, he fires his Shrike.): Missile away. (He banks the F-105 hard left.)

NAVIGATOR (Shouting): Break. SAM launch. Break.

(The pilot has started the turn while the navigator is still shouting. Suddenly conversation stops: the crewmen feel the effects of six, seven, eight times the pull of gravity. They are dragged deep into their seats. The flesh of their faces is stretched downward, their features distorted. Anti-gravity suits squeeze their legs and abdomens but are not enough. The men flex their upper bodies, tilt their heads to the side in order to prevent blood from being drained out of their brains. Still, they lose peripheral vision, their lines of sight narrow to a tunnel of light directly in front of them.)

At altitude, there was an accepted procedure for dodging SAMs: once the missile was sighted, the pilot dropped the aircraft's nose and dived as hard as possible in order to pull three negative G's and build speed to around five hundred fifty knots. When the missile turned downward, the pilot then went back up, climbing as hard as he could. The missile wasn't designed to follow that sharp reversal maneuver: if it tried, it went out of control and the crew was home free. If the missile didn't try to follow, then again the crew was rid of it.

The idea among Iron Hand crews was that with one quick close-in sidestep it was easier to avoid the line of a gun's muzzle than it was to attempt to outrun a guided bullet from that same muzzle.

(On the tape only the grunting and the panting and gasping of the crewmen is audible. There are sounds that could be whimpers, but listeners know that is impossible: cowboys and fighter pilots don't cry. The grunts and pants and gasps change in volume and rhythm as the F-105 twists through the sky to avoid the SA2 missile which can knock down an airplane by detonating within two hundred feet of it. Of course, while evading at low altitude the Iron Hand is being sniped at by AAA. Anything goes to escape. There is no written procedure when faced point-blank by death.)

NAVIGATOR (Relieved): Missed.

PILOT (Climbing and steering right and left through little twenty-degree check turns while rolling his head in every direction to make certain nothing is threatening him, like another SAM or a MiG): I think so.

NAVIGATOR (Emotionlessly): Hooray. (Less than three minutes have passed since the first red ring appeared on his RHAW gear scope.) We score with the Shrike?

PILOT: Close. Not sure. See what recce comes up with.

(In the background there suddenly is a high-pitched "scree" that repeats itself every other second.)

NAVIGATOR (Excitedly): One ring. Tracking. Seven o'clock. Oh, shit . . . Same site?

PILOT: Not sure. (He stands the F-105 on its left wing and turns sharply toward the source of the transmission.) Here we go . . .

Most SA2s that were fired nose-to-nose ended up as unguided. The Fan Song operators hoped for ballistic kills. As soon as their missile was launched, they temporarily went off the air. The operators knew the Shrike was a beam rider and they weren't going to provide it with a path straight to them. By stopping radar transmissions they made the Shrike another unguided missile. Because the Shrike had no memory, it usually missed the control van far enough so that the Fan Song crew was uninjured.

Therefore, the primary antagonists occupied each other with sparring but seldom scored a knockout. That was acceptable to the Iron Hand crews who considered their mission a success if they focused the SAM controllers' attention away from the strike force. There was one "however." As a result of pressing attacks too low, many F-105s were shot up by AAA positioned for mutual support of the SAM sites. The situation was another example of excessive courage sometimes proving to be self-destructive.

After bombing the Thai Nguyen steel mill at low level and then flying a Night Owl mission and then listening to Iron Hand tapes, Cy Allen was convinced that MiGCAP duty was a day at the races. Despite what the general preached, MiGCAP was MiG-killing and MiG-killing was glory.

7

In maneuverability the MiG-21 Fishbed was even with the F-4 Phantom. It was inferior in range and payload. Originally produced in the mid-Fifties, the MiG-21 resulted from Korean War experiences: Russian pilots demanded an "air superiority" fighter designed strictly for combat performance, with only enough armament to knock down an enemy fighter. To satisfy them, Mikoyan-Gurevich built what was fundamentally a small, fast airplane: fifty feet long, twenty-five wide, with a power plant that produced thrust equal to the plane's empty weight, eleven thousand pounds. In afterburner the engine pushed the airframe to Mach 2 at altitude, Mach 1 on the deck. The MiG-21 flown by the North Vietnamese was armed with a twin-barrel 23-mm cannon and four AA2 Atoll missiles, heat seekers similar to the Sidewinder.

The North Vietnamese air order of battle was comprised mostly of the older MiG-17 Fresco over which the Phantom held a decisive speed advantage. Like the Fishbed, the Fresco also was inferior in range and payload. However, the thirty-six foot long Fresco, which attained Mach 1 only in a dive, was far more maneuverable. It could out-turn a Phantom or Thunderchief all day. For firepower it had three 23-mm cannons: one mounted in the lower starboard nose and a pair beneath the portside; and it carried AA1 Alkali missiles. The Russian-designed fighter originally was intended to be used in defense of the homeland ("To protect Russia, that Mother!" Allen told Dobbs) and grossed only thirteen thousand pounds to the Phantom's fifty-four thousand. U.S. strategists decided their fighter would have to penetrate deep into enemy territory and perform both air-to-air and air-to-ground roles; therefore, the Phantom design emphasized range and payload.

"The rationale goes back to World War Two," Allen explained to Dobbs, "fly halfway across Europe to find a fight. World War Two's the last point of certitude, the last unblemished victory. Think about Korea. We had the F-86 Sabre, a real hot rod, built primarily for air superiority. It outkilled the MiG-15 something like ten-to-one—against pilots from Korea, China, Russia, and Poland—but the U.S. was stalemated on the ground and that made the politicians suspect of the entire war's strategy. And they control the appropriations. Ergo . . ."

Dobbs smiled at the Latin.

"Do you have to listen to every word?"

Dobbs nodded: "I write what you tell me to my dad. He claims we should still be on horseback."

Allen grinned: "There, you see, we're all strapped with outdated thinking. And that includes Russia. Little short-range jets are Stalin's dream-come-true." Several days later, Allen and Dobbs got trapped in a bizarre merry-go-round with eight Frescos, and Stalin's little dream became their nightmare.

* * *

The day started like many others, flying cover for 105s. Allen was Number Two behind Rocco Monge in an echeloned flight of four. The weather was raunchy, three or four miles visibility with a low cloud deck. They hadn't quite reached the Delta when, without fanfare, the RHAW gear lit up bright red and all hell broke loose. Dobbs shouted, "I got a missile ready-to-launch light," at the same time somebody shouted, "SAMs," over the radio.

"Launch," Dobbs said, "twelve o'clock. Jesus . . ."

A barrage of SAMs ripped out of the undercast and rushed skyward. Three or four voices called, "Twelve o'clock." There were eight missiles. Well out in front of the MiGCAP, they streaked straight upward, obviously unguided. "Scare tactics," a voice said.

"Six, six, six," Dobbs shouted. Simultaneously with the launch of the eight unguided missiles, a single SAM came up from behind the MiGCAP. The bad weather hid the solitary missile and the frontal barrage diverted attention long enough so that the warning came late. Allen had no idea of which way to go.

Three, Junior Eliot, shouted, "SAM, six . . ."

"It's through our altitude," Dobbs reported.

Provided its launch was detected in time, the method to evade a SAM was to execute a hard diving turn into it, then abruptly make a four-G rolling pull-up. Guided from the ground, the missile normally reacted to radical turn commands by yawing wildly and then tumbling out of control. The use of such evasive maneuvers along with ECM kept SAM effectiveness low: approximately one out of every fifty SAMs knocked down an airplane.

Dale Vestik, Number Four at twenty thousand feet, saw the SAM. He tried to execute a split-S. Basically, it was the wrong move. On top of that, he rolled inverted practically in slow motion, then paused before he pulled the aircraft's nose below the horizon. The maneuver looked as if he had to think through each step before he performed it. Like a person who danced by walking on numbered footprints, his moves were stiff and far from professional. At twenty thousand feet, Vestik had time to save himself. Even though his maneuver was not the proper reaction, a *snappy* split-S might have worked. Moving at half speed, Vestik wasted two or three seconds and that was a lifetime when confronted by the Mach 2 speed of a surface-to-air missile. The Fan Song operator got lucky and the missile's three-hundred-pound high explosive warhead detonated by proximity directly in front of Vestik's plane. Watching over his shoulder, Allen saw the F-4 emerge from the fireball with pieces spewing off of it. Instead of completing its maneuver, the plane headed straight down.

"Dale, punch out, punch out," Rocco Monge said over the radio.

The plummeting Phantom disappeared into the cloud layer about a thousand feet above the ground. There were no parachutes. The three surviving airplanes went into a loose orbit over the spot where Vestik crashed; the crews heard no emergency beeper. (Every parachute contained an emergency beeper which activated when the chute deployed. Over guard channel, the beeper broadcast a pulsating electronic howl that served as a cry for help as well as a beacon for rescuers.) "They've had it, one way or the other," Allen told Dobbs. "Goddamnit . . ."

Rocco Monge made the prescribed radio calls to Search and Rescue, but it was a foregone conclusion that a pilot shot down in the Hanoi area was lost. The best that could be hoped for was to see him when the war ended. Because of the concentrated defenses, crewmen agreed that there was no sense in risking, and probably losing, more people: a rescue helicopter pickup near Hanoi was impossible.

"Goddamnit," Allen said again. He had seen it coming: putting Lieutenant Colonel Dale Vestik in a fighter cockpit was a perfect example of how *not* to run an Air Force. The Air Force trained guys to be pilots; the best became fighter pilots; and the best of those—the naturals—didn't care to be much else. On the other hand, Dale Vestik—B.A., B.S., M.S., Ph.D. —was a natural logistics genius who happened to be taught how to fly. Shortly thereafter, he went off to a desk until, a dozen years later, a computer knocked the dust from his pilot rating and indiscriminately assigned him to the cockpit of a high performance airplane. By then, Vestik's brain rivaled Einstein's, but his body and reflexes couldn't keep pace with Grandma Moses. The computer didn't care: all it knew was that *every* pilot was required to fly at least one tour in Southeast Asia: Vestik filled a square! And forty-two-year-old, soon-to-be-promoted-to-bird-colonel Dale Vestik felt obligated to pay his dues by facing the enemy and was too much of an officer and gentleman to save his own ass by requesting reassignment to a machine he could handle. As a result, he sat there while a SAM ate him for lunch, and took a young backseater too. "Goddamnit . . ."

It was enough to make Allen gnash his teeth. It was a shitty day and he wasn't comfortable. After the decoy SAM launches, the strike force plowed in and radio chatter increased until it now sounded like everyone in the force was shouting directions and giving orders. It was impossible to know what was happening. Fighter frequency was as garbled as a Chinese schoolroom and he wanted to switch it off but didn't dare. More SAMs were being launched and even the normally cool Iron Hand jocks were screeching like a troop of baboons. All the strike force needed now was to be bounced by a swarm of MiGs. "Goddamn . . ." After being ignored by nine SAMs, he was in no mood to panic. At least, that was what he told himself. But he still wasn't comfortable.

Straining his eyeballs, Allen couldn't locate the first wave of F-105s egressing from the target. "Thuds are due out about now," he reminded Monge. He wished he had X-ray vision and could see through the clouds; there was always a slim chance that Vestik or his backseater got out at the last second. "Keep a sharp eye on that RHAW gear," he told Dobbs. "Where the hell are those Thuds?"

"Ten o'clock," Monge said. "That them?" Below, approximately two dozen airplanes were racing along atop the clouds.

"That's a lot of Thuds," Allen said to Dobbs and then identified the trailing aircraft as MiG-17s in hot pursuit of the 105s. "MiGs, eleven o'clock low," he radioed.

"Tallyho," Monge said. "Let's get 'em." The F-4 pilots jettisoned their external fuel tanks and dived at the MiGs. At two thousand feet, Monge and Allen flew in among the enemy planes which were milling to form a Wagon Wheel. Along the way they had lost Junior Eliot.

A MiG cut directly in front of them. Dobbs screamed, "Look out," and caused Allen more fright than the close call. Set on edge, he nervously tried to look everywhere at once while he stuck to Rocco Monge's wing.

Monge momentarily got behind a MiG and cut loose a Sparrow that curved homeward. Allen was about to say, "Nice shot," when the missile straightened and went behind the banking MiG. Monge later explained that the F-4's radar malfunctioned and broke lock at the worst possible moment.

By then the MiGs were in their Wagon Wheel and Monge and Allen were in it with them. Everyone was pulling a constant six G's in a ninety-degree bank. Designed for two or more MiGs, the defensive maneuver permitted airplanes to cover each other's rear area against attack while flying a circle in the horizontal plane. The North Vietnamese had simply modified the Lufberry Circle from World War I. In this instance, however, the MiGs were behind Monge and Allen and jockeying for position to fire at them. "The whole NVAF is on our ass," Dobbs said.

"Lead," Allen called, "I have eight bandits trapped at seven o'clock."

Monge reacted immediately: "Let's take them up." He kicked in top rudder and the big vertical slab on the tail lifted the Phantom in a high-G climbing turn. Allen stayed with him and the MiGs followed. The maneuver was designed to stall out the enemy planes which had smaller lifting surfaces. The formation had corkscrewed up to six thousand feet when SAMs rocketed from the ground. "Wrong move," Monge shouted. Locked in the Wagon Wheel, F-4s and MiGs flashed back to the deck.

Still pulling six G's in a ninety-degree bank, the F-4s tried for a shot at a MiG, any MiG. Mostly in frustration, Monge fired several Sidewinders that slued out of orbit and sailed off toward the horizon. The missile wasn't designed for accuracy under heavy G-loads. Flying fighter wing, Allen didn't dare fire for fear of hitting Rocco.

While Rocco was shooting, the MiGs were shooting too. They swapped lead and potted at the Phantoms with unguided Alkali rockets that harmlessly whizzed out of orbit. Nevertheless, whenever one passed wide abeam, Dobbs said, "Horse—shit." After about the tenth, he added, "What if one of those malfunctions and curves back on us by accident?"

The few times that Monge decreased the bank angle to sixty degrees and widened the circle in hopes of reaching a reasonable firing position, a MiG cut across the ring at full power and snapped a deflection shot with its 23-mm cannons. Muzzle flashes lighted up its nose. The F-4 crews sucked back into the smallest possible circle and watched the cannon rounds fly by like flaming bowling balls. To Dobbs, at least, the 23-mm rounds looked that large. "Cock—sucker," he called at each pass by the enemy.

The merry-go-round was nonsensical. The F-4s couldn't risk running for home because they couldn't build up speed quickly enough to prevent the MiGs from getting several shots at them. The MiGs couldn't break out because the F-4s would easily catch them. The only choice was to fly a tight circle and avoid giving the enemy a clean shot.

After countless orbits, the firing stopped. The airplanes circled counterclockwise as if in some endless, nightmarish race on a treadmill. The sun went in and the day turned gray. It was eerie. Dobbs said, "I don't like the feel of this."

Neither did Allen. The six-G load was killing him: with helmet, survival gear, and parachute, he weighed three-quarters of a ton. They had been stuck there for at least ten minutes; he needed both hands to hold the stick against his gut. Dogfights were supposed to end swiftly, decisively, he thought. Air Force statisticians found that in Korea the average aerial encounter lasted thirty seconds. They were really fucking up the average. Allen groaned from fatigue.

Monge said, "I have twenty-five hundred pounds,"

a few seconds before four MiGs plugged in their afterburners, racked around on the opposite wing, broke out of the circle, and were gone! Unexpectedly, the other four also made a break for it. It seemed that, after eleven or twelve minutes, everybody ran low on fuel at the same time.

"Alone," Allen said thankfully, "at last!" His laughter came out as heavy snuffles.

Dobbs said, "Maybe it's a trap."

"Let's head home," said Monge.

They found Junior Eliot safe at Ubon. He had been cut off by four MiG-21s and had juked through the weeds across North Vietnam before he broke free. At debriefing he said, "I outjinked everybody but one bloodthirsty fanatic. I was down in the tulies, hiding in the old ground clutter so he couldn't lock on with a missile, but it didn't matter to him; he came down in the weeds with me. The bastard was popping at me with his cannons, but I knew what he really wanted: silhouette me against the sky and fire an Atoll up my athhole." The listeners laughed. "We zigged up a narrow little valley and I kept thinking about trying to outrun him but had no room for pure speed. I got near the end of the valley and saw I had two choices: drive into the hills or hop over them and silhouette myself. Some choice! I went to max burner and popped over that ridgeline so fast and so low. I'll bet I cleared it by less than a foot. The MiG pilot fired anyway. I don't think he had a lock. A couple missiles passed over us when we were screaming down the far side of the ridge. I guess the MiG was low on gas because he broke it off there. I thought about doubling back and chasing his ass for a stretch. I figured he was out of missiles, then wondered if his buddies were still in the area. Everything considered, a standoff didn't seem too bad."

A few listeners nodded agreement.

Bob Slevin who was Eliot's backseater said, "I don't like that end of the stick. Cannons and missiles . . ."

"No shit?" Dobbs said. "Tell me about it!"

For three days Allen's arms were sore from hauling back on the control column. He told Dobbs, "I feel like I pitched a doubleheader, one game with each arm."

Dobbs didn't comment. He nursed a stiff neck for a week.

8

When Rocco Monge saw Pensy and Allen window-shopping downtown he mentally congratulated Allen: the woman had a distinct appeal, a Eurasian cast. She held Allen's arm as if they were promenading along a Parisian boulevard, rather than a dusty Ubon street. She probably had a French grandfather, Rocco thought.

Rocco didn't much care how the members of his squadron spent their spare time, as long as the activity didn't conflict with flying ability. Mike Hawk, for example, walked the line with his drinking. Junior Eliot performed at the other extreme, intellectually incapacitated by novels. (Although Eliot denied it, Rocco knew he'd seen Eliot with his nose in a paperback while he waited for Rocco and Allen to gas up on the way to Thai Nguyen.) Dale Vestik lived in the squadron administrative section, fussed over all problems, great and small. Or rather, he used to . . .

Rocco felt guilty about losing Vestik—and the backseater, Dick Strom. Rocco had gone out of his way to shepherd Vestik, to keep him close in anticipation that someday he or Allen or Junior, or even crazy

Hawk, might pull Vestik through a squeaky situation. And then like a pack of rookies, three of them let Vestik get shot from behind.

Rocco's mind tried to believe that it was bound to happen sooner or later. If Vestik had gone to Thai Nguyen . . . in Allen's slot, he wouldn't have recovered from being slapped upside down . . . faced off against the karst, he wouldn't have reacted quickly enough. . . . The hundred missions were a series of traps to eliminate pilots like old Dale, and pilots a lot better than old Dale.

The worst part of the shoot-down was the uncertainty of Vestik's fate—and Strom's. They were listed as missing in action—MIA—limbo for as long as the war lasted, perhaps beyond. In Strom's case uncertainty wasn't as dramatic: he was single. Sure, parents wept and prayed, but they had the consolation of each other, perhaps of other children. Vestik owned a wife and four children, rowed the same boat as Rocco.

From office bull sessions, Rocco had formed the opinion that Vestik's marriage was as rock steady as his own. Both men had married their college sweethearts, sired four children within eight years—two sons and two daughters each—and decided the balance and number was perfect. Surprisingly both also had expressed interest in a late-in-life baby, a child to raise after they retired, only to find dozens of inconveniences within such a plan. Laughingly they had tried to dissuade each other from their common dream. Rocco couldn't see a future without his Rose and their children. How did Grace Vestik and her sons and daughters view their tomorrows?

Total death in a limited war, Rocco thought. He was positive Vestik had understood that personal commitment and national commitment were two different things. Once a bod climbed aboard the big iron butterfly and swooped over the North, nothing was limited as far as self was concerned. National commitment might put limits on targets, and ordnance, and rules of engagement, but those factors had nothing to do with personal obligations within those confines. Once committed to battle, the obligation was made to carry out the assigned task with heart and soul.

Even when asked to fight with one arm tied behind his back, the military ethic dictated that a soldier still fight to the best of his ability, as hard as humanly possible. United States soldiers were in Southeast Asia to fight because it was in the interest of the United States that they did so. The reasoning wasn't dramatic, but it was correct: the soldiers went to work when the politicians failed.

Would his Rose or Grace Vestik agree?

Although Pensy believed she understood Americans, Cy Allen puzzled her: she had never encountered a man who found so much pleasure in basic activities.

When Allen sat down to eat, he expected to feast. Did he eat only once a day? Luckily, he didn't expect her to shop and to cook, willingly took her to her favorite restaurants.

He liked Chinese cooking best but seldom remembered dishes from previous restaurant visits, studied what should have been familiar menus as if he hadn't seen them before. Wanting to try everything, he selected a seafood or chicken and a beef or pork dish for each meal, always added "a side order of fried rice." That final touch angered her because, when she was a child, fried rice without the mixed meats and extra eggs that his included had been a meal in itself for her family. She thought it unfair that at one sitting his side dish alone was enough to feed a Thai family of four.

Perversely, when they dined at restaurants featuring Thai cooking, she ordered unusual delicacies, things she believed he would not enjoy: sparrow-sized birds roasted with their heads on; baked fish with staring eyes; once, an entire boiled eel that looked ready to slither off the plate. The only time Allen faltered was when she ordered an appetizer comprised mainly of highly seasoned, marinated chicken skins. He chewed a mouthful for minutes before carefully spitting it out. "Is this octopus tentacles or duck feet webbing?" he asked. Then he said, "I'm sure I can find a dish or two in the United States . . ." (As if he someday might take her there!) ". . . that you won't eat. Like pickled pig's feet." The suggestion of eating the unclean feet of any animal was an insult that made Pensy turn up her nose.

Waiters greedily watched Allen, made jokes about his bottomless stomach. Tinged with a jade green jealousy, their greed was based upon envy: they wished they could afford such a prodigious appetite. Speaking Thai, a giggling waiter said to Pensy, "He eats and eats. You must exercise all night long to keep him thin." Reading the sexual innuendo in his remark, Pensy pretended to ignore the man's words. When he brought the check, she told Allen, "No tip. I no like him." After refusing to say specifically what she disliked about the waiter, she sulked when Allen ignored her and overtipped.

Overtipping vexed Pensy: too much money spoiled the waiters, made them disgruntled by the gratuities of Thai customers who recognized true merit. How many years would it take for customs to return to normal once the Americans were gone?

Meals lasted hours, time that to Pensy was wasted.

She was accustomed to eating several quick meals, little more than snacks, throughout the day. In boredom, she sipped scotch while Cy ate. But alcohol provided little comfort. If she got drunk, he didn't care: he refused to chastise her for pleasing herself.

Unlike other Americans she had known, Allen didn't drink every day. And when he overdid it, he was a gentle, likeable drunk, reminded her of a Thai. To Pensy, the reactions of Thai and American drinkers were as distant as the locations of the two nations on a globe.

Thais drank for fun: when they got high, they stopped drinking, floated on a wave of alcohol, became happy, and let their worries drift away. They went to bed early, willing captives of alcohol's charm.

When Americans got high, they drowned the initial euphoria with more alcohol, continued to drink until they sank into anger and rage, depths of uncivilized bitterness toward things that were "not like this in the States." They stayed awake late into the night, fought the alcohol as if it were a beast they could conquer.

Differences in the morning after were equally pronounced. Thais awoke sober, happy to begin a new day, rid of past woes. Americans surfaced through hangover agonies of overindulgence, ached with residual poisoning of body and will. Many Americans she had known mysteriously faced the demon by partaking of the demon: Pensy did not understand "A hair of the dog that bit you." The morning after difference between Thais and Americans was the difference between innocence and guilt.

Would it have mattered to her if she had recognized that she was comparing an agrarian mentality to a technological mentality, comparing spirit to flesh?

There was a time, Allen told Pensy, when young and reckless he believed that non-stop drinking was the ultimate in fun and in creating chaos. Drinking used to bring out the crazies, he thought, and told her about a Saturday afternoon at college, the year after he and Betty broke up.

Smashed on gin, he wandered out to the campus golf course fairways, started shagging tee shots and throwing the balls back to the golfers, pegging them while on the run, like he was Carl Furillo or some other rifle-armed outfielder. That sporting event brought out the campus cops in a hurry. He led them a chase into the trees, through the roughs, and across the greens before they found him buried in a sandtrap with only his nose showing. (Did all that running actually cause him to throw up in one of the cups? But then, as he pointed out at the time, he did remember enough golf etiquette to remove the pin prior to holing out.)

Pensy didn't laugh at the narrative of his escapade and he said, "You have to hate golf to appreciate that story."

It seemed to Pensy that, except for eating and an occasional movie, Allen would have been satisfied to spend all of their hours together in bed. To her, he was obsessed with sex, an obsession based more on performing the physical acts than on attaining his own gratification. He participated as if sex was a game, she thought, a contest that pitted his physique against her central nervous system. No matter how many orgasms she had he always wanted to make her "come one more time," like asking for "a side order of fried rice." Worst of all, he knew all the right moves and, at times, it angered her when she responded to them. When she grew excited and traded him thrust for thrust, he smiled and called her "Thunderthighs," a name she considered a mockery.

She was angered more when he grew mentally

detached during sex: he seemed to operate on auto-pilot while his mind journeyed elsewhere. Had his imagination flown away to Vietnam? Or to the United States? To war or to another woman?

At those times she wondered what he did or who he saw on nights he was not with her.

Cy Allen was another opportunity lost, Pensy knew deep in her heart. He would fly his hundred missions over North Vietnam and then fly away to the United States. She never would see him or hear from him again.

She had received three short letters from a bachelor captain with whom she'd lived for two months. His letters had mentioned plans to return to Thailand, hinted of returning for her. But it never happened. She knew it wouldn't.

She wished Allen would be different from the others. One moment she believed he truly cared about her and understood her unspoken dreams; the next moment she decided he was agreeable with her because he was indifferent. Nothing would come of their relationship, she told herself to forestall disappointment.

Nevertheless, she frequently played a mental motion picture of herself in America, driving up to a ranch-style home with a broad front lawn. In what Hollywood movie had she seen such a setting? With the picture in her mind, she asked Allen where he would be assigned when he returned to the United States. "Nellis, maybe. Outside Las Vegas. You know, where everybody gambles day and night." He described the glitter and glamour of Vegas, the twenty-four hour lifestyle. The carnival world of Las Vegas added a party-filled Technicolor reel to Pensy's mental motion picture of her American fantasy.

9

The Red River Delta was never prettier. Widely scattered, fluffy white clouds dotted the landscape of green and rolling hills. A lovely, lovely scene, Cy Allen thought and said, "Nice day for a fox hunt."

"Can't see it on radar," Dobbs replied.

The Phantoms were flying a fluid four formation: two leaders were followed by their wingmen who spread vertically and horizontally. Lead and Two flew to the left with Three and Four about a mile to the right. The leaders scanned with radar and the wingmen searched visually while the four pilots randomly flew left and right, up and down, but still maintained the basic formation. The flight pattern best provided security from a six o'clock attack.

Allen saw a glint in the distance, then specks: "Look one o'clock, dead level."

Dobbs aimed the radar in that direction. "Bogies," he confirmed. "Twenty-one miles. Four of them."

"One o'clock. Four bogies," Allen called over the radio, then held the mike open and paused long enough for the others to strain their eyeballs before adding, "Twenty-one miles, according to radar."

"But *you* saw them first," Junior Eliot said.

Allen didn't reply. Finally, Dobbs said, "Affirmative."

"Too much," said Eliot and laughed.

"Let's check 'em out," Rocco Monge said and the four Phantoms turned toward the other aircraft.

"We have min overtake," Dobbs reported. The Phantoms and MiGs were headed in the same direction at approximately the same speed.

"They'll be to China before we catch up," said Allen.

"Turn and fight, yellow devils," Dobbs called for his pilot's ears only.

Seconds later Allen said, "I think they're turning."

"You kidding?" Dobbs checked the radar. The overtake velocity was a thousand knots. "Affirm. Head-on. Seventeen miles." The airplanes would close the distance in a minute. "I see only two."

Ballsy, Allen thought. They must be Chinese or North Korean instructors on loan; probably had two North Vietnamese rookies with them and ordered the kids to go home.

Rocco Monge and his wingman, Lenny Norwich, slid wide to the left. Allen nodded to Junior Eliot on his wing. The Phantoms dropped fuel tanks and lit afterburners. They were a shake too late.

The MiG-17 Frescos swept in high, dropped their tanks, and broke directly into Monge and Norwich. The enemy fighters turned tighter than the F-4s, got behind them, and opened fire. Monge called for a defensive split: he broke left and down, Norwich went right and up. The MiGs split after them. Monge scissored and his follower overshot him. By then, Norwich was taking hits from the other MiG.

Impacting rounds sparkled along his left wing. Allen saw flashes of light from the MiG's cannons.

Thick gray smoke trailed from the wing root of Norwich's Phantom. The fighter was coming apart. The MiG pounded away. Allen strained to get a bead on the attacker. Suddenly, Norwich's left wing fell off. The plane skidded sideways and lost altitude. The thought of being trapped inside an airplane in that condition created a hollow spot in Allen's stomach. The pilot's canopy popped free and Norwich ejected before the Phantom fell earthward like a boomerang out of control. The backseater rode it in.

Allen hastily fired a Sidewinder; he had no audio signal that indicated the missile sensor was locked onto the target and the heat seeker sailed off to nowhere. Then he was behind the MiG but the MiG pilot turned inside and ended up chasing Allen and his wingman, Eliot. The fucker was good, Allen admitted to himself.

Dobbs said, "He's right behind us."

"I know, I know." He called for a defensive split and the MiG came left with him while Eliot veered right.

"He's still behind us," Dobbs said.

"I know." He reversed his turns but the MiG stayed with him.

"That didn't shake him," Dobbs said.

Sweating like it was the fourth quarter, Allen wondered where Eliot was.

"He's lining us up," Dobbs warned.

Allen had no choice but to use his power and speed advantage. The Phantom had two big engines compared to the Fresco's one. He unloaded the F-4, which meant he reduced its G-load, and in afterburner accelerated to Mach 2 in a dive from twenty thousand to ten thousand feet.

The MiG-17 fell behind but continued to pursue. At ten thousand feet, Allen pulled back on the stick, sucked more G's than he wanted, and zoomed up to thirty-five thousand feet. At the top of his climb he saw the MiG, about six thousand feet below, run out of power and fall off on one wing. Instantly, Allen pulled the throttles out of burner, kicked rudder to fall off to his left, and turned into line behind the steeply banked, almost stationary enemy plane. At a distance of five thousand feet, he got a loud Sidewinder tone.

"You're in range," Dobbs said at the instant Allen fired.

"Skip it." He didn't need Dobbs' radar-guided Sparrows. A heat seeker would do the trick. The Sidewinder tracked perfectly and exploded in line with but short of the MiG's tail. There was a fireball that hid all but the wing tips of the MiG and Allen said, "Splash," but the fireball receded at once and the MiG looked no worse for wear. Allen had another strong tone and fired again. The missile streaked up the MiG's tailpipe and detonated inside the airframe.

The MiG broke in half.

Allen rejoined with Eliot and they found Monge. They couldn't agree on what happened to Norwich. "I saw him eject," Allen said, "but I didn't see him separate from the seat."

"No chute?" Monge asked.

"Affirm. No chute."

Eliot told them, "I thought I saw a chute open down low. Real low. But I'm not pos. Got only a glimpse. Could have been a cloud."

They orbited but heard no emergency beeper.

The MiG jocks had a tremendous advantage: when one of them abandoned a damaged plane, the minute his feet touched the ground, he was home. On the other hand, USAF aircrewmen landed right in the dragon's mouth.

"I don't think the guy-in-back got out," Eliot said.

"New kid, hunh, Trevorrow?"

". . . bitch!"

Low on fuel, they headed for a post-strike tanker.

Allen pictured Norwich's smoking F-4 skidding sideways through the sky. Jesus! Being shot up was bad enough. Bailing out, and evading enemy troops, then being captured, and confronting the uncertainties of imprisonment constituted quadruple jeopardy, at least. One of the events was enough for any given day.

Allen recalled the only time he had bailed out, ejected from an F-102 Delta Dagger, a sleek delta-wing Mach-buster . . .

He had been on a cross-country, flying a solo leg out of Hamilton Air Force Base, California, when around Elko, Nevada, the Duece started acting up. He aimed the bird toward Hill Air Force Base at Ogden, Utah, and went through his emergency procedures checklist from first page to last. Nothing he did corrected the fact that the airplane simply didn't want to fly right. Approaching Hill, he requested a flyby of the tower in hope that a controller would notice some external problem that he hadn't been able to isolate. When he came into view, a tower controller instantly spotted the malfunction: he screamed, "You're on fire!"

Allen later learned that the entire right side of his airplane had burned away: from the ground, the airframe ribbing was clearly visible. Apparently the fire had been burning internally. His instruments had given no warning.

The tower operator advised him to eject: "You're on fire from the wing root aft."

Allen looked over both shoulders but couldn't see flames although, if the controller was right, they were only ten feet behind him. Then he looked ahead and saw nothing but mountains. He didn't want to parachute into *there:* a guy could get killed in that terrain. Behind him was the endless, flat Great Salt Lake Desert. He banked the Duece into a one-hundred-eighty-degree turn. The plane had held together since Elko; it would probably last a few more minutes, he hoped. He tried not to think about it.

"You're on fire," the tower operator reminded him.

He told the controller his plans. Crossing the Great Salt Lake at seven hundred feet altitude, he prepared for ejection: took off his sunglasses and threw them on the floor, tightened his helmet's chinstrap and lowered its visor, swept checklist and inflight guide from above the control panel and pushed them to the floor. The moment he reached the opposite shoreline, he pulled back the throttles and raised the left armrest, which should have jettisoned the canopy. Nothing happened. He switched hands on the control stick, then jerked up the right armrest. Again, nothing. The canopy remained in place.

He broke out in a cold sweat. Was this a bad dream? Stretching upward, he hit the canopy with the heels of both hands. It didn't budge. He hit it again. Nothing moved. He was about to hit it a third time when from the corner of his eye he saw flames. He looked: the leading edge of the delta-shaped wing was on fire.

Fuck it, he thought and, for an instant, considered blowing himself through the canopy. The sight of the metal crosspieces directly overhead dissuaded him. What had gone wrong with his mind?

Calmly, he reached down in front of the left armrest, squeezed and unlocked, then lifted the emergency canopy jettison handle. In a wink, the canopy disappeared and he had a fleeting impression of lots of noisy air rushing around him.

Tucking feet and elbows in tightly, he simultaneously squeezed the triggers on both armrests. Either one alone would have done the job. He felt a kick in the ass like he had never felt before: a pain like an electrical shock shot up his spine and suddenly he had the most monstrous headache of his life. But he was out in the clean, cool, safe air. Moments later, his parachute deployed behind him.

He remembered survival instructors' briefings that claimed landing in a parachute was no worse than stepping out of a second story window. Then he crashed into the desert with a bone-shaking jolt. *That* desert wasn't sand! On impact, he bit his tongue, tasted blood. His hips went numb and his ankles and knees felt as if they had accordioned into his thighs. For several seconds he was afraid to look at his lower body. He lay stretched on the ground while he unfastened his oxygen mask and harness and wondered if his parachute had opened completely.

Eventually he sat up and took off his helmet. The visor was cracked. Cautiously looking down he saw that his legs appeared to be their normal length. He was able to move both of them. For no reason, he retrieved his overseas cap from a leg pocket and put it on. He noticed the right leg of his flying suit was ripped, looked inside, and saw his right knee opened to the bone. There was little blood. Pure white flesh that reminded him of a piece of cauliflower blossomed from the wound. The knee didn't hurt, either then or a short time later when a doctor closed it with fourteen stitches.

He leaned back on his hands and waited. The tower knew where he was. He expected a helicopter any minute. Half-buried in the ground near him were two blue objects, each the size of a fat nickel. They reminded him of the cork insets in the balls of flying boot soles. For comparison he looked at his right sole, then at his left; both his corks were missing. He pried the insets out of the ground and snapped them back into place on the soles of his boots. Second story window, like hell! Those survival instructors had neglected to tell him that the second story was eighty-five feet above the ground.

Headed for the post-strike tanker, Rocco Monge broke the silence: "Either of you see me blow up the MiG?"

"Negative," Eliot said. "Saw the one Colonel Cy got."

"That's nice," Dobbs said over interphone, which Eliot couldn't hear. "And what the fuck were you watching when that MiG was all over our ass?"

"Be cool," Allen told him, "you're still in the air."

"That makes three," Rocco Monge said. "Over the hump. Good show."

"'Good show'? What is this," Dobbs asked, "the RAF? Whatever became of 'Nice goin', mothafuck'?"

"Jerry, shut up," Allen said, then told Rocco, "Negative here also on yours."

"Maybe it's in the camera," Rocco said good-naturedly.

"That's tough," Allen told Dobbs. "Get one and can't confirm it."

"I don't know why the backseater's word isn't good enough," Dobbs said. "What about officer integrity?"

"Jer, this is for keeps, for history. Your name goes on the wall forever. Imagine a basketball game . . . the players call fouls on themselves . . . no refs—"

"I've played that way, plenty of times."

"You call every foul you committed?"

"I thought I did."

"Did your opponent?"

Dobbs didn't answer.

"See," Allen said. "Let's say the game's for the NBA championship. What—"

"I see where you're going. Score tied, one second to play, and all that. . . ."

"Certainly. The temptation to give yourself the benefit of the doubt is too great. Then there's always out-and-out cheating to consider. No . . . The system says only uninterested observers are credible."

To be awarded credit for a kill, a crewman had to submit a written claim within twenty-four hours of the event. A six-man evaluation board had ten days to process the claim at base level before forwarding it to the Seventh Air Force Enemy Aircraft Claims Evaluation Board where six other officers had twenty-four hours to deny the claim or to confirm it by publishing general orders giving credit for the kill.

Claims for the destruction of enemy aircraft were substantiated in one of four ways:

> Written testimony from one or more aerial or ground
>   observers,
> Gun camera film,
> Recovery of the wreckage of the airplane in question,
> Or some other indisputable proof of its destruction.

An enemy aircraft was considered destroyed if it:

> Crashed,
> Exploded,
> Disintegrated,
> Lost a vital flight component,
> Caught fire,

Confronted a situation from which recovery was
    impossible,
Or if its pilot bailed out.

Traditionally, credit was awarded to pilots (or to
gunners in multiplace aircraft) if they fired the weapon that destroyed the enemy plane, or if they caused
it to crash. The Vietnam War broke that tradition.
In the case of fighters with two-man crews, such
as the Phantom and the F-105 Iron Hand, both
flyers were credited with a confirmed destroyed aircraft.

Credit also was awarded for probable kills and for
damaged enemy aircraft. Pilots agreed that numbers
in those two categories weren't worth shit. Aircraft
destroyed in flight were the only things that counted.

It was Allen's turn on the tanker and he pulled into
position and hooked up with less effort than the
average bear used when driving his car into a neighborhood filling station.

Dobbs got a kick out of air-to-air refueling. By
slouching in his seat and snapping his head back and
forth, then holding it at a certain angle while staring
at the tanker's boom, he could confuse his eyes and
screw up his inner ear, thereby inducing one helluva
great case of vertigo: it made him feel as if the tanker
and fighter were in a vertical climb, speeding absolutely straight upward. The impression was strongest
and lasted longest on hazy days. Although he knew the
feeling was an illusion, to him it was as good as any
roller coaster ride.

That day he had built up a particularly good case of
vertigo, one that wouldn't go away. He heard the
boom operator say, "Sir, looks like your backseater's
passed out, or is in a trance."

Embarrassed at being caught at play, Dobbs sat up

and said, "I'm all right. No problem. I'm all right." He had to offer an excuse: "I was, ah, resting my head. Just resting my neck."

They had their fuel and Allen gave a thumbs-up signal to the boom operator who returned a Peace Sign.

"Fuck peace," Dobbs said over interplane frequency.

The boom operator rubbed one forefinger along the other in the direction of the fighter.

Dobbs said, "Shame on you too, gas passer."

The boomer grinned and Allen called for a disconnect. Eliot got his fuel and the Phantoms headed for Ubon.

After several minutes of silence, Dobbs said, "Everybody knows the pilot does ninety percent of the work. I don't know why the backseater gets credit for a kill. At most, he should get an assist, like in basketball: I help you score. Sometimes."

So that was what had Dobbs pissed, Allen thought. Dobbs obviously had been ready with the radar, ready for a Sparrow launch, and Allen had ignored him, completely bypassed him, and had gone with the Sidewinders.

"If the backseater got only an assist," Dobbs said, "that way, in cases like Rocco's, his word would be worth something. He wouldn't have anything to gain, or lose."

"Don't think that would work, Jer. He's still too close to the problem."

They ran through several checklist items in preparation for descent, then Dobbs said, "When you think about it, destroying the planes is the only thing that counts. It doesn't matter if anyone gets credit. Nobody up North is going to get credit for blowing away Norwich and Trevorrow . . ."

"Probably not," Allen agreed. "No survivor to make the claim."

". . . but it's still one less plane and one less crew for us." He sighed. "Fuckin' numbers."

"Nothing but, except at some point the numbers add up to glory. Don't you want to be an ace, Jer?"

Dobbs didn't reply.

"Think about it." Allen laughed. "Think about telling your kids, your grandkids, when they ask, 'What'd you do in the war?'"

Dobbs hummed noncommittally.

Two to go for the jackpot, Allen thought. He wanted those two more than he ever wanted anything.

10

When Allen and Dobbs landed, the F-4's crew chief and his assistants were waiting for them. Rocco had radioed ahead. The assistants helped the two flyers to unstrap. Meanwhile, on the left side of the fuselage slightly ahead of the engine intake, the chief taped a stencil and carefully spray-painted a hand-sized red star.

The moment Cy Allen's heels hit the ramp, the chief saluted, then grabbed his hand and shook it fiercely. "Thank you, sir."

Allen returned the chief's grin and tipped his head toward the star: "Shouldn't you wait until it's confirmed?"

"No, sir. When you get 'em, they stay got."

Other people crowded around, including the wing commander, Colonel Karl Schriber. There was a lot of back slapping. And good words. And champagne. Dobbs drifted to the fringe of the group, away from the limelight, until the photographers took charge. Then Allen hauled him back to the airplane and they posed: grinning all the while, they held up three fingers, pointed at the red star with the crew chiefs beside them, shook hands with Colonel Schriber, then stood alone with shoulders overlapping and Dobbs to the rear. "Good thing I'm taller," Dobbs said.

"Then that makes you ten feet two," Allen told him.

An instant before the photographers snapped that pose, Dobbs whispered, "You know, right on top you have a bald spot." The cameras clicked.

One photographer said, "Could we do that one over please, colonel. I know you're tired of smiling, but try to give us just one more." Dobbs laughed and, at last, was caught up by the moment.

Following a boisterous debriefing, they had a chance to pause while stowing their personal equipment. Grinning, Dobbs said, "Too much!" He shook his head. "Just too fucking much!"

Allen asked, "Can you take two more?"

"Maybe," Dobbs said. "But why stop at two?"

"Oh, ho!" A grin split Allen's face. "The killer instinct."

Dobbs reddened. He turned away, stripped off his G-suit, and hung it in his locker. After a moment he turned back and said, "I guess I still don't understand a lot of what's going on. That MiG today—ah—like that first MiG you got the other day—"

"We got."

"Bull. You got. That pilot ejected before the missile got there. Then, today, the pilot stuck with the airplane even after it was obvious he'd been had. I really expected him to go after he survived your first Sidewinder."

"Yeah. Shame he didn't. He was a good driver, a lot better than that other guy, the one who blew. Maybe that's why he stuck with the plane: figured he could get away, maybe even get another crack at us." Allen shrugged, "Who knows?" He smiled at Dobbs. "I'll tell you one thing, I was surprised when he tried to stay with us. That was asking for trouble. He should've been smarter than that."

"What I meant about that first guy was," Dobbs said, "he had to have started to eject *before* you fired. He wouldn't have had time to see the missile and then make up his mind. Would he, you think?"

"Some of the young Zips fly around with one hand on the ejection handle," Allen said. "They're spring-loaded. No self-confidence, not enough training. In Korea . . ." He looked down his nose at Dobbs. "May I discuss ancient history?"

Dobbs bit his lower lip, nodded.

"Late in the war, we had guys get kills without firing a shot. MiG pilots punched out as soon as an F-86 got on their tail. One jock from our squadron overshot a MiG and ended up alongside of it, flying formation; the MiG pilot saw the 86, did a double-take, and . . ." Allen flipped both thumbs upward. ". . . whoom!" He turned his palms outward and smiled: "Probably a rookie: being surrounded on one side was more than he could take."

"How was that again?" Dobbs asked. "'Whoom!'?"

"Fuck you, Jer. Look, I don't know what the master plan was late in the Korean War. . . . Hell, I don't even know what it was *early* in the war. Maybe the Chinese wanted their rookie pilots to get combat time. All of a sudden, the MiG pilots were the absolute worst. The Russians had gone home by then. They knew the war was winding down. God, the Russian airplanes were beautiful: pale blue bellies, copper tops . . . it was almost indecent to shoot at them." He smiled. "Want to hear a story about how bad the Chink drivers were?"

"In a minute," Dobbs said. He reached into the

back of his locker, pulled out a bottle of Ten High bourbon, and handed it to the older man.

"Where did this come from?"

"I bought it. Was saving it for when you got Number Five."

"My favorite. Neat." He punched Dobbs' arm. "You asshole." He took a long drink, caught his breath, and took another swallow before passing the bottle to Dobbs. "Ahhhhh . . . thanks. You didn't have to do that." He recaptured the bottle and had another drink before telling his story:

"Let's see, Korea. One morn, I spotted two MiGs above us—Fifteens—tooling along in formation, not paying attention, probably rookies, busy gabbing and feeling important, 'Hey, world, look at us, big jet jocks.' Of course, they said it in Chinese. We slipped in low and tight on them. It was so easy. Made me nervous. I kept clearing myself and gesturing for my wingman to do the same. Guy named Ralph Bova, really professional wingman. I kept expecting a forced-fed steel enema from one of the MiGs' buddies. Anyhow, I was on top of them when I opened fire, raked the fifties across them and got hits on both planes. They finished the job for me. Honest to Christ, they must have been China's answer to Laurel and Hardy. The guy on the left yawed to the right . . ." Allen was flying his hands. ". . . and the guy on the right broke hard left. Their wings locked. Like a good sport, I kept firing into them. They both sort of bucked up and their canopies smashed against each other. Locked together, they went into a flat spin, then rolled onto their sides and cartwheeled to the ground. They hit on top of a small hill, hardly burned. Real gimmes." The kills had been his ninth and tenth.

* * *

Long ago, after his victories in Korea, Allen had told the same story to his father, Nathan, when he returned home to Pittsburgh. Nathan had asked to hear the details of every victory. The father and son talked about war for days. It was then that Nathan showed Allen a yellowed copy of *The Pittsburgh Lighthouse* from 1918. A double-column story titled "Hero Born" with "Private Eli Mutie" as a byline ran down the left side of the front page. A poem led the story:

> The outlook, grim and deadly
>   For the Front Line Men that day.
> The Huns were coming over
>   And someone would have to pay.
>
> Young line troops, cowed and quaking,
>   Beneath fiery, mortal hell.
> Artillery and mortar shells
>   That fell, and killed, and fell. . . .
>
> The Huns roared into battle
>   Shooting, shouting as they came.
> The first to stand and meet them?
>   Nathan Allen was his name.
>
> Rifle, pistol, bayonet—
>   Hand-to-hand with deadly steel
> Nathan countered their onset,
>   Made the charging Germans reel.
>
> Picture thirty-seven Huns
>   Scattered o'er the slime and mud;
> Nathan standing over them
>   Splattered with their crimson blood.
>
> So when Chateau Thierry's
>   Just a spa for sipping wine,
> Once more France is wreathed in peace
>   (With Huns back across the Rhine),

Until the leaden clapper strikes,
Ringing out my final knell,
I'll remember Nathan Allen
And the day he gave back hell.

With Nathan seated across from him, Allen read aloud the story that followed:

"I saw a hero born yesterday. He saved my life and stopped a German advance.

"On the outskirts of Chateau Thierry, six of us Yanks from the Thirty-eighth Infantry Regiment waited in a makeshift post, a sandbagged shell hole, for the Germans to attack across the Marne. We expected the attack but, when it came, it came with a suddenness that was paralyzing. The German artillery laid down a short, intense barrage and the infantry followed directly behind it."

Nathan interrupted the reading: "That tactic developed by German General Hutier was new. Birth of the blitzkrieg! Until then, in World War I, days of bombardment preceded any push. I always found it difficult to imagine the scope of those earlier bombardments. At the Somme, before the United States entered the war, Allied artillery shelled for *seven days* before the British and French infantry attacked. The generals probably thought it prudent because their troops were attacking heavily defended and fortified positions: enemy infantry dug into trenches. Regardless, it always ended the same way. Fighting ultimately came down to man-against-man, hand-to-hand." Nathan gestured for Allen to continue reading.

"The barrage walked over us and the earth and air trembled from the concussions of bursting shells. I pressed my face to the dirt and prayed. Then one electric blue-white flash of flame and a crack, a crack like a hundred thunderbolts striking at once, with a blast of air as hot as the wave off an open hearth and as fierce as a tornado lifted me and hurled me through the air. I landed heavily and rolled along the ground. Breathless and bruised from chin to knee, I sat up. My nose was bleeding. I was stunned, paralyzed, shocked. My head rang maddeningly. I saw our lieutenant, Nathan Hale Allen, drag himself to his feet. Our corporal was sprawled against the side of the hole; he looked lifeless. Three other men who had been with us were gone—obliterated by the shell."

Nathan said, "In a funny way, it's still as clear to me as if it happened yesterday. I remember looking around, seeing the sprawled corporal—Schmedline, recognizing Eli Mutie seated in the mud with his bloody head flung back and staring vacantly. . . . I thought that both men were dead." He pressed his lips together and nodded.

"A moment later, a screaming German infantry-man charged over the lip of our hole, ran straight at the corporal, and bayoneted him in the stomach. That was the Hun's last act. Lieutenant Allen grabbed up a discarded rifle and bayoneted the enemy soldier through the throat."

"Poetic license," Nathan said. "It wasn't like that at all. That lone German infantryman was the fiercest bastard I'd ever seen: dirty, unshaven, red-eyed, screaming. . . . He drove his bayonet into Schmed-line's body again and again. Each time the blade punctured, it made a loud pop: 'Pop! Pop! Pop!' I leaned against the side of the hole and wondered how many times he was going to stick the corpse. I knew the German was going to do the same to me next but wasn't concerned about it. I expected to die. 'Pop! Pop! Pop!' The German cursed and bayoneted: 'Pop! Pop! Pop!' Suddenly I was outraged, felt uncontrollable anger: the German was mutilating, violating one of my men." Nathan lowered his gaze. "I bayoneted the German from a blind side. I doubt that the man ever saw me."

"The German went down but a tight wedge of his comrades poured into our post and Nathan turned on them. With a roar, he attacked. He dropped the first three Huns with gunfire and bayoneted two others. Three more Germans were on top of him by then; he clubbed and kicked two of them to the ground and brained the third."

"Oh, my God," Nathan murmured. He ran a finger along his lower lip. "That last man was so thin, sickly looking. I was enraged beyond reason. I tore his rifle from his grasp, swung it like a pick, and caved in the poor, frail bastard's skull with the stock butt. The man wore no helmet and blood spurted from his nose and ears. I remember he staggered with his knees together and toes pointed inward before he went down. It was nearly comical. I suppose that's why I still have that picture in mind. Actually by that point in the battle nothing mattered to me. I ran around stabbing, hitting, shooting . . ."

"Two more Germans followed and Nathan dispatched them with his pistol: in close-quarter struggles, he rammed the muzzle of his revolver against their bodies and blew them to hell. Then, from the bottom of the hole, he blindly lobbed hand grenade after hand grenade into the path of the attackers. He even snatched grenades from bodies of dead enemies. When he ran out of grenades, he grabbed up a pair of rifles and dashed to the rim of the hole. On his way, with an incredible shot from the hip, he drilled a Hun the instant the man's face appeared over the rim."

Nathan told his son, "I remember that at some point I smashed a man's face with a boulder. Eli must have missed that, or forgotten it. The fight was a wild nightmare. I had sensed only that as long as I killed Germans, they weren't going to kill me."

"Throughout the battle, Germans fired at Nathan from all angles and all ranges. In defiance of the Law of Averages he remained untouched by their bullets. I felt as if a host of Guardian Angels hovered around him to form an impervious shield. His luck was greater than humanly possible."

Nathan nodded to verify the story. "I emerged from that battle as a different person. I never openly admitted it but I believed that in some way I had been made bulletproof. I no longer gave a damn for the Germans or for their guns."

"Nathan crouched at the lip of our post and traded gunfire with the Germans. One wildly firing Hun rushed him from the right flank. In the classic bayonet movements of lunge-parry-thrust, Nathan slew the man: on the edge of the hole, outlined against the smokey sky, the combatants momentarily froze in a statue-like pose with the German impaled on Nathan's steel. Then the German dropped his rifle and Nathan ripped the bayonet upward and outward from the man's body.

"The lull came as suddenly as the barrage had arrived earlier. Nathan slid down to my aid. As fierce as he was in battle, he was equally gentle in administering to me. Because of his immediate care I was able to return to action within days."

Nathan smiled thinly. "Complete license there. When the battle ended, I still was outraged. And I was frightened. You see, I wasn't positive that it was over. Perhaps that was when fear caught up with me. I was confused. I craved more than the deaths. I wanted some greater revenge. It's difficult to describe. I walked about, examined the bodies. The faces were unrecognizable, all strangers. No face held the fierceness I had seen on that first German. A few men were only wounded, groaning. I felt no need to help anyone until I saw Eli seated in the mud and recognized that he was alive." The hand-to-hand fighting hadn't touched him, Nathan remembered. Outraged by that fact, he had grabbed Mutie's hair and screamed at him, something like, "Damn you. You sat there. You didn't help. You just sat there." Eli had said, "I'm sorry, lieutenant, I'm sorry. I couldn't move." His chin was covered with blood. Tears streamed down his muddy cheeks. He told Nathan, "I thought that if I moved and they saw me, they'd kill me." Nathan would never forget how Mutie had raised his hands—he raised his hands and *begged* forgiveness. Like a fool, Nathan had damned him again. Then he had sat beside him in the mud. He knew, until that German soldier's senseless bayoneting, he too had been resigned to die without defending himself. Nathan decided there was no need to relate to his son one moment of weakness on the part of a lifelong friend. Nathan shook his head in wonder of the past. Cy Allen resumed reading aloud:

"Shortly, our relief came forward led by a lieutenant colonel who counted thirty-seven Germans who were dead, dying, or wounded. The colonel saluted Lieutenant Nathan Allen. He said, "Lieutenant, I am going to see that you are awarded the Medal of Honor if I personally have to go all the way to Washington.""

There was a postscript to the story: the editor of *The Pittsburgh Lighthouse* promised Eli Mutie a reporting job when he returned from the war.

Cy Allen reverently asked, "How come you never showed me this before?"

"There was never a time that seemed appropriate. To me, it seemed as if it happened in another life; it had no place in this life, between us. I wasn't certain you'd understand, view it properly. A million reasons."

Pointing at the newspaper, Cy said, "You were my age when you did this."

"A few years younger. Twenty-two."

Cy Allen was physically larger, seemingly more powerful than Nathan, but at that moment he wondered if he was a match for the man. At the same time, he was filled with love and respect and admiration for his father, a warrior of heroic proportions.

"So much anger," Nathan said quietly. "That first German—he bayoneted my corporal over and over, ripped him to shreds." Nathan paused and studied his son. "I've seldom talked about these things. Maybe a little with Eli." He cleared his throat. "Until that German made me angry, I was prepared to die, expected to be killed. Were we all insane?"

Cy said, "It may sound strange but I never considered being killed—flying—in combat. It was mechanical. The worst I envisioned was having my plane destroyed, having to bail out."

Fear and death were strangely linked, Cy Allen had learned. Upon arriving in Korea he had believed that fear appeared only when death was imminent. By the time he departed, he knew the opposite: fear brought death. He had observed that men who worried most about dying were certain to be killed. In a like manner, men who believed they had everything to live for also died early in the game. The outcomes were fate's cynical way of easing the strain: they were practical jokes that the men played on themselves. Self-concern was fatal. Indifference was life.

In that regard, Cy's greatest trial hadn't come in combat. It had come on R&R in Tokyo when he took time to visit a fellow squadron member who had been wounded and evacuated from Korea . . .

A pair of drains running from the hospitalized man's abdomen were the first things that caught Cy Allen's eye, plastic tubes oozing greenish-brown sickness. A fecal odor touched Cy's nostrils, made him breathe through his mouth. His comrade's face was blanched to a whiteness that made Cy think "corpse."

The man perhaps read Cy's thoughts, said, "I'm lucky." He smiled weakly. "I have all the parts you can see." The smile transformed to rictus pain of memory: "When I first got here, I spent a week in Ward D, with the amputees. That place . . ." His eyes unfocused. "There're men down there . . . God, if you saw them." Tears filled his eyes. "I'd kill myself."

A tingle of apprehension shivered Cy's shoulders.

"It's—some of them—they couldn't kill themselves if they wanted." His friend cried out: "They're nothing."

Cy regretted making the trip. He passed on news of the squadron and excused himself at the first opportunity.

He left his friend's room and yet could not bring himself to leave the hospital, found himself wandering aimlessly down long corridors. Or did his wandering have subliminal direction? Had his friend's comments activated Cy's curiosity, triggered a natural attraction for the bizarre, the sort of morbid interest that drew a healthy person to a circus freak show? Whatever the case, Cy Allen wanted to see the unspoken horrors for himself.

Grotesque images, fragments of vanquished warriors crowded his imagination in endless, helpless, suffering ranks. And yet he suspected that the monstrosities of his imagination were far less hideous than the real beings in Ward D.

His wandering took him to the door of Ward D. Then his visions exploded in a burst of fear that stopped him from entering the door.

Unexpectedly, he identified with what he imagined: he saw himself chopped off at the waist, armless, faceless, blind, voiceless, unable to hear . . . A cold bony finger traced the contour of his spine. A spasm pulsed deep in his bowels, made him clench his sphincter. His jaws set. Blood pounded in his temples. He grew light-headed, warm, hot. Perspiring, he feared how he would react to horrors beyond imagination, the sight of living death. He feared being indelibly imprinted with the true view of the victims of war and being made forever conscious of his vulnerability. He feared psychological destruction: the loss of courage, the loss of a remote sense of indestructibility. Standing before the door, his left leg quivered. He shifted his weight but the muscular contractions intensified; his foot began marking time. His body was telling his mind to flee, to protect the vital self-image. He turned away from the door and limped rapidly out of the hospital.

On his final day in Tokyo, Cy Allen visited his squadron mate again, but only as a pretext for facing Ward D. By then he had decided that the amputees did not want strangers gawking at them. And certain things were better left unseen, his intellect told him. When he again faced the door of Ward D, he found the control to touch its handle, to pull it open far enough to enter. Then he walked away with composure. He hadn't told anyone about his actions. Now, he did not explain them to Nathan.

The episode was one that he chose to forget. . . .

Cy Allen tapped the yellowed newspaper: "Compared to this, what I did—shooting down planes—it's so very impersonal."

"I didn't recognize the face of any German I fought," said Nathan, "even that bastard with the bayonet. And I searched for him."

Cy tilted his head and leaned forward as if asking, "Why?"

Nathan glared at his son: "I searched for him because I wanted to make things even for what he did to my corporal. I intended to cut off his head and put it on a pole, or somewhere, some place where the Germans could see it." He relaxed. "I wasn't thinking clearly."

Nathan looked surprised when Allen laughed and said, "Last liar's the best liar," and told about his fifth kill in Korea. . . .

Two days prior to the kill, during a running battle, Allen saw an F-86 and a MiG-15 collide. They appeared to have enough time and space to miss each other; they were straight and level when they impacted head-on. Allen guessed that both pilots were checking six to confirm that they weren't being chased and took an instant too long. At their speeds, the closure rate was a third of a mile per second. Their fireball was still in the air when somebody said over the radio, "Ohhhhh, that's a tough way to get a kill." Allen wondered if either pilot had the image of the other plane transferred from eye to brain in time to recognize his fate, but not soon enough to act before being smashed to chum.

Two missions later, in the midst of a free-for-all, the same thing nearly happened to him. He was in a one-hundred-thirty-five-degree bank in the middle of a chandelle when he encountered another airplane headed in the opposite direction along the same arc. They were about a hundred yards apart when the MiG registered in his mind. It was one of the beautiful Russian jobs.

Despite the phenomenal speeds, Allen saw the other pilot: pale skin, western eyes. There was a jolt and the F-86's low, stubby right wing lopped off the MiG's canopy and slashed through its vertical stabilizer. The Russian plane went straight down and the Sabre jet limped home.

Years later Allen saw his first strobe light show and was reminded of his impressions from that collision. Three vivid images were trapped in his mind: one, the MiG pilot's eyes; two, the leading edge of the F-86's wing poised in front of the MiG's canopy; three, the debris with a green helmet in it. Never knowing for certain, he tended to believe that a head was inside the floating helmet.

After a long week, Allen got his next victory. He had difficulty accepting the fact that luck had made him an ace. The sixth victory resulted from skill. The moment that he slid behind the MiG-15, the enemy pilot bent it as tightly as he could. Allen had anticipated the move and was waiting. Smoothly the MiG crossed into his gunsight and he fired a long burst, six or seven seconds. The MiG shuddered under the hail of bullets. Rounds hit along the length of the plane: nose, canopy, wings, fuselage, tail. Smoke poured from the MiG. The crippled plane pulled into a steep climb, stalled, fell off to the left, and spun downward streaming smoke and flames. Motivated by curiosity and compassion, Allen followed the falling fighter. Around four thousand feet, the MiG pilot ejected and got a good chute. The lucky, lucky bastard, Allen thought and hoped his victim made it through the war.

In comparison, his first kill had been of an entirely different nature, bordering on butchery. Had he been a different man then? Could combat change a personality so swiftly? He had been up near the Yalu in a flight of four when they met eight MiGs. The Sabres tried to jump the MiGs at the same time the MiGs tried to jump the Sabres. Fantastic rat race! Cannon shells and .50-caliber slugs flew every which way.

A stream of 23-mm tracers with a few 37-mm rounds mixed in poured by Allen's canopy. The cannon fire was so close and so unexpected that he bounced an inch off his seat in a reflexive effort to leap out of the way. He glanced over his shoulder and saw a pair of MiGs on his tail. He went crazy. With a wildly pounding heart and a metallic taste in the back of his mouth, he executed every stunt he had been taught. All of a sudden he was clear, alone in the midst of chaos. Was his flying skill born of training or terror?

Then he saw a MiG turning, about four thousand feet below. He dived, firewalled the throttles, caught up, and slid behind the enemy plane, less than two hundred feet away. Fleetingly he wondered if the MiG pilot knew he was being tailed. Then primordial instincts flashed to the surface of Allen's mind, killer shark instincts that took control of his body and his desires. He had not suspected that such blood thirst cruised within his soul. There was no way he was going to turn that mother loose. He *wanted* to kill.

It took about two seconds to line up, then, looking straight into its tailpipe—blam!—he hammered steel into the MiG.

The enemy pilot stood his jet on a wing but Allen stuck to him. They were upside down, pulling G's, and Allen was still firing. Smoke poured from the MiG's tailpipe; the plane snap-rolled to the right before it slowed and its canopy came off. Allen wanted to get the enemy pilot before he ejected and he pumped everything he had at him. His six .50-caliber machine guns blazed a solid stream of fire, linking airplane to airplane. Fixated on his impacting rounds, he flew down the path of fire, nearly ramming the helpless MiG. At the last second, he broke the spell and jerked awake, pulled up, and saw his foe slumped in the cockpit. He banked back toward the target which was now trailing a thin line of smoke and cruising straight and level.

Carefully clearing himself first, he lined up and blew the MiG into a big orange and yellow fireball. His heart expanded as rapidly as the fireball, filling with a fearful awe as pieces of the MiG flew in all directions. His intention had been merely to knock the enemy plane from the sky, to send it to an earthly grave rather than let it aimlessly roam the sky like a Flying Dutchman. The malice that had driven Allen was tempered by a nameless fear. Did he subconsciously dread that someday he might be the victim of such violence?

His first kill. Only in the tumultuous and anonymous sea of war could such basic lust be legally gratified, he later decided.

"You consider those exchanges 'impersonal'?" Nathan had said skeptically.

"Yep," Allen said. He rubbed his hands together and looked at the ceiling. "No. Hell, I don't know. You give yourself a migraine trying to figure out this crap. Accept what happens. Let it go . . ."

Nathan bowed his head. "That's not always easy to do, to accept what happens." He brushed his nose with a finger.

"While you were away," Nathan said, "my friends were pulling for you to become an ace. People on the street would give me the thumbs-up sign. They'd wish *me* luck, tell me how hard they were rooting. Eli took it personally. He phoned every day with the latest news, hot off the wires. When the phone rang and I knew it was Eli, I feared bad news as much as I hoped for good news. I was proud of you. But I'll tell you the truth, all I wanted was for you to come back alive. I didn't give a damn how many planes you shot down . . ."

For minutes the men sat without speaking. Allen picked up the newspaper and reread the story about his father. He finished and asked, "How badly was Eli wounded?"

"Badly enough that he couldn't help. He did more than his share later," Nathan said in defense of his lifelong friend. "He won a Distinguished Service Cross in the Argonne."

Choked with admiration, Allen said hoarsely, "And you won the Medal of Honor."

Quickly Nathan said, "No. Definitely not. No." He took the newspaper and folded it. "As it turned out, I received the Distinguished Service Cross also." He sounded apologetic as he explained. "There was a time when I wondered why I hadn't received the Medal of Honor. I couldn't imagine anyone doing much more in a single encounter. I honestly believed that I failed to qualify for the medal because I lived through the experience."

"Ah, the mystique!"

"Correct," Nathan said. "After the war, the Army sent me a book that recounted the deeds of the Medal of Honor winners, and also listed the names of the DSC and DSM winners. I counted them and only one out of three Medals of Honor was posthumous. Most of the recipients were wounded, however, and the Medal of Honor winners did two of three things: first, at some time during the action, they took the offensive and charged insanely into the enemy's gunfire; second, they either rescued a buddy, or they killed Germans and took prisoners."

Allen nodded. "Above and beyond the call of duty."

Nathan also nodded. "After reading that book I realized that what I had thought was 'above and beyond' was instead a matter of me reacting to defend myself, fighting for *my* survival." Nathan's eyes fixed on his son. "We never took a prisoner. Not one in the whole war. When a German approached us with his hands up either Eli or I shot him—shot at him." Nathan smiled crookedly. "Insane. We drove Germans back to their positions, forced them to return to their guns or to retreat. One shot and they knew what was happening. Insane . . ."

"But glorious," Allen added.

"Perhaps. If a man makes it through untouched."

Between his second and third MiG kills over North Vietnam, Allen decided that his family was inexorably linked to America's wars of the Twentieth Century. His bachelor uncle, Patrick Henry Allen, a career soldier captured by the Japanese at the Fall of Corregidor in May 1942, survived the Bataan Death March and was a prisoner for nearly three years during World War II.

Twice a year the International Red Cross had telegrammed Nathan that his brother was alive on the island of Palawan. After the turn of the tide of war in the Pacific, the steady advance of American forces from island to island made Nathan's hopes soar. When the Americans landed on Luzon in the Philippine Islands in January 1945, Nathan celebrated; Palawan had been bypassed and isolated. A month later Americans landed there.

The Allens heard it at home, over a network-international radio hookup. American nurses with the Palawan invasion force called out the names of prisoners who had been rescued. The names were not announced in alphabetical order or according to rank. The Allens waited anxiously until, without warning, the list ended. Patrick Allen had not been called.

Months later two American soldiers wrote to Nathan. They had escaped from a thirty-two man work party minutes before the group, which included Major Allen, had been herded into an air raid shelter and burned alive. The island had been freed the following day. It took a year before Major Allen was identified through dental records and thus declared dead. His remains were buried in the Manila Military Cemetery.

World War I . . . World War II . . . Korea . . . Vietnam . . . Nathan . . . Patrick . . . Cy Allen: the family had paid its dues. Cy Allen had looked up "inexorably," wasn't positive it was the best word, but loved its ring. The Allen Family—Inexorably Linked to America's Wars of the Twentieth Century. Shithot! He had returned home once before as a hero; he was ready to do it again. He had a premonition: if he became the Vietnam War's first ace, he would be awarded the Medal of Honor. Nathan's rules no longer applied. All the rules were changed for this war. The more he thought about it, the more he believed that it had to be the Medal of Honor. It was the only award that fit. America needed a strong, live hero, a spokesman for what was an unpopular war. He felt destined to fill that role.

11

Gun-camera film substantiated Rocco Monge's second kill. The pictures were Hollywood quality. After debriefing and a stop by Personal Equipment, Rocco led Cy Allen, Junior Eliot, and the backseaters in a quiet attack on the Officers' Club bar. They were joined by Mike Hawk and his navigator who had flown an earlier mission. Hawk was his usual frantic self. Beer-soaked and grungy, he and several others had been making carrier landings until they heard about the loss of Norwich and Trevorrow.

"Carrier Landings" was a sport in which tables were pushed together until they reached twenty feet in length and then were washed down with beer, simulating the sea-swept deck of an aircraft carrier. Crewmen took turns making approaches and landings by using their bodies as aircraft. Approaches were initiated from a great distance. With arms extended sideways, a man ran at full speed toward the tables, then launched himself so that his body was parallel with the ground. The objective was to take off as far as possible from the carrier and land on the deck.

Impacts against the approach edge of the carrier

deck were common; damages ranged from broken noses and cracked ribs to crushed nuts and skinned shins. Failure to reach the deck eliminated a player from the game. A successful technique resulted in a belly-flop touchdown on the first table. Then, using only the toes as a tailhook, the aircraft arrested itself before sliding off the far end of the remaining tables. An overshoot also eliminated a player.

As the game and drinking progressed, the carrier was made shorter and shorter and slicker and slicker. The last man remaining in the game was declared winner, but he had to have style. Anyone who made less than a maximum-effort attempt anywhere along the way was eliminated by agreement among the other players.

The news of that day's loss had ended play.

Men who flew together tended to spend their off-duty hours together. Lieutenant Colonels Cy Allen and Rocco Monge usually could be found with their wingmen, Majors Junior Eliot and Mike Hawk. In a like manner, their backseaters stuck together. Although Greg Wiltrout was a pilot, he was only a lieutenant and, therefore, in limbo. He preferred to tag along with the pilots when he was invited, but he usually ended up with the other backseaters, Lieutenants Jerry Dobbs, Bob Slevin, and Pete Mansfield. Like college students, they sat and talked for hours. They also played handball, went to the movies, shopped for gifts for friends in the States, dined out, and got scrubbed and rubbed repeatedly. After a night on the town, Wiltrout invariably said, "Still not as good as a trip to the Chicken Ranch," and then recounted another "tale of tail," as Mansfield named the stories, at the famous LaGrange, Texas, whorehouse. Bob Slevin once asked, "As much as you were there, when did you find time for classes and football?"

Wiltrout's goal in life was simple, he wanted to lead at whatever he did. He found competition where it didn't exist. "Rocco's the best pilot in the squadron," he often said challengingly. It was his way of starting a conversation.

The others had heard his arguments too many times to take the bait. Mansfield agreed. "That's because he has such a great copilot."

Mansfield was nearly as large as Wiltrout; they would have been a fair match physically. Mentally, however, Mansfield was less involved. There were few things he took seriously.

"Rocco won't be pilot of your crew much longer," Mansfield said. With Mike Hawk, he often flew Rocco's wing.

"I can see it coming. You're going to take over any day, Greg." He looked at Dobbs and Slevin. "You guys ever notice? We're dogfighting and, the whole time, Greg's standing up in the back and looking over Rocco's shoulder. He never bothers with the radar, or RHAW gear, or anything in back. All he wants is to move into the front seat and pull that trigger."

"Bullshit," Wiltrout said. "Man, I do my job."

"Man, I've seen you," Mansfield said. "Remember who's on your wing. You practically crawl forward into Rocco's lap. He ever sneezes at the wrong time, zap! he's lost the stick."

Wiltrout smiled. "So what? I hate those navigator jobs. Man, I'm a pilot."

"No shit?" the other three said as one.

Wiltrout laughed. "You guys'll never understand the difference."

Bob Slevin said, "We do the same job you do, go the same places, see the same things."

"Right," said Dobbs. "Juke the same SAMs, eat the same flak."

With a smug look Wiltrout asked, "You ever get scared? I'd be scared if I didn't know how to fly, had to depend one hundred percent on somebody else. I wouldn't go for that. No way."

"I get a little scared when we're fragged to bomb," Dobbs said, "but I get really scared when I think that maybe someday I'll have to fly with *you* up front."

Wiltrout laughed. "Fuck you and the white horse you rode in on, masked man."

"Some of our bombing missions would scare the Pope," Slevin said, "especially around Hanoi. When we're headed up there to bomb . . ." He paused and looked carefully at the others.

He was the most conservative of the group. Married and the father of two children, he had worked for several years before attending college and entering the Air Force. "Everything about the plane sounds wrong to me. It's like I hear every turbine blade and can pick out the one that's going to fail. I can even feel things that are wrong with the plane. I could find a million reasons to abort. I keep thinking, maybe hoping, that we're going to abort at any minute. I'm willing to go, but . . ." He laughed self-consciously. He had an innocent appearance and resembled the young Montgomery Clift. "I'd be happier if we turned back. I keep thinking, you know, there's always tomorrow. Or the day after." He raised his eyebrows. "To be honest, I guess I feel that way every time we fly."

Throughout his speech, Dobbs and Mansfield nodded in a way that could have meant they understood him and sympathized, or they at last had proof that he wasn't as brave as they were. Whichever, Slevin didn't care. He knew that wanting to quit and quitting were two different things.

"Flying with Roc," Wiltrout said, "you never think about aborting. That mother'd go if the wings fell off."

Dobbs continued to nod. "Colonel Cy too."

"Hawk's the same. If Roc goes, he goes," Mansfield said. "He's still pissed we weren't scheduled low to Thai Nguyen with you guys."

"Be thankful. I hate that fucking place. When I think about it . . ." Dobbs clenched his teeth and couldn't finish.

Wiltrout laughed loudly. "I'd hate it too. Upside down at a hundred feet, not knowing how to fly . . . Man, if Allen had been wiped . . ." He shook his head.

"Look, Greg," Dobbs said, "just because you're the only one here who went through pilot training doesn't mean you're the only one here who can fly."

Wiltrout's eyes grew large. "Oh?"

Dobbs was sorry he had moved the conversation in that direction but he was committed. "I've refueled a couple of times. We all have." He looked to Mansfield and Slevin for confirmation. They deliberately ignored him. They saw he had put his foot in it and weren't going to soil themselves to rescue him. The bastards. "And we've flown letdowns and approaches . . ." He knew he sounded like a schoolboy saying see what I did. Nevertheless, he added, "I've even made a landing."

"Shithot," Wiltrout said. "And how many rolls you done, down on the deck?"

"Over the North?" Dobbs said. "As many as you."

Slevin moved the conversation backward to explain what he had confessed earlier. "When I mentioned that I think about aborting, ah, that doesn't cut any ice. I mean, like you guys, Junior's going—we're going. It's funny but after we hit the tanker everything seems to settle down. I stop hearing funny noises. The plane actually feels good to me starting about then. It's like I have a new lease on life."

"Pre-game jitters, man. Don't sweat it," Wiltrout said. "Even when I was a senior at A&M, I still got uptight before games. Once the ball was kicked off, everything settled down. It's the same coming off the tanker. You're committed. You're in the game. There're too many big things to worry about. No time to sweat the small stuff. Being tense is part of being involved."

"How come a cool guy like you knows so much about being tense?" Mansfield asked.

Wiltrout squinted and gave him what he called the Green Bay Packer, Jim Taylor look. "I remember from when I was a kid. Only time I get tense now is right before I drop a big one—in the crapper."

Siding with his fellow navigators even though they had deserted him a few moments before, Dobbs said, "I'll tell you one thing I don't like, that's being the spare airplane. We go through the motions, like everybody else, but I can't get completely involved mentally. Know what I mean? Like it's not really our turn in the barrel. It's like a bad joke. I keep thinking that if I have to go and there's a SAM out there with a particular name on it, I don't want to buy it by default. Rightfully it belongs to somebody else. Correct?"

"What do you know about being spare," said Mansfield. He called them as he saw them. "Allen, and Monge, you two never pull spare."

"We've caught our share," Dobbs said.

"Bull," Mansfield said. "Twice. No more than that."

Wiltrout gave Mansfield a hard look. "Hey, mouth, we're the first team. You ever see the Dodgers use Sandy Koufax in relief? Shape up your mind."

"You used the wrong example, man. You MiG-killers are more like running backs, not worth shit without a blocker, a wingman to keep your asses clean."

"Bite it," Wiltrout said. "If you're so busy covering us, what's Hawk doing shooting down a MiG?"

"Jealous?"

"Of Hawk?" Wiltrout sneered. "You gotta be shitting me." Then he smiled. "Pete, you better quit arguing, otherwise people might think you give a shit."

Mansfield relaxed, leaned back in his chair, and smiled broadly. "You got me."

"Right up the ass," Wiltrout said. "Which reminds me, I ever tell you guys about the time at the Chicken Ranch . . ."

So there they were, once again seated in the club, drinking. Allen had scored his third kill, Rocco his second, and Mike Hawk grabbed the floor and told the story of his kill—his first and only—that had taken place just a couple of weeks before but already was souring from retelling. Hawk was talking while gnawing a cuticle, really working it over. That was his habit whenever he was concentrating, or was expectant, tense. At pre-mission briefings, he chewed away like a three-star neurotic, twisting and turning a finger as if he were eating a chicken leg. The only time he stopped was when he ripped off a long strip of ragged cuticle and drew blood.

At one briefing, Rocco said, "Quit that," and slapped the finger out of his mouth. Hawk let fly an upward blow with the heel of his hand that landed high on Rocco's arm and nearly unseated him. The two old friends eyed each other and for moments it was touch and go. Lieutenant Bernard, the briefer, stopped talking and stood with his mouth open. Finally Rocco said, "Why you do that, eat your fingers?" Hawk shouted at him, "I can't stand listening to the same talk-talk-talk bullshit day after day. I want to get up in the morning and go out and do it." Lieutenant Bernard finished that briefing in record time.

Leaving the room, Rocco apologized and Hawk told him, "I'm sorry too, Roc. I get, you know, fidgety sitting through the same shit over and over." As squadron commander, Rocco had to ask, but said it in a friendly way, "Too fidgety to fly?" Hawk's face lit up. "Never, Roc, never." Rocco understood: once a body made it to the airplane the hardest part of the day was over.

Mike Hawk finished the story of his kill and everyone nodded. He ordered another round of drinks and, as soon as they were served, started the story again. Rocco grinned because he thought it was a put-on. Then he checked Hawk's eyes and, when he saw they had an oyster glaze, knew that Hawk actually was going to spell out every detail. In self-defense Rocco asked specific questions as if he had never heard the tale before, questions like, "What exactly did you eat for breakfast that day?" The others picked it up and bombarded Hawk with questions that had no bearing on the shootdown. He was too far gone to recognize what was being done to him and provided minute details in answering each question, until Eliot asked, "How long had it been since you'd last had sex?" Hawk sat up straight and said, "Now that's a strictly private matter." He stared at Eliot for several seconds before lowering his head and counting on his fingers.

After nearly a minute, he announced, "Sixteen and a half hours!"

Except for Mansfield who was disgusted, nobody cared that Hawk held center stage. Allen was rapt with visions of future glory; the navigators were engrossed in private conversations; and Rocco was too self-confident to need to go into detail over his score. Anyhow, Rocco hadn't had time to find the flaws, the subtle humor in his success.

Like most Air Force types who had proved themselves a thousand times, Rocco enjoyed relating stories in which he came out second-best despite giving his all. Air Force flyers labeled such experiences as "character building." Naturally, that was not always the case. When reminded of the character-building aspects of being shot down twice during his first twenty missions as a Forward Air Controller over Vietnam, Mike Hawk loudly declared, "I'm thirty-five years old and I'm so goddamn tired of building character that I could shit."

During his college years, Rocco Monge had quarterbacked the University of Pennsylvania football team and he loved to talk about that experience as much as he enjoyed talking about flying . . .

"I played for U-of-P," Rocco reminded listeners, "not Penn State, or the State Pen. The players we fielded were flyweights compared to the dreadnoughts that big schools like Penn State and Ohio State turned out."

His favorite story was from his senior year when Pennsylvania played Notre Dame.

"The Irish came to town—Franklin Field—and they were six-and-oh. We were like oh-and-six. We'd been slated as a breather, only we forgot and made the mistake of holding them to a seven-seven tie at halftime. In the locker room I was feeling cocky. The upset of my lifetime was in the making. I figured we'd win fourteen-seven. I visualized reading Red Smith's account of the game, his opening line: 'On a gray November afternoon, Rocco Monge led the University of Pennsylvania from the depths of ignominy . . .'"

Rocco paused and looked into the distance as if seeing a glory far greater than those around him could detect. Then came a frown that crushed his heavy, black eyebrows together. "The second half was like—the Saint Valentine's Day Massacre. I swallowed the pigskin so many times that I couldn't eat pork for six months. Drooling, toothless, green-shirted monsters were everywhere. I'm not small, but they dwarfed me. I'd take the snap, fade back . . . Fade, shit! I ran. A wall of green shirts was forever bearing down on me. I couldn't see over or around it. Six, seven, sometimes eight monsters rushing, fighting each other, pushing each other out of the way, stepping over my blockers, all the while focused on me and screaming, 'He's mine. I want him. Let *me* have a piece, my turn.' They fell on me, collapsed on me, pulverized me. I hadn't seen one of those ugly faces during the first half. About then, I realized that during the first half we had been playing the second and third strings, maybe the fourth. The monsters knocked me down, piled on me, then picked me up, guided me toward my huddle, and offered advice along the way, like, 'Try running dat halfback wit da clean shirt,' or 'Two more downs and you can punt,' or 'Before you try to pass again, you better make sure coach has a list of your next-a-kin.' And they laughed—'Ha! Ha! Ha!'—mirthlessly, and grinned toothlessly. The score was thirty-eight to seven at the end of the third quarter. Then the Death Squad disappeared. The second and third stringers came back and the final score was only about fifty to seven. I was surprised they let us keep the seven. A real character-building afternoon."

So there they were, once again seated in the club, and Hawk was answering stupid questions while trying to work his way back to the details of his one and only kill. All the while he was gulping whiskey. Rocco and Eliot drank beer and listened and laughed. At times, Hawk was a hundred-millimeter asshole, Rocco thought, but mostly he was good company and good in the air, dependable and loyal, which was what counted. In the air, Rocco considered himself tops. He believed Allen was the only pilot on base who was close to him in ability and smarts. But Allen was tough to know. Like most fighter jocks, he was a loner. By comparison, that fuckin' Hawk wore his heart on his sleeve. Asshole or not, Rocco liked him a lot. They had met during an earlier tour in Southeast Asia. . . .

One afternoon over South Vietnam, Rocco had watched his wingman crash-land a battle-damaged F-100 into the mountainous jungle northwest of Dak To. The fighter disappeared into the densely packed trees and there was no further communication with its pilot. Nevertheless, Rocco's intuition told him that a man down there had lived through a landing; he felt it was his responsibility to recover the man. He loitered above the crash site as long as fuel permitted, then was replaced by a Forward Air Controller in a Cessna 01 Bird Dog.

That night at the Tuy Hoa Officers' Club, Rocco brooded over the lost friend. After a half dozen drinks, he went to fighter operations, pulled out a stack of 1:250,000 charts, pinpointed the site where his wingman had disappeared, and studied the terrain. After a while, he returned to the club, had another half dozen drinks, then introduced himself to a Bird Dog driver named Mike Hawk who usually closed the bar. Hawk, who at the time was called "Lips" because he talked faster than he flew, lived life in accordance with his personal motto: "Anything for excitement." He went ape over Rocco's proposal that they unilaterally search for the downed wingman beginning at first light. By then, it was well beyond midnight.

Over more drinks Rocco and Hawk finalized their rescue plan—locate the downed F-100, then orbit until they raised help, hopefully an air rescue helicopter or friendly ground troops. Fundamentally they were playing by ear. Toward dawn, they agreed that taking an airplane without authorization was not a court-martial offense because they were pilots and the situation was an emergency. Before heading to the flightline, Hawk insisted that they shower and take two aspirins so that they would not be guilty of drunken flying. That was their last intelligent act of the morning.

Loaded with equipment, the two men walked out through the darkness, found a gassed Bird Dog with a clean Form 1, saddled up, and rode away. It was an hour before daybreak and nobody paid much attention to them. At sunrise they were orbiting what they thought was the crash site. The jungle canopy was an unbroken sea of green for as far as they could see. Rocco bailed out.

He had planned the move from the beginning. Wearing a parachute and survival vest filled with radios and flares, Rocco stretched forward, pulled the safety pins, and jettisoned the entrance door when the plane entered orbit. "Getting rid of this so we have a better view," he called from the rear seat at the instant he performed the act. Without pause, he pushed the front seat forward and said, "I'll call you on guard in five." Then he dived headfirst out the door.

Hawk's mind wouldn't accept what his eyes had seen. He didn't believe Rocco had jumped until he saw a parachute floating inside the orbit. Even then, he suspected it was a trick, some sort of practical joke. He flew closer and identified Rocco in the harness. "I never got so sober so fast," he later admitted. "I never expected that big turd to do something like that. Holy shit, how was I going to explain any of it? If that asshole got killed, I caught all the blame." The Bird Dog circled the descending parachutist until he disappeared into the trees. "He went out of sight," Hawk said, "and I waited and waited and waited and he didn't come up on the radio. It was a fucking nightmare. My entire career passed before my eyes, over and over and over. So many stupid, impossible things were involved in what we were doing that I tried not to concentrate on any of them. I just wanted to be drunk again, really drunk."

Rocco Monge had learned to parachute as a result of his own initiative. Early in his career, he finagled a quota to the Army's jump school at Fort Benning and then took thirty days of leave in order to attend the four-week course. At jump school, landing in trees was usually the result of a major fuckup by the aircraft navigator or by the jumpmaster. To jumpers, tree landings meant injuries. However, to Rocco, going into the jungle was no big deal: it was for his friend.

In recounting the episode, Rocco described his Laotian tree landing. "I did all those good things— legs tight together, arms raised and crossed in front of my face—I was ready. I went through the top canopy of jungle so cleanly that it surprised me. I decided to sneak a peek and looked down in time to take a faceful of tree. I swallowed enough leaves that I didn't order salad for the next six months. I guess that was when I went through the second layer of trees. My chute hung on that layer because I jerked to a halt hanging about thirty feet above the jungle floor. After a couple 'Oh, shit's,' I saw I could swing myself to the nearest tree. That was the good news. The bad news came when I wrapped a leg around the tree's trunk and learned it was covered with thorns, like ice picks. 'Well,' I told myself, 'if it was easy, everybody would be out here doing it.'"

Picking his way down the tree, Rocco developed a technique for kicking off thorns below him and then having a bare trunk to hug. He was about twenty feet from the ground when he kicked loose some rotted thorns and ants streamed from inside the tree. He didn't have time for one "Oh, shit." The ants were huge, the size of a thumb, and they swarmed over him. Unable to slap, he stepped up his rate of descent but the thorns stabbed and ripped him. The ants were eating him alive! For several seconds he climbed back up the tree but gained nothing because the ants were zeroed in on him and climbed faster than he did. Rocco said, "I felt trapped inside an adventure story in a pulp magazine. When something took a nip out of my scrote, that was enough for me. I bailed out of the tree." He made a twenty-foot free-fall that ended with a parachute landing roll and he didn't hurt himself. He had to undress completely before he was rid of the last ant. "A real search and destroy mission," he said. "I pinched the face off every little biter I caught."

By the time he finished, he was covered with welts the size of quarters. "I had welts on welts," he said.

While dressing, Rocco looked back up the tree and

ten feet above the ground he saw a thick, coiled python. Rocco's stomach turned over; he was thankful he had bypassed that trial. Then he noticed that the ants weren't bothering the snake. The python was resting there like he owned the tree. Rocco thought, Mother Nature sucks! He shot the snake in the head with a pen gun flare. The snake's head lit up like it was fluorescent, then it swelled and sizzled, and finally exploded. In retrospect, he was kind of sorry he did that. Then he called the orbiting Bird Dog.

Mike Hawk reported. "Out of nowhere, Rocco came up on guard channel and said, 'I'm starting to walk an expanding search pattern. I'll check in every thirty minutes. Hack!' He clicked off before I could say anything but 'Rog.' My career started passing before my eyes again."

Rocco Monge thrashed through the jungle for over two hours before he walked into a body seated at the base of a tree. He wasn't surprised by his good luck, but he was surprised when he didn't recognize the man.

The stranger, Ernie Bliss, stared at Rocco as if seeing a miracle. Bliss was an Air America pilot who had disappeared several days earlier. Search And Rescue personnel had no specifics as to where, when, or why his single-engine Turbo Porter had crashed. Both of Bliss' legs and one arm had been broken when he had been thrown from his airplane upon impact. He had landed near the base of a tree and settled there. Without food or a radio, he expected to die on that spot. Rocco hadn't heard about the missing airplane which was officially classified as civilian. Upon seeing Rocco, Bliss couldn't speak; he wept for joy. With his good hand he clamped onto Rocco's wrist.

Mike Hawk nearly fell out of the circling, doorless

Bird Dog when Rocco radioed that he had found a survivor but didn't know who the hell it was.

An hour later, a rescue helicopter out of Danang plucked the men from the jungle. Rocco had to pry loose Bliss' hand so that the injured man could be taken up in a basket. Rocco went up in a sling. He honestly didn't want to abandon the search. However, his body had reacted to the ant bites; the welts had turned to blisters and his face had swollen until he was having trouble breathing and seeing. The instant Rocco entered the chopper, Bliss again clamped a hold on his wrist. Bliss passed out when the paramedics shot him full of morphine but he hung on to Rocco until they reached the hospital at Danang. For weeks afterward Rocco wore a black and blue bruise that resembled a bracelet.

At Tuy Hoa the wing commander had conniptions and initially charged Rocco and Hawk with premeditated grand theft, plus a number of lesser charges like excessive chicanery and wanton mopery. By the time it ended, Rocco had a Silver Star; Mike Hawk received an Air Medal.

Monge never was satisfied with the outcome. At the end of the Vietnam War his wingman still was listed as Missing In Action. Throughout the years, every Christmas Rocco received a card from Ernie Bliss that included the message "Thank you again for saving my life." Rocco once wrote Bliss that the messages weren't necessary but the cards continued.

Accumulated booze finally caused Mike Hawk to run down. His audience sidetracked him with enough inane questions that he forgot his original intention. For a while the other men talked about losing Norwich and Trevorrow, and remembered Vestik. The conversation grew a little morbid. By then they had put away gallons of beer and whiskey. They had about decided to head downtown and make a real night of it when Mike Hawk said loudly, "I'd hate like shit to get shot down."

Hawk's backseater, Lieutenant Pete Mansfield, laughed. "Fuck yes! I'd hate like shit for you to get shot down too."

Mansfield was a big, blond, curly headed child who laughed at everything. Upon meeting him, Allen had judged the kid to be a fool. Dobbs told him, "No way, Colonel Cy. He finished first in the class ahead of mine at nav school. He's sharp. Take my word for it. It's just that he's in the Air Force for the fun of it. His parents are rich, really rich. They own distilleries, breweries, you name it. When he graduated from nav school, his folks showed up in a brand new Rolls convertible to see him get his wings—then gave him the car as a graduation gift. He doesn't have to be doing any of this."

Mike Hawk was running on. "I mean, I'd hate to be shot down and captured. Jesus, I'd hate to be captured."

"As much fun as you are," Mansfield said, "I'll bet the North Vietnamese would refuse to capture you."

Hawk ignored him. "Think how pissed off they must be up North. We bomb the shit out of them practically every day . . ." A couple of drinks were backlogged in front of him and he chugged one, farted loudly, then looked accusingly at Rocco.

Mansfield laughingly held his nose and said, "Hawk's voice is changing, but his breath's the same."

"You fucker, can't you be serious?" Hawk shouted.

"That's my cousin, So Serious Mansfield. People tell him, 'You're so serious, Mansfield.' I have another cousin, Crazy. People tell—"

"Knock it off," Hawk said. "I heard that shit a hundred times."

"Hey, Hawk," Rocco said gently, "lighten up."

"It's OK, Colonel Monge," Mansfield said. "The Hawk is in one of his moods."

"The Hawk is in one of his moods," Hawk mimicked. "Don't you be condescending to me, you fucking child. You ought to start thinking about what goes on up North—"

"Why? There's not a thing I can do about it," Mansfield said. "And I heard all this shit a hundred times too."

"Don't you ever wonder exactly what's happening? Maybe we accidentally kill somebody's family . . ."

"Tough shit," Mansfield said coldly.

". . . or really hurt somebody who doesn't even care about the war."

"I don't care about the war," Mansfield said, "so that makes it even."

"Jesus Christ, you asshole, think of the needless suffering we probably cause," Hawk said.

Mansfield banged the tabletop with the flat of his hand. "No. Fuck that. Oh, for—"

Rocco shook his head to silence Mansfield and said quietly, "Hey, Hawker . . ."

"I know, Roc, I know. Nobody wants to hear it. But sure as shit, I don't want to be a prisoner." From a time before Hawk started grade school, his Scottish-born grandmother preached two of her family's strongest beliefs to him: "A man never should be found on a battlefield with a knife in his back," and "A man never should be taken prisoner." Before he first imagined himself as a soldier, those beliefs were ingrained into Hawk's psyche as indelibly as his name. He hadn't questioned the old woman's legacy, her family's warrior creed. "May as well be dead," Hawk now said. "Better off dead."

"Horseshit," Dobbs said. "Where there's life, there's hope."

Hawk snorted. "Think so? Being captured is a life sentence. Those motherfuckers'll never let you go, alive. Think about some fucker who maybe had his family blown away and then he gets to be your guard." For a moment his eyes brightened and he focused on Cy. "Especially *your* guard. Brainwashing, torture, starvation, all that cheap oriental Commie shit. No thanks. Not this lifetime. I mean, put yourself in that fucker's place. How would you act?"

"Maybe you won't have a choice," Dobbs said. "What if you go down way up North?"

Hawk trembled as if he had been cursed. He glared at Dobbs, made a fist, and leaned forward. "What if *you* go down way up North, smartass?"

Dobbs backed off. "I meant, what if you have no choice, are just captured?"

"You always have a choice," said Hawk. "That's why we wear a fuckin' thirty-eight. You never have to be captured."

Allen disliked the conversation. It spooked him. Hawk's drunken mind was operating out of control, spewing subconscious thoughts that were best left unspoken. Over the years Allen had observed that when a man feared a certain fate, he usually suffered a similar doom. It was as if that man made an unwritten contract. By concentrating on his worst fear he willed it to come true. Such a man seemed to understand exactly what he was doing when he made that unwritten pact but he was incapable of controlling himself. He was trapped in a mental vortex:

It could happen:
>Don't think about it;
>Must think about it.

It could happen:
>Don't talk about it;
>Must talk about it.

It's going to happen:
>Think about it;
>Talk about it.

It's going to happen:
>Avoid it;
>Can't avoid it.

It's happening:
>Thought it would;
>Said it would.

It happened:
Always knew it would.

That was the way life appeared to Allen. Long ago he had decided that if a pilot could not think good thoughts, then he was better off not to think at all.

Rocco took Hawk home and tucked him in for the night. Then the others showered, put on civilian clothes, went downtown, and invaded the Ubol Hotel restaurant. In a fit of joy, Allen told the waiter, "Bring one order of everything." In Los Angeles, he had seen a friend pull a similar stunt. But that had been in a breakfast diner where a limited menu was posted on the wall. The Ubol Hotel menu ran six pages.

The waiter stammered something unintelligible. With a sweeping gesture, Allen told him, "Yes, yes. One order of everything." He held up a single finger, then flipped through the pages of the menu. "Bring all. We see all." He made another broad gesture with both arms. "Each man take what he want." The waiter grinned and nodded. "One time good deal for everybody," Allen said. "Bring check to me."

The waiters pushed six tables together and there still wasn't enough space for the food. The only dish that went untasted was something that looked like a gigantic bird's head. Mansfield studied it cautiously, then said, "Looks like somebody roasted a hawk."

After a while, recognizing that there was far more food than he expected, Allen invited the waiters to sit down and share with the flyers. By then it was late and the Americans were the restaurant's only customers. The waiters went through a heated discussion and then exchanged lots of laughs and shoves of encouragement before they carried extra chairs to the tables. Minutes later, the cooks and dishwashers joined the party.

Mansfield gave beaming Allen a long, long look and then told Dobbs, "Colonel Cy Democracy, champion of the common people."

Dobbs said, "These waiters'll probably remember this for the rest of their lives."

"Longer than they'll remember the war," Mansfield said.

Much later, climbing the hotel stairs with sweet, young Thai girls on each arm, Rocco told Cy, "To the victors belong the spoils."

Allen briefly pictured the face of Pensy-Betty, paused for a moment, then quickly brought up the rear. With an expression as innocent as Rocco's, he said, "Who cares how much it costs if it's for true love."

12

The very next morning when Pensy went out for breakfast, two bargirls who lived in Warin told her about Cy's extravagance at the Ubol Hotel restaurant and his trip upstairs with Rocco and the women. The bargirls acted sorrowful, pretended to be hesitant to speak, but Pensy knew that they were gloating. As soon as her back was turned, they would laugh openly at her bad fortune. The bargirls were squat and ugly Lao peasants, Pensy thought and acted nonchalant, as if the news did not affect her.

Inwardly she seethed. She generally did not associate with bargirls and massage girls, did not identify with the groups, but now the image she had of herself through their eyes was tarnished. Cy's actions had made a fool of her in the eyes of her inferiors.

She could not help but take an interest when they also told her that Cy had destroyed a third MiG. The feat alone meant nothing to Pensy. But to hear Cy described as "the Number One Air Force hero of the war" made her coldly proud. Wasn't he her man? More than ever she longed to own a piece of his life, to play a role beyond that of temporary wife.

As clever as she had been in manipulating men since Ronald Poindexter had abandoned her, she had not been clever enough to convince one of them to take her to the United States. Such an act involved marriage and, she knew, the marriage would have to take place before the American left Thailand. Banking on distant tomorrows was a worthless pursuit.

Pensy recognized that nothing from her culture had prepared her for filling the role of American wife. She could cook, but only Thai dishes. She could sew, but only simple Thai blouses and skirts. She could speak English better than most Thais, but still she felt inadequate when with a group of Americans.

If she went to the United States as a wife, she would go as an imposter. How long would it take for a husband to tire of her inabilities? And then what?

The idea of being divorced and stranded in America frightened her. She easily managed alone in Thailand, but she feared being alone in a nation of strangers. How would she provide for herself? She did not want to end up as a streetwalker.

In retaliation for Cy's betrayal, Pensy went shopping and filled the bungalow with lacquered furniture. By making the purchases, she regained a portion of self-esteem and reestablished her position in Cy's life as far as the eyes of the community were concerned. She justified the purchases by reasoning that they were her rightful rewards for her roles of surrogate wife and betrayed mistress.

Until then she had bought only basic pieces of furniture for bedroom and living room: couch, bed, chest of drawers. Now she bought end tables, coffee tables, another chest, and two oversized armoires. She selected the most expensive lacquer finishes in stock.

(The next day when Cy questioned the need for two armoires, she said, "One for you, one for me. Why not?")

Actually her purchases were investments for her future. When Cy departed she would sell back everything to the furniture broker. The deal already had been made. In the end, she would forfeit half the amount paid as rent for the furniture's use.

Cy thought he was in the wrong place when he next entered the bungalow. Before he could object to the new furniture, Pensy said, "If you no like, I send back." Then she cried. Her tears were real.

She had wanted to slap Cy's face, to scream at him, to make a righteous scene over his infidelity. At the last minute she had feared driving him away. Her anger dissolved in tears. Furthermore, she was nervous about the scope of her boldness in getting even. In the past she had been satisfied to milk Americans a little at a time. Now she had overdone it and she expected Cy to challenge her spending.

If he did, she was prepared to shout, "How much you spend on food for friends and *waiters?* How much you spend on Ubol room and Ubol girls?" If she found the courage . . .

Instead of challenging her, Cy gently took her in his arms, whispered, "We'll work out something."

"I try to make nice for you," she said. More tears followed. She couldn't believe that she was winning.

He kissed her wet eyes, said, "We don't have to pay it all at once, do we?"

"Half now," she said, "other half in maybe one, maybe two months," knew that she was gambling with her future. What if he left her during those months?

* * *

Later, while lounging around the squadron, Allen mentioned to Dobbs, "I think I'm about to corner the market on lacquered furniture in Ubon."

Bob Slevin overheard Allen and, eager to find bargains for his wife, said, "Is lacquer a good deal? Are you really into buying furniture?"

Allen felt foolish for raising the subject. He recognized how little he was getting out of his relationship with Pensy considering how much it was costing him. "Furniture's into buying me," he said. He visualized the crammed bungalow. It reminded him of—a temple?—a model home?—a furniture showroom, he decided. Was he again being led around by the dick? When would he learn?

Was Allen's third MiG (and consequential infidelity) or Pensy's buying spree the turning point in their relationship? Did one bring about the other, or did both serve merely as ready excuses? On the other hand, did such a relationship have a turning point, or did it simply run a straight line course from desire to satisfaction? From need to greed?

As pressure built in his quest for two more MiGs, he spent less and less time with Pensy. She responded by focusing more and more on herself, on her desires and needs. Subconsciously, Cy saw Pensy as he had seen Betty Vaughn in the years beyond the excitement of their college romance. Basically she was greedy. Consciously, Cy compared Pensy to his ex-wife, Clare. The longer their marriage had lasted, the more engrossed she had become with material possessions.

Was that the natural course of romance, he wondered, from affection to effects?

His relationship with Pensy approached its conclusion when traveling across Ubon became too unpredictable and too exhausting for him.

First, he had learned from experience, it was best to shower and change into civilian clothes before heading to town. Every time he had opted to forgo a shower on base, for unknown reasons the bungalow's water had been turned off or the water heater had gone out. Second, the trip itself was nerve-racking.

He felt he had more control when facing antiaircraft artillery fire than he did riding as a passenger inside a speeding, tiny Thai taxicab with his knees pressed against his chin. It was like being a Night Owl all over again. What demons possessed oriental taxi drivers? They plowed through the dense traffic of motorscooters, Mercedes trucks and buses, water buffaloes, and samlors on a one-track course that left the responsibility for getting out of the way to the other fellow. With the driver jamming the gas pedal flat to the firewall, the garish shop and restaurant fronts that lined the crowded road into town; the theaters, soccer field, park, and hotels of downtown; the central market; and the bridge over the Mae Nam Muo sped by in a fast-forward flash. What did the drivers think Americans expected? Had they somehow cultivated a belief that Western time was more precious than Eastern lives?

Once Allen jokingly offered a taxi driver ten baht for every dog he could run over. Moments later the taxi was up on the sidewalk and bearing down on a mutt poised with its leg raised against the corner of a building. He called off the joke by throwing a handful of coins and bills onto the front seat.

Along the bumpy route across town, construction proceeded unhampered by progress. Allen was convinced that Thai builders worked at a pace designed to have improvements ready for use in a future life, or two.

While the taxi bounced and yawed toward Warin,

Allen could have closed his eyes and told where he was by using his nose alone. Odors hit him in waves: the penetrating sting of the sidewalk vendors' charcoal cooking, the gray-smelling dust of the soccer field, the exotic reek of the central market, and the fetid bite of the river that was taste as much as smell. The odors were interwoven with the omnipresent fumes of oil, gas, and benzene, accompanied by the constant blare of horns.

Facing that sensory onslaught after a day of combat flying was like having a hangover and being set afloat on a storm-tossed garbage scow along with a drunken mariachi band. The ordeal made Allen question if the fleece at the end of the journey was worth the labor.

Returning to base was equally difficult. Taxis were scarce in Warin and he often ended up skittishly perched high in a samlor, the three-wheel pedicab of Thailand. Fundamentally, he disliked being propelled by the physical labor of another man, felt it degraded both of them. Normally he walked from the bungalow in search of a taxi but, within half a block, a samlor driver would pedal alongside, pace him, and question him with mournful sidelong glances and flicks of the head toward the empty rickshaw-like seat.

To Allen, all samlor drivers looked alike, resembled human machines. As a sort of uniform, they wore faded, practically colorless sleeveless shirts and short pants. Their thigh and calf muscles were sharply defined, had square corners, looked like bricks beneath the skin. Their bunched arm muscles resembled knotted hawsers, the size used for mooring ocean liners. And their universally battered faces held a resigned expression that anticipated rejection. Most of them shaved their heads. The drivers reminded him of aged club fighters who plodded straight ahead, willingly took dozens of stinging jabs for the pleasure of landing a single pulverizing uppercut.

Around his neck, each driver wore a thick 24-karat gold chain from which a gold talisman, usually a figure of Buddha, dangled. Some of the chains looked to weigh pounds. "Their life saving," Pensy said, "for life when they are old." "Aren't they afraid somebody will rob them?" Cy asked. Pensy laughed: "Everybody know, try rob samlor, you die quick." The men's lethal reputation made Allen feel a bond with them.

Therefore, when a samlor driver glided alongside, he couldn't long refuse the sad eyes, the almost invisible flick of the head. What choice did he have? To dismiss the man would have been heartless. To give him money and send him on his way would have been an insult to his pride.

To Cy, samlor drivers came to represent the true Asian spirit. They symbolized the toilers of the Orient, the uncomplaining laborers of North Vietnam who plodded year in and year out. Against stupendous odds, they knew only to get the job done. Their ceaseless efforts resulted in small gains spread across a lifetime. Yet time was immaterial. Effort ended only with death. Stoic human machines: Was that the enemy?

To watch a samlor driver hunch over his bicycle and rhythmically pump his way to the top of a long grade made Allen feel defeated. The drivers toiled as if today was of no consequence.

Allen told himself he was incapable of surviving, of earning a living as they did. What was their motivation?

13

The same as every other United States Air Force fighter pilot who was exposed to the concentrated defenses of North Vietnam, Cy Allen's combat tour consisted of one hundred missions. If things went right, he thought, that number would be enough. He'd needed only thirty-three missions to score three kills: eleven for one. Although the ratio leaned heavily in his favor, success wasn't certain. The figures were no guarantee that he would so much as see three, or two, or even one more MiG on the remaining missions. There were too many variables in this war.

He hated to think about it but he had no guarantee that he would fly the full one hundred. North Vietnamese defenses toughened every day. It wasn't his imagination either. Intelligence sources statistically confirmed that it was so. One hundred missions! It took eight to nine months to fill that square. Many men had done it. But the failure rate was constantly increasing.

Not long before, an eager lieutenant, an Air Force Academy graduate named Rich Carlson, defied all odds and logic in an effort to become the first flyer to complete two tours—*two* hundred missions over North Vietnam. Carlson was a bomber, a Thud pilot. He had unequaled luck. Airplanes were shot out of the sky around him while day after day he breezed through his second tour. One fine afternoon midway along in his second hundred, he outmaneuvered and blew up a MiG-17 with 20-mm cannon fire. Everyone in the Air Force was pulling for the kid's success. On mission one-ninety-eight, Carlson's plane was shot apart. He nursed the machine as far as Laos before he ejected. The Thud had had it. A rescue helicopter crew found and picked up Carlson. He had been shot apart as badly as his airplane. He died in the helicopter.

One hundred was one hundred, Allen thought. However, men fudged the number in both directions. Weather provided the opportunity. When clouds were out and targets socked in, some pilots were content merely to dip a wing over Mu Gia or Keo Neua Pass or any other spot along the border—thereby penetrating North Vietnam the shortest possible distance—and then salvo their bomb loads from altitude before calling it a day. Technically, that maneuver entitled them to log a "counter."

Allen didn't deny that occasionally a mission was easy, a so-called "milk run." He believed, however, that milk runs differed in quality. To him, an easy mission resulted from the enemy's desire not to shoot rather than from a pilot's desire not to be shot at.

Cy knew he could pick up extra chances for MiG-killing by not counting missions on the fringe, perhaps by stretching that a little farther. But what if he stretched it far out of shape and didn't count a bunch, then got five kills in a hurry and was left with a couple handfuls of missions still to go? Was his scoring system fair to Dobbs? Did Jerry care that much about becoming an ace? Damnit! Cy hated himself for pondering over such crap. A man didn't plan those things, he told himself. What happened happened. Accept it. Each situation differed. When the time came, he would do what was proper and honest. One hundred meant one hundred! But if he didn't get five MiGs . . .

A week later, he had Number Four—then lost it.

Eight MiG-21s attacked the strike force while it was making a right turn over Thud Ridge and, once again, preparing to line up on the Thai Nguyen iron and steel works. The MiGs flashed in from behind in two waves of four. They had remained unsighted until their leader opened fire . . .

"The entire setup is a horseshit deal," Dobbs often said. He wasn't alone in his estimation of the tactical situation. Most of the MiGs were based at Phuc Yen and Kep airfields, located southeast and east respectively of Thud Ridge, with a few at Gia Lam, practically in Hanoi. Being based at the scene of the action was a distinct advantage for the MiGs. Their fuel capacity permitted them only an hour of flying, which included five minutes of aerial combat.

The North Vietnamese Air Force held another, even larger advantage: the United States government decreed that American aircraft could not shoot MiGs on the ground. Enemy fighters had to be airborne before they were fair game. Furthermore, North Vietnamese air bases were restricted targets, meaning they were not vulnerable to attack.

Most of the targets around Hanoi and Haiphong also were restricted. Political and diplomatic considerations determined the sensitivity of North Vietnamese real estate and thereby established the restraints placed upon the use of air power. In 1964 the Joint Chiefs of Staff composed a list of the ninety-four structures and facilities vital to the North Vietnamese war effort. President Lyndon Johnson and Secretary of Defense Robert McNamara took immediate control of that list and, on a daily basis, dictated targets, forces, munitions, and strike times. Employing the strategy of Gradual Escalation they accelerated the tempo of the air war at a snail's pace. To "demonstrate determination" they ordered the same target to be struck day after day until it was pulverized; then they released another target from the list. In support of the strategy, Pete Mansfield sighed and said, "Too much is never enough. Remember, the more you run over a dead cat, the flatter it gets."

In March 1967, striking any MiG base was still a strict U.S. government no-no. There were occasions, however, when the Finger of Fate befouled the big picture, much to the delight of the aircrews. In one such instance, as part of a strike force Rocco Monge was leading a flight of four F-4s loaded with bombs and Sparrows. The group's intention was to fuck over the NVA barracks at Son Tay. Events did not transpire according to plan: MiGs jumped the strike force while it was inbound. Rocco ordered his flight to pickle their bomb loads and clean themselves for air-to-air. Had he preplanned it, he couldn't have executed better: the four Phantoms were over Hoa Lac and their twenty-four hastily dropped seven-hundred-fifty-pounders landed on the airfield. Four bombs cratered the runway, half a dozen tore up the parking apron, and the remainder destroyed and damaged nearby buildings.

Not until days later, while routinely reviewing reconnaissance photography, did Seventh Air Force Intelligence personnel spot the damage. Unwittingly, the same pictures had been forwarded to Washington.

Strike force commanders who had led attacks during the previous week were hit by letters filled with inquiries and accusations; one sly devil forwarded his pile of paperwork to Rocco who disavowed all knowledge of the event. Nobody was willing to accept blame, or to take credit for what were exceptional strike results. "A very fucked-up system," Rocco told Wiltrout.

At Seventh Headquarters, a four-star general actually jumped up and down on the photos of the battered airfield and shouted, "No, no, no. Damn the crews." Then he jumped up and down on his hat. After all, *he* was going to answer to the President and the Secretary of Defense for the error. The final irony of the accidental bombing was that Hoa Lac airfield was categorized as "under construction." It was not a primary installation and MiGs seldom had been seen there.

MiGs were under the direction of the NVAF Ground Control Intercept and the GCI operators understood the United States government's rules and restrictions as clearly as did the American pilots. There were days when GCI personnel deliberately kept the MiGs on the ground. The Thunderchiefs staggered through the SAMs and pounding flak while the Phantom MiGCAP orbited at altitude and its crew lusted over the untouchable targets parked clearly in sight along the ramps at Phuc Yen and Kep. The first time that Allen and Associate (Dobbs' current name for their crew) experienced it, Dobbs logged a dozen "Horseshits!" in less than five minutes.

The GCI operators calculatingly selected the time and place for encounters. When they scrambled the MiGs, the strike force was still approaching the initial point. Fresh and full of fuel, the MiGs were climbed out to the east, away from the Phantoms and Thuds.

Upon reaching altitude the MiGs were positioned high and beyond range of the strike force. Frequently the MiGs were only decoys. If chased, they ran for the protection of the twenty-five-mile-wide buffer zone on the North Vietnamese side of the China border. The United States government established that zone, which paralleled the border, and restricted American aircraft from operating there in order to prevent an accidental intrusion into China's airspace. In decoy situations, the Phantoms sometimes put a CAP over Phuc Yen and Kep and thereby denied landing privileges to the MiGs. While flights of Phantoms shuttled back and forth between the CAP point and tankers, the MiGs loitered in the buffer zone until they reached minimum fuel level. Then they would zing into Ning Ming, the closest airfield in China. The strictly Mickey Mouse game was worthy of infinite "Horseshits!"

The GCI operators unleashed the MiGs only when conditions favored them. While engaging in most of these ploys and counterploys, the MiG drivers were little more than puppets. Deep in his heart Allen believed that he was too good to be killed in a scrambling one-on-one encounter with some gook flyer. He had itchy moments, however, when he imagined an unthreatened GCI controller calmly vectoring one of his half-trained shit-for-brains pilots into a single-shot Mach-2 pass straight up his tailpipe. In a situation such as that, Allen would be spotting the enemy airspeed and altitude, which was the same as giving away Big and Little Cassino.

An all-out pass was the style with which the leader of the first wave of MiG-21s hit the strike force from behind. Traveling balls-out and spraying 23-mm cannon fire ahead of him, he had outdistanced the three other planes in his flight. Much later, Allen and Dobbs laughed about the pass: the Dink must have had adrenaline running out the ears. His pass was the closest thing to a kamikaze attack that Allen had ever witnessed. To make matters worse, the madman got results. His gunfire started one Thud smoking and made it dump its ordnance. Another Thud that didn't appear damaged dumped its load anyhow. Untouched, with its cannons blazing a steady stream of shells, the solo MiG barreled straight through the strike formation and zoomed out the front side. Most eyes were following the hit-and-run artist when the other three MiGs in his flight struck hard. One Thud took multiple hits and began losing altitude; two others salvoed their bombs. The lead Thud driver who was boss of the strike force shouted, "Get these fuckers off us." Then the radio was jammed with chatter.

Allen and the other Phantom drivers accelerated in pursuit of the three bandits whose leader was long gone. The Phantoms' move wasn't fast enough; the second wave of MiG-21s jumped their asses. Mike Hawk saw the bandits at the last second, an instant before they opened fire, and he shouted, "MiGs. Six. Break!" That lifesaving, although undisciplined and non-specific, call disrupted what remained of the strike force formation: everybody broke.

Cy Allen went hard left and down. Dobbs said, "Not us. We're clear."

"You sure?" Allen swiveled his head right and left. Spotting a MiG chasing a Phantom, he lit burners and rolled into a pass. The MiG fired an AA2 Atoll that left a trail of white smoke wide of the hard-turning F-4. "Jer, just make sure we're clear. I'll use AIM-nines."

"You're clear, you're clear."

Before Allen lined up, the MiG pilot saw him, broke off his attack, and flew for his life. The two airplanes went up and down and around and around. Allen turned off the logic in his mind and let his hand-eye reflexes steer; his chase followed as smoothly as if both fighters had been on rails. Locked in single combat the two aircraft drifted apart from the free-for-all.

The MiG driver tried every dance on the card and then made up a few new steps. Allen clung tightly to him and finally wore him down. As a last resort, the MiG jock made a straight-out dive for the inside of a cloud where radar and especially infrared would have more difficulty in tracking him. Allen fired one Sidewinder, asked himself, "What the fuck am I saving them for?" and fired two more.

The first missile passed over the MiG's tail, missed by about ten feet, and disappeared into the cloud beyond the target. Damning the missile, Allen wondered why it had come so close without hitting. The other two Sidewinders were on their way, looking good, halfway home, when over the radio a loud voice clearly shouted, "F-4, break hard right."

Instinctively Cy snapped the control stick to the right, racked the Phantom into a steep turn, then dived madly away from the target, found himself flying for his life. His mind raced, turbocharged. Had he fallen into the fighter pilot's oldest trap? While he was intent on destroying one foe, had another sneaked behind and lined up on him? He deserved to be in trouble. Twisting through space, his eyes grabbed patches of sky, expected to find a MiG on his tail, expected to find death chasing him.

Later, for the only time in his life, he regretted that his instincts had been that sharp.

He juked back hard to the left, and then right again.

He saw nothing but blue above and white below. From the rear seat Dobbs panted: "Don't think that was for us. We're clear. Nobody's after us."

"You positive?"

"Affirm, affirm," Dobbs said.

Certain now that the warning had not been directed at him, Allen's mind voiced words he never spoke: "Who called break?" It was a question forever unanswered.

He horsed the Phantom back to the heading on which he had launched the Sidewinders. Scanning the area where the MiG had been diving for cover, he was amazed to spot a man floating in a parachute, with a cloud for a backdrop. No MiG was in sight. From where had the chutist come?

Flying near, the two F-4 crewmen saw that the chutist was an Oriental. An old-looking guy too, wearing an out-of-date cloth helmet with goggles raised. He saluted the Phantom as it passed him.

"Horse, shit."

"Roger that."

Cy banked and returned the salute by waggling his wings. The MiG pilot grinned. Dobbs gave him the Peace Sign, then laughed at himself.

As it turned out, the person who indiscriminately called the break caused everyone to break and fly for their lives. As a result, nobody saw anything. Did Allen's Sidewinders hit or miss? What became of the MiG? When related to the absolute values of crediting aerial victories, the pilot in the parachute was not proof enough.

Allen and Associate claimed the MiG as destroyed but there was no way to substantiate it. Radio Hanoi announced no losses for the day.

14

Allen and Dobbs' inability to substantiate what would have been their fourth MiG kill of the Vietnam War was a small part of a disastrous morning for the 8th Tactical Fighter Wing. Events were in keeping with Pudder's Law: Anything that begins badly ends worse.

As usual, the crews on the early go rolled out of bed at two A.M. and dragged into the club for breakfast. They encountered the first omen: no coffee. The big, stainless steel machine had died in the night. The Thai waitresses, expressing terminal remorse and feeling personally responsible, fell over each other in serving tall glasses of pineapple juice to everyone. Cy Allen poured down one glass and found the ice cold juice a welcome change. Another hundred-hundred day loomed before them: one hundred degrees of heat and one hundred percent humidity. Bodies would use the fluid.

He was halfway through a second glass of juice when Dobbs said, "How can you drink that? If I did that on an empty stomach, I'd have the shits all day." The power of suggestion was too much: Allen felt his bowels churn.

Rocco ordered his standard: "Six scrambled very easy." He added: "Bring Hawk two over easy with a side of cuticle. Wait! Hold the cuticle. He's already working on an order."

Hawk ignored Rocco but, catching the attention of the club officer who was passing through the dining room, griped loudly about the dead coffee machine. In reply, the club officer picked up the breakfast tab for the table, five crews. "I'll make it back at the bar when you get home," he said with a smile.

"You bet. I figured it out," Hawk told him. "I already paid for your damn bar."

"You positive? It's solid teak."

"Cheaper than pine back home. And with the prices you charge . . ." The most expensive drink in the house was twenty-five cents.

"Hey, I bought you breakfast."

"Without coffee."

"Hawk—"

"I keep this club in business."

"You win. This afternoon, first round's on me," the club officer conceded and wished them luck.

At three o'clock the five Triple Nickel crews piled into a breadwagon van and chugged down to Intelligence for mission planning and briefing. The 433rd TFS crews were already there. The wing commander, Colonel Karl Schriber, was flying Lead for their flight of four and the crews felt the usual need to be extra professional and impress the boss.

Only four of the five crews from each squadron would fly; the extra crew was a spare that went if one of the primary aircraft malfunctioned and aborted. The spare crew went through all the motions right up to taxi. Murphy's Law dictated that when a spare crew failed to prepare adequately or didn't pay proper attention, it was certain to be called upon to fly.

During planning, much to Dobbs' amusement, Cy trotted off to the latrine three times. Normally he made a single pass, as he said, "to reduce the gross weight of the airplane, and what I reduced it by was really gross." That day's multiple offloads were another omen that went unrecognized.

In planning, the crews drew up navigational charts and flight plans, confirmed rendezvous times and coordinates (for F-105s and KC-135s), and agreed upon formations and speeds. Monge's flight was strictly MiGCAP. Since Allen's third kill, he always got that role and frequently wondered if somebody up there liked him. Colonel Schriber's four were hauling bombs and missiles. They spent extra time discussing sight pictures while studying month-old photographs that showed the target and surrounding AAA emplacements.

Then the ten crews got together and thought the unthinkable. "Anyone goes down," Colonel Schriber said, "everyone else watch for parachutes. Rocco, if it's my flight, we'll CAP low. You go high and call RESCAP. If you lose somebody, other way around." Rocco nodded somberly. The flyers had been through such briefings dozens of times but they listened intently because what was said pertained to each of them. Colonel Schriber finished: "When whoever's low gets short of gas, they'll go for the tanker and the others will come down low. We'll shuttle as long as there's a chance to get somebody out." Nineteen heads nodded agreement in a pledge of trust and faith.

At four A.M., the crews filed into the briefing room to get "the word" on enemy activity, friendly forces activity, weather, communications, Search And Rescue procedures, United States government restrictions on bombing and killing, and other information that seldom changed from month to month. Lieutenant Bernard obviously hadn't got "the word" that the wing commander would be present. The pressure of an impromptu command performance went straight to his feet: he opened the briefing by tripping on the cord connected to the overhead projector, then falling against and pushing the large machine to the floor. He did a job on it: the Fresnel lens shattered, the head assembly flew off and the glass in it cracked, the vertical support bent nearly ninety degrees, and the six-hundred-watt light bulb exploded. The destruction was enough to distract Mike Hawk from eating his fingers: "Jesus Christ, nice shot, Bernie," he said admiringly. Lieutenant Bernard melted.

It was the third omen but nobody recognized it as such. Allen did think, however, that in every man's life there were days that made no sense whatsoever. All effort was failure. When a man recognized he was in the middle of such a day, the sane thing to do was to return to bed and start again the following morning. Unfortunately neither Bernard nor he had that option.

A gentle rain was ending when the crews left Intelligence and headed toward Personal Equipment where flight gear was stowed. The rain was enough to max out the humidity. The crews had to be at the airplanes by five o'clock; then it would be getting light and things would begin to steam. Launch time was zero-six hundred hours.

Dobbs had a sign that he stuck on his locker door when he went to fly: it read, "Out to launch." Other than that, there was little humor displayed in PE. Most men concentrated on not forgetting something. Everyone ran and reran mental checklists. Emptied flight suit pockets of everything except Geneva Conventions identification card. Stuffed Escape and Evasion maps into lower left pocket, plastic flask filled with water into lower right, blood chit into thigh pocket. Then the important stuff. G-suit. Strap-on thigh note pad: filled with mission data, it was an extra brain if there was time to refer to it. Mesh survival vest containing two radios, flares, strobe light, signal mirror, sea marker dye, shark repellent, compass, mosquito netting, loaded revolver, honed hunting knife. Mae West. Overtop, nylon-web harness for connecting to the backpack parachute that waited in the airplane. Everything colored a bile shade, deep puke green. Topping it off, helmet with oxygen mask attached. A total of fifty pounds, at least. Dobbs said the equipment made him feel like a deep-sea diver.

The uniformity of the gear left little room for a personal statement. Men who needed to display their individuality did it by carrying their gun and knife on a low-slung, standard issue, brown webbed belt. Captain Luther "Lucky" Martin of the 433rd stood out from all others: on a hand-tooled belt in hand-tooled holsters, pouches, and scabbard, he hung two pearl-handled .45 automatics, spare clips, and a pearl-handled knife. Whenever he saw the rig, Hawk broke up and asked, "Hey, Luther, you gonna dismount and fight them on foot?" If he received an answer, it usually was a stiff middle finger.

The breadwagon van carried the crews to the flight-line. A crew chief waited in front of each Phantom. He already had inspected the airplane; most likely, he and his team had been up all night tinkering with it. Like other pilots, Allen reviewed the aircraft forms but was satisfied if the chief declared the machine fit to fly. At that point, a detailed inspection was impossible.

Nervous energy forced Allen to walk around the fighter-bomber, however. He respected pilots who were able to trace every stray volt through the airframe or who could recite the number of rivets on the vertical stabilizer, but that wasn't his style. He refused to sidetrack his mind with details that weren't his responsibility: he was a pilot, not a mechanic. He did what he had to do and expected others to do the same. For example, on his walkaround of the airplane, he sometimes paused to study the squibs and fuses and wires and toggles connected to the bombs and missiles without knowing exactly what he was looking for. Under the supervision of NCOs, young airmen had spent half the night hanging the weapons; he trusted those supervisors and airmen. Therefore, he walked around the plane, shook the external fuel tanks, leaned on the missiles, stroked the wings, and patted the nose radome. Finishing the tour, he gave the crew chief a big smile and a respectful nod. His body had gone through the motions; his mind already was in the sky, chasing a MiG.

Crews rotated airplanes and by coincidence Allen and Dobbs again had the bird in which they scored their first two kills. When they had walked by the left engine intake, the crew chief had paused and rubbed a hand across the two red stars stacked vertically on the fuselage. He was as anxious as Allen for another kill. Then it was time to climb the ladder. "All aboard," Dobbs muttered.

Now, hell was hot; maybe a half-fucked fox in a forest fire was hotter; but the inside of a cockpit during launch of a day fighter strike from any base in Southeast Asia was hottest of all. Even with the crew chief's help, Allen was soaking wet by the time he squeezed into the cockpit; attached the clips and rings and things which made separation from the seat automatic and reduced parachute deployment time to zero, thereby permitting him to eject at ground level, be knocked unconscious, and still survive; connected the hoses to his G-suit and oxygen mask; and finally strapped down shoulder harness and lap belt. Sweat dripped off his nose and chin, pooled in his ears. It was important to take time to get properly arranged. Once the canopy closed, a body had no space to adjust things. A twisted strap could become a major distraction after an hour or two of rubbing the wrong spot. Skinny Dobbs, settled in half the time, was already playing with his inertial system when Allen called for engine start.

Within minutes, the flightline's noise decibel level exceeded that of a Rolling Stones concert. The pounding of ground power units was joined by the rumble of twenty J-79 turbojet engines coming to life in rapid sequence and generating over three hundred thousand pounds of thrust. The noise was a wave, a wall of sound: it was the roar of a thousand hungry tigers set loose at sunrise.

Then the primary aircraft were ready to taxi. The spares sat and waited. Along the flightline, crew chiefs popped stiffly to attention and snapped perfect salutes to the men who were about to fly their warplanes. Allen returned his crew chief's salute. In the man's face he read a message: Get me another MiG! Dobbs raced through his checks: radar, missiles control, navigation system. "Got alignment. Everything looks good back here," he reported. The aircraft taxied from the loading area in takeoff sequence.

Near the runway the planes were guided into parking slots that faced them in the same direction with nothing in front of them. There, ground crewmen swiftly removed the flagged safing devices from missiles and bombs, held the red streamers aloft for pilots to see. Colonel Schriber's flight moved to the hammerhead; Rocco Monge's remained in the arming area.

The second hand ticked around to exactly oh-six-hundred and, with booming afterburners, the first two jets rolled down the runway. The next two immediately moved into position and, the instant Colonel Schriber and his wingman broke ground, they rolled. Rocco and Hawk skated forward to the hammerhead. Then the shit hit the fan.

The wingman in the element ahead of Rocco got off the ground but didn't climb. The wingman was a new troop, a captain named Bo Board. Not fifty feet in the air, he veered left of course, angled off across the countryside. Board obviously was in trouble, but there was no radio transmission. Rocco hesitated, then rolled. Cy Allen and Junior Eliot moved into takeoff position and had a front row seat for what happened next.

About half a mile from the runway, Board's airplane made a steep right turn, as if the pilot wanted to get back on course. The plane headed into the rising sun. In the turn, the aircraft began a shallow descent. It didn't have far to go. Over radio, a voice shouted, "Eject." A moment before the plane hit the ground, a seat and body popped from it and arced high into the sky. Dobbs gasped. "Backseater," Eliot said. There was a good parachute, briefly; the chutist touched down and the canopy collapsed an instant later. Not far away, the airplane had impacted in a fiery ball. Its ordnance exploded. Flames and smoke boiled upward. Rocco and Hawk were abreast of the crash which was clear of the runway heading.

"Let's roll," Allen said. The F-105s were depending on them.

"Roger that," said Eliot.

Scanning the instruments, Allen pushed the throttles forward to military power and pulled them back; then he again moved them forward to military power, slipped them left into the detent, then farther forward into afterburners: Boom! Boom! The Phantom leaped forward and accelerated down the runway until a hundred seventy-five registered on the airspeed indicator, then Allen lightly pulled back the stick. The jet fighter lifted off at one-eighty. Eliot was close behind.

They flew by the wreckage which was in the middle of a plowed field. Still wearing his harness with the collapsed parachute trailing from it, and with arms raised and both hands on his helmet, the backseater stood staring toward the fire. Smoke had risen to several thousand feet in altitude. It was black, dirty.

"Engine trouble?" Dobbs asked hoarsely.

"Or vertigo," Cy Allen said. They were climbing toward the morning sun. There definitely was a glare. He hadn't noticed it until they broke ground. But enough to kill . . . ? "Shit!" Fucking airplanes were unforgiving. Board had probably lost sight of his leader and was looking for him rather than checking instruments. If he remembered correctly, Board had been on only his fifth or sixth mission.

"Probably vertigo, hunh?" Eliot said over interplane.

They raced to catch up with Rocco.

The day brightened briefly. The rendezvous with the Thuds and then with the tankers were perfect. Allen had nearly decided that the day was salvageable when that crazy MiG-21 jock led his pack out of nowhere and ripped apart the strike force. By the time Allen finished his single combat and rejoined the others, the Thuds were outbound. Several of the bombers had been damaged; none had been lost. However, Mike Hawk and Pete Mansfield were down.

Their Phantom had been hit by an Atoll missile. They managed to stay with the airplane until clear of the Hanoi area. They ejected when the plane, entering its death throes, began a descending turn that Hawk couldn't control. Rocco had both of their parachutes pinpointed: they were on opposite sides of a long, steep spine topped with rocks.

Pete Mansfield had checked in from halfway up the western slope. He appeared to be in no danger, he said, and had no injuries he couldn't live with. On the eastern slope, Hawk was farther down the hill, near the treeline. He radioed that he heard voices in the trees and they weren't speaking English. He wanted Sandies ASAP.

Four Sandies—aka: Als, Skyraiders, and Spads— the oldest combat airplanes in the Air Force inventory —were inbound, leading an HH-3 Jolly Green Giant to the rescue. Colonel Schriber was high, talking to RESCAP, guiding the tiny armada toward the downed flyers.

By the time the Spads arrived, Hawk was in real trouble. He had moved a short distance up the hill after enemy soldiers appeared along the treeline and began encircling him. Enraged by the threat, Rocco made a couple of tree-skimming passes which frightened the NVA troops back into the trees until they realized the Phantom had no ordnance that could harm them; then they brazenly moved forward again. "I want a gun," Rocco shouted in frustration.

The Spads arrived in time to do his work for him. From wingtip to wingtip, each prop-driven airplane was pregnant with eight thousand pounds of hanging weapons; in addition, each had a pair of 20-mm cannons mounted in both wings. With Hawk directing them in Forward Air Controller fashion, the Spads blew the living shit out of the treeline. Again and again they swooped in and placed fragmentation and cluster bombs exactly where Hawk ordered. Over the North, the use of napalm was prohibited.

By the time the Spads neutralized Hawk's side of the spine, the Jolly Green had picked up Pete Mansfield from the opposite slope. Then the helicopter crossed the crest of the hill in search of Hawk. Withering groundfire poured out of the trees. The Jolly Green pilot slipped his craft back behind the protection of the crest and called for an encore by the Spads.

Rocco, who already had been to the tanker once, suggested: "While the Sandies work the treeline and keep their heads down, Hawk, you climb to the top of the hill. Pickup should be easy from there." The solution was made to order: in rapid succession, the Spads bombed whatever appeared threatening; hampered only by an occasional potshot, Hawk struggled up the steep, rocky slope. He was climbing a rock pile and, at times, took one step upward only to slide two steps backward. Junior Eliot laughingly said, "That's more of a workout than Hawk has had in the last five years."

The operation took a while, but it didn't matter: the Sandies had tons of ordnance and hours of fuel. The Phantoms cycled back to the tanker in pairs, making certain that four always remained over the rescue effort for MiGCAP.

Rocco was at the tanker when Hawk neared the summit. Maybe if Rocco had been there, he would have insisted that Hawk play it safe, go all the way to the other side. To those who were there, close looked good enough. Other factors influenced their thinking: first, the groundfire had diminished to random bursts at the Spads; second, the Spads had been working their asses off and were running low on ordnance, namely heavy stuff. With encouragement from Colonel Schriber, the Spads made a final maximum effort. Circling in close like frenzied sharks, they hammered the treeline with the ordnance remaining while the Jolly Green climbed out of the weeds and again crossed the top of the spine.

The chopper stayed low, lower than normal. Hawk stood facing up the steep hillside, stood on what was a rock pile. The helicopter's sling was lowered, trailing, ready for him. On tiptoes he stretched for it. Ten feet of space—a second in time—the blink of an eye before the sling came into Hawk's grasp. Instead, the powerful downwash of air from the rotor blades of the low-flying helicopter hit Hawk and pushed him backward. He flung his arms outward to break his fall, but there was nothing to stop him. Head over heels he tumbled down the steep slope and set off an avalanche of rocks. To the orbiting crewmen, the fall seemed to last forever. The world appeared to stop turning while Hawk, amid falling rocks, slid to the treeline.

The Sandies pulled off. As if on cue, NVA ground-fire raked the Jolly Green. The chopper took hits and a wisp of hydraulic fluid trailed from its fuselage. The wisp grew to a stream and the chopper fled toward Laos. A backup Jolly Green immediately headed inbound but by then it no longer mattered. The game was practically over.

Rocco returned from the tanker in time to see the conclusion. NVA soldiers materialized from every clump of foliage. Hawk stood tall to meet them. Practically ignoring the 20-mm strafing passes by the Sandies, the NVA troops rushed close to Hawk. They knew he now was theirs. Instead of surrendering, Hawk opened fire with his .38-caliber revolver. A pistol was no match for rifles. The troops shot him once and knocked him down; he regained his feet and resumed firing. Standing in the open, reloading, he got hit again. He clutched his side and staggered in a small circle. Apparently he took a third hit because he suddenly toppled over backward and landed hard, without breaking his fall. He managed to rise to his knees and gripping the revolver in both hands fired at the enemy soldiers. A fourth hit put Hawk down for good. He was last seen being dragged into the trees by uniformed North Vietnamese.

The F-4s orbited until the Spads cleared North Vietnam and then they headed for Ubon, via the tanker. The homeward flight was completed in silence.

The Jolly Green Giant helicopter crash-landed in Laos. In the official transcript of the incident, the pilot reported: "We lost hydraulics somewhere around the PDJ (Plain of Jars). I auto-rotated down, landing near a trail intersection. The aircraft tipped onto its right side immediately upon touchdown. I don't know why. Nobody was hurt. Everybody was strapped in. And the aircraft didn't burn. Even before that, I had a feeling we weren't going to fly it out of there. Because we were practically on the trail intersection, I deployed my crew so that each approach was covered. The crewman we had rescued earlier had trouble walking but he insisted on manning a position. I made certain each man was hidden and had a fair share of ammunition. Then I went back to the bird and carried off anything that might be of use in surviving. I was worried about a fire. In a way, to me, the situation was like working a Project X field problem. I kept trying to guess what kind of hazard would pop up next. After I cleaned out the bird and distributed the extra equipment to the others, I took up a defensive position too. All that activity took, oh,

I guess, five minutes. Then it got lonely as hell. I started worrying about troops coming down the trail and us not being able to tell whether they were friendly or hostile. I didn't want to have to wait for them to shoot first. I was sorry I hadn't paid more attention at Intell so that I knew what kind of uniforms guys on the ground wore. About then, I left cover and spread a marker panel near the wreck to help rescue aircraft spot us. What I did after that is going to sound crazy. You see, I felt I had to be doing something. We always carry a spare case of C-rations in the aircraft. So I passed out a carton of rations to each man and ordered everyone to eat lunch. Everybody ate lunch. During all that time, I had my copilot talking to Sandy Lead. He arrived overhead about the time we finished lunch and that made all of us very happy. At that time I checked my watch for the first time and thought it had stopped. I double-checked with my co. We had been on the ground a total of eleven minutes. Honest. It seemed like hours. All of a sudden I understood why guys on the ground are so damn anxious when we find them. I laughed at myself. I think maybe my co thought I was cracking up. A few minutes later the other Jolly came in, sat down on the trail intersection, and we climbed aboard. I've never been so glad to leave anyplace."

The Phantoms landed at Ubon. They had been airborne nearly six hours, twice as long as an average mission. Colonel Schriber touched down first and the five other survivors landed practically on top of him.

Just when everybody thought the last hand had been played for the day, God threw down a final trump card.

Schriber turned his F-4 off the runway and without warning braked to a stop in the middle of the taxiway.

The other two F-4s in his flight nearly tail-ended him. They were stopped, tucked in tight, with no space to maneuver. It was a mistake. They shouldn't have been following that closely. The taxiway was blocked. Rocco Monge's flight backed up behind them.

Eliot said, "Try putting it in reverse."

The jets were frying each other with the heat from their exhaust pipes and, sitting with raised canopies, the crewmen were being suffocated by the fumes. Rocco had enough nerve to say, "Lead, pull forward a few feet, please."

After long seconds, Schriber's backseater came on the radio: "Something's wrong with the colonel. He's not answering." Everyone shut down engines on the spot. The planes could be towed from there.

"What a terrible fucking ending to a terrible fucking morning," Dobbs said. "Now we'll probably have to walk in from here. This has to be the worst." He didn't know everything.

In the front seat of the lead Phantom, Colonel Schriber was dead: heart attack at age forty-six. As stunned as the others, his backseater reported that Schriber never spoke a word, never made a sound after touchdown.

It wasn't yet noon but the commander's death finished the day for the 8th Tactical Fighter Wing.

After supper, Rocco patched through to the Jolly Green pilot who flew that morning's rescue attempt. The pilot said he had been drinking, was in a lousy mood, was in no shape to talk. Then he told his story: "He (meaning Mike Hawk) was on those goddamn fucking loose rocks. There was all kinds of small arms, but with the Sandies working I thought for sure we'd get him out. We picked up the first guy so easy. I thought for sure we'd get the second guy without trouble. We came over the hill and the guy on the ground popped smoke before we called for it, like as soon as we came in sight. That was OK though. I thought for sure we'd get him. It looked really easy. Then we took hits before we got a chance to move down the hill. Fire was coming from right where he was. Otherwise, it was so easy. I thought for sure we'd get him out. The second time, when he was high up on the rocks and we were moving above him—we'd lowered the sling, were trailing the sling—he kind of leaped up to grab it while it was still pretty far away . . ." The pilot sobbed and Rocco told him that he wasn't to blame for Hawk's mistake. "But, god-damnit, he was so close," the helicopter pilot said. "I've picked up guys in lots worse places. He just lost his balance. Or the downwash pushed him over. I don't know. Maybe I should've been higher. No. He shouldn't have jumped. He should've waited until we brought the sling right to him. Oh, shit!" The man blew his nose. "Well, fuck, we really took hits then. I started down the slope anyway. I could see him sliding away from us. There wasn't any way we could stop him. There wasn't time . . . Somebody yelled we were leaking hydraulic. I remembered the other guy we picked up and wanted to get him out. Then we took more hits." He sobbed softly. "I'm sorry. I've been drinking. I shouldn't be talking. I feel like shit. That poor son-of-a-bitch on the ground . . . I'm sorry. I shouldn't call him that. I don't mean disrespect, you know . . . What was his name?" Rocco told him and he continued: "Mike Hawk. Yes. I see Mike stand up. After that fall, I'm surprised as hell. At the same time, all the shit in the world's hitting us . . . I don't know how the fuck we stayed in the air. I *had* to back off. I swear, the guy, Mike, he even waved me away. We crashed on the way out, around the PDJ."

Rocco said, "Thanks for explaining. We appreciate what you did."

"I feel like shit we didn't get him out." How could words express the futility of his day, his extraordinary sense of failure? It was as if he had killed a friend. Weren't they all brothers?

"Don't blame yourself. You did your best."

"Not good enough."

"We think so. You're ever at Ubon, look me up. I'll buy you a couple drinks, dinner. We owe you."

"Appreciate that," the helicopter pilot said. Tears were in his voice. "I'm really sorry about your friend."

Rocco gently cradled the receiver: "What a fucked way to lose a buddy."

Allen who had been listening on an extension nodded.

"Sandies would've had nape, they'd've burned down the whole jungle," Rocco said. "Infantry wouldn't've had a chance. Stupid rules."

"I wonder," Allen said. "Here we are, Americans in Thailand, humping for the South Vietnamese, making war on the North. . . . I don't know a single Vietnamese person. Not one." He took a pull from a bottle of Ten High bourbon, then slid the bottle to Rocco. "I'll probably fly my tour and go home without ever talking to a Viet."

"You can afford better. Why you drink this piss?" Rocco asked before he took a deep swallow from the bottle, then made a sour face.

"I like it."

"Good reason." Rocco took another slug.

During the Korean War, stationed in that country, Allen had met Korean military personnel and civilian workers on base. That setup made more sense to him. Of course, if he ended up as a Prisoner of War,

he'd meet enough Vietnamese to last him a lifetime. Damnit, he told himself, that was no way to
think.

"Hawk acted like he said he would," Rocco stated.
"Not many guys do that, act like they say they will,
especially in his situation. Plan it out, then do it. That
takes guts." He raised the bottle to eye level: "To
Hawk!" He drank, then slid the bottle to Allen who
caught it, said, "Hawk!" and also drank.

They were ready to call it a day, after only twenty
hours. They would finish the bottle on the walk back
to their trailers. Neither of them was on the next day's
flying schedule. Thank God for that; they could sleep
in. Rocco turned off the air conditioner and the lights
and they left his office. Outside, the temperature had
dropped to ninety degrees.

"Nice night," Rocco said.

They walked and shared the bottle.

Allen's deepest feeling, a feeling which nobody was
required to voice, was that Hawk definitely was dead.
He had been Rocco's true and honest friend and they
had failed to save him. "Rocco—I'm sorry."

"For what?"

"For Hawk."

"It's not your fault. He was my wingman."

"I know." Allen hoped that if his time came, he was
luckier or, at least, showed Hawk's courage. "I'm still
sorry."

"I know. Thanks." Then Rocco said what seemed
unimportant: "I guess I'm sorry too, for the one you
didn't get credit for." Would the destruction of an
enemy plane equate to the loss of a friend?

After all the things that had happened that day, Cy
nearly had forgotten the lost MiG. Did it matter?
Then his mind told him that if he shot down only one

more, today would stand out as the blackest of his career.

Not until years later did Dobbs learn that Pete Mansfield wrote the postscript to that disastrous day. Dobbs heard the story secondhand but, knowing Mansfield and his family situation, he believed every word.

Mansfield had his spine compressed when he ejected. It was a common injury. By the time he reached a hospital he was unable to walk. After repeated surgery and months of physical therapy, he again was mobile but was far from agile. The Air Force discharged him with a one hundred percent disability.

Two years later, Mansfield mailed a stack of twenty-four checks to the Veterans Administration and wrote: "Please accept these and stop future payments. I can now play polo all afternoon and make love most of the evening, both without physical assistance. Therefore, I believe it appropriate to forgo your financial support. Thank you for enduring whatever bureaucratic turmoil I am causing."

15

Cy Allen knew he had four MiGs. Dobbs knew he had four. And a North Vietnamese MiG driver knew he had four, or at least could testify that he had been a victim on a given day, regardless of the number. Nevertheless, he was credited with three and three it remained, not a fraction more. Dobbs jokingly called him "Colonel Three and Nine-Tenths" but only once. Allen's strained smile caused Dobbs to apologize in the next breath. Allen waved aside the words: "Jer, if you can't laugh about it, you just can't laugh about it. And I damn well can't laugh about it." Then he laughed a long and loud, honest laugh that eased the guilt Dobbs felt for being a wiseass.

Since the invention of the club (or was it money?) dreams of glory and conquest have lived within the soul of every man. Was the dimension of a dream determined by the ability of the dreamer? Or was opportunity the stimulus? Wouldn't this combat tour be Cy Allen's final call to glory?

Becoming the first ace of the Vietnam War meant everything to Allen. At his stage in life, approaching forty, the little he previously had accomplished dimmed to pale insignificance when he compared it to becoming the first ace. Sure, his basketball playing in high school and in college had been above average, even exciting at moments, but far from memorable years later. In Korea he'd made a flyby at Fame; however, he'd been neither first nor best. His feats were a footnote to the tales of Joe McConnell's sixteen kills and the fifteen victories scored by both Jim Jabara and Manny Fernandez. Those men were national heroes. He had ended up as merely one of the thirty-nine jet aces from that conflict. His recognition was local, limited to Pittsburgh newspapers and to in-house Air Force publications which the world at large seldom saw.

As far as other accomplishments were concerned, he didn't have a great deal to show for his life. He certainly wasn't wealthy, never expected to be. And the family he had organized was nothing to brag about now, seemed smashed beyond repair. Clare was raising his sons to be—well, not in his image. For example, while he was at war, the boys weren't permitted to write to him. What had become of so much love . . .?

Along the way, Allen had decided that once a man made up his mind to marry, nothing deterred him: for better or for worse, he found a mate. His courtship of Clare Coleman had been a whirlwind romance: to her he gave the love and tenderness that he had longed to bestow upon Betty Vaughn. They married three weeks after they met.

On their wedding night, after too much champagne and in the heat of passion, he called her "Betty." She let it pass. He covered his slip with, "Baby, baby,

baby. Oh, Clare, Clare, Clare." The next day he used her name in every sentence until she told him, "I know who I am. And I'm convinced you do too." His answer, "Yes, Clare. I see, Clare. Thank you, Clare," made her laugh.

Clare continued flying as an airline stewardess until she became pregnant. Until then, they frequently were apart. Their times together were a series of honeymoons. After two years, their first son was born. Two years later, Clare had the twins. After that, the marriage went downhill, took nearly a decade to run its course.

One big argument was that Clare spoiled their sons. Cy had grown up motherless. He knew that the love-me, pamper-me, understand-me, wait-on-me-hand-and-foot bullshit was unnecessary. He had been raised by Emma Durr, an old Kraut housekeeper, whose philosophy of child rearing had been simple: If the bone isn't sticking through the skin, you aren't hurt. He saw his sons as lazy, undisciplined crybabies. Clare was bringing up a litter of pussies.

Cy often hoped that things would improve as the boys grew older. He looked forward to sharing with his sons what he considered to be the "secrets of life." As it developed, the boys seemed to grow without him. The fact that he did not share his secrets made little difference to them: his ideas did not fit their world. When he gave them tomorrow, they saw it as today.

Clare, three sons, a house, and other problems of marriage distracted Cy from flying until, one day, he washed his hands of his duties as husband, father, and homeowner. He announced to Clare, "I quit. From now on, you take care of the kids and the house and the bills. I'm a fighter pilot."

He reverted to bachelor habits: flew at every opportunity, ate meals at the O-club, wasted weekends and evenings at the gym or at the bar with the other fighter jocks, had laundry done by the base facility: he again was self-sufficient.

He spent entire weeks in the BOQ rather than face the chaos at home. His house discouraged him: the place reminded him of Dien Bien Phu, just before it was overrun. He remembered watching Emma Durr keep house for his father: she boiled laundry in a copper caldron, stirred it with a cut-off broom handle, wrung it by hand, and hung it outside or, on rainy days, in the basement to dry. She ironed underwear. Clare owned every labor-saving device on the market and the kids still lacked clean T-shirts. Emma Durr had waxed floors on her hands and knees. Clare owned a four hundred dollar buffer, with enough attachments to win World War III, and the floors still looked like the Chicago Bears had scrimmaged on them, or maybe real bears.

He once said to Clare, "Women crossed the continent in covered wagons, without stoves, or dishwashers, or dryers—with nothing. Isn't that amazing?"

"And they died at forty," she said.

He said, "Don't try to build up my hopes."

To his fellow flyers he ridiculed her: "Clare's idea of a workout is to leave her air-conditioned house in her air-conditioned car and drive to her air-conditioned club—to take a steambath."

One evening at the O-club bar, he was bad-mouthing Clare when another major told him, "I wouldn't mind parking my shoes under her bed."

Allen said, "And I thought you had taste."

The major smiled: "You asshole, she's a good-looking woman."

"If you feel that way," Allen said coldly, "tell her, not me. She's home right now. Give her a call."

"And watch you shit a brick."

"I don't think so." The statement was a sigh of resignation.

The major said, "I was only joking."

"Skip it," Allen told him. Because he was unhappy, he thought, was no excuse for making some other poor bastard unhappy.

Cy Allen's decision to volunteer for duty in Southeast Asia was the coup de grace to their marriage: Clare called it desertion. She said, "You don't love me, you never loved me, and you probably never will love me."

He bobbed his head emphatically: "Not bad. You got two out of three."

He won the verbal games of a long home season, but she won the post-season championship in court. For a woman who didn't take care of things, she took care of everything he possessed.

The crux of their problem (as he saw it) was that the birth of the twins took away her figure and her appetite for sex. He remembered when he couldn't keep his hands off her and she loved his touch. When either of them returned from a cross-country, they were doing it before they got out of their uniforms. He used to drop dynamite loads—gully washers—loads that would have driven a cow to its knees. Of course, that was when her box was new and tight. Often they did it two or three, sometimes four times in a row without him taking it out between times. She had no belly then and it took no effort for her to push her hips up into his. It was as if it had happened a thousand years ago.

The crux of the problem (as she saw it) was Cy's

one-dimensional character. But wasn't flying the thing he knew best? Did anyone criticize DiMaggio for being only a ballplayer? Who dared to call Marciano a failure for being only a prizefighter?

Since his divorce Allen had reflected that the average man gained notoriety, became a pillar of the community, simply by remaining in one location, providing for his family, and rearing disciplined children. The solidarity of each household was the foundation for a neighborhood. Good neighbors built proud cities and, in turn, powerful states and a stable nation.

He questioned if the average Air Force career fit that scheme. Maybe the base commander hobnobbed with the mayor and the Chamber of Commerce took an airman to dinner every year or so, but in Allen's eyes the military and civilian communities were fundamentally sovereign.

During the years he lived off-base with his family, he had considered himself a visitor to the community. The natives were friendly but, knowing he would be gone in two or three years, maintained a constant distance, as if at any moment he might disappear. Allen helped maintain that distance: he preferred the company of other flyers, seldom gave himself completely to civilian projects or friendships. Hours at PTA or Scouts or Little League were like time in the stocks: he endured them until they ended. Church had no part in his life: God wasn't his copilot. And big business didn't interest him.

Allen was bored by the money-making concerns of civilians almost as much as they were irritated by military spending. Late at night, supported by drinks, civilians gave their "honest opinions" often enough:

"Flying around in those little jets" wasn't work; it was "sort of playing" and "cost the taxpayers, like us" a "big pile of dollars." Allen had endured numerous tirades on "military waste." Thereafter, he avoided the men who delivered them.

From Allen's experience, the loudest complainers were men who never had been face-to-face with an enemy bent on destroying them. They lacked any notion of the drama of combat. They tried to stretch their imaginations by wrestling with The Fucking Bomb, which was something no one could handle intelligently. That monster was beyond reason, beyond comprehension: Whoosh-Bang Everything Gone. Death in another realm. But that abstraction was what they most feared.

Allen believed the average civilian's life had been too easy for too long. Moreover, men who had been in service during World War II and Korea had lost sight of the military's role. They remembered only how they worked "good deals" and consequently "did nothing."

Allen was puzzled by the scorn the citizenry displayed toward the military establishment. Politicians in particular delighted in second-guessing military decision makers, right or wrong. And if a member of the Joint Chiefs of Staff so much as snorted in reply, he was doomed. Why did one group of public servants find it necessary to lord it so viciously over a similar group? In the early Sixties Allen wouldn't have been surprised to have picked up a newspaper and read that the Kennedys had marched the bemedaled Joint Chiefs before a firing squad. Couldn't citizens understand that the Joint Chiefs were fallible advisors exactly like the other fallible experts who served the President?

The civilians who stood aside and listened (then later apologized for their outspoken neighbors) were often men who had seen hard combat.

Chester "Chet" Russell was Cy's favorite civilian. It wasn't a fair choice. At heart, Chet would always be a part of the Corps. As a Marine lieutenant platoon leader, he won two Silver Stars and three Purple Hearts before being med-evaced from Korea. Summarizing his eight months in combat, Chet said, "I gave the Corps my youth and the Corps gave me my manhood." In speaking of his East Montgomery neighbors, Chet declared, "They are assholes. They know nothing of the world. Ignore them. Forgive them."

Chet was a muscular giant, six-six and two seventy-five. The first two times he and Cy got drunk together, he tried to provoke a confrontation; Cy ignored him. The third time, Cy said, "I know it's possible to be friends without seeing who's the better man. But you can't have it that way. You're asking me to shoot you right between the eyes. You are too big to fuck with in any other way." Chet puffed up his chest and scowled. Cy crossed the kitchen and from a cabinet drew an enormous wooden-headed stonecutter's mallet.

Russell saw the weapon and said, "A hundred and fifty-five millimeter hammer." He closed his eyes, chuckled until he was red-faced. Wiping his eyes and nose with the back of a hand, he said, "That might do the job." He finished the bourbon in his glass and admitted, "I get belligerent when I drink. People see me that way and back down, then sulk. If they give away their self-respect, why the hell should I respect them? They'd give away their lives to somebody hollers, 'Boo.' Act like a bunch of Frenchmen: eat shit to save their ass."

While Allen was a student at Air Command and Staff College, Russell was his best drinking buddy. Often they stayed up all night while exchanging details of their combat experiences, arguing about war in general, and talking about other military matters. Russell's accounts of hand-to-hand fighting reminded Allen of his father's exploits, only the locale and the opponents differed.

In the depths of his mind Cy questioned his ability to fight on foot. Despite what Nathan said, air battles were impersonal, eons removed from hand-to-hand struggles. Allen sized up Chester Russell as a foe. He fantasized himself into a situation where, dressed in a tunic of chain mail, he waited outside an enemy fortress. After a long siege, his army's bombardment knocked down a part of the fortress wall. Armed with broadsword and shield he led the charge through the breach. The first enemy warrior he encountered was scowling Chester Russell, effortlessly swinging a mace with a spiked head the size of a bowling ball. He grew fatigued by simply imagining the tremendous effort required merely to stay alive against the giant.

Clare, who then was yet to become the ex, thought that Russell was an "overgrown, obnoxious, cantankerous bully." She called him those exact words in the middle of one night when his drunken rowdiness wakened her and the three children. Russell told her, "That's what I like about you, Mistress Allen. Neath that gorgeous exterior beats the stone heart of a true killer." Naturally Clare's animosity made Russell that much more qualified as a drinking partner.

Allen tolerated most other civilians as, he believed, they tolerated him. Inwardly he laughed at their attempts to discuss air power and at their superficial dissertations on the subject. Mentally he questioned their motives for trying to impress him with their limited knowledge. He had read most of what had been written about air power and he first had debated its pros and cons in his own mind and later had hashed them out with peers for three months at Squadron Officer School and for nearly a year at Air Command and Staff College. In the end he understood that his thoughts were worthless: he would never be in a position to establish national policy. Furthermore, he doubted that he would ever have an input to establishing Air Force policy. Thinking at those levels was not his ultimate goal.

He was a journeyman flyer, nothing more. He sought only the finest war machine the Air Force could afford. He recognized that he was fortunate to be one of the chosen few upon whom his government expended vast sums of money so that he could duel in the sky with equally select men from other governments.

He appreciated aerial combat as its own reward. For that reason he decided he would be self-satisfied for the remainder of his life if he became the first ace of the Vietnam War. Although he expected to be honored and feted, he told himself that he would be contented to accomplish the deed, to down five.

If only he had substantiation for the last one—the lost one. From where he now stood two more kills loomed as high as Mount Everest; if he had but one to go, reaching his goal would appear as easy as stepping over an anthill. Goddamn all "ifs!" He was making himself nervous, flirting with a migraine by worrying about things beyond his control. When it happened, it happened. And if it didn't . . .

He knew that much of his reasoning was aimed at justifying a selfish ego. Had he contributed time and energy to his family and to the civilian community in amounts equal to what he gave to flying, he would have been "Father and Man of the Year." Such glory wasn't what he needed, however; to him, that was like being chosen "Best of Wimps." He wanted to be the war's most renowned fighter pilot—nothing more—and nothing less.

16

During March 1967, the month in which Cy Allen failed to get credit for what would have been his fourth kill, the United States Air Force scored only three victories over North Vietnam. In all three cases F-105 drivers shot down MiG-17s with 20-mm cannon fire. By the end of the month, the Phantom escort pilots were flying around in a haze of embarrassment: the bomber pilots had snatched their role and their glory.

"We're going to be hauling the bombs and the Thuds'll protect us if this keeps up," Rocco Monge said. The turnabout wasn't funny to the Phantom jocks; the Thud drivers loved every mission.

As a result of their air-to-air success, the Thud pilots became absolutely hostile. They sped to the target area, pressed hard to the bomb release line, then pulled up sharply with blood in their eyes, searching for bandits.

In April the U.S. Air Force killed nine MiGs. Seven of them fell to F-105s and their 20-mm cannon.

Rocco Monge and Cy Allen read accounts of F-105

kills and felt frustrated. The accounts clearly showed the advantage of a gun, particularly when a skilled and determined pilot aimed it. One F-105 pilot's account read:

"I was in afterburner. As I approached from behind, the two MiG-17s I'd selected lit their ABs. I had momentum on them, however, and rapidly closed to within three hundred feet. I fired a three-second burst at the trailing MiG about the time its pilot tried to turn right." (The F-105's Gatling–type Vulcan cannon had a six-thousand-rounds-per-minute rate of fire: in three seconds, the gun cranked out three hundred rounds.) "I saw hits on the trailing edge of the right wing and along the length of the fuselage. The MiG began torching from the tailpipe." (Commonly, flames rather than thrust blew out the tailpipe nozzle when, as a result of battle damage to the fuel system, raw fuel poured directly into the afterburner and ignited.) "The MiG reversed, showed me his left side, and I fired another three-second burst. The MiG pilot's maneuvers looked weak. He seemed locked in my gunline. It reminded me of a rabbit that panics and stays frozen inside the beams of an approaching car's headlights. By the time I finished the second burst, my range was about a hundred feet. I saw hits along the left wing, in the fuselage, and on the canopy. That MiG rolled over and started down." (In an attachment to the narrative, the F-105 pilot's wingman reported that he saw the MiG-17 strike the ground.) "The second MiG had gained on me by then. I accelerated and closed to within three hundred feet. From there it was exactly the same as the first one. The MiG pilot went right, I fired; he reversed left, I fired again. I saw hits on both wings, on both sides of the fuselage, and on the canopy. After the second burst, he straightened up, then executed a wild, really violent pitch-up. I went under him and came around hard left. I saw the MiG falling, tumbling, out of control. Then I saw him hit the ground." (The wingman also reported seeing the MiG-17 crash.) "I'd estimate the entire action lasted two to three minutes."

Another account by a lieutenant who was flying his fifth combat mission in a Thud also showed the advantages of a gun, even when skill was absent. The account read:

"It was the first time I'd seen MiGs. For the first few minutes I had no idea what I was doing. I was mostly trying to get loose from whichever MiG was chasing me. It seemed that every time I saw a MiG in front of me, there was another one behind me. I was flying like mad and burning fuel at a fantastic rate. Somehow I finally broke clear and then tried to start putting into practice what I'd learned in training. I tried to get behind one MiG but he out-turned me and ended up on my tail. He sprayed me with a short burst of cannon fire and that was when I jettisoned my tanks and ordnance and did some violent left and right breaks, all at the same time, and got away. I don't remember when I went into burner but, suddenly, I saw a MiG directly in front of me and I was closing very rapidly. The MiG pilot must have seen me because he racked it around and lit his burner. He was too late. I was overrunning him. I just started firing when I thought I was in range. I didn't even have my sights set up. I just held down the trigger and shot off his vertical stabilizer and half of his right wing. I went by him and another MiG jumped me and I started flying like crazy again. I never saw what happened to the MiG I shot." (Another pilot reported that the pilot of the MiG in question ejected shortly after the firing pass ended.)

Cy sailed the report onto Rocco's desk: "I had no idea what I was doing and shot off his vertical stabilizer and half of his right wing." He laughed. "Too much." (His memory refused to recall his panic prior to his first kill.)

Rocco reached inside his flying suit and sorted through the thick black hair on his chest, plucked out a gray one. "How did you like that 'hundred feet'?" he asked. "From that range you could kick the fucker out of the sky." With missiles it was possible to get too close to a target and, as a result, to have the missiles not operate properly, possibly refuse to fire.

Both Rocco and Allen knew that the surest kills resulted from outmaneuvering the other guy, sticking to his ass like flypaper, and from extremely close range hammering him to pieces with gunfire. Those kills were also the most satisfying. That was the old way and the old way was the best way for any pilot who could fly worth shit. "If we got rid of those missiles," Rocco said, "and got a gun pod, we'd be back in business."

In Korea, Rocco had scored a single MiG kill. He needed four more to become a career ace. The idea hardly entered his mind. As a commander he had team goals, not personal goals. Thoughts about ways to keep his troops alive occupied most of his mind.

Allen too wanted a gun. But he had mixed emotions about missiles. He favored, even liked, the AIM9 Sidewinders. He remembered the day he downed his first two MiGs and might have had two more if three of his four AIM7 Sparrows hadn't failed to fire. The Sparrows sucked. He disliked the coordination required between front and back seats: the pilot aimed the airplane and the nav controlled the airborne radar which locked onto the target and guided the missile to that target. After firing the missile, the pilot had to fly a profile which kept the enemy aircraft within radar range until the missile impacted. In comparison, the

Sidewinder needed no assistance from the guy in back. After launch the Sidewinder guided itself by seeking infrared emissions.

A mission on the First of April made up for Allen's earlier disappointment with Sparrows. The outcome of the flight was an April Fool surprise. . . .

That day, high over the Red River, a cirrostratus cloud layer curtained the sun and the world appeared to be illuminated by a sourceless glow of pure white light. Shadowless objects stood out in crisp definition.

Allen was leading a flight of four head-on toward four MiG-21s. The SAMs weren't out and the encounter held promise of a classic dogfight. Less than a minute before, Allen had sighted the MiGs conning, making contrails, as they came about to do battle. They obviously had seen the black smoke that trailed from the F-4's engines like a signature of arrival.

Unexpectedly, Cy felt something vaguely ominous. Neither group of fighters was in a position to gain an advantage. He had a premonition that the groups would do nothing but pass at high speeds. Ridiculous, he thought and pictured two heavily armored knights pointing lances from horseback, determinedly galloping toward each other, and then flashing by at full speed without making contact. Ridiculous . . .

The knights vanished when the MiGs opened up with their cannons at the same second in which Dobbs said, "Lock, in range. Fire! For Christ's sake, fire!"

Allen triggered his full load of Sparrows: three of the four radar-guided missiles worked. Microseconds apart and trailing white smoke, the trio of Sparrows leaped away from the well beneath the Phantom.

Because of the aircraft's high speed, the missiles appeared to float just beyond the F-4's nose. In that instant Allen analyzed the situation: the head-on firing angle appeared impossible; the probability of a hit, nil; nevertheless . . .

In a surrealistic suspension of motion, the MiG that Dobbs was tracking ran into the floating missiles, one after another: Boom-boom-boom. For a fraction of a heartbeat the enemy plane waited, suspended in space, then seemed to genuflect as the Phantom streaked beneath it in fierce majesty. Then the shattered plane fell to earth, an iron coffin.

A three-dimensional "4" as big and red as a barn overwhelmed Cy Allen's lagging mind. The numeral transformed itself into an enormous white 4 set in the center of a colossal red star. How had it happened so swiftly? He had not been prepared. The 4 disappeared, was replaced by Charles Demuth's painting, "I Saw the Figure 5 in Gold." Allen was happily stunned, as if he had won a contest or had received some great prize for no reason.

Then the scope of the achievement became visible: Dobbs and his radar had killed Number Four. Allen wouldn't have—couldn't have—made the shot visually. He had done nothing but instinctively squeeze the trigger when Dobbs ordered.

The credit belonged to Dobbs—and the radar.

Banked into a turn, the Phantom pilots saw the surviving MiG-21s going away. The action was ended. They had one kill for the day.

Cy glanced at the rearview mirrors: Dobbs was rocking from side to side like Ray Charles at the piano. Dobbs shouted, "They all hit? He didn't have a chance." He was breathless, gasping, choking, sounded on the verge of a stroke: "The most—unbelievable—greatest—luckiest—"

"It wasn't luck."

Dobbs laughed insanely.

"Drinks are on me," Allen told him, "for the rest of the year." He could think of no other words. He felt as if he now was the passenger and Dobbs was in command.

"Bullshit," Dobbs said. "Winner buys." He rocked his body and stomped his feet so violently that the motion shook the entire airframe. "I had him," Dobbs panted, "on radar. Had him cold. For a second, I thought you wouldn't fire. Oh, shit, if you hadn't fired . . ." Dobbs blubbered with laughter.

Where did he stand now, Allen wondered. His self-image as a single-seat fighter pilot appeared to be obviously transparent. Had technology altered his entire scheme of flying, his lifelong role?

Then he again watched Dobbs' rocking head and told himself, "Don't worry about it. Accept what happens. Be happy." And suddenly it was Christmas morning in the cockpit. . . . Allen smiled, faceless beneath his oxygen mask. He was achieving a child's dream in a man's heaven.

One more and Dobbs and he would become immortals. Demuth's painting came to mind again: The Figure 5 in Gold. Allen caught himself reflexively tapping his toes and nodding his head in time with Dobbs' stomping to the distant rhythm of a cosmic tune only he heard.

The very next day, Number Five flew straight into their laps.

17

Cy Allen and Junior Eliot were exiting behind the strike force and thought everyone was ahead of them until they received a Mayday call from an EB-66 Destroyer that had been left by mistake. The Destroyer had gone in deeper than normal to aid a flight of Iron Hands that had more SAM sites than it could handle. Allen and Eliot raced back and found the loner. "Wow, am I glad to see you two," the EB-66 driver said.

The Destroyer was no speed wagon. Tooling along at two-thirty indicated, the Phantoms kept overrunning the erstwhile bomber until they settled into an S-type weave behind it, sort of a fluid three formation. "This is expensive baby-sitting," Dobbs said.

They were at twenty-eight thousand feet. It was one of those days when a person could see for a thousand miles. Each time he turned, Allen rolled steeply in order to scan high and low aft. It was like a drive in the country. In the turns he saw Hanoi, the Delta's fan, Haiphong, all the way to the Gulf of Tonkin. When straight and level, he thought he recognized

Thanh Hoa, maybe even Vinh far to the south. "Super vis," he said.

"For you, it's always super vis," Dobbs said.

They were two-seventy at fifty from Bullseye (in everyday English: fifty miles due west of Hanoi) when Allen spotted a pair of aircraft that looked as if they were in pursuit. "Two bogies, six o'clock low," he called.

When confronted by a MiG, the slow, unarmed EB-66 had one defensive maneuver: the pilot put the plane into a spiraling descent. His intention was to keep the MiG from lining up on him in any manner and thus prevent the MiG from taking a respectable shot. At the same time, the EB-66 crew prayed that a friendly fighter came to its rescue before the spiraling plane ran out of altitude. The EB-66 hadn't been built to maneuver in the ways required for survival over the North.

Earlier in the year, Allen and Dobbs had watched a SAM cut an EB in half. The plane had wandered too near a launch complex and hadn't a chance to escape: the missile guided straight to it and the pilot was helpless to take effective evasive action. Futilely Dobbs had cried, "Look out."

The missile was a dud, didn't detonate. The apparent reprieve was a sham. The dud missile punched through the EB-66 fuselage's underside, exited slightly ahead of the leading edge of the vertical stabilizer, broke the plane's back, then continued upward, flew out of sight. The EB's empennage tore loose and spiraled out of control. The plane's front section continued in flight for several seconds, then slowly pitched forward over its nose and fell, belly up. Two parachutes blossomed before the inverted airframe impacted the ground. "The ECM guys bought it," Dobbs said, "never had a chance."

Allen had shuddered in empathy at the fate of the four ECM operators who were trapped inside their windowless compartment. Blind warriors who saw battle through a braille of electronics, they went to war only in hopes of surviving.

Now Cy Allen decided that he was going to save *this* EB crew and told Eliot, "Stick with the EB. Cover him, no matter what."

"Should I start down?" the Destroyer pilot said.

"Negative. Keep heading west. Follow Two's directions," Cy Allen said. "He'll stay with you all the way." Then he turned and dived toward the bogies. The Figure 5 in gold and a 6 crowded his mind. Later he wondered if visions of glory had obscured his reason.

Dobbs located the targets on radar: "Ten miles. Closure—looks like—eleven hundred."

"All yours, Jer." Allen swung the Phantom wide to the south. He switched interlocks in with the intention of letting the computer fire the missiles, then quickly flipped interlocks out. He'd have a quartering shot, couldn't afford that half-second delay while the computer made up its mind after he pulled the trigger.

At worst, he'd scatter the pair of bandits; maybe scare them off completely. He told himself that primarily he wanted to divert attention from the EB-66, but what he really wanted was a kill. If he missed on the first pass, he wouldn't be in too bad a spot to get behind one of them, if they were willing to play. Of course, Eliot then might have to protect the EB from the other MiG. No, probably not. Most likely the other MiG would double back and chase him. Was he going to end up in a sandwich? What if . . . Fuck it. Why was he going through all that? It would work out. When the time came, he'd do something clever.

"Eight miles," Dobbs said, "eleven o'clock."

The two bogies looked to be at an altitude around fifteen thousand. Allen turned, put them on the nose. Passing through twenty thousand feet, he suddenly had his second ominous feeling in as many days. In the middle of the eerie sensation, almost as if in a trance, he heard Dobbs' six mile call. His body and mind told him nothing was right. Weren't the target airplanes too close together? Didn't MiGs usually fly looser trails? But they were delta-wing, like MiG-21s . . . Cy hesitantly slid the throttles back to minimum afterburner.

"Four miles, twelve o'clock," Dobbs said.

Cy wasn't a champ at aircraft recognition. He'd usually avoided those classes, found them boring. However, he would have sworn the planes he was preparing to shoot weren't delta-wing MiG-21s.

"Two miles. In range, lock."

Cy watched the delta shapes while his mind's eye scanned nearly identical shapes hidden within a shadowy memory. He had no thoughts but those that traveled out on a line of sight, linked him to the planes he wanted to destroy. MiG-21s? No. SU-9s or SU-11s? Doubtful. Maybe Mirages? Not likely . . .

"In range. Lock," Dobbs repeated.

Allen's forefinger traced the curve of the trigger, but his mind refused to release a signal that would launch a weapon. He winced in anticipation. Suddenly the eerie sensation left him. The targets broke clear of his memory's shadows. "Jesus Christ, they're *ours*," he shouted. He'd recognized the bogies as F-102 Delta Daggers.

He racked up onto a wing, turned hard into them, rolled out parallel, slightly beyond and to the rear of them. The fuckers ignored him. For a moment he wondered if they had seen him. But how could they have missed him? They certainly weren't drones. Then he figured it out: They didn't want to see him because they didn't want him to see them. The fuckers weren't supposed to be over the North.

Stationed at Don Muang, outside Bangkok, the F-102 role was limited to combat air patrol over Laos to protect KC-135 tankers and B-52 jungle blasters—on an outside chance that a MiG roved that far. These two Dueces were poaching, free-lancing, hunting for a MiG to kill, seeking extracurricular thrills and glory. And they nearly had lost their asses . . .

Dobbs laughed, said, "They're still in range."

Allen broke away, rammed the Phantom into max burners, boomed skyward to reach Eliot. A cold rage filled him. He was angry at the ignorance of the F-102 drivers, but more than that he was angry with himself, with his inability to identify a target until it was nearly too late. The cold rage settled achingly into his stomach. He felt a cramp. Was he getting an ulcer over this ace business? He craved a drink, a long swallow of raw bourbon.

Dobbs said, "If you'd've shot one down, how would you've logged it?"

"From jail, I suppose." If he had destroyed a friendly, a hundred enemy planes would not have redeemed him, Allen thought.

18

In his heart Allen knew he had five MiGs. But a voice inside his mind insisted he didn't. He had four and Dobbs had one. The fighter racket no longer was a one-on-one encounter, the voice said. The MiG jocks flew solo, but the Phantoms were two-man teams.

In his heart Cy Allen knew that his two-man team had five MiGs. But that same inner voice told him it didn't. Officially? the voice asked. Had Dobbs and he been credited with five destroyed enemy aircraft, beyond a shadow of a doubt? No, he admitted, and "officially" was the only thing that mattered.

He was surprised when at a remote base such as Ubon a half dozen or so civilian reporters showed up on his doorstep. They knew about the one he lost and they thought it made terrific human interest news. "Do you think Hanoi would respond to a telegram requesting information regarding a specific airplane shot down on a specific day?" one reporter asked.

Cy smiled: "Doubt it. Radio Hanoi claims I haven't shot down even one. None of us has."

Nathan sent clippings from *The Pittsburgh Light-*

house that told of Cy's exploits. Eli Mutie sent identical clippings, plus one from *The New York Times*. Cy was chagrined to see that the stories incorrectly identified Dobbs. In one he was called Jerry Debbs; in another, Jeffrey Dobbs.

Cy also received letters from other well-wishers. Chet Russell wrote several pages that indicted the United States president and his aides specifically and the U.S. populace in general. Among the letters was the first and only fan mail of Cy's life. A boy from Gresham, Oregon, wrote:

> It makes me proud to read about your victories. We need men like you. I'm 16 years old and am striving to become a pilot for the United States Marine Corps. My only wish is to kill Commies and get rid of people like the Viet Cong.
> Please keep up the good work.

Baby brother Ty Cobb sent a most alluring message from Miami, a letter that with a stretch of the imagination also could have been ranked as fan mail:

> Dear Heartthrob,
> I think you are some kind of beautiful and I hope you knock down the whole sky over North Vietnam.
> At this end, the war stories of your heroics are vaguely reminiscent of a breathless Army Information Officer giving an up-to-date body count after the last savage counterattack by the Big Red One—and as the saying goes, "If you're going to be one, be a BIG RED ONE."
> I am on company time and, according to the First Law of Allen, that is a perfect time to finish personal business. No, I guess that's the Second Law. The first is: "The flesh is everything." Thus, on a slow day around the ol' condominium sales office, ol' Ty Cobb,

ex-boy-jock, ex-boy-pilot, and present-day hotshot-boy-sales specialist, beach Don Juan, correspondent and corespondent, takes pen in hand . . .

The job is dull—you wouldn't believe—but the money is *extremely* good. And the off-duty fringe benefits are sensational.

Rather than risk being accused of tormenting a GI by describing all the soggy details, let me say that I meet a lot of very nice ladies who I see again and again and I am quite satisfied with my lot.

I feel mentally healthy—and will not burden you with the psychological repercussions of my divorce lest you retaliate with specifics of a similar nature. Truce?

Which reminds me . . .

I picked up a girl in a bar the other afternoon—she wouldn't sit on the bar stool and later I found out she didn't have panties on under her mini and her cheeks would have stuck to the leather—and she told me I was so mentally healthy that I scared her. Scared her? Oh, well.

And now for the good news.

Planning is proceeding apace for your homecoming extravaganza. I am most anxious for you to get back and get down here and sample what I have lined up for you. Never before has one man had so much pussy waiting on his arrival—even after I told them about your incurable clap. There is a complete mythology building.

I already am planning a giant orgy to be called "The Festival of the Seven Virgins and South Florida Watermelon Eating Contest." Cast of hundreds auditioning weekly. Selectees engrossed in further body-building exercises.

Meanwhile, try to curb your appetite. If you are logging lots of east-west landings, you might get a friend to take a few pictures of your cock so you have something to remember it by next year after it rots off.

I looked for you on the Bob Hope Show and

thought I saw you once in a crowd scene outside a latrine. What were you doing in that sailor suit?

Skill and planning, babe.

Ty

Cy recognized the invitation as no idle boast. Ty Cobb was four years behind him in age, but he was light-years ahead in making money and making out.

Best of all, however, Cy received letters from his three sons. They too were proud of him and basked in reflected glory. Clare included a note in Frank's letter, wished Cy luck and success. What had changed her attitude? Was her message some type of overture? Did she still care? He was touched by guilt the next time he made love to Pensy, felt almost as if he was cheating on Clare. That was something he never had done, no matter how badly the marriage went.

The attention he received was tempered by a factor Allen did not understand. Most of the stories about his exploits were short, to the point. They took up no more space than the recap of a ballgame between two out-of-town teams. If he did become the first ace, was it possible there would be little recognition and few rewards? But hadn't he told himself that he would be satisfied merely to accomplish the feat?

From what Allen read in magazines, Americans were developing a hatred for the Vietnam War. Hadn't Frenchmen done the same while their Army was engaged in Indo-China? And in Algiers? The problem with this war was that there was no visible enemy villain, no single person to represent a foreign nation threatening America. Skinny Uncle Ho certainly didn't personify a despicable foe. According to the press, people in South Vietnam loved him as much as people in the North. Ho's tranquil old mug could pass for Charlie Chan's grandmother. If anything, his frailness worked against the United States. The way it appeared, the underprivileged were being slapped around by the wealthy, and that was by-god un-American.

Was that the image the world would have of him? If that was the case, Allen questioned the honor of being the first ace. Under perfect conditions, playing the hero was a strange and difficult role. . . .

During World War II, Eli Mutie had made certain that Cy met Sergeant Charles "Commando" Kelly, Medal of Honor winner from Pittsburgh's North Side. Cy had expected to meet a man who was ten feet tall, maybe had fangs that dripped blood. In reality, Kelly turned out to be another happy-go-lucky North Sider. He wasn't even natty, wouldn't've stood out in a squad of GIs, except for the pale blue ribbon with the five tiny white stars above his left breast uniform pocket. Kelly shook Cy's hand and nodded. Cy had anticipated hearing a chilling war story or receiving some message that no other man could deliver. Instead, Kelly faked a punch to Mutie's midsection, bounced several soft hooks off his arms, and joked about being owed a couple beers for another public appearance. Then he shook Cy's hand a second time before excusing himself and strolling away.

Now, Cy smiled to himself at the memory of the jaunty, carefree figure. Although he had not been impressed at the time, and had seen Kelly only once, he vividly recalled him twenty-two years later. Did he remember the man or the medal?

When he returned from Korea, Cy Allen had been a minor celebrity. He had given interviews and made speeches before civic groups and private clubs. His favorite speech had been at a Pittsburgh Press Club luncheon. Nathan had been there; Eli Mutie arranged everything. Pictures of Lieutenant Allen and accounts of his aerial feats were featured on the first page, second section of that day's edition of *The Lighthouse*. Cy believed that his speech had won the listeners' hearts and minds long before some weenie of a staff officer determined that there were civilian hearts and minds to be won.

He had opened his talk by playing the role of devil-may-care pilot: "A combat fighter jock leaps out of bed every day at the crack of noon—doom—dawn! Breakfast is two aspirins and a barf—not always in that order. Either way, it purges the systems. Our planning is based upon the KISS principle: Keep It Simple, Stupid. Every mission briefing is the same: kick the tires, light the fires, and try not to run over anything on the ground; first man off is Lead; after you're airborne, shoot down anything that's dumb enough to fly in front of you. One day, our commander got three French hens, two turtle doves. . . . Actually, tangling with the enema—I mean, enemy —tangling with the enemy is the easiest part of the day. Usually, fighter pilots are destroyed by drinking whiskey and chasing women all night long in order to maintain the image."

He graciously avoided controversy. An obviously hostile reporter asked, "I've heard that Korean pilots who bail out are machine-gunned while hanging in their parachutes. Have you ever done that?" Several men in the audience booed the question but Allen silenced them with a wave of his hand.

"I think," he answered good-naturedly, "you saw the same war movie I saw when I was a kid." He hoisted his pants with his forearms and did a Cagney: "Yooooou—dirty-Japs!" Smiling, he said, "I've never seen it happen, in real life, on either side. Why hurt some joker you know you can beat? Let him go home and get another airplane, then hope you meet him again." The audience applauded his answer.

Another reporter asked, "Is it true that every fighter pilot thinks of himself as the absolute best, the greatest?"

Turning solemn, he replied: "Definitely not. We know our limitations. I've never considered myself the greatest, not even second. I rank a humble third . . ." He smiled warmly. ". . . behind God the Father and Jesus Christ."

As part of another answer he had said, "Along the Yalu, all over North Korea and China—" He stopped as if confused, stuck his tongue in a cheek, then said, "From as high as we fly, you can see far into China." The audience laughed with him. "The landscape is cold and barren, desolate—sort of like Philadelphia. If you crash there, it ruins your whole day. And you have one helluva long wait for a Crosstown." Any Pittsburgher who had waited for a streetcar in the dead of winter knew exactly what he meant, he thought; the statement drew appreciative laughter. Eli Mutie captioned his account of the speech, "Streetcars Scarce on Yalu."

He had wrapped up the afternoon by telling them: "Combat is exciting. Flying per se is exciting. My heart hits high gear the moment I climb into a fighter cockpit. Roaring down the runway, blasting off into the wild blue still gives me a thrill. Believe me, every fighter pilot knows that the challenge is there— constantly. In high performance aircraft you die one of three ways: the enemy kills you, the airplane kills you, or you kill yourself. Some of the best died far from any battlefield. The challenge is always there. And we love it."

Eli Mutie had written it exactly as he had said it.

The role he had played hadn't been easy. When he first returned to the States, he had sincerely tried to communicate to people exactly what aerial combat had been like. He had been twenty-six years old and filled with the certainties that accompany limited insight. He displayed brashness but it had been tempered by an honest enthusiasm for flying. Therefore, listeners tolerated him. He soon learned, however, that they didn't want to hear details of killing and dying. Details were unimportant. They respected him as a war hero. For them, that was enough. Therefore, he adopted a jocular attitude toward combat. The public ate up that approach. Citizens who had been dissatisfied with America's involvement in Korea chose to ignore him, the same as they had ignored the war. Nobody publicly protested.

Now, citizens who were disgruntled by the Vietnam War openly opposed the United States government. They tolerated nothing and nobody. Respect was gone. As Allen saw it, a hero from Vietnam would have to play a role different from any in America's history. He had only vague ideas as to what the new role entailed. The manner in which America had seemingly changed within less than a year puzzled him.

Heroes! Men larger than life? In retrospect, Cy questioned the image. Too often a hero was a professional who had devoted a decade or more of hard work to becoming an overnight sensation.

Allen recalled the only World Series he saw in person, the 1960 encounter between the Pittsburgh Pirates and the New York Yankees. Again, Eli Mutie had arranged it: box seats for the four games at Forbes Field in Pittsburgh, and then an unexpected bonus.

The Series went down to the final inning of the seventh game. The score was tied, 9-9, and Bill Mazeroski, who wore the number "9," watched Yankees pitcher Ralph Terry finish his warmup throws, then stepped into the batter's box to lead off the last of the ninth inning. The first pitch was wide and Mazeroski barely moved as it passed him. The second pitch came in high and fast. Mazeroski swung and hit the ball on a low trajectory toward left center field.

"Oh, my God," Nathan said and leaped to his feet. Every person in the ballpark seemed to rise with him. There was a hush that lasted for a tick of the clock.

The ball stayed on a low trajectory. Yogi Berra, the Yankees left fielder, moved to the base of the ivy-covered wall. The ball disappeared over the wall to the right of the big Longines clock mounted above the scoreboard. The atmosphere was filled with one gigantic roar of joy. Mazeroski grabbed his hat from his head and started running. The clock above the fence read 3:36.

Allen was swept with a feeling of pure physical pleasure. Goose pimples broke out on his forearms. He shivered with delight. He turned and saw Nathan grinning madly: the corners of Nathan's mouth curved grotesquely upward and every line in his face was compressed toward his eyes which were tightly squinted so that his nose pulled down over his lips. The expression produced an unrecognizable clown's mask. Eli Mutie was grinning as stupidly as Nathan and a thin string of drool stretched from his lower lip to his necktie. He squeezed his Stetson in his hands and watched Mazeroski run the bases.

Nearing second, Mazeroski triumphantly waved his cap in the air. The clock above the fence read 3:36. Time had stopped.

Cy grabbed his father and hugged him. Large tears were running down Nathan's cheeks. "You all right?" Allen shouted.

He had to hold his ear directly in front of his father's mouth before he heard him say, ". . . so damn happy, just so damn happy."

Mazeroski rounded third base and was grinning with his mouth wide open. His running stride changed to sort of a gallop. Fans rushed onto the field and chased him homeward. Casey Stengel, the Yankee manager, walked to within twenty feet of the third base foul line and watched to verify that Mazeroski stepped on home plate. Mazeroski stomped on the plate and his teammates swarmed over him. The clock above the fence read 3:36.

Cy had an arm around his father who was weeping for joy. Mazeroski's life was distilled into one unforgettable moment, Cy thought. In front of more than thirty-six thousand spectators he reached the highest moment in his career, in his life. That moment was the essence of his existence as a ballplayer and as a man. With one swing of the bat he captured the jubilant admiration and love of every Pittsburgh follower and gained baseball immortality.

People pranced across the infield. They danced without music but many were in step. Perhaps they unconsciously heard some universal song of victory. Men and women hugged and kissed on the field and in the stands. Many had to be strangers. Cy watched one man pass through the crowd and hug every woman he encountered. Symbolic rape? He laughed at the idea. To the victors go the spoils! Why not? People scooped up infield dirt and by the handfuls poured it into their shirt and pants pockets. The bases had disappeared from the field. A man in a snap-brimmed hat and an expensive-looking sport coat was digging up home plate with a shovel; two policemen were assisting him. They had dug a hole about a foot deep and were straining to free the white rubber plate which looked to be anchored in concrete. Cy pointed and shouted to Nathan, "I wonder if that crazy SOB brought that shovel with him." The well-dressed man was looting in broad daylight, Cy thought and wondered if the mad, victory-starved fanatics would burn down the city. He remembered VJ-Day in 1945. Nathan had taken him into the heart of Pittsburgh on that day; now he planned to take his father there tonight.

Eli Mutie pulled his two friends by the arms: "Come on."

"No, no," Nathan shouted, "you two go."

Mutie again pulled Cy's arm.

"Where we going?"

Nathan shoved his son: "Go with him. I'll wait right here."

Mutie forced his way out of the box, down the aisle, and onto the field with Cy holding fast to his belt. People milled every which way but Mutie had direction and purpose. Waving an arm, he caught the attention of one of many policemen who were keeping fans out of the Pirate dugout. The policeman and Mutie exchanged a greeting and then Mutie and Cy were inside the dugout and headed down a corridor beneath the stands. Mutie had his Press Pass out and ready. It was worthless. They came to a halt amidst unmoving reporters and photographers massed before a door. Mutie backed off, built up momentum, charged into the crowd, and towing Cy behind him burst into the Pirate dressing room. Confusion reigned.

A tall ballplayer sloshed a bucket of water over a gray-haired man dressed in a business suit. Mutie laughed and shouted, "Mayor Barr. That's Mayor Barr."

The grinning ballplayer shouted at the mayor, "Ya old bastard, ya shouldn't come in here if you don't wanna get wet."

A towel hit the mayor. He wiped his face and said happily, "That's all right, all right. I wore an old suit."

"It looks like it," another player shouted and hit the mayor with a second bucketful of water. Then newsmen, cameramen, Pirate officials, and the many hangers-on were drenched.

An Italian-looking player grabbed a hat off the head of the next man who entered the room, pulled the hat tightly down over his own head, and poured champagne over himself while screaming, "Yipee! Yipee! Nine big ones! Nine big ones in the kick."

Mazeroski kissed his bat time after time for the photographers. Then he answered questions. "Yeah, a high fastball. Yeah, I was swinging for the fence. I was trying to ride it out of there. What? What? What did I think? I was too happy to think. I guess I didn't think anything. I can't begin to describe how I felt when I saw the ball clear the fence. Yeah, this is the biggest thrill I ever had. I was so happy! When I saw the ball go over the wall, I grabbed my hat and started running. I never thought this would ever happen to me."

Allen felt out of place. He didn't belong in that dressing room. Things weren't what he wished them to be. He wanted Mazeroski to be more articulate, to make a revelatory statement that added infinite dimension to the event. At the same time, he felt a twinge of envy, a touch of jealousy. He compared

Mazeroski's career to his and for a minute they appeared to correspond:

> Minor leagues—Pilot training.
> Spring training each year—Transition training into a new fighter.
> The long season of game after game—The combat sweeps day after day.
> Games in which he failed to score—Air battles in which he failed to destroy an enemy plane.
> Victory—Victory.
> Defeat . . . Death, probably.

The correlation broke down there. Baseball was a game. It wasn't deserving of glory of the first magnitude.

Cy Allen would have given anything he possessed to have performed his combat feats in front of forty thousand fans. His glory had been gained in the broad, spectatorless skies of Korea. But if he had been before a crowd . . .

He imagined forty thousand fans rising from their seats when he locked onto a MiG and poured machine gun fire into it. He imagined the collective "Awwwww . . ." when the enemy plane burst into flames; the prolonged "Ooooohhhhh . . ." that accompanied the MiG's smoking dive earthward; and then the sustained cheers that deafened when the enemy plane crashed in a ball of fire and burned. He wanted that. He wanted to land, step from the cockpit, and circle the bases or jog a victory lap while the spectators screamed their approval, and admiration, and absolute delight. He wanted that and, he realized, he would never have it. His father had stood next to him and had publicly wept in gratitude for the deeds of a stranger. Yet his father had never been present at any of his times of combat recognition: his medals for gallantry and for achievement had been pinned on him in quiet ceremonies attended by fellow officers. A secret life.

The mood of the dressing room shifted. The initial, mass, frantic outbursts and overreactions were dissipating and the players seemed to be settling down to serious merrymaking. It was becoming a private celebration that only the ballplayers deserved to share. Cy felt uncomfortable, considered himself an intruder. He said to Mutie, "Let's get out of here, OK?"

"Certainly. Whenever you're ready. I came down—I wanted *you* to see this. Hell! Who am I kidding? *I* wanted to see this."

Recalling Mazeroski's inability to speak in memorable terms led Allen to three "absolute conclusions" which, to him, perfectly explained human behavior. His first conclusion: *Heroes were surprised by their heroics.* Mazeroski had been doing a job; he happened to do it best when the situation was most critical. He achieved the dream of every boy who ever swung a bat: to hit the winning home run in the last inning of the seventh game of the World Series. The odds on reaching the situation that provided the opportunity were staggering. To get there and then to produce to the maximum was too much to comprehend. That revealed the second conclusion: *Reality rarely equaled dreams.* In a way, Cy had always understood that. He never looked forward to achieving goals—until now. Tomorrow had always been far away. He lived his life today. Yesterday was forgotten. Therefore, his third conclusion: *Doers didn't remember details.* They were swept up by the activity of the moment. They took no time to reflect, didn't stop to write memoirs. He was suspicious of persons who later recalled many tiny details of settings for events in which they had been performing under stress.

There were but two settings from his life that he remembered vividly. Regarding both, he had been merely an observer, an unsuspecting spectator.

The first scene was the Grand Canyon. Alone, driving to a new assignment, he made a side trip to the south rim of the Canyon. Arriving at Grandeur Point minutes before the sun touched the western horizon and having no idea of what to expect, he had been stunned by the view. The colors, the depth, the distances were beyond comparison to anything he had previously seen. He stood at the rim until long after dark. Then he checked into the El Tovar Hotel and went directly to bed. He arose in time to return to the rim before the first light appeared in the east. When sunlight crept down the Canyon, the beauty of the changing pastel colors made him shiver with pleasure. Alone, he felt that he was watching the creation of the world. He absorbed the colors and the depth and the distances to the best of his ability, but something was lacking in his understanding. In an effort to add a personal dimension to what he saw, he found a golf-ball-sized stone and, with all his might, flung it toward the distant north rim. The stone fell from sight so very close in the foreground that it seemed as if he had dropped it at his feet. The futility of his gesture awed him. The scale reduced the colors to insignificance. He felt as if he had attempted to throw a stone across the Universe.

The second scene was the Grand Canal in Venice, again at sunset. On vacation, he checked into the Danieli Hotel, went straight to his room, and showered and changed for supper. Walking onto the hotel's dining room balcony which overlooked the Grand

Canal, he had been dazzled by the sun's golds and yellows and oranges and reds and pinks—but predominantly golds and pinks—that reflected off the water. Boats, island, and buildings were swallowed in the shimmering brilliance of the colors. He felt as if he had stepped inside a piece of gold, had been transformed and momentarily became part of its warm and glistening beauty.

He was saddened by the thought that his mind had recorded so little of what his wonderful all-seeing eyes had viewed. He tried to recall other striking scenes, other vivid images from his life. The effort was as profitless as trying to recall pages from old issues of *National Geographic*.

My God, what was becoming of his mind? He was trying to pass his life before his eyes! Was he preparing to die, or was he being reborn? Whichever, it wasn't his normal style. Alone in his room, he laughed at himself. Was he taking himself too seriously, especially now? An ace was not a hero per se. The feat of destroying five enemy planes was no proof of character. Fighting for personal glory was no different from fighting for personal survival. His father had taught him that much about combat.

Fuck it all! He didn't need to understand any of it. For whatever the reason, he still wanted to be the first ace of the Vietnam War.

As fate would have it, he didn't get a single shot at a MiG during the remainder of April.

19

May of 1967 fulfilled sweet dreams for seventeen USAF pilots. They downed sixteen MiG-17 Frescos and five MiG-21 Fishbeds for twenty-one victories, the greatest monthly total of the war. One Danang Phantom light colonel and his backseater grabbed the headlines by bagging three MiG-21s within three days. The feat was extra spectacular because the two flyers downed one MiG with a Sparrow, one with a Sidewinder, and one with cannon fire. The Danang Phantoms had been fitted with an external pod, the SUU-16, which contained a Gatling-type 20-mm cannon capable of grinding out six thousand rounds per minute. Phantom units in Thailand were promised similar equipment before the year's end which, Allen decided, wouldn't help him. By that time, he would be Stateside. During May, the Danang crews racked up eight victories and he wondered how in hell they got that many. Those crews were supposed to be bombing groundpounders in South Vietnam and the flyers from Thailand were supposed to be the MiG-killers. To top that, the damned Thud drivers got six more in

May: four with 20-mms and two with Sidewinders. The month's niftiest mission was flown by an F-4 jock who destroyed two MiGs with only seventy-eight rounds of 20-mm ammunition. Rocco's reaction to the news was: "McNamara hears that, he'll limit everybody to forty rounds per MiG. If one guy can do it, we all should be able to."

Allen was troubled by what was taking place. Why did the Phantoms in South Vietnam get gun pods first? Who decided to hang Sidewinders on bombers? Every action seemed designed to undermine his quest to become the first ace. Roles were being reversed. The goddamned war was fucked-up beyond belief.

May of 1967 was a nightmare for Allen. When it ended he had a total of eighty-two missions and still only four victories. He hadn't killed anything since April Fools' Day. Shut out for twenty-six counters plus seven weather aborts, he had never felt more out of step in his life. When he flew, the MiGs didn't. It was as simple as that. If he stayed home, the MiGs came out en masse. When he went out in the morning, the MiGs came out only in the afternoon. When the MiGs were out in the morning, he had a late takeoff and they were gone when he arrived. To make matters worse, he hadn't been scheduled to fly on either the thirteenth when USAF pilots killed seven MiGs or on the twentieth when they downed six more. "What's going on?" he asked Dobbs. "The war is passing us by."

His time to score another victory was limited: a tour ended after one hundred missions over North Vietnam. It had taken him—them!—fifty-six sorties to get four kills. Then twenty-six counters clicked by with nothing happening. Dobbs had predicted that they would get their fifth kill on their sixty-ninth mission: "The public information officer will ignore that number, but I am going to point it out, loud and clear."

"Me too," Allen said uneasily. He didn't like to speculate in specific terms about future combat events, especially about future kills. He compared his situation to the late innings of a no-hit baseball game: no professional discussed it aloud, made plans on it. To do so was a jinx.

On the sixty-ninth mission Allen was jumpy. The night before, he hadn't slept soundly which had been a new experience. From the beginning he had accepted combat with a clear mind. He had never looked forward or backward to a degree that deprived him of rest: large, conscious doses of anticipation, fear, or guilt had been unknown quantities until then. Once a flyer worried about what *might* happen tomorrow, Allen thought, he was wide open to worry about what *could* have happened yesterday. The more he struggled not to think about any of it, the more specific details (forgotten close shaves and near misses) crowded into his mind from the past. He silently damned Dobbs' rookie predictions, his witless hex.

When the sixty-ninth mission passed without event, he was relieved. He would have been strangely uncomfortable, felt cheated in some way if Dobbs had called it so easily. A touch of the mystique would have vanished from combat flying.

By the time they reached their eightieth mission, Allen felt pressure. He almost believed he was never to see another MiG. He hated the days that he didn't fly because he feared he was missing a chance at a MiG; he hated the days he did fly without so much as sighting an enemy plane. Aerial encounters, even without kills, at least burned off the accumulated adrenaline and tension. Milk runs left Allen worn down: his eyes burned from scanning the sky; his back ached from the weight of personal equipment; in places, his body was rubbed raw by the parachute harness and survival vest; the oxygen mask pinched his face and the helmet pulled his hair. Never before had he noticed the fatiguing aches and pains of routine flying. Throughout his career, flying had been fun. Now it was an unrewarding, thankless *job*.

There were times when he believed he could sleep forever. But when he flopped into bed, his mind was wide awake. Yet his body was exhausted. Even his hair felt tired. Maybe he had grown too old for fighters, he thought. The day after Hawk had bought it, Rocco had said, "War's like having children: it's for the young guys." After all, both Rocco and he turned forty this year and—damn that Dobbs! He was responsible for the waves of self-doubt. Damn his predictions. Allen knew better: never anticipate, never be disappointed. "Forget tomorrow," he told himself nightly. The act made him think of the day to come all the more, which in turn brought unwanted memories.

Drinking a *little* more than usual didn't help much. Drinking a *lot* more than usual was the answer. Plenty of bourbon shut down his imagination, cut off his thinking. If he dreamed, at least he didn't remember it.

Pensy and he frequently drank away the evening. They would go to a restaurant and before ordering food might have five or six drinks. When dinner arrived Pensy ignored it, kept pouring down scotch. Cy matched her drink for drink. There were moments when he thought she liked him better at those times, enjoyed seeing him out of control.

One night he hired a samlor and, while the unhappy driver trotted alongside and protested, Cy pumped the vehicle back to Warin. Throughout the trip, Pensy sat in back, laughed, shouted orders to both men. When they reached the bungalow, Pensy said, "He lose much face. All his friends tell him he sick, can't carry big farang like you." Later Cy decided he could have hired the samlor contraption for a week for as much as he tipped the mortified driver in compensation.

Sex in an alcohol stupor left Cy physically drained but emotionally unsatisfied. Under heavy influence Pensy was icily aloof, unreachable. Cy's inclination to touch her was dulled by a stubborn desire for her to touch him, to reverse roles and to ease his psychological burden. Who owed who? Who was holding back? As it was, the nearness of sex drove them farther apart.

Self-esteem kept Cy from flushing himself away night after night, however. He definitely wouldn't get wiped out the night before he flew. If he didn't owe that much to himself, he at least owed it to Jer. Those dry nights were the toughest.

Cy Allen wondered if the glory was worth the price. Aerial combat: action compressed in space and time: a rolling, turning, climbing, looping, diving, spinning race across the vast, open, endless reaches of sky while attempting ultimately to outmaneuver an opponent and thereby gain the advantage in that killing zone which focused into a scant few degrees, a short distance (even with missiles) for a period no longer than a squeeze of a trigger. He had logged hundreds of hours of practice for each minute of dealing death, an inordinately disproportionate ratio. Seventeen years of training for two seasons of combat that distilled down to fourteen definitive encounters—fights to the finish—which lasted a grand total of, perhaps, at most, thirty minutes. His lifetime—forty years—for half an hour of glory.

On each subsequent mission he risked everything. His first loss could be his final loss.

He hated his thoughts during his MiG famine.

In that period, Cy Allen frequently "went to the movies." The 8th TFW scored seven kills in May. Late at night when he couldn't sleep despite the booze and wasn't flying the following day, he walked to Photo Intell and reviewed gun camera photography of the latest kills. Alone, he ran the short film strips dozens of times and often caught himself talking to himself ("Yep, Cy, that's what a MiG looks like. That's a MiG all right.") or offering advice aloud ("You got him. What are you waiting for? Fire!"). None of that shit was healthy, he knew; however, the sight of enemy aircraft being destroyed satisfied some basic need, sick or not.

In a similar fashion, he "broadened his reading" by reviewing every USAF after-action report that the 8th TFW Intelligence section received. There was something to be gained by knowing how other pilots performed. He recognized most of the details that were imprinted on men's minds in the heat of an engagement, and he found amusement in the unconscious humor that emerged when the men related those details to a debriefer. Many lines leaped out at him:

    . . . the MiGs popped up out of the clouds. Unfortunately the first one to pop through came up at my six o'clock position.

. . . we were about Mach 1.4 with the MiG about as fast, in afterburner. I was low on him and believe he was unaware he was under attack.

The MiG jock had a terminal case of tunnel vision as he bored in on the EB-66 without checking behind him.

I pulled in deep at six, descended to two thou to get a good look-up angle for the radar, then placed the pipper on the trailing MiG at two miles—ten degrees off-angle, five hundred fifty knots, two G's—and used auto-acquisition to get a full-system radar lock on.

The missile started guiding in a corkscrew manner, then straightened out, made a small correction to the left then to the right, and, from there, guided straight away with just a little flutter.

The MiG then went into a series of frantic turns, some so violent that the aircraft snap-rolled in the opposite direction.

It was beautiful. The MiG was diving toward the ground with flames coming out of its tailpipe. It wasn't afterburner. He was on fire. Right behind him was that great, great, huge Thud with fire breathing out its nose. It looked like a shark chasing a minnow.

. . . two large balls of flame exited the MiG's tailpipe.

I noted a gray cloud of smoke, tinged with pink.

The smoke looked like taffy streaming from the rear of the MiG.

. . . a brilliant white fire streaming from the left side of his fuselage. It looked like magnesium burning, with particles flaking off.

The MiG-21 erupted in a brilliant flash of orange flames. As the wing fell off, the MiG swapped ends and stalled out.

The MiG seemed to blow up on the spot. The second missile powdered it and it broke into many disorganized pieces.

. . . a large reddish-yellow fireball that sustained itself for several seconds while trailing sparks behind it. The entire fire pattern was about two hundred feet long.

I then turned back left and observed another MiG-17 with no left wing in a nose-down snapping spin. The left wing was about fifteen hundred feet above the MiG and slowly tumbling downward.

. . . I saw debris and a man in the air.

. . . a man hanging in a bright orange and white parachute of a square pattern.

. . . saw a yellow chute go by.

There was a yellow canopy . . .

. . . a dirty yellow parachute . . .

. . . a pastel orange parachute . . .

The MiG impacted the ground in what appeared to be a rice field. He spread in flames across a large area.

The after-action reports also included descriptions of friendly losses:

Two called, "They're shooting," and seconds later his aircraft was on fire. I saw him crash about a mile from the target. No parachute.

. . . we lost sight of the MiG-21 and, a moment later, an F-105 got hit with an air-to-air missile. The pilot ejected.

I felt and heard the SAM hit Lead as much as I actually saw it. There was this awesome "thud," like nothing I ever felt before. Then there were two clouds:

a brown one, and a yellow one that turned into a fireball and kept getting bigger and bigger. Lead yawed hard right, flew through the fireball, and emerged as if nothing had happened. Then I saw his aft end was burning and pieces were peeling away. He slowed down and went into a flat spin. I saw one parachute.

Survivors also reported:

. . . we were hit by a missile and immediately went out of control, flopping from side to side. Fire started coming in the back of the cockpit. It seared my canopy with bubbles and I couldn't see anymore. The airplane slowed down and went into what felt like a slow spiral to the right.

. . . felt as if the entire aircraft was on fire. It was bucking violently. The control stick was rotating in a circular motion. I assumed we were totally out of control and I ejected.

The gun camera photography and after-battle reports constituted the proof of a world unseen by the average man, of a blood sport in which few participated and in which even fewer gained fame. Allen was humbled and felt privileged to be part of it. For the first time, he was on the fringe rather than at the center.

During May, Rocco Monge had scored another victory, nothing spectacular. He caught up to the MiG whose pilot obviously wanted nothing to do with an exchange and blew it to bits. There was no doubt that it was a valid kill. The Fresco pilot ejected before Monge fired; to be exact, he went out as soon as

Monge pulled within range. Both planes were deep into the buffer zone along the Chinese border by that time. Rocco admitted it to Allen: "We were gaining slow but sure and I guess we weren't paying too much attention to navigation. After we nailed him, I got a fix . . . Well, shit, you know."

Rocco also hadn't been paying too much attention to the airborne radar early warning station, an EC-121 Constellation which had been orbiting over the Gulf of Tonkin. The EC-121 controllers supposedly alerted U.S. aircraft to MiG threats; more often, they monitored U.S. aircraft to ensure they did not violate off-limits airspaces. While chasing the MiG, Rocco switched off his IFF and nullified the EC-121 controllers' ability to identify his aircraft. The controllers saw Rocco's code disappear from their scopes but they continued to skin paint his airplane with scan radar. They saw he was in hot pursuit and understood what was happening.

They screamed their lungs out: asked him to recycle IFF, told him to squawk ID, demanded that he alter heading for positive identification, and finally ordered him to reverse course. They might as well have been shouting in a vacuum. Rocco never answered. He blew up the MiG, silently came about, and sped to a tanker.

In his after-action report Rocco stated, "So Goliath killed David. What else is new?" He declared temporary IFF and radio failure. It didn't sell. The entire time, his wingman had been tooling along behind, covering him against bandits.

Rocco took a light ass-chewing from the director of operations. When the colonel who ran Intelligence jumped on his case, Rocco dismissed the whole thing as stupid because that non-rated weenie wasn't in the chain of command. He walked off and left the man talking to himself.

Monge was eleven missions ahead of Allen, nearing the end of his tour. The victory was his third. Gun camera film had confirmed his second which nobody witnessed. He had scored his first on that January morning when their squadron killed four. Rocco explained his current attitude to Allen. "I don't care any longer. This is my last trip over here. If they want to, they can court-martial me. I don't think they will. They know the rules suck. Anyhow, I'm too close to finishing. But they're welcome to. They won't be getting a virgin. You know, I didn't go into China—I think. I guess they could take the squadron away from me. . . . So I don't make full colonel . . . I can live on what a retired LC gets paid—I think."

That night's celebration at the O-Club was marred by the new wing commander's ambivalence: pleased that Rocco scored the victory, he was unhappy because he had to answer to higher headquarters for one of his men's obvious lack of self-discipline, and a squadron commander to boot. With several belts under his belt, he told Rocco, "Tomorrow morning. Oh-seven-hundred *sharp*. Be in my office. We'll settle this once and for all."

Rocco made it to bed around four but, like a good soldier, rolled out at six-thirty. He leaped under a cold shower before putting on a sharply creased uniform, the first time since arriving at Ubon that he had gone to work in anything but a flying suit. A ten-minute walk halfway across base didn't help his head or humor. As usual, he stopped outside the wing headquarters building and admired the wooden red stars nailed above the portico. From habit, he counted them: twenty-two. The one representing his kill from the previous day was up there, he noted. He couldn't be in too much trouble, he hoped.

Adhering to the Air Force adage that "If you're not five minutes early, you're late," Rocco walked into the wing commander's outer office at five minutes to seven. Nobody was there.

Rocco sat and nodded through a hangover. At five after seven he peeked into the commander's office, just to be on the safe side. It too was empty. He remembered the old college rules: a person waited five minutes for an associate professor, ten minutes for a full professor, fifteen minutes for a doctor. How long did a lieutenant colonel wait for a wing commander? The answer was obvious: forever.

At seven-fifteen the commander's secretary arrived: "Colonel Monge! What are you doing here this early? And so dressed up?" She made a pot of coffee and Rocco considered prostrating himself at her feet in gratitude. At seven twenty-five the rest of the staff arrived.

Rocco was slouched in a corner, nodding, sipping coffee, when the wing commander strode through the door at quarter to eight and pleasantly greeted his secretary. Upon seeing Rocco, a glimmer of surprise lighted his eyes. Without another word, he entered his office. A few minutes later, the secretary answered the interphone's buzz, then called to Rocco, "The commander wants you, colonel."

At Ubon, walking in to see the wing commander was like walking that last mile to the electric chair. The man's office was fifty feet long. The wall to the left was teak paneled. The wall to the right was a series of picture windows that looked onto the flightline. Immediately inside the door and to the right was an average-sized desk manned by the Director of Operations who sat with his back to the windows. Rocco smiled weakly at the bird colonel seated there; the bird winked in reply.

Then Rocco made the trek across the highly polished teakwood floor leading to the massive teakwood desk from behind which the wing commander ruled. Like going to see the viceroy, Rocco thought. His black rubber heels squeaked against the spotless wood and he hoped he wasn't leaving a trail of scuff marks. Halting five feet from the desk, he saluted stiffly. The commander made him hold the salute for several seconds, then answered by quickly touching his forehead above the right eyebrow.

Drawing himself upright, the commander frowned, scowled, glowered, huffed and puffed, played his role to the limit.

The act was wasted on Rocco who already had been defeated by his hangover. Furthermore, Rocco was standing at attention and, as the drill manual described, focused somewhere in the distance.

Sensing that he wasn't getting through, the commander hit his desktop with a fist, glowered anew, then slammed the desk again. "What do you have to report?" he shouted. Another hit: Thump. "Don't just stand there . . ." A harder hit: THUMP. ". . . tell me something." THUMP-THUMP.

Rocco Monge inhaled deeply. Waiting had been enough punishment. Without the coffee he would have died. Now the desk-pounding made his head throb in a different quadrant. He said the thing foremost in his mind: "Tell you something? Do you know you were forty-five minutes late?"

The wing commander's jaw dropped.

At the other end of the room, the DO grinned. Realizing what he had said, Rocco groaned loudly, bowed his head in shame. The loud groan finished the DO: he laughed and fled the room.

Following that the commander discussed the problem in an adult-to-adult manner. Rocco made no excuse, admitted he was wrong, accepted his punishment. What did he care? He killed the MiG. Nobody could take that from the squadron. Rocco ended up with a letter of reprimand that went into his personnel records for a year.

Cy Allen didn't even share the thrill of victory that resulted in May when the United States government declared MiG airfields to be valid targets, on a controlled basis. Twenty-four MiGs were destroyed on the ground, blasted to pieces by the bombs of F-105s. In a series of closely coordinated attacks, follow-on forces raced in behind departing strike forces and caught the MiGs on the ground while refueling between sorties.

From a MiGCAP position, Cy watched enviously. Planes destroyed on the ground counted for nothing toward becoming an ace, but he would have enjoyed wasting his share just for the sake of killing something.

20

On the first day of June, Allen spotted a pair of
MiG-21s from above. He sagged with relief. Then,
before Dobbs located them on radar, he lost them
beneath a cloud deck.

In desperation he took his wingman down to
search. Racing aimlessly along a valley, he cursed
himself for losing sight of the enemy. "Two, watch
six," he snapped at Junior Eliot. "Jer, keep a sharp eye
for SAMs." He popped up high enough to scan the
other sides of the mountains bordering the valley
and—sparks touched his heart—to his left was a
MiG.

An F-4 was on the MiG's tail but wasn't firing. The
two planes were jinking. From an off-angle Cy joined
the chase. He was behind the other Phantom but well
to the side of it. He banked slightly left and lined up
on the enemy plane. All of his switches were set and
he got a growl in his earphones which indicated that a
Sidewinder had locked on to something. The MiG
looked like the only hot spot ahead of him. He made a
fast visual check to ensure that the other Phantom

hadn't crept nearer and somehow entered his field of fire.

The moment he looked back at the MiG, the enemy pilot ceased evasive maneuvering and lined up with the runway at Kep. The MiG pilot obviously hadn't heard the latest word, probably still thought that if he landed, got on the ground, he would be safe: the American government's rules would protect him.

Cy didn't agree with the tactic: it was a stupid move even if the old rules applied. The MiG couldn't get down fast enough, couldn't outrace a missile. "Asshole," he muttered and fired a Sidewinder.

A microsecond later a missile streaked from the other Phantom.

The airborne MiG was dead. The only question was which missile would arrive first.

Cy didn't have the straight shot. His missile arced slightly left and, in so doing, lost the microsecond advantage of launching first. There was a moment in which he feared that his curving Sidewinder had altered its choice and now intended to knock down the other F-4's missile. Then it didn't matter.

The two missiles reached the MiG-21 simultaneously, tried to squeeze into its tailpipe together, detonated and tore off the empennage and fuselage all the way forward to the trailing edge of the wings. What remained of the fighter pancaked onto the threshold of the runway—Splat!—and exploded—Blam!

"Holy shit," Junior Eliot said from the wingman position, "I don't fucking believe it."

The three Phantoms pulled tightly together, echeloned right, and made a low-level flyby down the length of the runway at Kep, acted like it was an Armed Forces Day demonstration. At that point Allen recognized that Rocco Monge was flying the other shooter.

Without discussing it beforehand and while talking to different debriefers, Monge and Allen each claimed the MiG on behalf of the other. By then Junior Eliot had told the base what had happened. He called it the dead heat to end all dead heats, the perfect photo finish. After his account no other story could be circulated without raising suspicion.

At the debriefing, Rocco heard Allen giving him credit for the victory and said, "Wait a minute. I think your missile got there first. Honest."

"I don't agree, Roc."

"If you take it, that's five. That's it."

"With a big asterisk."

"Oh, Colonel Cy," Dobbs said, "take the fucker. You got one coming from—"

"Horseshit, Jerry. That one has nothing to do with this one." They weren't balancing a bank account, he thought. Goddamnit, why had he wasted seconds in clearing his field of fire? He hadn't had a choice, he realized and considered how distressed he would be if he had accidentally hit Rocco. He couldn't've lived with that.

"Dobbs's right," Rocco said. "It's your kill. What's fair is fair."

"Rocco, don't give me that. Life's not fair. You know that." Be cool, Allen told himself. It wasn't Rocco's fault that things worked out the way they did. Cy wanted to end the discussion, feared that from the depth of his disappointment he would say something that would alienate his friends. Allen spoke calmly: "Look, I'm not taking the fucking thing. I don't want five that way. I don't want bullshit from anyone, ever."

Rocco understood. The man didn't want doubt to mar his feat. In Rocco's mind, Babe Ruth hit sixty homers in a season and that still was tops; Roger Maris' sixty-one were forever tainted by additional games. It was the same thing here. But there was another angle too. "Cy, if I take the fucker, then luck out and get another, I'm in the same boat."

"Not if you get the fifth one clean. That's the one that matters." Allen reached across the debriefing table and crumpled Rocco's debriefing form. "Don't give it to me. Please." He stood. "I don't want to talk about this anymore."

However, the wing commander arrived at that moment, just in time to stick his nose into the debate. He wanted a decision, a clean-cut verdict. Rocco already was on the wing commander's shitlist and didn't help matters by telling him, "With all due respect, sir, let's let the Intell weenies sort it out. They'll probably be a hundred percent wrong but they'll be emphatic as hell. Cy and I'll be at the club when the pictures are ready."

The gun camera photography settled it. The two short film strips were mirror images of each other. On Monge's, his missile was halfway home when another streaked in from the right; on Allen's, his missile was halfway home when another streaked in from the left.

The Photo Intell experts synchronized and ran both strips simultaneously, stopped action frame by frame, and took an hour to critique what in reality lasted a few seconds. When all was said and done, the best the photo experts came up with was a tie.

Junior Eliot shouted, "I said that three fucking hours ago."

"A tie is a tie is a tie," said Cy Allen.

"Like kissing your aunt," Rocco said.

Junior corrected him: "Sister."

"No way," Rocco said. "That's incest."

The three pilots were half in the bag by then.

"Where's Dobbs?" Allen asked.

"He and Wiltrout and Slevin left after the first showing," Junior said. "They listened to me. I called it a tie the second it happened."

The decision stood up. It meant that Allen and Monge split the credit for the kill, an old Air Force custom. They had contributed equally to the destruction of the enemy aircraft. According to regulations, there was no other way to log it. Allen had four and a half MiGs; Monge, three and a half.

Back at the O-Club Rocco said, "I didn't see you over there to the right. Honest. Didn't see you until after I fired. If I had known . . ." He spread his arms in a gesture of hospitality.

Cy nodded: "One more second . . ."

Rocco laughed: "That's what *she* said."

"After the MiG splashed, Jerry pointed out that *you* made a pretty fat target on radar."

"Big. Not fat," said Rocco. "Shouldn't've told me. Now we know to watch out."

Seventeen missions left to do it, Allen thought. Rocco was down to six.

The party didn't last all night.

Dobbs wrote the details of the half victory to his father.

He remembered how his father used to preach that the military existed for the benefit of commissioned officers—the same as hospitals were for the benefit of doctors, courts for lawyers, and insurance companies for salesmen—despite the hoopla about serving the nation.

Dobbs told his father:

You deserved to watch the gymnastics that went on while the staff tried to decide who should get credit for the MiG. The way everybody was arguing made me wonder what this war was really all about.

A while back I said to Colonel Allen that destroying the target is all that counts and it doesn't matter if anyone gets credit. He gave me a lecture about glory. I guess I should have known better. I've decided that the Air Force is for the benefit of pilots. And Colonel Allen is the ultimate pilot.

He is in extreme heat over a fifth MiG. He wants it so badly that I'm afraid he's going to do something really crazy. More than that, I believe he wants to get it alone. I mean without my help. I had a radar lock-on during the attack and I didn't tell him so that he had a chance to shoot a Sidewinder—the *pilot's* missile. Sometimes I wish I didn't have to go fly with him. He'd be happier alone.

Now I'm sorry I didn't speak up when I had the lock-on. I honestly believe that if we'd used the Sparrow we'd have shot down the MiG before Colonel Monge had a chance to fire. Colonel Cy hesitated way too long. I could hear the Sidewinder growling, ready for launch, and he kept on doing all kinds of unnecessary things. I don't know if he was slow because of nerves or tension or reflexes or what.

I hate to tell you but Colonel Cy has been drinking a lot lately and that scares me too. I don't mind if he gets drunk when we're celebrating, but now he gets smashed every night, for no reason.

We have seventeen missions to go and that will be enough for me, one way or the other. At this point I kind of wish the magic number was ninety.

Dobbs signed the letter, "Your loving son, Jeffrey Debbs." While addressing the envelope he had a fleeting vision of Rocco shooting down a pair of MiGs, reaching five first. The mental picture gave

Dobbs a perverted thrill, as if he found enjoyment in another person's agony. After all, wasn't Colonel Cy making far too big a deal out of becoming the first ace? Wasn't Rocco equally deserving? In fact, wouldn't he make a worthier hero? Was that the way he should feel? Wasn't he being disloyal?

He wanted to ask Cy: "Can't you measure success in another way?" But then he decided that such a question was not the type a lieutenant navigator asked a lieutenant colonel pilot.

21

No normal course of events could result in the misfortune he had encountered in his quest for five MiGs, Allen thought. Somewhere in heaven the gods were having a rollicking, back-slapping good time at his expense. They were dangling him on strings that threatened to hang him.

He decided to take a few days off to get his bearings. He hadn't seen Pensy for nearly a week. Thinking he would surprise her, Allen went to the bungalow shortly after noon only to find her not there. He established a routine that he repeated for three days: arrive at the bungalow in the afternoon, sit around for several hours, sip bourbon and let his dissatisfaction toy with his emotions, then leave in anger when Pensy didn't show.

On the third day, Bau who was their teenage housegirl ran after him, bowed low before him in the middle of the street and said, "Pensy other room. I get." She ran off toward Ubon.

Cy drew one swift conclusion: Pensy was sharing her time (or was it his time?) with somebody else. Cuckold, he thought and felt pierced by the stares of

262

every stranger on the street, instantly believed that everyone in Warin had known of the situation except him. Another lover was the reason Pensy had stashed him out of sight in Warin, he decided. Her excuse about lower rent had been a fabrication.

Feeling disappointed more than angry, duped rather than betrayed, he didn't wait for either woman to return.

If he had confronted her, Pensy might have confessed to such manipulations. In the past, in separate bungalows, she had simultaneously served daytime and nighttime husbands, pilot lovers from Night Owl and Triple Nickel. The tactic was a necessity. By overlapping lovers, she avoided being left alone—and subsequently without income—when one man ended his tour of duty. But she had not behaved that way with Cy. She had been alone when she met him and she had intended to remain alone until after he departed. But didn't she subconsciously hope to depart with him? Wasn't that the reason she had played it straight? Would he have believed her?

The next day Cy went to the bungalow at the normal time. He was prepared to end the arrangement.

Pensy was there, greeted him with a tired smile, paced jerkily about the living room, kept asking, "How you?"

He judged her nervousness to be an admission of guilt.

Then she told him that he had made her pregnant and he found himself adrift in an ethereal void between belief and disbelief, between responsibility and unconcern. His sense of morality seemed to expand and to come untethered in the same instant, as if it were a rapidly inflating hot air balloon straining to escape society's pull. The idea of conception pumped new life into his withering spirit.

Paradoxically the lift of new life set his spirit free, set his flimsy morality adrift as if it were floating beyond his grasp. Was this a test? Not a test of his concern for Pensy, he thought, but a test of his relationship with the future. He tried to see a way in which the problem (or was it a solution?) related to another MiG. Wasn't a life or death quotient contained within the situation?

Then he wondered how Pensy could be certain the baby was his. How could he be certain there was a baby?

Suddenly, surprisingly, truth didn't matter to him. He saw that literal interpretations of events had prevented him from reaching his goal. In his case, the truth wasn't the truth. Without the strictures of unflinching truth he now would be the war's first ace. Truth was his enemy.

"Maybe I have baby," Pensy said.

"If that's what you want," Cy told her, "it's all right with me."

"Yeah? Who take care of it?"

"I will." His words rang like a pledge. "I'll take it back to the States."

"What about baby's mother? You take her too?" It was Pensy's best shot. After firing it, she ran into the bedroom.

The shot ruptured Cy's balloon. Everything fell earthward with Cy strangling in the cables, strangling in his own words. Silently he followed her, shaking his head. He was untrained for this type of combat.

She was waiting, knew what his answer would be: "See? Maybe you change mind, not take baby too."

She had thought through the problem, Cy realized. Was the situation beyond his control? Was his whole life beyond his control? He said, "If it's my child, I'm willing to take it."

Pensy's eyes widened, her nostrils flared: "What you mean? Sure, is your child." Her mouth turned down: "See? You no want either."

Cy felt as if he had been attacked from blind six, had been hit before he saw a threat. His whole world seemed aflame, about to fall in ruins. Pensy was right, however. He was not prepared to become a father again. He had enough children. He was too old. How would he explain a Thai brother or sister to his sons? People would laugh at him. And yet, if she was telling the truth (as much as he desired to ignore it, the truth remained inescapable), she had a life inside of her that was part of him. "What's one more life?" a cynical voice within his mind asked.

Pensy glared at him: "Maybe I have and I keep. Then what—coal-nell?"

Trapped, he said, "Do you want the baby?" He couldn't believe she wanted the burden of a child.

She turned her back to him: "What you know. How come you take baby United States but no take mama?"

Was there no end to his dilemmas? He had enough on his mind. This was too much. "Goddamnit, I don't need this," he said. Should he ask her to get rid of the baby?

Pensy turned and squinted at him: "Why you goddamn? You no want baby? Maybe I have, give to Bau. She know is your baby. She call it superbaby, coal-nell flyer's baby. She say, 'You no want, I take.'"

"Give it to Bau," he said deflatedly. "Give it to anyone." The words seemed to come from another person. Inwardly he did not believe she was pregnant. And yet he was suffocating in a self-created moral vacuum. How had he arrived there? Where had he crashed? He felt isolated, so beyond reach that his plight became laughable. "I don't care," he said.

Didn't he have more important concerns? He felt the ironical certitude of a man about to be hanged from a gallows of his own design. "Send it to Uncle Ho." His life and thoughts were out of balance.

"See? You no care about nothing. You just want kill. Have no heart!"

No heart? Her words struck with the authority of antiaircraft fire. He never had thought of himself shaped like that, without a heart. What did she mean?

"You go Vietnam, how many people you kill? Some my family live in Vietnam."

Was it true? Was she part Vietnamese? Cy didn't know. He had listened to her stories without recording them, had stored no details of her life in his mind's memory bank. She was as much a specter, a shadow without substance, as the pilot bodies he saw in the MiGs over North Vietnam. He heard himself say, "We don't kill anyone over there . . ." He laughed because the statement was so transparently false. ". . . deliberately."

"You just give massage with bombs," Pensy said. She threw herself across their king-size bed, clutched her stomach.

The argument was absurd, Cy thought, beyond belief. His whole world seemed insane. Dropping onto the bed, he roughly wrapped Pensy in his arms and legs. She made a sour face and struggled weakly for a few moments. Quietly he said, "The only family you have in Vietnam are the monkeys in the trees." He hooted softly.

"Not so," she whispered.

Cy continued hooting and, recognizing that she wouldn't try to escape (her body felt as limp as his spirit), he freed a hand and picked through her hair as if preening her. Was he mad?

After a time she said, "You monkey," and gave him a smile of resignation and defeat.

He silently accepted blame for their shame. Unconsciously rubbing his nose along her neck, he inhaled her fragrance, found that a harshly civilized metallic bite had invaded her flowery jungle aroma. Clasping her tightly, he wished that she would cry so that he could join her, let their tears mingle.

She said, "You never take me United States."

Cy thought of his sons. Of Clare. "Right," he said, "never."

"What about baby?"

"Is there a baby?"

"What you think?"

He paused: his magnificent eyes could not see across the inches that separated them. His mind was keyed to recognize only deception. He studied Pensy's face and then shook his head: "No."

"You wrong," she said.

"Then whatever you do is up to you." Had he ever had answers to problems that involved the women in his life, or had he accepted the courses of action they chose?

Pensy lowered her eyes, then lowered her head, nested against his chest. She sighed deeply. In a voice he barely heard, she said, "I need money for hospital, for doctor."

Pensy said she would be gone for a week, perhaps ten days. She took the train out of Warin Chamrap, sat upright in a day coach during the twelve-hour ride to Bangkok, checked in at the Chulalongkorn Hospital, underwent dilation and curettage. In the recovery ward she listened to taped lectures that explained how to avoid future pregnancy. The postpartum program tapes were played over public address loudspeakers so that everyone in the ward, both women in her category and women who had birthed full-term babies, had no choice but to listen. Conversation was forbidden while the tapes were playing.

The abortion was Pensy's second. The first had been performed in Ubon by a furtive Chinese midwife who had forced Pensy to miscarry by filling her with a solution of plant extracts, herbs, honey, gin, and cayenne. Pensy had been sick for weeks; afterward, had felt unclean for months. The Chinese woman had ministered only on nights when the moon was visible, had made Pensy hold the fetus during a ritual designed to prevent another unwanted pregnancy. Pensy's hands would forever remember the fetus' dead reptilian texture.

After the first pregnancy, for a time Pensy had dreamed of an extra soul trapped within her: a child crouched inside her chest, played with sticks and stones as toys, much as she once had done. If she did not bear a live child, would the soul remain in the limbo of her body until she died? Then would it be set free as a mate with her own soul? Pensy's doubts created a question of wondrous proportion: Was that the manner in which twins formed?

Even before the miscarriage she had worried about the extra soul within her. Was the transmigratory voyager bound upward or downward? The economic quadrant of her mind had said that an American child—even a child who was half American—had to be rising toward Nirvana. But her mind's psychosocial quadrant had declared such a child to be a mongrel (less than a true Thai, it would be less than a true Buddhist) and therefore headed downward.

Occasionally Pensy still wondered if the extra soul

had departed her body or waited inside for another opportunity.

Pensy had fewer reservations about the second abortion. The staff members of Chulalongkorn Hospital overwhelmingly sanctioned her decision, made her feel that her action had social acceptance and government approval. The head nurse granted her a free night of rest in a hospital bed before the long train trip back to Warin. A second doctor gently counseled her about a future visit to the hospital in order to be fitted for an intrauterine device.

During the return trip Pensy stopped at her parents' home outside of Sisaket, rested for several days. In all, she was away from Cy for exactly one week.

At Warin, the bungalow owner told Pensy that Cy had paid the rent for three months in advance. Bau said that she too had received wages for three months.

Pensy lived exclusively at the bungalow during the next ten days.

Cy did not return.

22

On June Sixth, the MiGs departed North Vietnam, left completely, flew off to China or elsewhere. After losing twenty-six MiGs in the air and twenty-four on the ground in a period of thirty-six days, the Chinese and Russian advisors probably suggested that all pilots be given additional training. It was the normal course of action when their puppets suffered heavy losses. The same thing had happened in Korea. And it had happened before in Vietnam.

In February 1967 the United States had suspended bombing for six days in observance of Tet, the Lunar New Year. When bombing resumed, the MiGs were kept on the ground for the remainder of the month. February had passed without a MiG being destroyed. An Intelligence briefer reminded the USAF crews that the NVAF also had been grounded from July 1965 to April 1966. Nine months! Allen's heart shifted into low gear. With a month of flying remaining, he had a single question: How long would the present MiG stand-down continue?

To compensate for the loss of its MiG fleet, North Vietnam continued to increase the number and manning of its AAA and SAM sites. USAF Intelligence reported that defenses now consisted of seven thousand antiaircraft guns (23-mm and larger) and one hundred seventy SAM complexes. Many pilots had believed that the flak could get no thicker. They were wrong. And SAM sightings doubled.

Meanwhile, the number of bombing missions had been stepped up. The U.S. government removed more targets from the restricted list. As one American four-star general told a Senate subcommittee: "For all practical purposes, we have driven the MiGs out of the sky." In the eyes of the narrow-minded, the USAF was unopposed in its effort to "destroy the North's ability to support operations against South Vietnam."

After a week, MiGs ventured down from China on training flights and practiced Ground Controlled Intercepts. GCI was a five-step procedure. First came the *scramble* which, in this case, got the MiGs off the ground and to altitude. Second was *positioning* which vectored the MiGs to the targets so that they arrived at an advantageous spot. In classic dogfighting, the best position was high and diving out of the sun. The third step was *transition:* speed and altitude were adjusted as necessary for the *attack,* step four. The attack consisted of four maneuvers: turn to attack heading, acquisition of target, firing pass, and turn to escape heading. The fifth and final GCI step was *recovery* of the MiG to a safe airfield.

The MiG-17 practice intercept runs were unfinished snap-up maneuvers. The fighters approached the strike force at low level and extremely high speed, climbed quickly, but while still beyond firing range executed a hard breakaway and fled. The MiG-21 practice intercepts were normal high-altitude, high-airspeed approaches filled with energy for wham-bam hit-and-run passes. Because all MiGs broke off the GCI maneuvers prior to the firing pass, they posed no threat to the strike force.

On the day it was confirmed that the MiGs had departed North Vietnam, MiGCAP flights were canceled. All F-4s that went North had their pylons loaded with bombs. In the fuselage well, they carried four Sparrows, just in case. If the strike force was challenged by MiGs, the F-4 pilots were briefed to jettison the bombs and engage.

The change resulted in Rocco Monge finishing his combat tour as a bomber pilot. He didn't mind the transition in his squadron's role, but he was angered by the manner in which he received the information. A full colonel from the targeting shop at Seventh Air Force telephoned him and said, "It looks like the Wolfpack's glory and glamour have come to an end." The colonel pronounced the words spitefully, in a voice filled with unsuppressed glee.

Earlier in the year, with one phone call Rocco had made the man an enemy by questioning Seventh's wisdom in sending the same crews to the same targets along the same route at the same time day after day after day. In his estimation, the element of surprise had been forgotten by the planners. After a particularly bloody morning in which the strike force ate several waves of MiGs, dozens of SAMs, and tons of AAA rounds while traveling the route it had traveled all week, Rocco telephoned the colonel and said, "My five-year-old nephew would have your tactics figured out by now." He spoke on behalf of the F-105 drivers who were far more vulnerable than the MiGCAP crews. It was his opinion that the Thud drivers were taking unnecessary hosings.

The colonel was infuriated by having his judgment questioned: "You fighter pukes think you run this war, think you run the Air Force. I'm telling you, you don't! Targeting is our business. Your job is to fly what we tell you. We have information you don't have. We know things you don't know. We . . ." Rocco recognized the personality type: insecure. He tuned out the voice and, seconds later while the colonel was still talking, decided that he had initiated the call and therefore had the option to terminate it: Rocco gently hung up the receiver. The colonel called back immediately. Rocco put the phone in a desk drawer and let it ring continuously for half the day without answering.

Now, the colonel was off again. "From this day, you MiG-killers are nothing but bomber pilots," he said gloatingly. "And don't you forget it. Let's see how many headlines you get now. You'll go where *I* send you. Is that clear?" When Rocco didn't answer, the colonel said, "You better not hang up."

Rocco calmly said, "Sir, I finish my tour in about a week. I want to return to my family as much as anyone. But, I'm telling you, sir, I'm detouring through Saigon on my way home. If I find you, I'm going to break your fucking neck with my bare hands. And I'm big enough to do it, sir. You don't belong on our side." Then Rocco quietly placed the phone inside a drawer.

Rocco did detour through Tan Son Nhut. The colonel was "somewhere up-country on an inspection tour" according to his assistant. Rocco phoned Allen from Saigon: "I can't find that piece of shit. I thought about leaving a log in his desk but knew he'd make some poor airman clean it out. The same with wetting down his room. His housegirl would get stuck with cleaning up." Rocco lowered his voice, grew confidential: "I checked his personnel file. What I'm going to do—when I get to the States—I'm going to kill his wife and kids."

Cy was stunned. "Hey—a—wait—wait a minute." Had the Roc completely flipped? "I—I wouldn't—ah —hey, look . . ."

Rocco's laughter nearly burst Allen's eardrum. "You may be the best flyer," Rocco yelled, "but you're sure not the fastest thinker." He laughed again. "You know me better than that." He chuckled. "That's one on you, Cy. All I know is that it's a small Air Force. Someday, somewhere, I'll find that turd."

"And flush him."

"You bet. Good luck, guy."

Rocco's hundredth mission over North Vietnam was another flight through a rather impressive array of fireworks. Cy flew his wing. Their target was Gia Lam airfield, on the edge of Hanoi. Rocco was as relaxed as if they were headed downtown to Ubon Ratchathani. "At last, I'm going to bomb a MiG base legally," he said. Diving through the flak on the bomb run, he observed, "You'd think the Russkies and Chinks would get tired of paying for all this."

Gia Lam already was cratered by Thud-delivered three-thousand-pounders dropped on previous strikes. Even with the MiGs away, it was satisfying to plaster their home. Cy imagined how much better it would be with MiGs trapped on the ground. Then he felt duped: Why hadn't they done this during all those months when the MiGs were home?

The day's effort was one of those miracle missions: nobody in the strike force got hit.

Rocco had told Allen that if anything came anywhere near them, he was going to take a shot at it. They had been tail-end Charlies en route to the target.

Leaving the area, Rocco insisted on swapping positions: "You lead. I had my chance inbound. You see anything, shoot. If there's time, I'll shoot too." They fell behind the rest of the formation. Sure enough, a pair of MiG-21s appeared high and far away. Allen saw them first: "Bandits. Two o'clock, high."

He watched the MiGs roll into their dive and then he banked sharply toward them and lit burners. Seconds later, the MiGs racked into a steep turn away from him. The range looked impossible, at least four miles. When he rolled out, he was lined up nicely, however: "Lock? In range?" He recalled reading or hearing that the missiles would travel ten miles.

"Negative," Dobbs said.

Rocco said, "Take a shot at the sons-a-bitches."

Dobbs laughed.

Without another thought, Allen squeezed the trigger four times. Three Sparrows flew from the Phantom. The other emerged stillborn from the well and fell to earth. There was hope in Allen's heart that some power greater than he would fly the missiles to their maximum range and have them destroy one of the targets. His mind, however, recognized the reality of what he had done: the missiles were merely unguided projectiles that already were scattering and falling below the flight altitude of the MiG-21s. Dumb, he thought. He had wasted the weapons.

Rocco said, "Nothing ventured." Continuing to accelerate he fired his Sparrows. Four launched and scattered. "There go a dozen Cadillacs," he said. "I hope they at least start a forest fire or something. Tough shit, world."

They were the last two on the post-strike tankers. Dropping off the boom, Rocco said, "Let's jog down, take one more look at Laos." Turning left, they headed southeast over the Laotian panhandle. A few

minutes later, the two F-4s were the only aircraft in
the sky. Rocco dipped below Allen's airplane and
called, "You're clean. No ord hanging."

"Affirmative. Thanks."

Rocco slid out wide, then slipped back high. "How
do I look?"

"Clean."

Rocco moved far to the side and lagged behind.

Allen was irritated by what he considered a lot of
unnecessary maneuvering. "What the hell's he gonna
do next? Keep a sharp eye on him, Jer." He thought
they had headed over Laos to sightsee.

"I think one of my throttles may be jammed,"
Rocco said. There was no concern in his voice. "I'm
going to back off, get behind you, and . . ."

The words ". . . get behind you . . ." rang Allen's
bell.

Rocco had intended to say, ". . . and chase your ass
all over the sky." He got out ". . . chase your ass . . ."
when Allen broke back and into him, hard. Really
fucking hard! Thin contrails arced off his wingtips
before he zipped under Rocco who also broke back,
but not quite as hard. Trying for a scissors, Rocco
mistimed his reversal and went by the other fighter.
Without time for an "Oh shit," Rocco broke this way
and that way, did it all, worked his ass off, and when it
was over Allen was locked on his tail like he was a
bitch in heat. Rocco didn't know exactly how he had
arrived where he was.

"We're leading the parade," Wiltrout complained.
"What the fuck, how did he do that to us?"

When Allen initially broke into Rocco, he hadn't
bothered to warn Dobbs who was wondering if Rocco
intended to rat race when he said, ". . . chase your
ass . . ." Before Dobbs had time to ask or to think or
to brace or to flex, Allen abruptly tore back the stick

and they were off. Tremendous, unexpected G-forces smacked Dobbs and his vision went from normal to black. Allen scored a clean knockout on his back-seater. Moments later Dobbs came to and was more frightened than he ever had been in an airplane. His stomach was trying to squeeze through his asshole. His balls weighed fifty pounds each. How the fuck had the Phantom's wings stayed on, he wondered.

They were in a dive. Directly in front of them, in an effort to get Allen off his tail, Monge was scissoring and barrel-rolling and striking attitudes that Dobbs didn't recognize. The two jets went through five thousand feet and Dobbs decided that his life was about to end. At their speed and dive angle, he saw no way they could avoid hitting the ground. An obituary line, "Lieutenant Dobbs was twenty-four," passed through his brain.

Rocco chopped power and jerked up his airplane's nose at the same time speed brakes popped out from the Phantom's gray belly. The jet fighter pancaked, mushed, shuddered in flight. Rocco had gambled on an overshoot by Allen. It never happened. Anticipating Rocco's actions all the way, Cy matched him move for move. The two airplanes leveled off a hundred feet above the trees. Speed being relative, they seemed to hang in the air for a long moment. In Dobbs' imagination, Allen had enough time to take several large bites out of the other plane's ass. With a cannon, he could have picked it apart. Then Rocco poured the coal to his machine and Allen instantly followed. If the flight had been choreographed, it couldn't have been tighter and smoother.

They went down into the trees, below the level of some treetops and between jutting karst formations. "Trees're above us," Dobbs said and wondered why he had bothered to speak. Tensely leaning forward, his asshole was clenched as tightly as his hands. He'd be shitting foam rubber for a week. His mouth was dry, his throat filled with sourness. He wanted to clear it, wanted to shout, "When the fuck is enough enough?"

Rocco's jet wash was cutting a wake through the treetops. He was blowing down the jungle. And Allen was on his tail, drafting in his slipstream. Rocco stood his plane on a wing and snaked around a chunk of jagged karst. For a second he disappeared. Allen racked through the same turn and Rocco popped back into view. Then they tore away down a valley, skimming the trees, juking, jinking, gone berserk.

Dobbs was sweating, happy, excited, a fucking nervous wreck. How had they known there wasn't a chunk of karst behind that chunk of karst? Had it been there, none of them would have ever known. It was just one more risk. Well, shit, Dobbs realized, they didn't care! They didn't care because they knew exactly what they were doing. Any other pilots would have killed themselves by now. Most likely Rocco had studied that terrain every time he crossed it and had the patterns of landmarks, the highest karst and deepest valleys, engraved in his mind. Dobbs didn't doubt that Rocco had picked that specific area to rat race in hopes of sandbagging Cy.

Dobbs relaxed. Everything they did was a risk. Their life was madness. Their profession was death. Why should their play be any different? He was on the ride of rides, a ride he would remember and talk about for as long as he lived. He was with the world's greatest fighter pilot, chasing probably the second greatest, and *whipping his ass raw!* What the fuck else was there? What more to be said? "Go, Cy," he shouted.

Rocco broke hard one more time, again around a

tall piece of karst that formed the edge of a plateau. That magnificent son-of-a-bitch Cy Allen cut the corner tighter and, in a ninety-degree bank, gained ground in the turn. He passed so close to the vertical wall of solid rock that Dobbs involuntarily ducked his head. Around the other side of the karst, a waterfall dropped from the plateau to the valley far below. Allen forgot Rocco. In a majestic diving, curving, sweeping, zooming flight path he arced through the waterfall's spray. For a second or two the canopy was shrouded by mist. To Dobbs, that short segment of flight was magical. In a mystical moment they were baptized with droplets of immortality, transposed into deathless eagles.

Rocco climbed above the treetops, throttled back. "Bingo fuel," he announced. They had just kissed the tanker, Dobbs thought, they had plenty of fuel. Then he understood: the game was ended, the winner decided. It was time to go home.

Allen slid in tight, to the rear and side of Rocco, exactly where a good wingman flew. Everything now seemed to take place in slow motion, Dobbs noticed. Rocco looked over at Cy, raised a gloved thumb, said, "Hold what you got. No tricks this time." He banked wide and dropped back, came up from behind and snuggled into the wingman position. The planes hung motionless in a glacier of space. Then Rocco threw a salute to Cy.

Dobbs couldn't imagine a more chivalrous gesture. He suppressed a cheer. Instead, with mist in his eyes, the words he managed to get out were a whisper: "Beautiful. Fucking beautiful." He wanted to live forever, to fly like this for all his days.

Monge and Wiltrout were finished. Following the mission, Rocco no longer was looked upon as the squadron commander and Greg wasn't just another backseater. Now they were far more important. They were fighter pilots who had lived through one hundred missions over North Vietnam. They were Red River Rats.

When they climbed down from their Phantom for the final time, their squadron mates soaked them with a firehose, then made each chug-a-lug a bottle of champagne while the group chanted his name. Rocco spilled most of the champagne down his chest. "Drinking that is tough as flying any mission," he said. He hugged Allen. "Where's that piss you drink?" Somebody handed Allen a bottle of Ten High. Rocco grabbed it, tore off the cap and threw it away, then took a long swallow. He shivered from head to toe: "That cuts the sugar."

It was Rocco's day. Along the way he tried several solo MiG Sweeps of the O-Club. The beefy lieutenants who normally were his partners formed against him and crushed him time and again. Even arm-in-arm with Wiltrout he was no match for them. By nightfall Rocco was knee-walking.

At one point in the celebration he steered Allen to a corner: "You hear, the North Vietnamese put a price on our heads."

"You kidding?"

"Hell, no. An Intell guy told me. Just you and me, he said." Rocco looked around warily. "You know my price, the price they put on me?" His question was rhetorical. He looked into Allen's eyes for a long time before he told him: "Fifty thousand dollars. Dead or alive." He nodded. "Fifty thou. Christ, I don't earn that in two years." Rocco smiled crookedly: "Fifty grand. For me!"

Allen barely could wait to hear. "How much they offer for me?"

For several seconds Rocco acted as if he hadn't heard the question. Then he said, "You sure you want to know?" He couldn't restrain himself any longer, however, and grinned from ear to ear: "Ten thousand. No shit. Only ten—for you."

"Come on . . ."

"I shit you not, Cy." Rocco was delighted. "Ten grand." He wrapped a heavy, hairy arm around Cy's neck and hugged him fiercely. "Don't let it get you down. I still respect you." Spasms of laughter choked him.

Unwittingly, the squadron's lieutenants gained a measure of revenge for Allen by talking Monge into going to town for a final scrub and rub. Rocco passed out on the massage table. Like well-disciplined officers, the lieutenants walked off with Rocco's clothes and money, abandoned his naked and penniless body. Nobody learned how Rocco managed to get back to base. Nobody had the nerve to ask.

23

With eleven missions to go, Allen computed his chances for becoming the first ace in so many different ways that he gave himself a headache. Dobbs didn't seem to care about MiGs. He appeared to be contented by simply dropping bombs and coming home. Going through the SAMs and flak was enough excitement for any sane person, he said.

After Rocco finished, Allen loitered behind during egress from North Vietnam. The MiGs he sighted were on the fringe of the Phantom's operating area and didn't challenge the strike force. His remaining missions dwindled to ten, then nine, eight, and finally seven. By then he was lagging so far astern that Junior Eliot spoke up from the wingman slot: "Colonel Allen, I'll be glad to request a tanker to come up here if you want to spend the night."

What he was doing wasn't normal, Allen thought. He was setting himself up to be attacked, asking to be shot at. His behavior differed in other ways too. Dobbs made him see that.

Sitting at the club bar after Number Ninety-three, he asked Dobbs who had come from the base theater late show, "How did we get so close without doing it?" Since Rocco finished, he had seen Dobbs only when they flew. "You don't care, do you?"

"I care," Dobbs said hotly. "Damn right I care." He leaned forward. "It's not over yet."

"You believe that?"

"Don't you?" Dobbs hesitated, cut his eyes around the bar, then looked into Allen's face and spoke rapidly: "Look, I don't mind being set up, being made a target. It's worth it, if we get to shoot back. But if you keep getting shitfaced every night like you've been doing since Rocco left, and if we ever tangle with a MiG, he'll eat your lunch."

"Now wait—"

"There's a difference between heading down the chute to drop bombs and tangling air-to-air. Surviving bomb runs is mostly luck; the other's skill. And your skill is turning to shit."

"Hold it right there, *lieutenant.*"

"Blow it out your ass, *sir!* I ride with you. Remember? I have to go where you go."

"That's enough, Jer."

"If you fuck up, I pay too. Remember MacDill? My glasses? Well this time you better rethink—"

"That's enough, damnit!" Allen slammed down his glass and it shattered.

The Thai barmaid rushed to him: "You OK, Colonel Allen? Let see."

He waved her away. The broken glass had made long, shallow cuts in the ends of three fingers. His throttle hand, not his stick hand, he thought. He sucked the cuts, spit out grains of glass.

"Want 'nother, Colonel Allen?" the barmaid asked.

He shook his head: "No. No, thanks." She smiled and moved to another table. Grabbing Dobbs' arm, he said, "I ought to kick your ass."

283

"How about a little one-on-one at the gym?"

Lightly: "Fuck you, Jer."

"Save it then. Take it out on some MiG driver."

Cynically: "You think?"

Dobbs gave him a withering stare.

Seriously: "Let's have one more then and call it a year. In here, I mean."

Dobbs thought about it, shrugged, nodded.

Allen ordered two double bourbons and water. When the drinks were served, he said, "You really believe we're going to get one more? Up there, I mean."

"Yes." In an attempt to lighten the mood, Dobbs said, "Have you ever known me to be wrong?"

Remembering the prediction that they would score the fifth victory on their sixty-ninth mission, Allen said, "I've known you not to be right." He smiled and asked, "Is that the same thing?"

Dobbs shrugged.

Allen clinked his glass against Dobbs': "Winner buys, professor?" He said it without understanding that he was betting against his own good fortune.

"Rog. Winner buys."

Cy Allen hated the bombing missions. They were the worst part of the year. He was finishing on a sour note. He had bombed the Xuan Mai army barracks, the Ha Dong supply depot, the Yen Vien and Bac Le railroad yards, the Dai Loi railroad bypass bridge, and the Yen Bai ordnance depot, and (almost forgot!) the Dap Cau railroad and highway bridge. He wondered if he would remember any of the names a year from then.

It was the dry season over the North and the target areas constantly were clear. As long as its airplane was flyable, a crew logged a counter every day it was scheduled.

With only bombing missions to look forward to for the next seven flights, he wondered if given the opportunity he would walk away, leave early with his four and a half confirmed kills. Unfulfilled love often made a more interesting story.

Bombing missions were punishment.

On his way to Ubon, Allen had spent one night at the Chao Phraya Hotel, the United States military billet in Bangkok. He had shared a room with a fellow pilot. Allen already was asleep when the man arrived; a loud voice asked him, "Are you awake?"

Opening his eyes, he saw in the darkness a person stretched out on the other bed. "Yes," he answered.

"Would you like to talk?" the shadowy figure asked.

It was a request more than a question. The man sounded sober. "All right," Cy said. He glanced at the luminous dial of his watch: two A.M.

"Where you headed? Going home?"

"No. I'm on my way to Ubon."

"I'm headed back to Korat. I've been to the States. I just escorted my brother's body home, for burial. He was an Army captain, killed in Vietnam, near Pleiku. Ever been to Nam?"

"No." Allen restrained himself from adding that he had been in Korea. His role in the conversation appeared to be that of a listener.

"I hadn't been there either, until I went to Danang to pick up my brother's body. Taking him home was the saddest thing I've ever done. Our parents, my mom and dad, they never stopped crying. He had a full military burial. It was perfect."

The silence that followed lasted so long that, thinking the man had fallen asleep, Allen whispered, "You awake?"

"Yeah." He sniffed back whatever had stopped him. "My brother was only a year older than me. We were practically twins, the only children my parents had." The next words came slowly, evenly spaced, but in a grimly determined tone: "Now I'm going back to Korat to finish my tour in 105s. I have thirty-one missions to go." His rate of speech picked up and, Cy guessed, the man finally got to what he wanted to say from the start. "I'm not looking forward to going back. Not at all.

"We fly over the North. Going back up there will be the toughest thing I've ever done. Anybody who hasn't been up there can't imagine how bad it is, especially around Hanoi. I've rolled in over downtown Hanoi eleven times and every time is as bad as the one before. It's something you never get used to.

"The whole time you're inbound you worry about SAMs or MiGs. But the bomb run is what really gets you. Nearing roll-in, your heart starts pounding, you can hardly breathe. You can see guys ahead of you diving through the flak. It's so thick, the sky is black. I wasn't over Germany in World War II but, from what I've been told, North Vietnam is twice as bad. And I'm talking about just the flak!

"I've seen antiaircraft guns track a plane all the way through a dive and breakaway. The plane's flight path is actually outlined by a trail of flak clouds. The worst is when guns crisscross on you. One chases you from behind, and one comes up from the front, and maybe two others are off to the sides. The gunners traverse their fire so that at a given time they all come together at a single point. If you happen to be at that point . . .

"The really worst part is that the lower you get the faster the rate of fire you're exposed to. The fifty-sevens and thirty-sevens hammer that shit at you faster than you can count. I mean, when you get to bomb release altitude, it is really hot! Everything is happening at once. You're trying to stay in the chute, and trying to fly around the flak, and thinking about SAMs and MiGs . . . It's almost impossible. It's a wonder we hit anything.

"And the targets! They're worthless. What I mean is, they're so insignificant. And we have to hit them again and again because our bomb loads are puny. There has to be a better way to do what we do. I mean, more efficient, cheaper, and a lot safer." He sighed. "One nuke would do it all." He forced a laugh. "I'll tell you the truth: I almost didn't come back —from the States. I really didn't want to go back up North."

Allen said, "Isn't there a regulation or something about a sole surviving son, about being exempt from combat?"

"Yeah, there's something like that. But I don't want that. You see, I have to go back. It's hard to explain. It doesn't have anything to do with my brother. I'm not going to avenge him or anything. I know that's impossible. The person who killed him is somewhere in the South. Maybe dead by now. Who knows? What I mean is I have to go back and finish my tour. It's something I *have* to do. I don't want to do it. But I have to do it. You understand?"

"Yes." The man desired confirmation; now he had it.

"I'm going to do it. I'm going to finish my hundred. Then I'm getting out of the Air Force."

Allen doubted both statements. Chances were that the man wouldn't last one hundred. If he did, he wouldn't leave the Air Force.

"I appreciate you listening to me. I couldn't talk to

my parents." The man stammered for a few moments, then said, "You know, I'm not a . . ."

Allen expected him to say "a coward."

". . . afraid. It's just, sometimes, I don't understand the sense of what we do." He exhaled loudly. "I don't understand the military mind."

In the morning the man was gone. Cy never saw his face or learned his name or rank. That was the way it had to be, he decided, if the conversation had worth. He changed his mind: the man would make it through his remaining missions over the North.

While hating the bombing missions, Cy Allen came up with several radical ideas concerning military duty. First, he questioned the drafting of men in peacetime, but could devise no alternate solution. He dismissed the concept of an all-volunteer military as too extreme: nobody would voluntarily join the Army, he concluded.

Second, if the United States was going to draft men in peacetime and insisted upon fighting other nations' wars, he thought that only volunteers should be used in combat. Thus, the scope of America's involvement would be limited to the number of men who believed in the cause.

Third, he believed that men who volunteered for such combat should have an easy way out once they had done their "fair share." Although few Air Force commanders admitted it, Korea and Vietnam were gigantic training exercises. To career personnel, they were times for gaining glory, establishing a combat reputation, cementing a career, getting promoted. The higher the rank, the better the chance for individual recognition and fame, and the less likely the chance of being killed. Because the outcome of the fighting was unrelated to the security of the United

States, the lower rankers deserved an escape hatch, an exit from combat as uncomplicated as stating, "I've done my share. I've had enough."

What constituted a fair share was moot, always had been, always would be. For flyers who operated in high risk areas it was a given number of missions; for other flyers and groundpounders, a given length of time. Allen envisioned a fair share as a constantly recomputed figure, an average rather than a fixed number. Once a fair share number was attained, a man was free to leave when he chose. Anyone who cared to stay beyond that number could do so for as long as he desired. . . .

Allen remembered a lieutenant named Ralph Bova who had been an exemplary wingman in Korea. Bova eventually gravitated to his wing and they flew nearly twenty missions together. Then Bova asked for his support in talking to their squadron commander, Major Moose Garrison. Knowing that Bova had about a dozen missions remaining, Allen expected him to request upgrading to element lead to get first crack at the MiGs for a change. Instead, Bova told the commander, "Sir, I want to go home."

Major Garrison laughed: "Get the fuck out of here."

"I'm serious," Bova said and placed several pages of numbers on the major's desk. "These are the combat statistics of our squadron's pilots for the past year, dead and alive. I've flown more than the average, both in missions and in hours. Now, I want to go home."

The major frowned, picked up the papers, and flipped through them. "Bova, you haven't flown your hundred."

"Why do I have to fly a hundred?"

"Because it's a nice round number," Allen said and drew a scowl from Garrison.

"I've already done my fair share, sir," Bova stated.

"Your fair share is one hundred missions," Garrison told him. "Don't make me say it again."

"That's an arbitrary number, assuming you're not killed, seriously wounded, shot down and captured, grounded by illness, or recalled for compassionate reasons. When you consider those factors, you come up with an average number that changes slightly every day. For our squadron, during the past two months, that average number has held constant at seventy-nine. I've exceeded the average and I want to go home, now."

Moose Garrison studied Bova before he said, "That ain't the way it works, sonny." He looked at Allen. "Tell him how it works."

"I'm not sure, sir. What Ralph says sounds pretty good."

The Moose growled, then snapped, "Shut up, Allen. Keep out of this." He aimed a finger at Bova: "You said squadron average. What's the Air Force average?"

"I don't know, sir. I couldn't get those figures. I assume it's close to ours."

"You *assume?* How do you know your assumption is valid?"

"I don't. But I do know that the Air Force average is some number less than one hundred. I've allowed ten percent for error in my computations. The squadron average is seventy-nine; I've flown eighty-seven, ten percent more. Now, I want to go home."

"Will you stop saying that!" Garrison shuffled through the pages of statistics. "Did you include my hundred and thirteen missions in here?"

"Sir, after a hundred you're on your own and fall

outside the mandatory parameters. Figures over one hundred have no statistical validity."

"Statistical validity, my ass!" Garrison threw the papers onto his desk. "You rework those figures and you include every mission . . ." He slumped in his chair and ran a hand across his bald head. "What am I doing?" He flipped the pages with a forefinger. "That isn't some staff study. Your figures are bullshit. Only one hundred counts." He looked at Allen: "Right?" Immediately, he raised a hand: "Shut up. Keep out of this."

"Sir," Ralph Bova said, "I want to go home, now."

"Get out of here," Moose said, then in the same breath reversed himself, "No, wait." He rested his elbows on his desk and cupped his face in his hands. "You afraid, lieutenant?"

"No, sir. It's just that I've done my share."

The major fired questions: "You want to be grounded? You got battle fatigue? You want to turn in your wings? You got family problems? You on the fuckin' rag or something?"

Bova disgustedly shook his head. "Sir, I just want to go home. I'm tired of sleeping in a fucking tent."

"No shit? Well so am I," Major Garrison said. "Boy, I'll say! But this is the only war we got right now, so we have to make the best of it. You see that, don't you?" He didn't wait for an answer. "Now you two scram before I get really pissed off." Before Bova or Allen moved, Garrison said, "Wait a minute. Allen, you still want him for a wingman?"

"Yes, sir."

"Then keep his ass out of my office. Now git!" Nobody moved before Garrison ordered, "Wait a minute." He jabbed a finger at the paperwork. "Who else's seen this?"

"Nobody," Bova said.

"You certain?"

"Why would I lie?"

"I don't know. You have another copy?"

"No, sir. I don't even have the worksheets. Threw them away."

"This is it, hunh?" The major thought about the problem for a while. "Your old man a congressman or anything? You want a few days off in Japan?"

"No. I only want to go home."

Allen laughed.

"I told you to shut up, Allen." The major put the sheets of figures into his desk. "Keep him out of here and you'll both stay out of trouble. Now go away, pronto."

Ralph Bova finished his hundred.

Going home early, even by one day, seemed extremely logical to Cy Allen following Mission Ninety-four. The target was the railroad car repair plant in the center of Hanoi. A steady stream of SAM warnings occupied the crews all the way in and out. It was a bad day in every respect: two Thuds were destroyed by SAMs, one F-4 was downed by AAA, and another F-4 ran out of fuel before reaching his post-strike tanker and crashed just short of Laos. To finish the day, a damaged F-4 tore the dog pecker off one tanker boom because the nozzle failed to automatically disconnect when the F-4 momentarily slipped out of control. The F-4 landed with ten feet of aluminum pipe protruding from its topside. The feat wasn't a first. It did, however, provide the only smile of the day.

On taxiing by the F-4, Allen said, "A unicorn!"

Crazy days, he thought. A few missions earlier an F-105 had been hit by a SAM that failed to detonate. The missile impacted and imbedded itself into the aft section of the Thud's fuselage, tore everything to hell. After overcoming his initial shock, the pilot established the aerodynamics of the new configuration and labored home. The Thud landed routinely with the SAM hanging from its bleeding ass. When repairs finally were completed, the crew chief changed the name painted on the side of the airplane from "Sweet Baby Sue" to "Magnet Butt." Crazy days!

Still studying the pipe protruding from the Phantom, Cy Allen said, "If it's not one thing . . ."

"It's two things," Dobbs said. "At least it's not us. Aw, shit. Six to go . . ."

". . . and counting," Cy added. Bombing missions *were* punishment, he thought again. What had they done to deserve them?

24

Mission Number Ninety-five tested the other half of Pudder's Law: Anything that begins well has to get worse and end badly. Allen and Dobbs were on the early go. The O-Club had plenty of coffee, rich and hot. Allen made but a single trip to the latrine during mission planning. Lieutenant Bernard's briefing was uneventful. Except for a little thin, scattered stuff, the sky was clear and the visibility unlimited from Bangkok to Chungking. Every F-4 rolled on time and got airborne safely, joined up with the Thuds a minute early, tapped the tanker practically to the second.

Inbound to the target, of course, there were no MiGs. The ECM pods hanging outboard in place of the F-4s' starboard external fuel tanks hummed in unison and saturated the ground radar screens with one big blob of a return that made it impossible to accurately detect azimuth, altitude, and range of the strike force. The few SAMs that roared from the deck seemed to lack purpose. The large radar-controlled AAA pieces, scary as always, were well off the mark. Even the smaller guns seemed uninterested, used low rates of fire, were inaccurate. The flight was a milk run. "If they all were like this," Allen said, "I'd go for another hundred."

"Sure you would," said Dobbs.

The target was nothing to get excited about, the Yen Vien railroad yards. Everyone in the strike force had been there before, some before that, and a few even before that. Dobbs wondered if the NVA gunners failed to show interest because there was nothing to defend. He said, "I have the strange feeling that the North Vietnamese have bypassed and no longer need what we just bombed the shit out of."

Heading for Laos, Allen and Eliot were tail-end Charlies. Exactly as on Rocco's hundredth mission, Allen spotted a pair of MiG-21s high and far away: "Bandits. Two o'clock, high. Hold this heading." He eased back the throttles.

The MiGs looked like they couldn't make up their minds. Staying high, they sneaked closer and worked back to the Phantom's four o'clock position. Suddenly they dived.

Allen saw them roll into their attack pass. Waiting for them to fully commit, he counted to five, then forced himself to count to five again.

"Here they come," Eliot warned.

"I know. Let's clean up." The two Phantom pilots dropped their external tanks and Cy called for minimum afterburner. He wanted the MiG jocks to see them light up, wanted them to think that Eliot and he were going to try to outrun them. The MiGs had closed to about two and a half miles when he stood his F-4 on a wing and bent back toward them.

The MiG drivers should have gutsed it out, completed their high-speed, one-shot pass. Instead, after the briefest hesitation, they turned away from the Phantoms. The hesitation permitted Allen and Eliot to narrow the separation. The poor bastards probably were under the direction of some GCI radar operator who couldn't make up his mind, Allen thought. The GCI operator's error was the MiG drivers' loss, and his gain.

The MiGs split. The one to the left headed northeast and started down. The other held his altitude and went east. "I got the one on the left. The other guy's yours." There was a one- or-two second pause before Eliot acknowledged and broke in the direction of his prey.

Lieutenant Colonel Cy Young Allen followed the MiG-21 down. He was willing to settle for one shot with a Sparrow missile. He knew he shouldn't be pressing his luck by heading north, but he needed only a single kill to become the first ace of the Vietnam War. No guts, no glory, he thought.

The Fishbed and the Phantom passed through five thousand feet and antiaircraft artillery opened up on both of them. The dumb bastards were shooting their own man, Cy thought and remembered seeing a MiG-17 blown out of the sky by an SA2 Guideline when an NVA ground commander salvoed his missiles into a dogfight.

Around a thousand feet, the MiG pilot went crazy: turning, twisting, dodging. . . . Allen slowed to keep from overrunning him. He worked into a good lookup angle, held the MiG atop the nose radome despite the enemy pilot's frantic scrambling. Come on, Jer, he thought. What was happening back there? "In range?"

"Affirmative."

A beat passed, then two, but Dobbs said nothing more. Goddamnit! "Lock? We locked, Jer?"

"Affirm. In range, locked."

The missile came out of the well cleanly, then drifted slightly right. The MiG juked left and the Sparrow lost track, went ballistic and harmlessly sailed wide of the target. Goddamn, Cy thought, something fucked up but he didn't know what. Too many G's?

"Still locked, in range," Dobbs said.

Flying as if he were mad, the MiG pilot dived into the weeds, jinked into a box canyon. The fool was going to fly into the ground and finish the job for him, Cy Allen thought. He again was closing on the MiG, getting too close. Tracers from groundfire crossed over both airplanes. Allen jerked back the throttles but was late; he passed the MiG.

"Goddamn! You see him, Jer?"

"Hunh?"

"I lost the son-of-a-bitch visually." The bastard was probably behind *him* by now, Cy thought. He racked around to the right. "Do you see him?" he shouted.

"No! I lost him too."

"Check six and—" The F-4 was in a ninety-degree right bank and doing five hundred fifty knots when a 23-mm shell punched through the pilot's cockpit canopy cover and tore open Allen's body from his right shoulder to his left abdomen, slightly above the hipbone. The shell exploded against the fuel control panel.

The explosion and the roar of wind filled the cockpit with horrendous noises. Sucked from every crack, dust and dirt swirled around Dobbs, made him squint. They had been through this before, he thought.

Over interphone, Allen screamed. Gasping, he called, "I'm hit, I'm hit, I'm hit." Involuntarily he groaned and sobbed.

In the back seat of the Phantom, First Lieutenant Jerry Dobbs hung tight and wondered what exactly had happened. The sounds made by Cy Allen reminded him of a soundtrack from a Hollywood dramatization of a World War II battle in which masses of men charged toward enemy machine gun positions and were mowed down amid high-pitched screams of pain and low-pitched moans of agony. He felt as if he had been through this too before. He nearly told Allen to stop the theatrics. Then Dobbs saw that the airplane was aimed at the ground.

With both hands, Dobbs yanked back the control stick. G forces crushed him into his seat and he flexed the muscles in his upper body; his sight was squeezed to tunnel vision. The ground, the hillside rushed at him. Then the aircraft's nose pulled through the horizon and Dobbs saw blue. Somehow he had scooped out what little remained of the airspace in the canyon. Centering the stick, he rammed the throttles to full power. The Phantom climbed rapidly.

"I'm hit, I'm hit, I'm hit," Allen cried again.

I know it, I know it, I know it, Dobbs thought. "Don't worry," he said. "I've got it. I've got the airplane." He felt surprisingly calm and confident. He wasn't sure why. Originally, two pilots were assigned to an F-4; the less experienced pilot was put in the rear and taught navigator skills. When the Air Force ran short of pilots, honest-to-God navigators were assigned to the back seat. Initially, the pilots derisively named them "GIBs"—Guys In Back. That was how Dobbs got where he was today. He wondered if upper echelon policy makers had ever thought to teach basic pilot skills to GIBs. Blaming his predicament on some obscure "They" didn't help, he told himself. He was thankful that Allen had given him stick time now and then.

His pull-up maneuver had taken them out of the U-shaped valley. They had barely cleared the crest of the ridgeline on the valley's east side. That was behind them now, Dobbs thought. In a sixty degree climb, he pointed the jet toward the nearest clouds, thin stuff but better than nothing. Ground fire followed them upward. He hoped the MiG had gone home. Wind roared into the cockpit and he believed damage to be extensive; he expected the airplane to come unglued at any moment. They popped through the thin cloud deck at fifteen thousand feet. Dobbs felt the airspeed slacken and saw that Allen had reduced the throttles to idle. Dobbs leveled the airplane.

After thousands of hours of flying, Allen instinctively executed his duties when, for moments, he regained consciousness. Dobbs' actions blended with his own thoughts. "IFF—Emergency," he said. "Guard. Guard." Dobbs switched the UHF radio to Guard channel. "Guard," Allen said again.

"We're on guard," Dobbs told him. There was no reply. Under control, the aircraft idled along at twenty thousand feet. If they had to eject, Dobbs thought, he preferred to do it over rugged terrain; that way, they would be away from people on the ground and less likely to be captured. Fleetingly he wondered what animals would be down there.

"Oh, God," Allen said, "I'm not going to make it." He was having difficulty breathing. "I'm not going to make it." He sounded resigned to his fate and unafraid. "Not going to make it."

Dobbs didn't know what to say. The words of encouragement that came to mind seemed hollow. After a long pause, he said, "Let's get the hook." Eventually they might have to land, he thought; if they had to land with battle damage, he wanted the hook extended in order to engage the runway barrier and stop the airplane. He remembered watching a fuel-heavy F-4 land without a tail hook. The airplane took out the runway barrier, skated out of control off the side of the runway, tore off its landing gear, knifed across the infield, and sliced in half a maintenance breadwagon. The two crewmen miraculously survived the wreck, but eight men in the maintenance vehicle were killed. "Colonel Cy, you have the hook?" Dobbs asked but got no answer.

Without warning, Dobbs felt spooked. He was afraid to touch anything, particularly the throttles. For some reason, Allen wanted them in idle. Dobbs couldn't afford to get into a shoving match over them. Although the front and back cockpit throttle controls were mechanically linked, the pilot had a break-out capability which permitted him to release and override pressure from the backseater. When the pilot did that, he broke the mechanical linkage and the man in the rear was left without control. Reconnecting the linkage was an involved process that took close coordination, far more than Dobbs expected from a semiconscious pilot.

Suddenly Dobbs noticed that they were headed northeast. Hell, he thought, they probably were over China! How could he have been that dumb! Forgetting his fear of touching anything, he altered heading to the southwest, toward Thailand, and pushed the throttles to military power.

"Invert, Chevy Lead," Allen called weakly over guard channel. "Chevy Lead. Mayday, mayday, mayday. We're hit and we're . . ." His voice trailed off.

"This is Invert Control. Go ahead, Chevy."

Allen remained silent.

"Invert, Chevy Lead," Dobbs said. "My pilot's hit. We need a direct vector to the nearest field, probably NKP."

Seconds passed. "Chevy Lead, Invert. Turn to heading two-three-zero."

Dobbs said, "We're squawking Emergency," before

he realized that Invert controllers already saw it on their scope. Otherwise they couldn't have vectored him. Why was he always one step behind? Two-three-zero! He altered five degrees right and thought it was a fluke that had put him so close to the proper heading. He still had no way of assessing the extent of damage to their jet but thought that, as long as the plane held together, every second in the air was several hundred yards of walking through jungle that they wouldn't have to do in order to get back to Thailand.

Allen gasped, mumbled, "Can't breathe."

Dobbs fretted: he had to get back to Thailand. If they ejected over the North or over Laos, Cy wouldn't have a chance. Dobbs pushed the throttles into afterburner and minute after minute they raced along at full speed.

It seemed like forever before in the far distance he saw the Mekong River. Retarding the throttles, he let the airplane slow, then reported, "Invert, Chevy Lead. I have the river in sight."

Invert relayed him to Nakhom Phanom Ground Control Approach. The new controller asked, "Will you accept a ten mile straight-in approach?"

"Affirmative. Anything. Be advised, this is the navigator flying this airplane. I want all the help you can give me. What's the field elevation?" What a stupid question, he thought instantly. Totally unprofessional. He sounded like some civilian pilot.

Calmly, reassuringly, the GCA controller told Dobbs exactly what he needed to know and exactly what he had to do. He made it sound easy. Dobbs had sat through countless GCAs; he knew what had to be done. But it was nice to hear it again. The only things required of him were to listen and to do as he was told. He didn't have to be perfect. He just had to get the plane on the ground, hopefully in one piece.

Out of nowhere, Junior Eliot pulled alongside him. "You were really booking it across Laos. I couldn't catch you." Eliot studied the other plane. "How's Colonel Cy?"

"He's alive," Dobbs said, then hoped it was true. Cy had been quiet for some time.

"Except for the hole in your canopy, you look clean," Eliot told him.

GCA called and Dobbs followed instructions. He was ready to turn to final approach when he thought about the landing gear and flaps. From the back seat, he could lower them only with the emergency pneumatic system; however, such action caused the aircraft to lose utility hydraulic pressure and, as a result, the engines *auto-accelerated to full power* in order to cool themselves. Auto-acceleration occurred regardless of the position of the throttles; with the engines at full power, it was impossible to stop the airplane on the runway.

He recalled also watching an F-105 Iron Hand attempt to roll out under full power after landing with battle damage. The Thud slashed through the barrier, went off the end of the runway, sheared its gear, and skidded forward on its belly until it came to a klong. At that spot, the nose of the Thud dipped into the ditch and hit the opposite bank; the front of the airplane broke off. The front section with the pilot in his seat was crushed beneath the aft section which crossed the ditch with the navigator still riding in it. An instant later, both sections were enveloped in a fireball.

Worried about lowering the gear and flaps, Dobbs turned the Phantom onto final approach, ten miles from the runway. Allen said, "Field in sight."

"You all right?" Dobbs shouted. "Colonel Cy!" There was no response. "Gear and flaps down,"

Dobbs shouted. He waited several moments, then repeated, "Gear and flaps down." They were on guide slope. He had set up a smooth five-hundred-feet-per-minute rate of descent. "Gear and flaps," Dobbs said two more times. He saw Allen's head bobbing over the stick. Nothing happened, however.

They were six miles from touchdown when unexpectedly Dobbs felt and heard the gear lower. His indicators showed both gear and flaps were down. The auto-acceleration problem was solved. He swelled with confidence.

"Down," Allen mumbled. "Got hoo-ook."

For two heartbeats Dobbs wasn't certain what he had heard. When he understood the last word, a chill passed through him. He had forgotten the tail hook! His confidence dissolved. He had been flying with a false sense of security. Spooked again, he thought he detected pressure on the control column. He feared Allen was trying to fly the approach. He placed a hand behind the throttles because he also feared that Allen might suddenly pull them to idle and cause the plane to crash. Every few seconds, he released the stick to see if Allen was moving it. "You all right, Colonel Cy?" he asked each time. The stick didn't move. He received no answer. Was he with it or not? "You all right?" he continued to ask between calls from GCA.

Dobbs craned his head from left to right. As tall as he was, with the aircraft in a nose-high attitude he couldn't see forward and find the runway. How was he to see? What was he to do? On trust, he listened to the controller and continued the letdown: heading, airspeed, rate of descent. Maybe he didn't need to see? He hoped the runway was in front of them.

At three hundred feet altitude he felt a sharp, forward bump on the control stick. He pulled back to counteract the force and, at the same instant, saw runway on both sides of the airplane. He held the stick where it was and flew the Phantom onto the hard surface. The fighter hit and stuck, settled without a bounce.

Dobbs moved the throttles from ninety percent to idle power. The landing hook caught the arresting cable and the aircraft stopped in the webbed barrier. The backseater couldn't shut down the engines. Rescue personnel would shut them down, he thought, then realized they still weren't safe.

Below the pilot's seat was a lower ejection handle which simultaneously fired both seats. If left uncovered, rescue people could inadvertently hook the handle and kill them. He winced at the idea of making it as far as they had and then being blown away by accident. "Lower guard," Dobbs called again and again until his eyes focused on the fuel gauges and he was struck speechless. Four hundred pounds of fuel remained, about four minutes of flying time. He had forgotten about fuel and had lucked out. A sinking spell hit him, followed by a new wave of relief.

With engines running, the airplane crept back from the barrier while ground crewmen swarmed toward it from the right. The mechanism for opening the canopy from the outside was housed on the left of the fuselage. After motioning several times without being understood, Dobbs opened his canopy, unstrapped, climbed and stretched forward, and activated the switch that raised the pilot's canopy. Straining farther, he grabbed the throttles and cut the engines. What the hell, how would the ground crew know? NKP didn't have F-4s, he thought.

Ladders appeared on both sides of the plane. Dobbs shouted at the first man to reach the cockpit, "Lower guard, lower guard, lower guard," and the man gave an exaggerated wink before lowering the metal guard over the dual ejection handle. At least one guy had it together, Dobbs thought. At last, they were safe.

To Dobbs it seemed as if one hundred hands levitated the slumped form of Allen from the front seat. Hands under his wrists, forearms, elbows, and shoulders raised him upward; hands slid behind his back and knees, under his thighs and buttocks to lift him from the cockpit. Hands supported his head and neck. Hands held his calves, his ankles, his feet. Hands lowered Allen, still in a seated position, from the airplane and gently set him on a stretcher.

"That's Cy Allen," an airman said quietly.

"Jesus Christ, look how white he is," another said and made a sign of the cross.

When a young, thin doctor tried to make him lie down on the stretcher, Allen came awake with a ferocious scream. "Let him sit up," the doctor shouted.

"Let him sit up," a senior sergeant shouted in turn. The sergeant wore eyeglasses three-quarters of an inch thick; Dobbs wondered if they were bulletproof.

Pairs of airmen double-timed to each end of the stretcher. They grasped the handles and lifted; then, the pairs discovered they were facing each other. "No, no," the doctor shouted. "Put him down."

"Put him down," the senior sergeant echoed.

"You two," the doctor said and pointed, "about-face, turn." All four stretcher bearers turned. "No," the doctor cried.

"No," the senior sergeant bellowed.

The doctor looked skyward and said quietly, "For God's sake, you four men face in the same direction and carry the stretcher to the ambulance."

After another false start, they accomplished the task. Dobbs followed the medical personnel into the vehicle.

The senior sergeant jumped into the driver's seat, slammed the ambulance into gear, and accelerated rapidly before the rear doors were closed. He drove straight off the paved surface and across the runway infield. Dust rolled in over patient and passengers. The vehicle bounced and yawed on the uneven grassy area. The doctor examined Allen who had again lost consciousness. "I don't know," the doctor said. "I don't think I can handle this." He attempted to insert an IV fluid needle into Cy Allen's forearm but the vehicle's erratic motions stymied him. "Slow down," he shouted at the driver. In response, the driver swerved the ambulance back onto the paved road and the top-heavy vehicle leaned far to one side. "Slow down or you'll roll us over," the doctor shouted. The driver continued speeding. After several tries, the doctor slipped the needle into Allen's arm a moment before the driver slammed on the brakes in front of the base hospital emergency area. Everyone, except Allen, toppled forward.

During the ride, Dobbs stared in fascination at the deep wound across Allen's chest. What he saw reminded him of a freshly opened deer after a hunt, only one cut diagonally rather than straight up the middle. He was surprised by the amount of blood. There was a lot but he had expected far more. Quite amazing! The innards were really exposed to the elements. He often had tried to picture what the human anatomy looked like inside. This was nothing like that. A white object about the size of a thumb hung inside the cavity and Dobbs wondered what it was. It moved up and down when the ambulance bounced, and it flopped from side to side when the ambulance swayed. He wanted to ask the doctor about the object, but he felt guilty for being more curious than concerned. He thought that his attitude bordered on sacrilege. Feeling a need to contribute something positive, he shouted, "Doc, he had a lot of trouble talking and breathing. Maybe he has a punctured lung."

The doctor nodded. "I don't think we're prepared to handle this here," he said. First out of the ambulance, the doctor told a waiting chief master sergeant who was the hospital administrator, "I don't know if I can save him. Prepare a Jolly Green. I'll do all I can and then we're going to get him to Udorn."

The chief was gone instantly.

Still in a seated position and apparently unconscious, Allen was carried to an operating room. At least twenty people were in the room when the doctor cut away what remained of his flying suit and then probed into the wound with a long needle-like instrument. Allen jerked, his eyes popped open, and he loudly asked, "Doc! What're you doing to me?" He thrashed about with his arms and legs.

"Hold him," the doctor ordered. Two or three men grabbed each arm and each leg.

"What're you doing to me?" Allen asked again and struggled with the men holding him. He jerked one arm free and snatched the instrument from the doctor who snatched it right back.

"Damn, he's quick," an airman said.

"This is no good," the doctor said. His uniform shirt was soaked with sweat. "Stretch him out. Tape him to the table." It took the efforts of a dozen men to hold Allen and tape his arms and legs so that he was unable to move. Dobbs hadn't realized Cy was that strong. "Anyone not involved in operating room activities leave now," the doctor ordered. He told

Dobbs, "I'm going to do all I know how for him. I'll clean him up and close him up as well as I can. Then he's going to Udorn in a Jolly Green."

Dobbs nodded. Outside the operating room door, a Catholic chaplain stopped him and asked, "What religion is that man?"

"None. He doesn't have a special religion."

"Then how do you explain this?" The chaplain held up a small, strangely shaped piece of metal.

At first glance Dobbs thought it was some kind of fancy identification tag. After several seconds he recognized it as a Saint Christopher medal that had been badly bent and punched through. Dobbs shrugged.

The chaplain stared at the disfigured medal with a rapture usually reserved for miracles. The chaplain elevated his chin and declared, as if addressing a multitude, *"This* was found near your airplane."

Dobbs shrugged again. Then it dawned upon him: the priest was looking for another "medal that deflected the bullet from the heart" story.

"Are you certain," the priest asked, "about his religion?"

"As much as I know it disappoints you . . ." End the fairy tale forever, Dobbs thought. ". . . I'm positive *that* does not belong to Colonel Allen."

In the priest's eyes, the light went out.

Dobbs laughed and said, "Excuse me." He headed back to the airplane to retrieve classified maps and documents that he had forgotten. On top of everything else, he did not want to be charged with a security violation.

A tall, gray-haired lieutenant colonel fell in step beside him. "Did you get any?"

"What . . . ?" Dobbs asked.

"I'm Clark Carter, Chief of Intell. Did you get a MiG—today—before you got hit? I saw a Sparrow was gone . . ."

There was a chance Allen wouldn't live; he had probably flown his last combat mission; it would be fitting if he finished as an ace, Dobbs thought. If he claimed that the last MiG they were chasing had flown into the ground, nobody could deny it. There was no other witness. "Yes," Dobbs said with lowered eyes.

The lieutenant colonel slapped Dobbs on the back and squeezed his shoulder: "Great! That's great!"

Intelligence officers would check the camera films, Dobbs thought. Everybody in the whole fucking Air Force would check the films! And they would find nothing. At most, a miss. "I think. I'm not—ah—I'm not sure," Dobbs muttered. The final verdict wouldn't be made on the basis of his word. He said distinctly, "We chased a MiG-21 down on the deck. We were on top of him, lined up. Colonel Allen fired once. Then we got hit and everything went ape shit. I lost sight of the MiG. I thought I saw a fireball on the ground. The MiG could have flown into the ground. I honestly don't know. Everything was," he looked at Clark Carter and threw his hands in the air, "you know."

"You think you have anything in the camera?"

"I don't know. I doubt it. Probably not."

"Damn," Carter said. "You want to claim it?"

Dobbs shrugged. If he were Allen, he wouldn't want to win that way. "No," he said. "If it's not in the camera, I don't see how we can."

"Damn!" Carter said. "It would have been a helluva finish for Allen. Damn . . ."

Dobbs felt he had done all he could: he had left room for doubt—room to build a legend around

Allen. He stopped in his tracks. If he made Cy an ace, he made himself an ace. How had he overlooked that fact?

Carter stopped too. "What's wrong?"

Dobbs looked the other man straight in the eye: "Sir, after having time to think it over, I'm positive we didn't get one."

Approximately forty-five minutes after they landed, an unconscious Cy Allen was wheeled from the operating room. "That's all I can do," the doctor said noncommittally. "No vital organ was punctured, or damaged in any way. There is bone damage. Whatever hit him missed his heart by a quarter, maybe half an inch at most. Now, a Jolly Green is ready to take him to Udorn." He shook Dobbs' hand.

The world's longest flesh wound, Dobbs thought. Unreal.

The chaplain approached Dobbs and asked, "Are you traveling with him?"

Dobbs nodded: "Sure."

"I don't think you should do that."

"Why not?"

"Because you're going to see something you'll never forget."

Tired of the man's interference, Dobbs asked, "What's that?"

The priest said, "You're going to see a man die."

You vindictive prick, Dobbs thought. He turned his back on the priest and jogged to the ambulance.

Cy Allen remained unconscious until the helicopter was halfway to Udorn. He opened his eyes; they had a glazed look. Recognizing Dobbs, he lifted a hand and motioned him closer. Dobbs placed an ear against Allen's mouth. The beat of the engine and rotor blades directly above made it impossible to hear.

310

"Gonna make it," Cy Young murmured.

"What?" Dobbs shouted.

"Thanks—to—you." It was the only time he ever thanked Dobbs for saving his life.

"What?" Dobbs shouted. "What did you say?" Allen stared up at him without speaking. Dobbs grinned broadly and yelled at the top of his lungs, "That was really super when you got those gear and flaps down." He laughed loudly. "And I almost shit when you remembered the hook."

Epilogue

During his month in the Udorn Hospital, Cy had a recurring dream in which he was in a casket, but he wasn't dead, and Clare and his sons stood silently staring down at him as if he were dead. The worst part of the dream was that he could not speak: he wanted to tell them that he loved them.

Each time he awoke from the dream he felt a hardness inside, as if his stomach was a stone, as if his heart was filled with pebbles. Why had he always chosen adventure, the lure of unknown tomorrows? Wasn't his family his first responsibility?

Cy returned to Ubon for two days of processing. By then Dobbs—who received the Silver Star for saving Cy and the Phantom—was gone. Nobody mentioned that Cy had five more missions, if he wanted them.

On his last afternoon at Ubon, he returned to the bungalow in Warin. It appeared smaller than he remembered, much bleaker. New tenants occupied the fading building. He sat in the dusty courtyard and recalled a time when he had felt his strongest affection for Pensy.

They had been at a movie theater, watching a story

about American soldiers in Europe during World War
II. Pensy had whispered: "If I can pick my life, I be
a soldier, go around world, make love to women in
all countries." In that minute he had felt bonded to
her, believed that they were identical: warriors at
heart.

Now, alone in the courtyard, lost in the solitude of
his intellect, he questioned if he had been correct:
Was he a warrior at heart?

He had tasted his own mortality and he did not like
it.

That night over a drink at the O-Club bar, a new
Night Owl lieutenant colonel pilot asked, "What did
you do to a woman named Pensy?"

"You know her?" Cy said guardedly.

"She gave me a rub the other afternoon at Sabi-
thong's. She found out I was a Phantom jock and
asked if I knew you." He grimaced. "She said, if she
ever had the chance, she'd cut out your heart." Cy
remained silent. The Night Owl sucked on a tooth,
then said, "I were you, I'd steer clear of her. She
sounded serious."

What had Pensy expected from him, Cy wondered.
What had he failed to provide? Even before the
conversation, Cy had wondered if somehow he had
traded their child for his own life? Or had the child's
death negated his fifth victory? Was there a link?
Despite his questions, deep inside, he never was
totally convinced that Pensy had been pregnant.

The week Cy spent in Miami couldn't have been
better if he had destroyed the entire North Vietnamese Air Force single-handedly. Every woman that he
met recognized him as a hero.

During his last night there, while Ty Cobb and he
were group-groping through six very pneumatic
young ladies, Ty said, "This is the best I can provide."

Cy nodded approvingly: "In that case, I guess I'll be moving on in the morning."

He was going back to his sons, he had decided. And hopefully to Clare.

Rolling Thunder operations against North Vietnam were halted in mid-February 1968; attacks on the North did not resume until four years later when the United States launched Linebacker operations.

During Linebacker, five United States aces were crowned. All were F-4 Phantom crewmen.

The first American aces of the war were Navy Lieutenants, the team of Randolph Cunningham and William Driscoll, who brought their total to five with three kills on 10 May 1972.

The United States Air Force had three aces, all captains: one pilot and two backseat navigators. America's leading ace was one of the USAF backseaters who scored six.

The North Vietnamese Air Force claimed fifteen aces. Tops was Colonel Nguyen Toon with thirteen victories. He flew both the MiG-17 and MiG-21 before being killed in action by Cunningham and Driscoll.

Does Toon's spirit now wait in the body of a future flyer, perhaps another ace? Or did he above all men find Nirvana in the skies of his homeland?